ZANE PRESENTS

A DEEPER BLUE

PASSION MARKS II

Lee Hayes

ALSO BY LEE HAYES

Passion Marks

ZANE PRESENTS

A DEEPER BLUE
PASSION MARKS II

LEE HAYES

SBI

STREBOR BOOKS

NEW YORK LONDON TORONTO SYDNEY

Strebor Books
P.O. Box 6505
Largo, MD 20792
http://www.streborbooks.com

This book is a work of fiction. Names, characters, places and incidents are products of the author's imagination or are used fictitiously. Any resemblance to actual events or locales or persons, living or dead, is entirely coincidental.

Cover design: mariondesigns.com

ISBN-13 978-1-59309-047-0
ISBN-10   1-59309-047-1
LCCN 2005920187

First Strebor Books trade paperback edition December 2005

10 9 8 7 6 5 4

Manufactured in the United States of America

For information regarding special discounts for bulk purchases,
please contact Simon & Schuster Special Sales at 1-800-456-6798
or business@simonandschuster.com

"Love is just a misunderstanding between two fools."

—TIMOTHY LEE

Dedicated to Adrian

Thank you for being my bridge over troubled waters.

ACKNOWLEDGMENTS

Damn, it seems like only yesterday that my first novel, *Passion Marks,* was released. Here I am with book number two. I want to thank the readers and fans of *Passion Marks* for the astonishing support they have given me over the past couple of years.

Now, to my NURF'ers: I would have never finished this program without you. Now, we have our Master of Public Administration degrees and we can and will conquer the world. Special thanks to: Octaviano aka O-town (for talking me off the ledge many times and for the good times). You are my brother and my friend. Danny (for being cool and calm), Audrey (for letting me vent my frustrations), Baaba (for keeping on task with assignments), Debbie (for checking on a brotha as a buddy would), Joyce (for understanding my pain in stats and econ), Michelle (for volunteering to be my surrogate baby mama…LOL), Leticia a.k.a. Ruth Ann (for IndyGoes4u and for being a blast) and Traci a.k.a. T-Scott for laughing with me. And thanks to Tyrone, Njemile, Cliff, Aquilino, Liz, Susan, Ron, Soloman, Sherazade, James, Jomel, Anthony, Carolyn, Monifa, Saran, Laura, Sholonda, Felicia, Kim, Mario, Ibelice and Dr. Nurf for making this journey extraordinary.

CHAPTER 1

Pussy don't fail me now, Cerina Ford thought as she watched Temple's naked body glide with ease across the bedroom. The cool confidence of his steps and his raw sex appeal drew him into her so much that she was barely able to contain herself. Nervousness grew inside her, along with unchecked desire, making for an explosive combination. She feared her unbridled passion and lust would shoot forth like a geyser and lay her low.

Temple had just gotten out of the shower and his still damp body glistened with moisture. The lazy illumination from the candlelight provided precisely the right amount of radiance. From a distance, with his body half-covered in shadows, he looked like Adonis—faultless in every physical sense. His honey-colored skin, cherry-red lips, bald head, and perfect abs drove her wild. As she took a deep breath, she tried to inhale him from across the room so that he could be a part of her forever. She could feel herself getting hotter, and if she didn't get him to quench this fire below soon, she'd soon overheat.

With desperate anticipation, she watched him. She felt like a drug fiend waiting for the next hit to bring marvelous satisfaction. It wasn't drugs that she desired but, nevertheless, her addiction was authentic. In her wildest fantasies, she could not imagine a more perfect or beautiful man. The thought of this unique specimen rocking her with his powerful body was more than she could handle. Sexually, she was past overdrive. It had been a few days since she last felt her man inside her, and tonight she would do *whatever* was required to satisfy her aching desire.

She continued watching as Temple went about the simple business of drying himself off. Occasionally, when the weight of her stare bore through him, he would shoot her a quick look as if to say *hello,* and she'd lick her lips in enticement.

All of her thoughts at this moment were of him and sex. She thought about how her entire body came to life each time he pushed his thick flesh into her willing spot—it was an unmistakable feeling of intense joy that set her soul on fire. She was lost in lust and didn't want to be found. She needed his heat—now. She wanted all of him—every inch of him—and she wanted every inch of him inside her. She wondered how much longer would she have to wait. She didn't know how much longer she could be teased by his nakedness. She wanted that dick. She longed to wrap her lower lips around it so that he could feel her desire and the inferno that awaited him.

She knew he was playing with her now. He knew she was watching and longing for him, and yet he kept walking back and forth in front of her as if he were oblivious to her heavy desire that hung in the air like a thick bar-room smoke. She wanted to be ravaged, rocked, pounded, banged; she wanted to sweat, moan, scream, scratch and shriek insatiably and uncontrollably. She wanted to see his face contort while he pounded her because then she knew her power. When he was inside her, she knew that he was inside joy—a joy she thought only she could provide.

She continued lusting.

She continued waiting.

Temple smiled with artificial interest.

She knew that he was tired after a hard workout at the gym but, still, she needed to be satisfied.

He now stood in the middle of the room with the towel moving slowly from his neck and then to his chest before moving down to the lower part of his anatomy. He was teasing her. She smiled. To tease her, he made his dick wave; he knew she was in heat. She motioned for him to come closer. The candlelight danced a slow jig and outlined his six-foot frame as he took a few steps closer to her, his dick leading the way.

She kneeled on the bed awaiting his imminent approach. Her breathing accelerated. She slowly lowered one strap of the silk nightgown that covered her body. She looked seductively into his eyes to let him know that she meant business. She licked the tip of her right middle finger and used it to gently caress her left nipple, which was erect. She never broke eye contact—not once. She moaned a deep moan and rolled her head back as the electric waves moved throughout her body.

He liked to watch.

She licked her lips and beckoned him with her tongue. He remained still, watching her—watching her perform for him.

Before completely removing her gown, she reached over onto the nightstand and brought a glass of wine to her full lips. She traced the edge of the glass with her tongue before taking a drink. She let the wine spill and run down her chin, between her full breasts before making a trail leading to Pandora's Box—that's what he named her pussy. Her fingers followed the trail made by the wine and were soon lost inside her joy box. Eye contact was broken, for a moment, as she affirmed the joy of self-pleasure. She inhaled deeply, tilted her head backward, and Temple watched her eyes roll to the back of her head. Her breathing was heavy with a moaning that originated from a place deep within desire.

Temple, standing with an impressive erection, stroked himself as he watched her perform. She knew that he enjoyed watching the freak in her and they had a stack of videotapes of their sexual escapades to prove it. She removed her fingers and inserted them into her mouth, enjoying the flavor of her sugar. She licked her fingers with a ravenous delight and called him over to her, yet he did not move. She knew he wanted to keep watching the show and listening to the sounds of masturbation.

After a few moments, she removed herself from the bed and seductively walked over to him. She went over to claim her prize. She rolled her tongue around her lips and gazed into his eyes. She stood before him momentarily, while fingering herself and enjoying the moment of pleasure. Then, she stuck her fingers into his mouth to share her brown sugar, and he eagerly sucked her fingers and tasted her.

She kneeled before her Temple and was ready to worship at his altar.

She took him fully and hungrily into her mouth and aggressively pleasured him. She loved the way he tasted and she knew that he loved the way she worked him. His deep moaning testified to the skills she possessed. Without restraint or hesitation, she pleasured him with her entire mouth. She sucked, blew, nibbled, licked and tasted all of his manhood. She rubbed her nipples as she looked up into his brown eyes. He watched her devour him.

She lowered herself onto her back and pulled him down on top of her. She pushed his head between her legs and gasped when she felt his tongue connect with her spot. He ate her as if it was his last meal. Eagerly he devoured her, and her moans caused the walls of their apartment to vibrate. She couldn't control the spasms she felt, and she simply could no longer endure this intense oral presentation. She pulled his face into hers and wildly kissed him. This was not the extent of what she was looking for. She wanted his thrusts. She wanted him inside her before she overheated and melted, leaving behind a puddle of lust and steam.

When she felt him enter her, she wanted to weep—the unadulterated pleasure of penetration touched her soul and made her want to shout with a holy joy. Temple was her saint and her savior, and she willingly gave her lust to him as an offering. She wrapped her legs around his waist and pushed himself into her with a force that she felt in the small of her back. This heat, this passion, this power, this love was hers to own and she would never let it go.

He kissed her deeply. His tongue assertively worked her mouth—she wanted to let out a scream of pleasure, but his tongue did not relent. He pounded her hard and she dug her nails into his back, marking her territory. He grabbed her hands and held them against the floor and continued plowing into her box. The sound of flesh slapping against sweaty flesh filled the room with rhythmic palpitations. His body rolled like a snake, hitting all the right spots with the perfect amount of thrust. The more he pounded the more she felt as if she was about to explode. The intensity increased with each push, and she knew she would come very soon. She didn't know how much more she could endure. Time and space lost all meaning as she neared her peak. The vibrations of his body told her that he was near his moment, too. She wanted to feel his release. She knew it would be hot and powerful. Their vibrations deepened, and they moaned louder. She screamed, and her body shook violently. She announced her climax with a banshee-like yell that echoed throughout the apartment. The sounds of her pleasure escaped the confines of the room, rolled down the stairs in a dense fog and filled every conceivable crook and crevice.

Now, she wanted him to come. She wanted it all—every last drop—and he gave it to her. His release inside her was forceful as his body shook violently. Moments later, as he lay on top of her, his body still experienced residual waves of pleasure.

After her lust was consummated, they lay there, incapable of speech, basking in the afterglow of their release. She knew this was love. Never before had she known such pleasure or desire for a man. Until she met Temple a year ago, she could never have imagined loving someone so completely and unselfishly. She turned her head to look at Temple, who stared blankly at the ceiling while trying to recover. She watched his chest rise and fall as air entered his body vacated his body. Simply watching him breathe was an event for her.

"Baby," she said in an almost whisper as she tried to recover the gift of speech. "I love you so much. You know that, right? What we have is special, and I would do anything for you."

"Well, you keep doing what you just did, and we'll be fine," he said with a coy laugh.

"I'm serious. I love you. I want you to know that. I want you to always know that."

Temple heard her words but, as usual, did not reciprocate affection to her satisfaction. He cared for her, as he had cared for many others, but love was not something to which he'd ever surrender. As usual, she was left emotionally empty by his casual words.

"You are my baby." He leaned over and kissed her forehead. "Not that I'm complaining by any means, but what got into you tonight? You were so hot—you were like a wild woman."

She smiled.

"Watching you after your shower did it. You know how your body turns me on."

"Oh, so it was all me?"

"It's always you."

Temple leaned over again, kissed her lips and stood up. He grabbed her by the hand and helped her off the floor before leading her to the bed. She could not have been any happier or any more satisfied. She climbed into the bed and tried to pull him in with her, but he resisted.

"I'll be right back," he said.

"Where are you going?" she asked even though she knew the answer. Each time they made love or had sex, he'd quickly race into the shower as if he needed the cleansing properties of soap and water to erase the memory of his transgression with her.

"I'm going to take a quick shower. It'll only take a minute."

She wanted to pressure him into staying with her a few more minutes, but she didn't. She didn't want to shatter her bliss with an argument. After all, she had become accustomed to his style and knew that he'd go to the shower after they finished. She had tried to adjust to his habit but, still, it was difficult for her not to be offended. Just once, she'd like for him to lie on her or near her for longer than a minute after they had spilled love's juices.

Cerina allowed a menagerie of blissful thoughts to drift in and out of her head. She sat back in the comfort of her own bed and thought about all the other men, the tragedies and the disappointments of her life. She pondered the failed loves and the heartaches and the lies and the deceit from others who claimed to love her, but none of those men were real. This moment with Temple made all that seem so insignificant—this moment was real.

Cerina knew that Temple, like most men, had his faults. He was surely not as affectionate as she'd like, and his employment history was patchy, at best. He sometimes worked as a personal trainer when he felt like it, but his gigs never seemed to last very long. He wasn't working right now, but as long as he was looking for a job, Cerina was satisfied. She had resolved herself to being the breadwinner for now, but she told herself that would change as soon as he found the right opportunity.

Women were also drawn to him like ants to a picnic, but that wasn't his fault. He exuded masculinity and sexuality through no additional effort of his own. His magnificent and cocky gait turned heads as he stalked the city streets and when he stretched out his powerful arms, it called out to all those in need of shelter from the storm. Temple was the kind of man who left women and men equally weak-kneed, teary-eyed, and breathless. When he stormed into their lives in a magnificent flare of passion and hope, he bedazzled them with glorious splendor that burned hot, but lasting only long enough to empty their wallets. When he left them, they were dazed, dizzied, bewildered, scattered and sometimes ashamed that they had been caught up in his rapture.

Women were overt in their flirtations with him in the presence of Cerina—men were a bit slicker—but Cerina always knew when someone was checking him out. The joy that he took from the attention used to get under her skin. But, she understood now that the attention he received made him feel special, and he needed that. As long as he was coming home to her, she had no complaints. Men will be men, and being in a relationship doesn't mean they are ever going to stop looking at other women. She could accept that because she wasn't immune to recognizing a fine man when she saw one but, at the end of the day, she took pride in the fact that he was hers and hers alone. All those other bitches who smiled wildly in his face couldn't compete with what she offered him. They could kiss her ass because if they got within sniffing distance of him and made the wrong move, they'd have to answer to her. She was not opposed to fighting to protect her man.

She tried to not think about all those times in the past in which infidelity marched directly into their lives, took an offensive stand, and threatened to destroy all that she had built with Temple. They had some rocky times in the beginning. On more than one occasion, she was ready to throw in the towel and give up on him and love altogether. Love had never been her best friend, and her faith in it had waned. All those sappy love songs about roses and sunshine and the fairytales had no meaning for her. But something about Temple would not let her let him go. So she stayed. At first, she stayed out of loneliness. Then, she listened to her heart and remained in the struggle to make him hers.

As she lay in the bed, she thought about how far they had come and all that they had dealt with in order to build a lasting and meaningful relationship. In the beginning, she recalled several nights of him coming home late smelling like some other woman's pussy. It didn't matter whether or not he showered before returning home because she could always tell. She had smelled enough pussy while working as an exotic dancer—a stripper—at the 202 Club, one of D.C.'s most popular gentlemen's clubs, to be able to smell it despite his attempts to cover it up. And she hated him for it. She hated him for making her feel like less than a woman. She hated him for going out for the loving that he could easily get at home. She knew how to put it down on him and could not understand why he would choose to go to some other woman.

On those nights when he would surreptitiously enter the house, hoping to avoid her gaze and her rage, she knew he had been with some other woman. Then, curse words flew like daggers, furniture was overturned, and tears of anger were shed. On those nights, neighbors who had been snatched from their sleep by the melee next door, often called the police to bring an end to the commotion. And, on occasion, one of them or both of them went to jail. The last time it was Temple, who in the heat of the moment had slapped her across the head so hard that she lost hearing in her right ear for almost a day. For that offense, he was jailed and placed on probation for two years, and he was still paying the fees—or at least Cerina was paying the fees for him.

That fight started when he left her at the club after her long shift. She was scheduled to get off work at one a.m. because she had worked almost twelve hours that day to earn enough money to pay rent and to help Temple with his child support—he had two children, a boy and a girl—by two different women, but he hadn't seen either of them in years. She was dog-tired and her feet were aching from the stilettos that she had worn while doing her onstage gyrations. Temple, who kept her car while she was at work, was to have picked her up from her late-night shift. When she walked outside the club into the frigid winter night, chills raced up her spine from the cruel and wintry breezes. The 202 was located on the edge of town in an industrial and rundown part of Southwest Washington. It was an area where no one would dare venture more than two blocks from the club out of fear for their lives and personal property.

She walked outside several times only to be greeted by the steely grip of winter's unforgiving grasp. The wind blew her hair and made her long for warmer days. She walked up the sidewalk to the end of the street and looked around to the corner to see if he had parked the car and come inside looking for her. She thought maybe she had overlooked him in the crowded club. When she asked the security guards had they seen him, they replied no. After many calls to the apartment and to his cell phone—all which went unanswered—she gave up. Exasperated, she waited for her girlfriend Nicole to finish her shift for a ride home. That was two hours later.

As soon as she walked into their apartment, she smelled it. *Pussy. And it wasn't hers.* She found Temple in the bed sound asleep. She screamed for him to wake up, but he simply waved her away and rolled over, oblivious to her anger. She immediately dropped her bag and went into the kitchen and grabbed a glass of water. She poured the glass of cold water all over him and the bed and he jumped up like a thief in the night.

"What the fuck is your problem?" he screamed.

"My problem is you! How the fuck you gonna leave me at the club! I got off two fuckin' hours ago!"

He looked at the clock, feeling cold, wet and confused.

"Damn, baby. I'm sorry. I set the alarm, but I guess it didn't go off."

"You had some ho in here, didn't you? I know you did because I can smell her!"

"What the fuck you talking about? Calm down."

"You left me standing outside the club in the cold while you were fucking some bitch in the house where I pay rent, and you expect me to calm down? You must be out of your fuckin' mind!"

"Cerina, stop trippin'. I fell asleep. That's it, okay?" Temple removed his shirt and moved in the direction of the bathroom to get a towel to dry himself off, but Cerina did not budge out of his way.

"I'm out there shaking my ass so that we can have a place to live and to help you pay your fucking child support, and you treat me like shit. You can't even pick me up in my own car. You are a sorry mothafucka! I'm so sick of this shit!"

"I'm sick of you always accusing me of fucking somebody! If I was gonna fuck somebody, you'd know! I told yo ass I was sleeping."

"Temple, you so full of shit! Stop lying. It's all over your face, and you can't even look me in the eye."

"I ain't been fucking nobody!" he yelled.

"I'm trippin'? Why it smell like straight pussy up in here? I ain't been here in ten hours, so I know it ain't mine!"

"Stop acting all paranoid." Temple walked around her and into the bathroom and grabbed a towel. Cerina ran behind him and snatched the towel out of his hand before he could use it.

"Bitch, you better stop trippin'." Temple's anger began to rise and he pointed his finger in her face to let her know that he meant business.

"Oh, so, now I'm a bitch?" She was trying to push his buttons.

"You trying to start some shit, and I don't feel like fucking with you tonight. I'm sorry I forgot to pick you up, but you're home now. Get the fuck over it."

She reached out and slapped him hard across his face. By reflex, he returned the slap and knocked her into the bathroom door. He stepped over her and tried to move to the living room, but the battle had only begun. She jumped up like a wild woman and threw herself into him. He tried to restrain her, but her limbs were out of control. She was kicking, screaming, punching and scratching at him, occasionally landing a serious blow. Temple pushed her onto the couch, and she rolled over it and fell onto the floor behind it. Before she was able to pull herself up, Temple picked up and put on a pair of sweat pants that he had left on the floor.

"I don't have time for this shit. I'm outta here. I'll be back tomorrow to get my shit, you crazy bitch."

"You ain't gonna leave me. I'll kill you first!"

As he reached for his shoes and the keys to the car, she picked up a ceramic kitten from the coffee table and threw it with considerable force into the back of his head. He stumbled, feeling the blood running down the back of his neck. He turned to face her, not completely understanding what had just happened. She ran toward him and tried to jump on him. He snatched her out of the air by the neck and shoved her into the wall so hard the paintings rattled.

"You need to quit before someone really gets hurt up in here!" She felt his fingers applying more pressure to her neck and knew that she was gasping for air. For a quick second, everything went black for Cerina as she struggled to free herself. He released her, and she slid down the wall, gasping for air. Moments later, the cops arrived, and Temple was arrested.

He never admitted to cheating that night, but they both knew. And, as far as she knew, that was the last time.

❧❧❧

When he got out of the shower, he kissed her on the forehead and said, "I'm gonna get something to drink. You want anything while I'm down there?"

"No, but hurry back. I miss you already." He offered a half-smile and turned to leave. "Temple," she said as he turned to her, "don't ever leave me."

"I'm not going anywhere, baby."

Temple didn't bother to put on a robe. He allowed his nakedness to fill Cerina's eyes. He knew she loved watching him from behind, so he took his time walking toward the door. His plump ass reminded her of a couple of well-developed cantaloupes, and his sculpted back offered the right amount of definition. On his right shoulder the tattoo of a black scorpion—indicative of his Zodiac sign—stood out on his caramel skin.

Temple walked into the kitchen and turned to face the stairs, listening for any sounds emanating from her room. He heard Cerina rustling around, but did not worry. He grabbed the black cordless phone off the wall and began to dial. He listened impatiently as the phone rang several times before there was an answer.

"Why aren't you over here?" the voice on the phone chimed in before he could gather his thoughts.

"I thought I was gonna be able to get away, but I can't. I think I'm stuck for the night," Temple said in a whisper.

"Stuck? This is the second time this week you've been *stuck*. What the fuck am I supposed to do? I'm getting really sick of this shit."

"Baby, I know. I'm sorry, but Cerina—"

"I don't want to hear about her. This is about you and me. Fuck Cerina." Temple felt the venom in the voice. More than anything he wanted to go, but he knew after their lovemaking session he'd have to move heaven and earth to get her to understand that there was some other place he needed to be. Quite frankly, he wasn't up for the fight. He learned a long time ago that life is all about balance. If you are able to keep the scales balanced, then you are able to get away with a lot. It is only when the scale tips to one side that suspicion is born. Leaving now would create a world of suspicion and contempt.

"I have everything set up over here—candles, wine, strawberries and whipped cream. You know you want me to put cream all over your body and lick it off—starting with your nipples. You know how you like that." The voice changed from anger to seduction, and Temple felt himself getting aroused at the thought.

"Damn, baby. Don't do that to me. I'm getting hard by merely thinking about you!"

"You still saying no?"

"There's no way I can. Let's do it tomorrow. She's gonna be at the club until really late. I promise tomorrow everything will be alright."

"Guess I'll have to find someone else to play with then."

Click.

The sudden sound of the dial tone rang in his ear. As he turned to hang up the phone, there was Cerina.

"Who was that?" she asked.

"Oh, uh, that was Darren. I forgot that I was supposed to take him over to his sister's house in Fairfax tonight. I told him I could do it tomorrow, but he was still pissed." She stood there and looked at him for a second. He leaned in and gave her a kiss. He inserted his tongue into her mouth, and she pulled him closer.

"Baby, you want something to drink?" he asked. Temple went around her and opened the refrigerator door looking for something cool. He took a glass from the cabinet and poured some orange juice. Cerina glanced curiously at the phone and then at Temple as she took him by the hand.

"Come on. Let's go back to bed."

CHAPTER 2

"**D**anea, I have no idea how we got here," Kevin Davis said as he sipped on a cup of green tea. He had started drinking tea a few months ago because he'd heard of its medicinal value and these days he needed something soothing to calm his often inflated nerves. With all that had been going on in his life, peace of mind was invaluable. "Daryl and I are having serious problems. Something is going on with him and I don't know what to do. We have been through so much together that it's hard for me to understand why he won't talk to me now. This shit is pissing me off. I try to talk to him, but he shuts down every single time. He seems content to live like this, but I don't know how much more of this I can take. We're supposed to be happy, damnit! Instead, I feel like a part of me is dying."

"How long has this been going on?" she inquired out of deep concern. Her heavy tone reflected her desire to get to the bottom of their problems. Danea always felt that she could solve the problems of the world if given the opportunity, and Kevin had relied heavily on her friendship and counsel over the past few years. Kevin wished that she could utter some incantation or wiggle her nose and make all of his problems with Daryl disappear in a puff of smoke. Even though her words of advice had proven themselves priceless over the years, he wasn't convinced that today she could offer the kind of abiding hope that he needed to weather this storm. In his soul, he felt that the dark days had already lasted too long. At this point, all that he was sure of was that he was tired of being confined by feelings of helplessness. He knew that he couldn't fix their problems by himself, and if Daryl had resolved himself to misery, then their demise was imminent.

"On and off for the last couple of months. Things had gotten better so I figured it was a momentary thing. Now, whatever *it* is won't go away. He is distant, inattentive and truth be told, we haven't had sex in a couple weeks and that's unusual for us—even our kisses are passionless." Kevin's speech slowed as if his next words required time and deliberate effort to escape from his mouth. "It feels like sometimes he doesn't even want me to touch him. When we're in bed and I reach out to him, he freezes up, as if my touch is unwanted or unfamiliar. I don't know if you know what that feels like, but there are only so many times I can be rejected before I start to take things personally." He watched the steam rise from his cup of tea, swirl around in the empty space, and then dissipate into nothingness. If he and Daryl didn't do something quickly, the same thing would become of their relationship and the life that they'd built together.

"We all have moments where we need to sort things out on our own. I'm sure he is not intentionally shutting you out or rejecting you. Is there anything going on with him at work?" Danea felt there was a lot that Kevin wasn't sharing with her, but she didn't want to press the issue. She knew there were always three sides to their story: Kevin's side, Daryl's side, and the truth.

"See, that's the thing. I have no idea. He hasn't said anything about *anything*. He comes home and it seems like all of the conversations we have are forced, or we end up arguing about something stupid. I can tell that he's not really interested in having a conversation with me. If I've done something—or didn't do something—I wish he'd tell me so I can make it better. All of this not knowing and wondering is tearing us apart. I can actually *see* the distance between us. I can see us growing apart, as if our emotional distance was something I can reach out and touch. Can you imagine what that feels like?" Kevin breathed a forceful sigh as a way of expunging his pent-up emotions. The negative energy that had taken refuge in his soul felt like poison pulsing and racing through his spirit. "It could be work, it could be me or it could be that he's having an affair—"

"Kevin, don't even think that," Danea chimed in with flared passion. "You know Daryl would never do anything like that to you. He loves you more than you could imagine. Why would you say something like that?"

"Because it may be true. I can't think of another reason why he's acting so strangely. I can't believe I'm in a position to think that he's cheating, but things aren't adding up. We aren't having sex, we don't talk, he comes home late sometimes talkin' about he was working late or had a late night at the gym. Danea, do you that know he's started taking his calls in the other room, as if I wouldn't notice? I haven't said anything to him about it, but I'm sure he knows I've noticed this big change. I remember the days when we'd be cuddled up on the couch and his cell phone or mine would ring and whoever could reach it would pick it up and answer it. It was no big deal. Now, when we're in the room together and the phone rings, he checks the caller ID and either leaves the room to answer it or he turns off his phone. What kind of bullshit is that?"

"Well, that may not mean anything."

"And, he has this strange fixation with the Internet. There were a couple of times when I got up in the middle of the night to get some water or go to the bathroom and he wasn't in bed. Last week I walked downstairs and found him asleep at the computer in his office and when I walked in, he woke up and hurriedly closed the screen he was on. Another time, I could have sworn I heard moans coming from his office—sexual moans. I think he was jacking off, probably to porn on the net. If he's jackin' off to porn on some sex site, should I be concerned? Is that cheating?"

"That's not cheating, but it's definitely a sign that something ain't right in your relationship. If he's using porn as a substitute to having sex with you, then that's a deep problem."

"I agree. If we were having normal relations, then I wouldn't be as concerned. I know men are visual creatures and we like porn, and masturbation is a part of our lives and I'm cool with that. I enjoy a video from time to time and I like touching myself as well, but I don't use that as a substitute for having sex with him."

"Men are some strange creatures," she said with a laugh.

"Tell me about it. All of these changes within him are scaring me. He never used to do any of those things. Now, I find myself watching his every move to see if he's gonna slip up and say or do something I can call him out on. This ain't healthy, and it's really frustrating. I try so hard to trust him, but I can't get rid of this feeling that there's a reason why he's pulling away from me. I really think he's cheating. And, I think I know *who* it is."

Danea paused; not sure whether or not she wanted to inquire. "Who is it?"

"I think something is going on with his teaching assistant, Amir. I've only met him once; when I went up to the school. I was planning on surprising Daryl on his lunch break. I rented this hotel room at the Wyndham not far from the school, and I thought we'd get a little freaky on his lunch break. I wanted to send him back to work with a big smile, and plus I wanted to do something special to try to bring us back together. When I walked into his office unannounced, the surprise was on me. I walked in and Amir was there. I felt like I was interrupting something—something more than English papers and grades. It wasn't anything that was said, but it was the feeling in the air. You should have seen the looks on their faces. It was like getting caught with your hand in the cookie jar. And, when I explained to Daryl that I was stopping by for lunch, he wasn't exactly bursting with excitement. The strangest part was when Amir excused himself. It really felt like Daryl wanted him to stay and wanted me to leave. I mean, I didn't expect him to do a cartwheel, but he could have at least feigned some interest—fake a smile or something. I mean, I was there to show him love. I ended up feeling like I had done something wrong. Needless to say, the romantic afternoon I had planned never happened. Even after I explained to him what I had in mind, he brushed it off as if it wasn't important."

"Damn," she said out loud before she realized it. "Did you see or hear anything else?" She hoped the overwhelming feeling Kevin described was misplaced but, as a woman, she knew how powerful intuition could be.

"Nah, that was it. I don't think I could have handled anything else. I wanted to get out of there as soon as I could. And I did."

"Well, that's not enough to conclude he's having an affair," she said, trying to sound reassuring, "but it is enough to be concerned about."

"I don't know what I'm supposed to think. All I know is something isn't right and I have this really sick feeling in the pit of my stomach. I love Daryl with all my heart, but I will not sit around and be played like some violin. I've been through enough relationship drama to last me a lifetime. At least when I was with James, I knew what to expect. This shit Daryl is pulling now is driving me crazy. I know I won't deal with infidelity."

"Have you asked him about Amir?"

"Danea, of course I have. Don't you think I'm smart enough to do that?" he said with corporeal irritability.

"Don't bite my head off. I was simply asking."

"I'm sorry. I'm frustrated. I don't mean to take it out on you. I don't know what to do." He moved over to the bay window in the den and looked blankly out at the snow falling gently to the earth. Each wondrous flake floated through the air before adding its own individuality to the winter blanket now covering the Washington, D.C. streets. It was barely December, but the fierceness of winter had already taken its toll on the region. As far as Kevin was concerned, the bitterness of his failing relationship stung far worse than the cold winds outside. If they didn't work hard, and soon, to fix whatever the problem was, then they would go down in the annals of history as another failed love affair—that was not a distinction Kevin desired. After surviving the horrors of his last relationship with James Lancaster, the lover who viciously tormented and physically abused Kevin a few years back, Daryl was like a breath of fresh air for him after a year of barely breathing while he lived with the maniac. Only after James perished in a church fire did Kevin finally feel free, but the scars on his body would always be a reminder of his personal hell.

"Daryl is the man who I have always loved and always dreamed about. I have built my life around him, and I thought we'd be together forever. Now, I'm not so sure. Why is it so hard for people who fall in love to stay in love?" His question was rhetorical in nature. "I don't understand what happens. What is it that suddenly appears and destroys everything? Danea, I love that man. I'd give my life for him, but I don't know what's going on. We can't make it if we continue down this path. Something has got to change." There was a noticeable pause on the phone, and he imagined the wheels in her mind spinning rapidly in search of a solution.

"When you two argue, what are you arguing about? Maybe that's a place for you to start. It may not be what he's saying, but what he's *not* saying during those conversations."

"Danea, I'm not Ms. Cleo. I shouldn't have to figure out his feelings. We have known each other for years—he was one of my best friends before we became lovers—and he knows me as well as I know him. This shit we're going through is crazy. I don't want to get into the business of looking into a crystal ball to try to figure out what my man is going through. He's a grown-ass man and he needs to be honest with me. I can't fix the problem if I don't know what it is."

"I'm glad you're not Ms. Cleo, 'cause if you were, you'd be unemployed or working as a greeter at Wal-Mart, I'm sure."

"See, you wrong for that," he said as they both laughed. "But seriously, our arguments have been largely inconsequential. He makes little snide comments about living in D.C. I don't think he was completely sold on the idea, but after all that happened in Houston with James, I had to get out of that city, and he knew that. When we talked about moving together, he agreed. I don't think he's adjusted well, but hell, we've been here two years— you'd think he would have settled in by now."

"What about his job? Does he like it?"

He thought for a few seconds. "As far as I know, he likes it. He complains about it like every-one does about their job, but I honestly don't think that's it." Before they relocated, Daryl had been teaching English Literature at a college in Houston while taking classes to receive his doctorate in Educational Administration. After he graduated, they relocated to Washington, and Daryl applied for a job at the University of the District of Columbia. He had been hired as a Professor of English Literature and a year later he found himself chair of the department. "Maybe he's tired of me. I know I haven't given him as much attention as I would have liked to, but running the restaurant and trying to open this center in Keevan's name takes a lot of time. I've tried to make the best of the time we have together, but he ain't willing."

"Maybe he's only lonely. You should do something special for him."

"Well, the last time I tried to do something special, I felt like a fool. I don't know if I can go through that again."

"Put that incident out of your mind. I think you should do something sweet for him tonight like run a nice bath with candles and wine—something simple, to let him know you're thinking about his needs."

"I don't know, Danea." Kevin continued gazing out of the window, feeling as if the ground was shifting underneath his feet.

"Look, Kevin, you have nothing to lose and everything to gain by doing this."

"Why do I always have to be the one to make the first move?"

"You can't be responsible for his actions. All you can do is your part and hope he responds in kind. Take this chance, step out a little bit and I bet you'll be surprised by what happens."

"Yeah, I guess you're right. With this snow coming down, I suspect he's on his way home now. The entire city is shutting down." Kevin tried to convince himself to swallow his pride and take another step at fixing their broken relationship. In his heart, he truly felt that after the fiasco with trying to surprise Daryl with lunch it should be Daryl who made the next move. "I'm so tired of feeling like this. What if he's really cheating on me? What will I do?"

"Stop talking like that. He isn't cheating on you. You guys have got to start talking and work this thing out because I'm not letting you break up. I'm not having that shit." He forced a small, dejected laugh and tried to let the force of her words provide some comfort. If only she did have the power to keep them together he would have elicited her services months ago. He moved over to the mantelpiece and looked at the picture of him and Daryl that was taken last year in Rehoboth Beach, Delaware, a popular gay vacation destination spot. In the picture, they were all smiles—those were happy days. Daryl stood behind Kevin with his arms clasped around his chest as if he was protecting him from the world. Back then, joy radiated from them. *Funny how things change.*

"That's enough about me," he said, as he abruptly changed the subject. "I saw your new video yesterday on BET, and let me tell you, it was hot! I don't know who found all those sexy-ass men, but I know you were in heaven when they all started grinding on you. I think I got jealous," he said jokingly.

Danea's interest in singing had budded into a full-fledged career. She was discovered while singing a karaoke-style song in a New Orleans bar a few years back when they all went to the Crescent City for a weekend trip. Since then, she had had two number one singles, and her CD, simply titled *Victory* after her first single, had achieved platinum status. She hadn't missed being an attorney at all.

"Let me tell you, it felt so good that I was about to pay all of them to keep grinding! If I wasn't engaged, it would have been on and poppin'," she said in her susta-girl voice. Her boisterous laugh was like music to his ears. It was nice to hear laughter and to know someone else was happy. "By the way, how is the fund-raiser coming along for your New Year's Masquerade Ball extraordinaire?"

"This has been more work than I imagined. Last week I took out ads in a couple of local papers announcing that you'd be performing at the party and ticket sales spiked. I mean, at one hundred dollars a pop, I wasn't sure how the D.C. community would respond, but so far so good. Apparently, you have diva appeal, and I'm going to use it."

"Me a diva? Never that," she said playfully. "But for real, I'm excited about the benefit. I know you've put a lot of work into organizing this to raise money for Keevan's Room. I'm thrilled to be a part of it."

Kevin was working to create a non-profit organization in the name of his deceased brother, Keevan Davis. The organization was called Keevan's Room after Keevan's favorite novel, *Giovanni's Room*, written by James Baldwin so many years ago. Keevan's Room would serve as a shelter and counseling center for victims of same-sex domestic violence. In most cities, there were many places women could go to seek shelter from an abusive partner, but the options for males were far less comprehensive. Kevin, being a survivor of abuse, wanted to help others so they would never have to go through anything similar to what he had experienced. Kevin was trying to raise an additional one hundred fifty-thousand dollars for the organization and, through various fund-raisers, he was close.

There was so much work that still needed to be done. At some point in the process of trying to figure out how to create this organization from scratch, Kevin decided it would be more advantageous to partner with an existing city organization. In particular, he sought out an organization that provided gay social service programs and already had a base of clients, name recognition, and possibly office space. Kevin had already invested one hundred-thousand dollars of his own money in the program for its start-up and had organized a couple of fund-raisers, including the upcoming masquerade ball on New Year's Eve. It wasn't going to simply be another New Year's Eve party. It was going to be *the* New Year's Eve party.

Over the past several months, Kevin finally was able to make a solid connection with Crown Services, a local clinic that provided HIV/AIDS and counseling services to the Washington, D.C. area. Now, they were in the final stages of the contract, and Kevin could sense the end of the line.

"I have no doubt you will deliver a wonderful performance. I saw you on *Good Morning*

America performing in their concert series a couple of weeks back and I was quite impressed. But, you know I know you can *sang*. Make sure you don't let your newfound celebrity status go to your head."

"You don't have to worry about that. Curtis keeps me humble."

"And speaking of Curtis, how are things? Are you still *givin' him something he can feel?*"

"You so nasty," she replied, "but I'll tell you this, I know my man is satisfied."

"So, everything is still cool with having your fiancé as your manager?"

Danea knew Kevin had concerns about the arrangement when she first signed her record deal and announced Curtis as her manager. Kevin told her never to mix business with pleasure because of the countless stories of love going bad and spoiling a business relationship. He didn't want to see Danea go down that path, but she was a smart woman and had been a great attorney before her career change. Kevin knew she would never let herself be played by a man—again.

"It's great. It means I don't ever have to look too far for what I need." They both laughed. "Listen, I've got to run, but we'll talk soon, okay?"

"I hope you know how proud of you and happy I am for you."

"You know I love you. Give my love to Daryl. And, y'all better work it out," she said as she hung up the phone.

He sat down by the window and looked up at the muted gray sky for answers to one of life's biggest mysteries: how do you make the love last? He remembered what it felt like to be happy, but those days were laid out behind him like yesterday's news. Now, here they were, in the trenches of heartache and neither he nor Daryl knew exactly how they had arrived in this valley.

He walked over to the stereo, found one of his favorite soundtracks, put it in the CD player and turned up the volume. He moved slowly back over to the window to watch the falling snow and listened as Aretha's voice evoked a flood of emotion within his soul. When she sang, her voice echoed with a sadly hypnotic flare as the cheerless words of the song filled his ears. Unfortunately, Kevin could relate firsthand to what she sang. He sat back and continued to stare into the sky, waiting for his answers, yet no answers came.

He believed he should be living his dreams. Here he was, in Washington, D.C., living in a wonderful home with Daryl, and yet he felt a thousand miles from happiness. A bluesy, melancholy midnight melody echoed in his head and drove him to madness. He thought about how far he had come over the years and all he had been through. He had survived the death of his identical twin brother and because of the pain and guilt he felt, he ended up in the clutches of an abusive egomaniac—James Lancaster—who abused him physically, mentally, and sexually. James had become his lover at a time when Kevin was too weak to fight back and too guilty to care. But, he survived. He survived losing jobs because of James's antics, and when Kevin finally did leave him, he survived James's crazed stalking, the death of his unborn child at James's insane hands, and the shooting of some of his friends during Tony and LaMont's commitment ceremony. James had tried to kill them all. Yet, they survived. And here he was, alive to tell the tale.

After all of that, he swore he'd find true happiness. And he did in Daryl. When they finally got together three years ago everything fell into place. The happiness and joy that had eluded them both for years was finally realized. The empty spaces were filled, the loneliness vanished, and they enjoyed the most amazing love affair with life and each other. They blended together, almost in perfect harmony.

But now, everything had changed. The love that used to provide comfort was slipping away without explanation; the feeling of elation they used to experience in each other's presence was fading. With the music still blaring, he walked over to the mirror on the opposite wall. He wished he could will away all of the bad times, but sorrow, like joy, becomes a part of who you are and no power on this earth could erase its effects.

As he stared into the mirror, he looked at his face and tried to determine if he was the same man who fell in love with Daryl or whether everything they had been through had somehow altered his very nature. Externally, he still looked the same, with a low-faded hair- cut and smooth brown skin. He was an avid runner and even ran track when he was in college. Even though he was separated from college by several years, he still maintained his runner's build: powerful thighs with a sculpted upper body. His face had changed only slightly, with the addition of a few permanent passion marks left by his former lover. He examined the scar above his left eye. It was a painful reminder of his journey and lessons in life. He took his right middle finger and traced the mark—he could almost feel James slamming the black cordless phone into his face. As happy as Daryl had made him feel in the past, he still would never forget James. *Never.* He would always have memories of abuse and violence. He would always remember living in fear. A part of him would always cringe at the simple utterance of the name James. The specter of James would always be reflected back at him each time he looked in the mirror—they were inextricably bound, in life and in death.

CHAPTER 3

DarkBroNDC: So, when are we gonna hook up?

NuttyProfessor: I never said we were going to meet.

DarkBroNDC: What, you scurred? LOL

NuttyProfessor: I ain't neva scurred! LOL

DarkBroNDC: We can meet for drinks or coffee, or something…

NuttyProfessor: The *something* is what I'm concerned about.

DarkBroNDC: Don't worry. I only bite if you want me to.

NuttyProfessor: LOL…you so silly. I will admit, though, that I am curious about the man behind the name. Who is this DarkBroNDC? As far as I know, you could be a serial killer…LOL

DarkBroNDC: Trust me, I ain't crazy, but I will give you the opportunity to meet me.? We could meet one night at that club Republic Gardens at 14th & U Streets. We could do a happy hour. I'll even treat you to a few drinks.

NuttyProfessor: Hmmmmmm…

DarkBroNDC: What does hmmmm mean?

NuttyProfessor: It means I'm thinking about it. I'll let you know. It can't be today because of the weather.

DarkBroNDC: I know this cold shit is a trip. I'm from Florida and I ain't ready for all this. I'mma need you to keep me warm.

NuttyProfessor: I gotta go. Hit me up later.

DarkBroNDC: Wait…I have a question for you.

NuttyProfessor: What?

DarkBroNDC: What kind of underwear you got on…?

NuttyProfessor: Stop being nasty…

DarkBroNDC: I'm not being nasty. Just wondering if you're a boxer or brief kinda guy. I don't wear drawers at all…LOL

NuttyProfessor: You are cra-zay! Man, I gotta roll. Got work to do.

DarkBroNDC: Answer the question before you leave.

NuttyProfessor: Briefs.

DarkBroNDC: That's what I thought. Check your email. I sent you something. And, forget work. With this white stuff falling it's time to head to the house! Holla.

NuttyProfessor: Holla.

***

"Damn, the snow is really coming down," Daryl said out loud as he looked out of his office window at the university. He logged out of the instant messenger program that allowed him to chat with DarkBroNDC. He had listened to the weather report this morning and the entire D.C. area had been placed under a winter storm watch. The weather forecasters indicated eight inches of snow were possible over the course of the next day or so. When he left for work that morning, a few flakes had begun to fall and then stopped an hour later. Heavy snow was not expected until the evening rush hour. He looked at the clock on his computer and realized it was only half past noon. As he looked at his screen, an email popped up from the school president indicating the school was officially closed and everyone should head home before the weather got too bad.

He decided to log into his personal email account to see what DarkBroNDC had sent him before he left the building. When he opened the email, he was surprised to see a picture of a beautiful dark-skinned man with a dazzling smile and bright eyes. After the weeks of Internet flirtation, he finally could put a face on the mystery behind the screen. He wasn't quite what Daryl had imagined, but Daryl was—by no means—disappointed with the picture. For a fleeting second, he entertained the thought of actually arranging to meet him at Republic Gardens at some time in the near future, but the responsible side of him knew that would not be a good idea. Their conversations had been far from innocent.

Daryl started packing his bags, not quite ready to be at home, but he didn't want to be stranded in his office due to inclement weather. He didn't get much sleep last night because of the fight he had with Kevin over what amounted to nothing, as far as he was concerned. He knew things had to change because he couldn't live like this too much longer.

He had hoped that Kevin would have called him at some point so they could have made up before he got home, but the only voice mail he received was from one of his students regarding a late paper. He wasn't sure what kind of mood Kevin would be in by the time he got home, and he really didn't feel like dealing with all of the tension that had mounted since last night. Things had been pretty sour between them for the past couple of months and, for the first time in their relationship, Daryl wasn't convinced they would survive. Nothing major had happened in terms of cheating or anything like that, but the distance between them was more than noticeable, and neither of them was quite sure why. Life happened. They were both busy people, and their lives were seemingly on divergent paths, so much that there were days they barely saw each other. Kevin was busy running the restaurant and trying to open Keevan's Room, and that took up so much time. Daryl was gunning for a promotion at work and put in extra hours to secure the post. Even in the midst of their busy lives, their commitment to each other had remained constant, but cracks in that foundation were beginning to show.

Daryl gathered his belongings, not sure when the school would reopen, and prepared to shut down his machine. Before he did, he took one last look at the face on the screen. The face that looked back at him was perfect, and there was something bewitching about his eyes. Even before he had received the picture of DarkBroNDC, Daryl found himself daydreaming about meeting this stranger for a simple conversation.

Weeks ago, Daryl had placed an ad on a website for gay men in the hopes of meeting someone, some friend, who he could chat with from time to time. At least, that's what he told himself. Although each personal ad on the website www.adam4him.com provided an email address to contact the person, at no point had Daryl ever responded to an ad, and he had no intention of doing so. He liked to read the ads and look at the pictures people often posted to accompany their profile. Daryl spent many hours laughing at the crazy and sometimes sad ads he read. The pictures were often revealing and the ads very sexual in nature. Most people listed personal information within their profiles and many of them revealed explicit details relating to the size of their dicks and their favorite sexual positions. Daryl often laughed because the Internet had truly revolutionized dating and put sex on the fast track. Simply by clicking on a profile, you could determine if you wanted to meet the person based on the information they listed. It was a cold and dehumanizing way of existing, but the website was a sign of the times. Daryl passed a lot of time browsing ads until he received a message from DarkBroNDC and their Internet friendship was born.

Daryl heard a knock at the door and commanded the person to enter.

"Hey, Dr. Harris," the familiar voice called out from behind the slowly opening gate. It was his teaching assistant, Amir. "I wanted to make sure you knew we are officially closed because of the weather. I didn't know if you had checked your email, and I saw your light on as I was passing by. I just thought I'd check," he said with a welcoming smile.

"Yeah, I got the email, and I was shutting down this machine to get out of here before it gets bad. I'm glad I didn't drive today. I hope the Metro isn't crowded because the last thing I want to do is sit underground for a half-hour waiting on a crowded-ass train."

"Well, I have my car today," Amir said.

"You drove today? Didn't you know it was supposed to snow?" Daryl asked playfully. "You kids like living on the edge, don't you?"

"Lucky for you, I'm a man who likes to take chances. If I hadn't driven, then I wouldn't be able to offer you a ride home. I have to go through your neighborhood anyway, so why don't I drop you off?"

Amir's pleasant personality always made Daryl feel better. He was one of those individuals who could turn a frown into a smile simply by his presence. Maybe it was the disarming Southern accent that made him feel familiar and comforting, or maybe it was the fact that, in spite of his polished good looks, he was humble and sincere. He was about five feet eight inches with smooth, milk-chocolate skin and a tight, high booty Daryl found himself staring at each time Amir walked away. Daryl found Amir to be very alluring, and he knew Amir had an unspoken crush on him, but it was not anything Daryl felt he would ever act on. At twenty-five, he thought Amir was a bit too young for him—even though Daryl was only thirty-two. And besides, he had a man at home he adored—most of the time.

"Only if it's no trouble."

"Of course it's no trouble. Anything for you, *Mr. Harris.*" When Amir spoke his name, he spoke with just enough inflection in his tone to bring his attraction right to the surface and there was something about the way his lips moved that made Daryl quietly smile.

"Let me get my bag and coat."

Daryl and Amir walked out of his office, down the stairs and out of the building into the snowy day. The light flakes twirled magically through the air before settling onto the earth.

"How's Kevin?" Amir asked suddenly. Daryl knew he wasn't terribly interested in how Kevin was doing, but far more curious about how their relationship was faring. Daryl had to admit he was flattered by Amir's tacit interest. It made him feel desirable; something he had not felt from Kevin in quite some time.

Daryl had run into Amir one night at the Bachelor's Mill, one of D.C.'s more famous black gay bars. He had had a fight with Kevin and simply did not want to be in the house with him anymore. Like the river finds the sea, he ended up at the bar, trying to drink away Kevin's harsh words. When Daryl entered the establishment and paid his cover charge, he immediately went upstairs to order a strong drink. If there was one thing you could find at the Mill, it was a strong drink. He ordered an Absolut vodka and cranberry juice, but ended up with a plastic cup full of vodka and a small splash of cranberry; added mainly for color, no doubt. Daryl had taken a seat at a table in the back by the patio and tried to be inconspicuous. He didn't go out very often because he didn't want to risk running into one of his students. He never considered himself "in the closet," but he didn't want to create an awkward situation for himself at the college.

Daryl saw Amir walk into the room and proceed to the bar, but he did not attempt to hide. Instead, he sat there, took a gulp of his elixir, and smiled at Amir as he turned from the bar and noticed Daryl sitting. It was the first time they had run into each other at a gay club.

"He's doing well," Daryl said plainly as he brought himself out of his reflection. "He's probably closing down the restaurant even as we speak. How is your friend? I forgot his name."

Daryl knew that Amir had noticed his not-so-subtle attempt to deflect his inquiries. Daryl didn't want to talk about his relationship with Kevin. It wasn't appropriate. He had always tried to maintain a professional distance from Amir, but ever since that night at the Mill they had begun to divulge more and more personal information to each other. Daryl was actually beginning to see him as a friend; not merely his teaching assistant.

"Who? Antonio?"

"Is that the one you met at the gym?"

"Yep, that's him, but we don't talk anymore. I think he was trying to run game, and you know I'm not into all of that. Every single time we tried to get together, something would *happen* to come up and we'd have to reschedule. I have never had to work so hard to get someone to have dinner with me, so I figured that either he was full of shit, or the universe was telling me to back away. Either case, I got the message. I can't believe it's so hard to find a good man in D.C. Everyone is always talking about how they don't play games and they aren't looking for players, but the ones I've met since I've been here have their issues or are big Internet whores. All these damned sex parties and hook-up sites make it very difficult to find someone who's about more than sex. I'm beginning to think everyone needs medication and therapy. I don't know how an entire city gets to be full of crazy folks—maybe they put something in the water here in D.C." They both laughed. "I mean, the only man I've met who I really like has a lover."

Amir turned and looked at Daryl as he spoke. A dull silence fell upon them and, in those few seconds of silence, Amir had put everything on the table. Silence often says far more than words. "It's like the ones who like you are the ones you don't like, and the ones you like are already taken. This dating and relationship thing is for the birds."

The brutal honesty of Amir's words caught Daryl off guard because he had never been so overt in his approach to him. Yet, Daryl let the words dwell in his soul and momentarily fill the void left by Kevin's emotional distance. They walked in silence the remaining steps to Amir's Toyota Corolla that was parked on a side street right off Florida Avenue. Amir opened the doors and they got into the car, both trying not to notice the subtle exchange of glances between them.

"I have to let the car warm up for a few minutes," Amir said once they were comfortably seated in the car. "I didn't mean to make you uncomfortable back there."

"Trust me, Amir, I'm not uncomfortable. I'm actually really flattered by your words but—"

"Yeah, yeah, I know. You got a man and I'm your teaching assistant, blah, blah, blah. I've heard it all before. I know all of that, but I can't figure out why I can't stop thinking about you." They sat in the car, staring at each other in the charged atmosphere. Daryl tried to resist the attention aimed at him, but he couldn't help but be drawn into this man. "You are often the first thing on my mind when I wake up in the morning and usually the last thing in my head as I fall asleep. If I told you about some of the dreams I've had about you, we'd both be embarrassed."

Amir leaned closer and closer to Daryl until their lips were close enough to meet. As Amir approached, Daryl thought of Kevin. He knew that the split second before he and Amir kissed would define the kind of man he would become. In that passing second a thousand questions raced through his mind at supersonic speeds. Was he willing to risk the life they had built and was he willing to lose Kevin's love? Even though they were having problems, Daryl knew he wasn't ready to let Kevin go. In that endless second with nothing between his lips and Amir's, everything he used to feel for Kevin came rushing back to him. Was he ready to betray the man whom he had prized for so many years and forsake their relationship? If they kissed, how far would it go? Would he be able to stop? How would they work together after this? How would he live with the guilt? Was he ready to become the kind of man who cheated? *Temptation is a motherfucker and it always comes in such a pretty package*, he thought.

"Amir," Daryl faintly said. With the simple utterance of his name, he backed off. They backed off.

For the rest of the ride home, they sat in virtual silence; letting the music from the radio fill the car with thumping sounds. This was the first time he and Amir had gotten that close, and Daryl was relieved he had been able to resist his advances. For the first time, he realized he wasn't immune from or incapable of infidelity. He had been tempted in a way he had never been before and that scared him. He really wished he was home because the longer he sat in the car with Amir, the more his mind began to think about things he shouldn't wonder about. In spite of Kevin, he was sinfully captivated by the possibility of Amir.

In spite of his lustful desires, this moment with Amir made his love for Kevin stronger. He really missed him and who they used to be together. They used to have such fun and their love was easy, like the breeze. Daryl thought about what could have happened had he kissed Amir and what it could have meant for him and for his life. He had never been one to cheat, and anyone who says cheating *just happens* is a liar. It doesn't just happen. There are as many opportunities as there are seconds in a day for someone to make the right choice. People always say, after they get caught, that the affair didn't mean anything to them. He could hear Kevin's stinging voice telling him if he was willing to risk the life they had built together over something that didn't mean anything to him, then that must mean Kevin meant even less. They had their problems and Amir was very attractive, but he was unwilling to lose Kevin over this man. The price of a simple kiss was far too high. But, the flesh is weak.

Daryl retraced his journey of love and life with Kevin from Austin to Houston to D.C., and he thought about how their love had grown slowly over time. It had aged like a perfect bottle of pinot noir. He thought about the first time he kissed Kevin and how wonderful and soft his lips were. He thought about the first time they made love and the magic they created. He thought about Kevin's favorite song—the song that became *their* song. He remembered that night in Houston a few years back when he surprised Kevin with a romantic dinner on the rooftop of a downtown skyscraper. He had a table set up with Kevin's favorite meal and, when Kevin came out onto the rooftop, Daryl serenaded him with the song. Before Kevin saw him, he *heard* him. And that was the night that "I Feel Good All Over" by Stephanie Mills became their song, and it had never been more appropriate.

As Amir navigated the narrow and weathered D.C. streets, Daryl tried to understand why he felt so disconnected from Kevin. It wasn't anything that suddenly happened. It was more like a growing infestation they failed to address. Maybe they were restless and simply not wanting to be settled anymore. Straight couples are said to have a seven-year itch in regards to marriage. After seven years, they were more prone to an affair or a divorce. Daryl always joked that one year in a gay relationship is like three years in a straight one. So, maybe the restlessness was their seven-year itch. Or, maybe it was being in a new city, with new friends and a new job. Or, maybe it was something entirely different. Kevin had been extraordinarily busy with the restaurant, and there were times when Daryl felt alone and lonely. Kevin definitely hadn't given him the attention he was used to and their sex life had slowed considerably, but that shouldn't have been enough for him to place himself in a situation where he could be tempted. Half the battle of remaining monogamous is to remove temptation, he always told himself. In any of his past relationships, Daryl made sure he didn't put himself in situations where he could be tempted, and he knew getting in the car with Amir, feeling the way he was feeling when he left the office, was a bad thing. Yet, he did it anyway. Daryl felt awful about allowing himself to be tempted.

As they approached the place he called home, the snow fell down in big white, spiraling balls. He felt as if his guilt was raining down on him in a fit with sudden fury. Amir slowed and eventually came to a stop in front of the door. They exchanged a few heavy glances and said their goodbyes. As Amir drove away slowly and the snow poured down on him, Daryl took a deep breath as he came to a most unsettling realization. He wasn't feeling awful because they had almost kissed. He felt awful because they had not.

CHAPTER 4

Kevin was draped across the chaise lounge next to the window in the bedroom of their Capitol Hill Victorian townhouse as he waited for Daryl to arrive. The speed in which the snow fell had accelerated and Kevin had expected Daryl to be home some time ago. According to the television weather reports, most businesses, including city and federal agencies, had closed almost two hours ago. He hoped Daryl was okay.

He looked around, mesmerized by his life and what they had achieved together. After convincing Daryl to leave Houston for D.C., Kevin remembered how they faced the daunting task of finding a house in their new city. D.C was a bastion of liberalism and had a prominent and active gay population, including a couple of openly gay men on the city council. Dupont Circle, the famous and sometimes notorious gay haven on the northwest side of the city, had become very trendy as more and more straight, yuppie, white couples moved into the area and drove property values to an all-time high. That area did not appeal to either of them. The Capitol Hill area, also a prime prospect for gentrification, had yet to feel the full thrust of change, and property values in that area remained somewhat lower. Not only that, but the neighborhood was experiencing redevelopment at a slower pace than some other parts of the city which helped to maintain the history and character of the area.

When they first laid eyes on the Old World, four-level Victorian townhouse, they instantly fell in love with it. The red brick and strong stone frame added texture and character, and it served as a stark contrast to the modern home Kevin lived in with his past lover in Houston.

When they entered the house for the first time with the real estate agent, the house exhaled a puff of stale air, as if it was the first time in years it had breathed. They slowed their approach so they could take in all of the building and its unique characteristics. Their minds ran wild on the possibilities of what this place could become with a little work. They imagined new paint, wallpaper and the combination of a couple of rooms to make a larger, more open space. Once the fruits of their imaginations had ripened, they imagined living there for many years to come.

The entire third level of the house was the master suite complete with a huge bedroom, which was by far larger than any room either of them had seen in a house. They decided it would be the perfect backdrop for their new life together. Kevin fell in love with the double-sided fireplace—one side of it could heat the bedroom and the other the master bath, which contained a huge black marble tub that could easily fit four and a large walk-in shower with gold trim. On the second level there were two rooms that could be used as guest bedrooms or office space and an open space that would serve as the den with a bar they could stock with the finest liquor. The doors to the balcony were right behind the bar, and on a nice summer evening they could have a drink and sit out on the balcony and look at the world. Immediately, they made an offer and the deed was done.

Kevin finished off his cup of tea and knew he could be using this time to go over the books from the restaurant instead of reminiscing. He got up from the chaise and walked into his office downstairs. Six months ago, Kevin made an offer to purchase his favorite restaurant in the Eastern Market area of D.C. because he had always dreamed of owning one. Ninety percent of new restaurants failed within the first few years, so Kevin didn't want to take the chance of losing money on a business that statistically was almost doomed to failure from the beginning. Instead, he wanted to purchase an existing restaurant and learn the business from the inside out.

The restaurant was a Latin and Cuban mix with a warm and inviting environment and friendly staff. It was simply called Jose's. The Eastern Market area, within a few blocks of the United States Capitol, was enjoying a new burst of life as more people moved into the neighborhood. After months of haggling, the offer Kevin made was finally accepted three months ago because the owner decided he wanted to retire and return to his native country of Colombia, and he didn't have family here to whom he could leave the business.

When the purchase was completed, Kevin didn't make any major changes; in fact, he kept most of the staff, including the restaurant manager—Mr. Martinez—who was teaching him the business. When the sale was first announced, Mr. Martinez threatened to quit because he was under the impression the owner was going to sell the restaurant to him. Apparently, he and the owner had held previous conversations about it and Mr. Martinez had made him an offer. Fortunately, for Kevin, his offer was too low and he had no way of raising the extra cash to make a viable counteroffer. Kevin had to convince Mr. Martinez not to quit and ensured him that he would still be able to run the restaurant. At first, he offered a lot of resistance and attitude but, after a few weeks, he understood Kevin wasn't going to fire him. Kevin's powers of persuasion brought him to his corner—that and a twenty percent raise.

The sound of footsteps coming up the stairs broke Kevin's thoughts. Kevin backed away from the computer to meet Daryl at the door.

"Hey, baby, how are you?" Kevin said. Daryl gave him a quick kiss on the lips and they took the extra flight of stairs to the bedroom.

"It is so cold out there. The snow is really coming down—again," Daryl said as he hung up his coat and moved to the bed. He let out an audible sigh as he plopped down onto the bed and started to remove his shoes. "I hope Amir gets home safely."

"Amir?" Kevin asked.

Daryl sensed uneasiness in Kevin's tone, but ignored it. He purposely mentioned Amir's name in an attempt to put Kevin at ease so the next time he mentioned Amir, Kevin wouldn't be put off.

"Yeah, he was passing through the neighborhood on his way home and he offered to drop me off."

"Oh, I see." Kevin's tone more than hinted of discomfort.

"What does that mean?"

"Nothing."

Kevin tried to hide his annoyance at the mentioning of that boy's name. Kevin didn't feel threatened by him, but he knew Amir had a thing for Daryl, and Kevin wasn't sure if he was the kind of person who would make a move on someone's man. Each time the name was mentioned, Kevin felt as if Amir inched his way a little closer to Daryl.

"Baby, please don't start. You know Amir is my teaching assistant. That's it. I don't know why you don't like him. What has he ever done to you?"

"It's not what he's done to me, but what he wants to do to you."

"You have no reason to say anything like that. Have you ever seen him do anything inappropriate? Huh? Have you ever heard anything flirtatious come out of his mouth?"

Daryl's defensiveness caused veins to slightly bulge in his neck. This wasn't their first conversation about Amir, but there was something that wouldn't allow Kevin to let it go. He knew there was something hiding right beneath the surface of Daryl's professional relationship with Amir.

"Of course not; considering I've only met him once. But that doesn't mean he hasn't or won't try something sooner or later."

"What, you think he's made a move on me?"

Daryl folded his arms and glared at him. He wasn't really looking at him, but more like trying to look into his head; wondering how he could have such a strong sense about someone he'd seen only once. He recalled that day when Kevin tried to surprise him for lunch and, even though nothing was going on, Daryl felt what Kevin felt when he walked in the room. Part of Daryl's attitude was his fear that Kevin could see past his defensive walls and know that Daryl, too, was attracted to Amir. In spite of his defenses and his shields, Kevin knew about the lust lingering in Daryl's heart.

"If he had made a pass at you, would you tell me?" Kevin shot back.

"I don't know when you became so damned suspicious. I am not interested in that boy. He is my assistant. Period."

"If you didn't give me reasons to question you, then I wouldn't. Your eyes light up when you mention his name."

Daryl panicked. "What the fuck are you talking about? This is so pointless. If you're looking for proof that I've done something wrong, then keep looking. When you find it, let me know. I can't believe you said that shit." Daryl turned his back to Kevin as he walked over to the closet and threw his shoes into the darkened room.

"I know what your eyes look like when you're excited about something. I used to see that same look in your eyes when you looked at me."

"What do you want from me? What do you want me to do, quit my damned job, or better yet, fire Amir over your suspicions? I'll simply walk up to the dean and tell him that my jealous lover doesn't like my teaching assistant and I'll request that he assign me someone ugly. Will that make you happy?"

Kevin stared at him; almost at a loss for words. He was battling for Amir and, in spite of all his heated words, Kevin still knew. And, Daryl knew that Kevin knew. The truth is not something you can run from forever. Here, it was a naked force that would not be denied in spite of Daryl's anemic attempts to cover it. Kevin knew he hadn't been intimate with the boy—his spirit told him that much—but he wanted Daryl to at least acknowledge the validity of his suspicions, which Daryl seemed incapable of doing. Daryl remained steadfast in his denial of any attraction toward Amir and that only fueled Kevin's suspicions.

"The *gentleman* doth protest too much." Kevin took liberty at altering the famous Shakespearean quote, and Daryl threw his hands into the air in a defeatist motion. This whole conversation had been blown out of proportion, as far as Daryl was concerned. When Daryl came home, Kevin didn't have any intention of discussing Amir or anything related to him, let alone arguing with Daryl. Yet, they found themselves in the midst of a great battle in which neither of them would win. They had gotten so much into this cycle of arguing that they often forgot what they were arguing about. Usually, at the end, when both sides had retreated to their respective sides to tend their wounds, neither of them could remember how the battle had started. Yet, their warm blood still flowed and neither side could claim victory.

"Baby," Kevin continued, "I don't want to fight with you and I didn't mean to start anything."

"Well, you did," he shot back quickly, still very engaged in battle and firing his artillery.

"Damn, can you let me apologize?" They both stopped and looked at each other; each of them too proud and too angry to let it go. Kevin took a deep breath and moved toward the window in the room. In a faint voice, his hollow words still rang out. "You're changing right before my very eyes."

"What am I changing into?"

"Someone I don't know. You're so defensive about everything. I don't know what's going on with you."

"If I'm defensive it's because you see suspicion in everything I do. Nothing I do or say anymore is right or good enough for you. Every time I mention Amir, or mention that I want to go out, you immediately get this look in your eyes like you don't trust me. That hurts. I remember when we first started dating and everything was so great between us. I remember telling you that I needed you to love me for who I was right then, and not for who you wanted me to be. I couldn't promise you that I'd ever be any better than I was back then. That's how I loved you—for who you were and not for who I wanted you to be. I knew that if you never changed I could love you exactly the way you were. We both agreed to that. This is who I am. I have not changed. If anyone has changed, it's you, but I need you to trust and believe in me again."

Kevin paused. "You haven't changed? Do you remember yesterday when we ran into that dude from your gym?"

"Yeah, what about it?"

"Do you remember how you introduced me?"

Daryl rubbed his head and thought about it for a minute while he tried to figure out Kevin's point. "Yeah. I said this is my friend, Kevin. What about it?"

"Friend? You introduced me to one of your gay friends as a *friend* and you don't understand why that is a problem?"

"Why don't you explain it to me?"

"Daryl, I am much more than your friend. We have been together for three years and you haven't introduced me as your friend in years. I am your lover, your partner and I used to be your baby, but now I'm simply your friend. I've been demoted."

"You're making too big a deal of that."

"Am I? Have you ever heard of a man introducing his wife as his friend, or vice versa? I have earned the right to be called more than your friend. Now, if you were introducing me to one of your colleagues or someone who didn't know you were gay, then I'm fine with you introducing me that way. But, in a gay setting or to other gay folks, I am not simply your friend; unless that's how you see me."

"You know I see you as more than a friend and I'm sorry if I said that—it slipped out."

"I'm sure."

"I don't know what's going on with us."

"Me either. All I know is that things are different. You are different. I don't think you like me, let alone love me anymore, and I can't love you if you won't open up and let me."

"I have always loved you. Never doubt that, but you're changing, too. You say you don't know who I am anymore. Well, sometimes, I don't know who you are. You seem so happy to be residing in this big house and owning your restaurant that you have forgotten about me—about us."

"I'm not going to apologize for wanting a better life. After all of the shit I—we've—been through the last three years, you should want to live well, too."

"Yeah, but we didn't *earn* this money or this house—"

"Oh, I earned every cent of this money—"

"But, not from a job."

Kevin could not believe those cutting and permanently damaging words had escaped from Daryl's mouth. Daryl's verbal shards of glass cut deep and once his poison-laced words were said, they could never be unsaid. Daryl was acutely aware of all the abuse Kevin had suffered from James. Upon James's death, Kevin was truly surprised when he found out he was the benefactor and James had bequeathed him most of his property and money. James was truly an evil man but, in the end, Kevin knew James had loved him the only way he knew how. And, it was unfortunate that his love was expressed with fists.

"Is that what all of this is about? You don't want to live in this house I bought for us because James left me some money when he died? Is that what this is really about?"

"It's about that and the fact that you never even talked to me about the money."

"What was there to talk about? He left me a lot of money. I took it. It was a no-brainer. What was there to discuss?"

"I didn't feel like I was a part of your life then, and I don't feel like I'm a part of your life now. Since Keevan died, you have a way of pushing everyone away; regardless of how close we try to get."

"What the fuck are you talking about? Why are you bringing my brother into this conversation? This has nothing—nothing—to do with him. This is about you and me. And, if I have been distant, you haven't wasted any time trying to fill the void. I'm sure Amir will be everything you hoped I would be."

Once again, they stood in silence, each calculating where to go from here. Kevin realized he had been forever changed by the death of his identical twin brother several years back, but he never anticipated Daryl would use that as a weapon. In the past, the mere mention of Keevan's name was enough to shatter Kevin's soul, but he was much stronger now. However, he still didn't want anyone using Keevan's name to win points in an argument.

"You know what; I have a lot of work to do so I'm going to my office to finish up there."

Kevin walked over to the computer and started gathering up his papers. Daryl walked over to him, grabbed him by the waist and pulled Kevin into his body. Daryl inserted his tongue into his mouth and for a fleeting second Kevin fought back, but his desire rose. Kevin never could resist him. Kevin kissed him back with rage and fury and pushed him onto the bed with force. He didn't bother to take the time to unbutton Daryl's shirt, opting instead to rip it open. He immediately started licking, kissing and biting Daryl's nipples as Daryl grunted with pleasure and pain. Daryl then rolled Kevin onto his back and, in record time, Kevin was naked and Daryl was straddling him. Moments later, they found themselves fucking with passion and earth-shattering fury. Moans and grunts escaped from their mouths as their bodies burned and turned. Their experience was forceful and heated and animalistic. As Daryl pounded his flesh into Kevin, Kevin grabbed Daryl by the head and forced his lips into his mouth. He licked and kissed and bit Daryl's lips with such power that he drew droplets of blood. But, they didn't stop. The bloodlust was beyond their control. The anger and pain that had swelled within their souls fueled their rite as their relationship was spread out on the altar. This sexual ritual was an attempt at saving what was left of their lives together. The pounding of flesh and huffs of breaths and drops of blood and sweat came together in a cacophonous symphony of desire and rage. It was their sacrifice, but neither knew if it was enough.

t took a couple of days of unseasonably warm temperatures for the snow to melt enough for the city to return to some semblance of life. The past few days saw the mercury rise to hit the lower-fifties, but on this day the bitter cold returned with much attitude. Even the icy temperatures failed to cool hot-heated drivers who wanted to vacate the city at the end of a long workday. Snarled traffic and angry drivers who were prone to road rage made the mad dash home at the end of the day even more cumbersome. Mounds of dirty and knotted snow were piled up on the sides of streets like small urban combat hills. These snow mounds were the result of city snow crews clearing the major roads by pushing the snow to the curbs. It would take days, maybe even weeks, depending on the weather, for the mounds to melt away completely. Even still, brave Washingtonians confronted the sharp breezes and went about their evening tasks.

When Daryl left work, he decided to unwind in a familiar area of town. He knew Kevin would be at the restaurant and he didn't feel like going home to an empty house. Even though they argued incessantly, sometimes loneliness was worse. Ironically, even when Kevin was home, it still felt empty and he felt alone.

After searching for what seemed like an eternity for a parking space in Dupont Circle, he finally succeeded and hurriedly parked his car on the side of the road near P Street Beach, a neighborhood park near the bar. He put the car in park, snatched his gloves off the passenger's seat, and exited the vehicle. He zipped across the street as the light changed from red to green and vehicles started in his direction.

When Daryl walked into The Fireplace, which used to be one of his favorite bars, a strong sense of familiarity overcame him. It had been several months since he had been out to this bar and, when he did go out, typically he would go out with Kevin as a couple. But today he was being pulled there, not out of desire, but out of a need for attention. He checked his watch. It was almost six-fifteen p.m. He planned on being there only for a short time since this was meant to be a happy hour excursion. When he looked around the bar, he felt slight pangs of guilt and a contradicting sense of exhilaration. He felt as if he was doing something wrong because Kevin would not approve of his visit to the bar. Yet, somehow, he was excited. It was a very odd sensation, something that tingled in his bones, but even still he did not slow his pace as he made his way to the back of the bar and upstairs to the room that was frequented mainly by black men.

As soon as he walked into the interior of the upstairs bar, his lungs were assaulted by thick cigarette smoke. R&B music blasted from the speakers that hung diagonally across the bar from each other. Aside from the fresh coat of red paint on the walls, the place looked and felt the same; even after being away for months. The same faces that lined the stools around the bar when he was a regular were still sitting at the bar. Daryl wondered whether or not they had ever left.

He made his way through the crowded room and stood in the corner by the mirror. Slowly, he removed his gloves and his hat and tried to shake off the chill he had encountered outside. He surveyed the room, still not sure what he was doing there, but assessing the situation. The room was filled with a variety of men of all sizes and shapes and ages. Quite a few old men gaily sauntered through the room, most likely looking for some young stud they could liquor up and then use to satisfy their ancient needs. Daryl could only laugh out loud recalling a warning about old men from his first lover's best friend Jeremiah—who was an old man himself—about predatory older gentlemen. "Be careful when you go out. Don't let them old men buy you nothing. All they want to do is get you drunk and then *have* you. Old men will give you worms." Daryl never quite figured out what he meant by "worms," but it wasn't something he ever wanted to discover.

As usual, intermixed within the crowd were a few obligatory straight women who most likely had become regulars in the bar themselves. For some women hanging out with gay men was the highlight of their lives. They were introduced to the bars and clubs by their gay friends, who felt it was okay to bring straight women to gay establishments. It's great to have female friends, Daryl always thought, but why a straight woman would choose to spend so much of her time in a gay bar was beyond him. Straight women had thousands of clubs to choose from and he didn't always like the idea of them invading places that were meant to be sanctuaries for gay men.

Daryl decided it was time to make the most of the happy hour and take his place in line at the bar. As he moved through the crowd toward the bar, he tried to ignore the glances of people checking him out. He smiled and thought, *I still got it*. When he got to the bar, he placed the order for his drink.

"How much?" Daryl inquired.

"Nothing. It's already been paid for," replied the bartender. Daryl shot him a confused look. "Someone paid for it already."

"Really?" Daryl was quite surprised. "I think I'll pay for it myself."

"It's a free drink. Take it and enjoy it," the bartender said as he pushed the drink toward Daryl.

"At least tell me who bought it."

"He'll let you know, I'm sure."

With those words, the bartender turned his back and took another order from the other side of the bar. Daryl stood there, slightly confused, but also intrigued by this simple and unexpected turn of events. He moved back into his corner by the mirror and took a sip of his drink. The very potent drink caused his face to wrinkle as he took his first sip.

"Ahh, I see we have a virgin here," a voice said to him. Daryl turned to his left and there was a man who must have been in his late-fifties smiling at him.

"Excuse me?"

"I can tell by the look on your face that you haven't had a Fireplace drink before. They'll knock you on your ass if you're not careful."

The man, with salt and pepper hair and a full gray beard, actually wasn't that unattractive, as far as older men go. He stood about six feet, was very well-groomed and had all of his teeth, which was a good thing. Daryl tried to mask his smile when he thought about that.

"I'm not new here. It's been a while though."

Daryl wondered if this man was the admirer who had pre-purchased his drink. He wanted to ask but then didn't want the old man assuming credit for an act of kindness he didn't commit to score some points.

"If you know the Fireplace like I do, then you know you haven't missed a thing. It'll always be the same." Daryl nodded his head in polite agreement and secretly longed for the old man to go away. "Where is your boyfriend?" the old man asked with little discretion.

"He should be here in a few minutes." Daryl lied without hesitation as he looked at his watch, pretending to wonder what was keeping his man away. "He must have gotten caught up at the office, but he'll be here soon."

Daryl couldn't tell if the look on the man's face was incredulity or disappointment. The man lingered for a few moments making small talk before finally excusing himself. Like clockwork, the old man was on to his next victim. At this point, Daryl decided he needed a different vantage point. He picked up his coat, gloves, and scarf and headed downstairs where the light was a bit brighter.

He found an empty table over by the windows and the burning fireplace. He looked out onto the streets and watched people move with deliberate speed to their destination—it was far too cold to loiter. He remembered when he and Kevin first moved to the area and would frequent this bar during the summertime. The place was packed on Thursday and Sunday nights to the point that it was almost impossible to maneuver through the small bar. On those occasions, many people chose to fill the sidewalks outside of the bar, to see and be seen. Kevin and Daryl enjoyed being with each other, being amongst friends and enjoying the moderate summer evenings. He missed those days.

"Is this seat taken?" a stranger asked, pulling Daryl back into the moment. Daryl was slightly annoyed that someone had interrupted his thoughts but, in a crowded bar, distractions were plentiful. When he turned to answer the stranger, he was awestruck by the incomparable good looks of the man. His annoyance suddenly vanished and he fought back a smile.

"Not at all."

The man pulled out the wooden bar stool, set his drink on the table and made himself comfortable. "Thank you. How are you this evening?" he asked.

"I'm fine and you?"

"Doing much better now. I thought I had lost you."

"I beg your pardon?"

"I saw you upstairs through the crowd and wanted to meet you, but then I saw some old dude all up in your face. Next thing I knew, you were gone."

"I don't know who that dude was, but I really didn't feel like being bothered by him. It's like you can't go out and have a drink without some busted raggedy-ass man trying to holla at you."

"I know what you mean. I like coming here because of the drinks and some nights are really cool, but other times these fools be up here sweatin' you hard. That's one of the things that caught my attention about you. You didn't look pressed about anything. You came in, found a spot, ordered a drink, and chilled. By the way, you can thank me for the drink anytime you're ready."

The stranger smiled as he took a sip of his beer. Daryl watched him bring the nose of the bottle up to his full red lips.

"You bought my drink? You didn't have to—"

"I know I didn't have to, but I wanted to."

"Well—" Daryl stopped abruptly, realizing he didn't know the stranger's name. "What's your name?"

"Temple."

"Temple?"

"Yes, Temple."

"Well, Temple, thank you for the drink. Your next one is on me."

"What if I wanted something besides a drink?"

Daryl didn't answer the loaded question. They both took another sip of their drinks. Taboo thoughts of Temple filled Daryl's head.

"Temple is a very interesting name," he finally said. "How did your parents come up with that one?"

Temple looked Daryl directly in his eyes. Usually, when he was asked that question, it irritated him, but not this time. Daryl intrigued him. He wanted to tell the story, but he didn't want to sound too cocky. He smiled again.

"Why are you smiling?"

"Just smiling at you. The look on your face tells me that you really want to know the answer."

"I never ask questions I don't want to hear the answer to."

"That's a good policy. I'll keep that in mind."

"So, what's the answer?"

"It's such a stupid story, but my mother said that all through her pregnancy she couldn't think of a name for me. She was going to name me after my father, but his name is Horatio and she hated that name. So, when she finally saw me and they placed me in her arms, she said I was the most beautiful baby she had ever seen and she knew that when I grew up people would want to be around me, or as she put it, 'they would worship at my temple.' So, that's what she named me—Temple."

"Wow. That's interesting. Is it true?"

"Is what true?"

"Do people worship at your temple?"

Temple's face lit up and his dimples made their first appearance. Something about Daryl— the way he spoke, the way he chose his words, his sincerity, his honesty—excited Temple in ways Cerina couldn't.

"I've been known to baptize a few people, but that was then. This is now. Over the last few years I've learned what's important about life."

"What have you learned?"

Even though he didn't believe it necessarily, he wanted to tell Daryl what he thought he wanted to hear. So, he said it. Something he rarely said. "Love. Life is all about learning and loving."

"You're a bit of a romantic, I see."

"You can say that."

"Would you like another drink? You're almost empty."

Temple looked at his bottle. "Sure, why not. How about a Long Island?"

"Coming right up."

Daryl walked around the little table toward the bar. As he walked, Temple stared at his ass, and he could tell through Daryl's slacks that it was nice and firm. Temple had always considered himself a butt man; regardless of which gender he was entertaining at the time. He thought Daryl was about the right height—five feet eleven inches—and the right size for what he had in mind. He could imagine himself getting naked with this stranger and doing every debauchery imaginable. He wanted to reach out and touch his butt, run his tongue up and down his spine, while the muscles in Daryl's back tightened. He wanted to kiss his perfect lips; even though Temple wasn't much of a kisser when it came to men. He thought kissing a man would make him gay, because kissing was so intimate. With Daryl, he would suspend that rule and let his tongue do gymnastics in his mouth.

Daryl made his way through the crowd and took his seat at the table next to Temple. He placed the drink down in front of this unfamiliar and hypnotic person. When Temple reached for the drink, their hands grazed each other and the electricity between them was undeniable. Daryl felt heat move swiftly up his arm, to his shoulder, and down his chest before finding a final resting place between his legs. He took a deep breath. And another one. And another one.

They both lost track of time during the next hour. Daryl placed all invading thoughts of Kevin and his relationship in a little box and tucked it neatly in the back corners of his mind; he enjoyed the moment and the freedom that it brought. It was amazing how he was able to compartmentalize his relationship. Temple, not the least bit concerned about Cerina, wanted more from this man than mere conversation. His cell phone had vibrated a few times throughout the evening, but he ignored it, as he usually did when she called.

The duo sat close enough to smell each other and Temple secretly sniffed Daryl's expensive cologne. Daryl carried himself in a way that suggested to Temple that he had money and resources and Temple thought he had found a great catch. Daryl had an aura of class that made him even more alluring to Temple. Maybe Temple thought he had found that attractive "sugar daddy" he was looking for to help subsidize his income. He knew there was only so much money Cerina could make swinging around a pole.

When Daryl finally glanced at his watch, he realized it was much later in the evening than he had anticipated and it was now time to go.

"Temple, as much as I've enjoyed this conversation, I've got to get home."

"You're not leaving me all alone, are you? It's too soon. Stay, have another drink with me," Temple said as he grabbed Daryl's hand.

"As sexy as you are and as much as I'd like to, I can't. I have to get home."

Daryl, during their hour-long conversation, had failed to mention Kevin in any substantial manner. And Temple didn't mention Cerina, either.

"Let me guess. You got a man at home?"

Daryl paused momentarily as he pondered whether or not to tell the truth. "Yeah, I got a man at home."

"You don't sound too happy about it," Temple retorted.

And, he was right. "Well, it's cool. It is what it is."

Temple looked so disappointed that Daryl actually considered staying for another round of drinks. He thought about it for a brief second, but reason won out over lust.

"Well, having a man doesn't mean you and I can't be friends," Temple replied. His words dripped with desire and sex and sweat. Daryl knew that if he didn't leave now, he wouldn't ever leave.

"Unfortunately, Temple, I've got to go." Daryl stood and grabbed his coat.

"When can I see you again? I'd like to spend some time getting to know you."

Damn, Daryl thought. One part of him wanted to escape the temptation and slide out of the bar without any hope of seeing this man again. No exchange of numbers or email addresses or anything that would facilitate further contact. He could remember this evening as two ships passing in the night. But, the other part got exactly what he wanted—the invitation. Daryl put on his coat, scarf and hat, and wondered whether or not he'd be strong enough to resist. He knew, unequivocally, that the best way to remain faithful and true to your relationship was to avoid temptation. He also thought about going home to Kevin, the emptiness that rested in their bed, the distance that had become a tenant in their home, and came to the conclusion that, in spite of their lingering difficulties, he loved Kevin more than he had ever loved anyone. Yet, at that moment, with Temple gazing lovingly at him, his love for Kevin wasn't enough. Temple grabbed one of the cards off the table and wrote down his name and his cell phone number. Daryl then grabbed a pen from his bag, wrote his cell number on a cocktail napkin, and quickly exited The Fireplace, partly ashamed, partly excited, and fully aroused. He had made a conscious decision to play with fire. He hoped he wouldn't get burned.

As Daryl scrambled down the busy street toward his car, the pangs of guilt he had felt walking into the bar had multiplied and were now tugging at his conscience. But, he was tired of feeling guilty. He felt guilty browsing the personal ads online. He felt guilty about being attracted to Amir. He felt guilty about coming out to The Fireplace for a simple drink. He didn't want to feel guilty anymore. So many thoughts swirled around inside him: guilt, excitement, passion, pain, thoughts of pleasure and thoughts of love. Outside, the cold wind cut across his face. Once inside the vehicle, he put the key in the ignition, turned on the heat and leaned back. He needed a moment to collect himself. The magnitude of what had just happened rested heavily upon his heart. What he felt in that smoky bar with Temple was by far stronger than anything he had thought about with Amir. He was in the danger zone and he knew it.

He thought about when he and Kevin finally got together after so many years of waiting. When Kevin hugged him, he knew he was home and no one would ever be able to tear down what they had built together. Slowly, but surely, over the last year or so, the bricks had begun to crumble and it wasn't caused by any outside influence—the foundation was corroding from the inside out. And now there he was, sitting in a car, outside of a bar actually contemplating the possibility of what could be with another man. He hoped and prayed Temple wouldn't call. In his heart, he knew that he would.

❀❀❀

Temple sipped on his drink for a few more minutes and let thoughts of Daryl dwell in his mind until he realized he was late for his evening with Cerina. He knew he'd catch hell for being late, but somehow he didn't care. He knew all he'd have to do was lay the pipe right, and she'd get over it. He poured the rest of the liquor down his throat at exactly the right moment. He could see some dude making his way toward him. The man looked like something from the Addams Family and Temple could see his ragged smile through the crowd. His teeth were dull and spaced far apart in his mouth like he had a tooth every now and then. He made eye contact with Temple, who had proceeded to put on his coat and gather his belongings. The man walked right up to him, smiled, stood there for a few seconds. Temple barely acknowledged his presence and exited The Fireplace.

He stopped right outside of the bar and reached into his pocket for the keys to his cousin's car and found the lone cigarette he had bummed from some man upstairs. Sometimes, when he drank he liked to have a cigarette to enhance the effects of the drinks. When he put it to his lips, he realized that although he had a cigarette, he didn't have a light. He searched his pockets hoping he had inadvertently picked up one of the books of matches that were scattered throughout the bar, but came up empty-handed. Right as he was about to turn and re-enter the bar, a voice caught his attention.

"Need a light?" the beautiful woman asked of him as she raised her lighter up to the cigarette dangling from his mouth. His heart stopped. After she lit his, she then took a cigarette out of an expensive-looking gold case and put one in her mouth and lit it, too. Temple forced a smile. Never, not even in his wildest nightmare, did he ever expect to hear that shrill voice again. It sounded like fingernails on a chalkboard as far as he was concerned. It made the hairs on the back of his neck stand at attention and the shiver in his spine wasn't due to the wind. When he finally exhaled, the smoke slowly left his mouth and hung frozen in the air as if in suspended animation.

"Thank you," he said, trying to hide his shock.

"You're welcome," she replied with a catty smile.

They exchanged mutual glares at each other as the hate of years past drifted to the surface on this cold evening. Even though the temperature was in the low-twenties, the cold did not faze either of them. They stood and smoked; in silence. Temple had hoped he'd never have to lay eyes on her face again, but there she was, in Washington, D.C., and there they were, outside of The Fireplace, smoking cigarettes as if their union were natural. In spite of the fact they had shared a few previous past encounters, they had never been friends. They were too much alike to be friends and too scandalous to be lovers for long. They were birds of prey—opportunistic, cunning, and poisonous.

Slowly, Temple eyed her from head to toe. He remembered vividly the kind of body she had and all the power she held between her thighs. They had shared some explosive sexual encounters in the past but he knew that wasn't why she was here. He noticed a small, two-inch scar on her right cheek and she had lightened her hair to the point that it was almost blonde. Temple usually hated black women who dyed their hair blonde, but it blended well with her light skin. Beyond that, she hadn't changed a bit. Her breasts stood at attention and looked like a couple of melons strapped to her chest. He wanted to sneak a peek at her ass, but dared not. Temple could not believe that after all the time that had passed and all they had been through and the hate they shared for each other, she still turned him on. He hated being attracted to her but then he remembered how that hate fueled their encounters—it made their sexual relations explosive.

"How did you get that scar on your face? Did some woman finally cut you for fuckin' her man?" Temple asked with a slight jab.

She looked at him with scorn. "I was in an accident—a fire."

"Sorry to hear that. As vain as you are, I'm surprised you didn't rush to the nearest plastic surgeon and have it removed," he said.

She sucked her breath. "You should know about vanity. And, for the record, I'm leaving it there for a reason," she said plainly. When she spoke those words, her eyes dulled and her demeanor changed. From the look on her face, Temple knew there was a story there.

"Even still, you remain the most beautiful woman I've ever known."

She gave him a perfunctory *thank you* and exhaled. The next few moments were filled with silence as Temple waited for her to speak. He knew they hadn't run into each other by coincidence. With her, there were no coincidences. So, he waited. She had a flare for the dramatic so this tension-filled moment would serve her purpose well.

"What are you doing out on a cold night like this? Shouldn't you be scheming to get some old lady's Social Security check?" she finally asked.

"I've moved on to bigger and better things—you taught me that." They both smiled. "I'm sure you didn't come all this way from Houston to have a cigarette with me. Why don't you tell me what you're doing here?" Temple could no longer bear the suspense and the growing warning in his heart.

"Don't be in such a hurry. You act as if you have no time for an old friend."

"We were never friends, and I don't have time to play these little games with you."

"Who's playing games? Games are for children and I'm all woman. What I have in mind is something far better than a game." She looked at him and the sinister glint in her eyes sent another chill up his spine. Whatever her reason for tracking him down, he knew it couldn't be good.

"What do you want from me?"

"I want to make you an offer you can't refuse."

"And what if I do refuse?"

"Let's not go there, baby. Just do it for me. Otherwise, there's a judge in Houston who'd love to know your whereabouts."

He paused. He knew one day his past would catch up to him. He didn't expect it to be so soon. "What makes you think I won't disappear again?"

"Honey, you're not hard to find. It took me all of four days to track you down. All I had to do was follow the wake of destruction and broken hearts. And, besides, this will be very enjoyable for you."

"What exactly do I have to do?"

"First, tell me about the man you were talking to in the bar."

"Who? Daryl? Just some dude I was *working*."

"You like him?"

"Why?"

"Answer the question. Do you want to fuck him?"

He hesitated. "Yes." His short reply was punctuated with passion.

"Well, this is gonna be the makings of a beautiful working relationship." She took one last drag from her cigarette and let it fall to the ground. "Let me buy you a drink so we can discuss my offer in greater detail." She didn't wait for a response from Temple. She simply took him by the arm and led him away.

CHAPTER 6

Temple's heart sank low in his chest as RaChelle led him down the street. It was very strange that she was holding onto him as if they were a happy couple out doing some late-evening shopping. She was talking as if they really had something to say to each other. As they walked underneath a pale, starless December night, Temple gritted his teeth and wondered what she wanted from him. He was not about to get involved in another one of her schemes.

They walked into the swank Mimi's American Bistro on P Street and followed the hostess to a seat in the back. The restaurant, dimly lit with a Mediterranean flare, was a unique spot in the city because each night starting around seven, the wait staff would bellow out a mixture of songs in between serving food. Temple's first date with Cerina was at Mimi's and he remembered a small-framed white woman who *sang* Natalie Cole's "I'm Catching Hell." Her voice brought the patrons to their feet in a thunderous applause that continued for what seemed like several minutes. The woman blushed slightly, bowed and continued on to her server duties as if it wasn't anything special.

"This is one of my favorite spots when I come to this dreadful city," she said as the hostess walked away.

"What are we doing here?" he asked impatiently. He wanted her to get to the point because he didn't want to be around her any longer than he had to.

"Relax and have a drink with me." He could never relax with RaChelle because she always had a motive; like now. The moment you let down your guard and relaxed was the moment she'd pounce on you like a jungle cat.

"I've already had several drinks this evening and I'm late," he said.

"Cerina will be fine a few more minutes without you," she offered with a wink. Temple was about to ask her how she knew about Cerina when the waiter approached. He knew she had a way of finding out every detail of someone's life so he wasn't exactly surprised when she dropped Cerina's name.

"Good evening. My name is Cameron and I'll be your server. May I get you something to drink?" The waiter, appearing to be in his mid-twenties, paused for their response. Even before he had approached their table, Temple and RaChelle each had sized him up from across the room. They both had a talent for spotting attractive men and assessing their situations. He stood about five-feet nine-inches tall and had the most enchanting midnight-black skin either of them had seen in a long time. They both stared at him for a few seconds, mesmerized by his unconventional face. His facial features were distinctive—his nose was wide, his lips were full, and his teeth were pearly white. A sparkle danced in his deep-set eyes, but in spite of his boyish good looks, they concluded he wasn't worth the time of day for either of them—he was *only* a waiter.

"I'll just have water," Temple replied.

"I'm not drinking alone. We'll have two martinis."

Immediately, Temple's temperature started to rise as a result of RaChelle's take-charge and bossy attitude. Now, he knew he'd need that drink.

"How did you find me?" he asked as soon as the young waiter turned his back.

She did not reply. Instead, she focused her attention on the latest waiter to take the mic and start singing. Temple searched RaChelle's face for meaning and explanation, but found that pain and bitterness had replaced her sexy appeal and smile. He didn't know exactly what had happened, but he could tell that something weighed heavily upon her heart and was beginning to take its toll upon her face. Upon closer inspection, he noticed a few thin wrinkles originating in the corner of her eyes. She was too young for wrinkles, he thought, and attributed the premature aging to whatever darkness she carried. He tried not to stare at the scar on her cheek, but he couldn't refrain. It detracted from her beauty, but somehow it made her look…human.

Halfway through the martinis, she began to speak.

"The man you were speaking to in the bar—Daryl—I know him from Houston and I need your help."

"What kind of help would that be?"

"Stop interrupting me and I'll tell you."

Temple grimaced.

"He is part of the reason I have this scar on my face."

She spoke those words in a simple, matter-of-fact-manner that was as casual as ordering from a menu. As she spoke, she took her index finger and traced the scar on her face. She stroked it as if it brought her some unspoken comfort. Temple raised one eyebrow out of curiosity and to a lesser extent, out of fear. He had witnessed her wrath and wondered momentarily what Daryl—his new love interest—had done in the past to wrong her. And, he wondered how she'd get her revenge. She always got her revenge. She leaned back in her chair, gulped the rest of her martini, and motioned for the waiter to bring her another one.

"Maybe you should slow down with the drinks," Temple said.

"Maybe you should mind your own fucking business," she snapped.

Temple glossed over her abrasiveness and gave her the moment. "What did he do to you?"

"It's not really about him. He's only part of the problem. It's about his lover—Kevin."

"Wait. I thought you knew Daryl. You're confusing me. What did Daryl do to you?"

"What he's done to me is not really your concern. All you need to know is your part of the plan."

He audibly sighed and tried not to get frustrated. "I don't like the way this sounds."

"Quite simply, I want you to do what you do best. I want you to fuck Daryl. I want you to make it so good that he falls in love with you. I want you to do a complete number on him—body, mind and soul. I want you to break them up. I want Kevin to know what it feels like to lose the one he loves the most. It'll be easy for you; you're gorgeous and his relationship is on the rocks. And Daryl is restless. That's why he was in The Fireplace. All you have to do is make him feel important—*woo* him and he'll be yours. That's the good part about men—y'all are so easy. Stroke your little egos and make you feel important, and you can have anything you want. I want Kevin to suffer. There is no worse pain than having your lover cheat on you. Trust me, I know. And that's only the beginning. By the time I'm done, Kevin will wish he never met me."

"If Kevin is the one you're after, why not go after him? Why are you fucking with Daryl?"

"Because I always go for the hurt. It'll hurt Kevin far more to lose the thing he loves the most. Trust me; I know what I'm doing."

"I really don't want to be involved in this madness. I've changed a lot. I'm trying to get my life together. I'm not into that kind of shit anymore. You'll have to find someone else for your little revenge plot."

Her wicked laugh filled the room and echoed off the walls. "Give me a fuckin' break! You don't have a job and you're living with some bitch that swings around a pole to make money. She takes care of you, and you're still fuckin' every Tom, Dick, and Susan. How does that constitute getting your life together? You're the same player you used to be. I'm surprised you'd pick a lowly titty-dancer this time. Usually you go for the money—lawyers, doctors, and businesswomen—but you've downgraded, and that's fine, if that's what you're into these days. I don't know if that means you can't compete here in D.C., or if you're too damned lazy to set your sights higher."

Temple's glare said more than words could ever convey. The last thing he needed was her ass coming into town, spying on him and telling him what was wrong with his life. He didn't need her throwing that shit up in his face. But, clearly she had done her homework on him. He wouldn't have expected anything less from her—she was *always* prepared.

"I'm not about to get caught up in any more of your schemes. What we had was in the past and I'm not about to travel the same road with you. I won't help you."

"Temple, baby, don't make this difficult. This will work out for us both if you work with me. And, if you work Daryl right, you could possibly get your hands on some of his cash," she said as she rubbed his hand. "I know you're looking for a replacement for Cerina; someone with a bit more class."

"I'm not interested in his money." Temple knew that wasn't entirely true.

"Since when? Money and dick are the only things you're really interested in, but since I can't offer you the latter—"

"Fuck you. I'm outta here."

She took a sip of her martini. "I'll give Judge Kent your regards—and your address," she said as he stood.

He stopped. That was a name he hadn't heard in a long time, and it wasn't a name he wanted to get reacquainted with. He sat back down. "I'm listening."

She reached into her bag and pulled out a colored folder. Temple watched with interest as she pulled out her big guns. "Let's see," she began, "I hear they love pretty boys like you in prison." She pushed the folder over to him. He picked it up and thumbed through the sheets. Page after page after page he saw his former life in black and white—it was a life he had hoped to forget. Quickly, he closed the folder. He didn't need to see any more to know exactly where she was going with this. The dirt he dished out in the past was now being shoveled right back into his face. You can't run from the truth forever.

"The good judge has issued a warrant for your arrest. I'm sure he'd like to know exactly where you are. You're a pretty popular man in the state of Texas and you're wanted for a whole list of felonies, including fraud. How much money did you get from that old woman in Houston? I hear it was in the neighborhood of fifty grand."

Temple's heart threatened to punch through his chest as he remembered the violent night he had spent in jail when he was arrested for drunk driving a few years back. He remembered how the foul stench of urine and vomit and blood clogged his nostrils. He remembered the hungry and sexually charged stares of rough and rugged men whose primary desire was getting a piece of the new guy. Luckily, RaChelle pulled some strings with one of the judges she knew and had him released that night; even though it was the weekend. Jail was not an experience he was eager to repeat. He was far too pretty to do time.

He couldn't risk it when the district attorney filed charges with the grand jury and they indicted him on grand larceny charges about the missing fifty thousand dollars from the widow he had wined, dined, fucked, and robbed. He didn't think it was theft because she had willingly given him the check. Well, she was under the spell of his dick and the drugs he put in her drink. Temple fled the city in a blaze of shame. He couldn't go to jail. He knew he'd never survive a Texas prison—he'd kill himself first. He landed in D.C. and tried to remain low-key. He had made a comfortable life for himself a thousand miles away. Now everything was about to be undone.

"In spite of their unhappiness," she continued as if she hadn't mentioned his warrant, "they love each other. Your job is to destroy their relationship—to have an affair with Daryl and get him to fall in love with you, among other things."

"What other things?"

"I'll tell you later about those." Temple swallowed hard. He was in between a rock and a hard spot. When he got Daryl's number, he knew it would only be a matter of time before he got into his pants and his wallet. But, this was different. He wouldn't be the boss. He'd have to take orders from her.

"Let me be clear, Temple. I have absolutely no interest in sending you to jail—I couldn't care less about what you did in Texas or what you're doing here. If you do as I ask, then you'll never hear from me again—ever. If you resist, well, let's just say the Texas Department of Corrections is notorious for its in-house *hospitality*. And, don't try to run from me and disappear like you did when you left Texas. I found you in D.C.—I can find you anywhere because I will make it my life's mission to see you stand trial and go to jail. You don't want that. I don't want that. I know you don't want to spend the rest of your life running and looking over your shoulders for men with handcuffs. And, furthermore, I don't have the time or patience to chase you, but, make no mistake about it," she said as she leaned in closer to him, "if you run, I'll make the time. If you don't believe anything else, believe that. All I want is your help." Temple knew she was a woman of her word. He was tired of running and hiding. "But the bright side of this is that once I'm done with you, I'll make sure your charges are quietly dropped." She had Temple's full attention.

"And, how are you gonna do that?"

"Temple, you know I have my ways. I've caught Judge Kent in some very compromising positions with one of Houston's finest hookers. He's up for re-election next year and if his bitch of a wife finds out he's had yet another affair—with a hooker, mind you—he'll lose everything—his wife, his job, and a good deal of his money in the process. He doesn't want that."

"You really are a scary bitch," he said.

She winked. "You have no idea."

She made a formidable adversary, and he had to admire her gamesmanship. She had all the angles covered. Not only was she blackmailing him into helping her, she went the further step of holding out the proverbial carrot in front of his face. He needed those charges dropped. Once the charges were dropped, Temple would be able to walk around and not cringe at the sight of every police officer or unmarked car. He had no choice but to go for it. He wasn't sure what Daryl or this Kevin had done to incur her anger, and furthermore, at this point, he didn't care. He was glad he wasn't her primary target. *Hell hath no fury…*

CHAPTER 7

T hat same evening, Cerina looked at the clock for the tenth time within the last few minutes. It was half past nine, and Temple had not yet arrived. Her anger had reached a boiling point and she needed to find a way to calm herself down. She couldn't believe he was three hours late and had not bothered to call. She didn't ask much from him; merely a little respect from time to time. They had had countless arguments in the past about his lack of consideration, and his lateness showed a complete disregard for her feelings. She struggled with finding a way to deal with him and the way he treated her. She wanted better and even felt that she deserved it, but did not know how to get that better treatment from Temple. She thought she could love him back to where she needed him to be. She hated fighting with him, but found it difficult to remain civil during these times. She wasn't sure exactly how she was going to react when he finally walked through the door.

Earlier in the day, Cerina had spent a lot of time in the beauty shop getting her hair and nails done so she could look her best for her special evening with Temple. She even bought some sexy lingerie, a pair of handcuffs, some body oil, and a blindfold for their anticipated night of passion. She looked and smelled good, but it seemed it would all be for naught since Temple was a no-show.

Each time she heard a car door slam she'd run over and peer out of the window to see if it was Temple. She waited with baited breath each time she heard the squeal of tires or saw headlights, only to be disappointed when one of her neighbors or some stranger would walk away from their car. Her nervous energy was rising to a peak, and she didn't know what to do.

She rushed over to the dining table and verified that the setting was perfect. With deliberate effort, she made sure the silverware, plates, and glasses were in perfect order. Wine was chilling in the ice bucket, but she finally decided to put it in the refrigerator. She sat down at the table in her slinky lingerie and took another gulp of the wine she had freely poured herself earlier. Sitting alone at the table, having a glass of wine, only added to her frustration.

She pushed away from the table and walked into her bedroom. She hadn't checked the answering machine since earlier in the day and, for a second, she thought maybe he had left a message. She hit the blinking red light and gasped as she listened to the nurse from her doctor's office. She thought she had deleted that message earlier, but she must have saved it instead. She hit the delete button and the machine announced, "No more messages."

She took a seat in front of the vanity mirror in the corner. She studied her face. She examined its contours, its tiny pores, its fine lines, its symmetry, and her coffee-colored complexion. Her skin, in spite of her health, was without blemish because she went to great lengths to keep it smooth with a variety of products and a weekly facial. Her mother had always told her that a lady always had to look her best. Before she had become strung out on crack, her mother was an extraordinarily beautiful woman, and although Cerina hated her more than words could describe, she always remembered the little beauty tips her mother would give her in passing.

There were times in Cerina's life when faint memories of her mother would creep out from the corners of her mind. Usually, she beat down those thoughts because the burden of thinking about that woman was too much for her to bear. She remembered that her mother was beautiful, yet she could barely remember her face. It had been fifteen years since that fateful day in the mall in Baltimore when her world suddenly changed. Her mother had taken Cerina to the mall and disappeared without a trace. She sat eleven-year-old Cerina on a bench and told her to wait until she came out of the restroom. Cerina never did see her come out of that restroom, nor did she go into there to seek her. At her age, she did exactly as her mother told her or she'd risk the beating of a lifetime. Four hours later the mall was closing, and Cerina was still sitting on that bench when a security guard approached her and inquired about her mother. She told him that her mother had been in the restroom for a long time and when he entered, the room was empty, and there was no sign of a struggle or foul play. He alerted the police, who never were able to find her mother. She was simply gone. Cerina, in her heart of hearts, knew her mother had abandoned her. She didn't cry and she didn't say very much afterwards about it. In fact, part of her rejoiced because she would no longer have to endure the beatings and the harsh words inflicted upon her by the woman she called Mama. The police called her father, who reluctantly came and picked her up. Even in her father's custody, she knew she was alone in the world. He had remarried, had other kids, and made Cerina feel like an outcast.

Cerina picked up the brush and stroked her shiny shoulder-length hair. With long smooth strokes, she tried to let go of her tension. She wanted to brush all those unpleasant memories out of her head forever. She longed to see Temple's face and to feel the warmth of his embrace. He could make her forget the past. Those memories, those painful images from her past, had worked themselves into her spirit for the night, and she suddenly felt despondent.

She looked at the clock on the wall. Temple was now almost four hours late for their evening with no phone call. She knew he'd show up eventually. All of her life she had been alone. This was no different. Her mother abandoned her, her father despised her, and Temple neglected her. Yet, she remained in complete love with Temple; partly because she simply didn't want to be alone. She had decided that having a piece of a man was better than having no man at all. She silently hoped one day he'd reciprocate her love. She thought if she loved him enough, then one day he'd love her back. Until then, she'd continue stroking her hair. And waiting patiently.

Her mother's piercing voice echoed in her mind again. She could hear her sour words as if she were in the room chastising her. Cerina remembered her mother yelling at her about being "too friendly" with the boys in the neighborhood. At that age, Cerina didn't know what her mother meant by being "too friendly." Cerina merely wanted to be like her mother and was simply repeating the behaviors she had learned from her—her mother was quite popular with the gentlemen of Baltimore.

Cerina thought about all those times when her mother referred to her as a "ho" or a "lil' bitch." She could hear that banshee-like voice yelling at her from across the room. "I saw you out playing with that Chandler boy today! Did you raise your dress for him? That's the only reason why he'd want to play with you! Did you let him touch yo' stuff, ho? Lil' bitch, you hear me talking to you!" She was called that so many times she had begun to think that was her name. Cerina could never understand why her mother would deny her love—the only thing she'd ever asked for. At least with Temple, she had love. It may not have been her ideal version of it, but she knew love like that only existed in fairytales and she lived in D.C.—a far cry from Wonderland. Temple loved her the only way he knew how, she thought. And, she was grateful for that.

When Cerina placed the brush on the vanity, something strange happened. She watched her hand hover over the brush and she trembled. She experienced a memory so vivid that it felt as if she was living in that moment again. Her eyes were fixated upon her hand. She saw her fingers morph into something strange and unsettling. She wanted to break her gaze, but something held her there. She could feel the touch of another hand on top of hers and the hairs on her arms rose like the hair on the back of a cat that sensed danger. Suddenly, she wept. Uncontrollably. The tears flowed from her eyes in a steady stream. They rolled down her cheeks and vanished into the white cloth that covered the table. She did not want to relive those memories—that pain would always be kept private, locked away in the deepest part of her consciousness. It took a lot of strength and concentration, but she was able to bring herself out of that moment. When she came out of her trance, she swore to never go to that dark place again.

In a flash, anger swept away her sadness and she focused her thoughts on Temple. She thought about how freely she had given everything to Temple. She had given him her time, her love, her body, and a lot of her money to help solve whatever crisis was going on in his life at the time. In another flash, anger turned to rage that ravaged her soul. With one fell swoop of her arms, she knocked over every item on the table. Her brushes, combs, powders, and perfumes flew across the room and crash-landed onto the floor. She screamed as her madness continued.

Running on anger, instinct and adrenaline, she tore the clothes from the hangers in her closet and screamed with a ferociousness that would have startled even the calmest ocean. From where that raw emotion originated, her mind tried to forget.

She reached into the top of the closet and pulled down the brown music box that was the only decent thing left from her childhood. In those moments of darkness and despair as a child, she'd retreat into her room, open the box, and watch the little dancer spin around in ecstatic circles of light and hope to some unfamiliar Spanish tune. She carefully studied the construction of the box and its deep mahogany color. When she opened the box, the little dancer—forever happy—once again twirled gaily around. This box, throughout both her childhood and adulthood, had comforted her. To calm her down during her fevered moments, she usually kept two emergency cigarettes tucked away beneath the blue velvet cloth. Frantically, she tore away at the cloth only to find that she had no cigarettes.

Instantly, the walls of loneliness and the weight of misery closed in on her. The room began to spin and she fell to the floor in a fit. The walls on the other side of the room somehow moved closer to her. She crawled into the closet and sank into the corner, pulling her knees into her chest. She stayed in the closet for a few moments, but she needed her fix. She needed a cigarette. She jumped up out of the closet and grabbed her keys from the dresser. In a mad dash to save her life, she yanked a long coat from the closet, slipped into a pair of heels, grabbed her purse, and headed out the door in a flash. In times of great turmoil, the magic of that inhalation was all that could soothe her.

She didn't remember driving down the street to the store, but somehow she found herself at the grocery store a few blocks from her house. She raced inside, weaving between people who stood in her way. She looked like a woman possessed, her hair scrambled about her head and makeup stains on her face. She didn't care. She needed that fix to make her anxiety dissipate. In order to buy cigarettes, she had to stand in line and get the cashier to retrieve her pack from the glass case, which was kept under lock and key at the service desk. Quickly, she scanned for the shortest line.

She stood there, carefully remembering her breathing techniques she had learned from the therapist she saw only twice. Slowly, she inhaled and exhaled, but that didn't seem to help. Adding to her frustration was the lady in front of her making small talk with the cashier as if they were old friends suddenly reunited. Cerina's patience was being tested. She continued to breathe, but that didn't help. When all of the lady's items were scanned and the total tallied, it was then that the lady decided to reach into her purse for some money. She dug and dug and finally was able to pull out her wallet.

"Excuse me," Cerina said with heavy irritation, "what is the problem here? This is an express line. You need to get it together."

The lady turned and glared at her for a second, rolling her eyes in disgust. She took her finger and pulled a lock of blonde hair behind her ear. "You'll have to wait your turn," she said.

"You're holding up the fucking line. I know this isn't your first time in a store."

"You need to wait your damned turn," the lady snapped. It was all Cerina could do not to take her fist and punch that woman. The lady turned back to the cashier, huffed, and mumbled something under breath. "What is the total?"

"The total is thirty-six dollars and seventy-three cents, bitch. Are you fucking blind? I can see it from here. And, why the hell did you wait until all your shit has been rung up to finally look for your money? I guess it never occurred to you to have your wallet or credit card in your hand while she's ringing up your shit? Did you think this shit was free? You fucking people think the world revolves around you, but I'm here to tell you, bitch, that you're gonna meet the wrong person on the wrong day and you're gonna get fucked up. Have some goddamned consideration for everyone else in line." Cerina's voice had begun to carry and people were beginning to stare.

"You need to calm down. Did you just get out of jail or something?" the lady asked sarcastically.

"No, I didn't, but if you don't hurry up, I'mma catch a case 'cause I'mma beat yo ass. Pay for your shit and get the hell outta here before I get really upset."

The lady looked at Cerina and saw the crazed look on her face and decided not to push it. She handed the cashier two twenties and waited for her change. On the way out, she turned and pulled a few strings of hair out of her face again and said, "Have a nice day."

Cerina flipped her the bird. When Cerina finally got her pack of Newports, she didn't bother to get her change. She stepped outside, quickly grabbed a lighter from her purse, and took a long deep drag of that cigarette. It was like heaven. On her second puff, a car pulled close to the curb where Cerina stood. The window slowly rolled down to reveal the lady from the store. She looked at Cerina, and Cerina looked at her.

"Fuck you, bitch!" the lady screamed as she sped off.

Cerina, enjoying her moment, wasn't bothered by her comment. She had her cigarette and was lost in a nicotine-induced calm.

She had tried many things over the years—prayer, chanting, exercise, singing—but nothing had the same effect on her when those memories from the past broke through the barriers in her mind and tormented her. She stood on the curb in the cold, inhaling and exhaling. It was the most powerful thing in her life next to sex with Temple. The nicotine entered her body, and it was like magic. She took another long drag, exhaled, and felt herself regaining her composure.

With her sanity seeping back into her body, she was now embarrassed. It was as if some other personality had taken control as the real Cerina sat defenseless in a dark corner in her own mind. In that moment, if that lady had said the wrong thing, Cerina was sure she would be in handcuffs now because she would have tried to knock her teeth down her throat. Because of that horrible scene, she knew she could never return to that store…nor would she ever want to.

When Temple finally did arrive, it was close to midnight. "Baby, I am so sorry. Things got a little hectic at my cousin's house. His girlfriend was trippin' again and they got to carrying on and—"

"Don't worry about any of that right now. Come on in."

Temple allowed himself to be pulled over to the couch by Cerina. He knew where this was about to lead but wasn't sure if he was ready to perform. Then, he thought about Daryl and started to get aroused. He pulled her into him and kissed her deeply. Before they knew it they were naked and fucking on the couch.

CHAPTER 8

NuttyProfessor: You're up late, aren't you?

DarkBroNDC: Yeah, got some work to finish for a meeting in the morning. Why r u up so late?

NuttyProfessor: Couldn't sleep.

DarkBroNDC: You want me to come over and rock you to sleep?

NuttyProfessor: LOL…thanks, but I'll be fine.

DarkBroNDC: Where have you been lately? I haven't seen you online in a minute.

NuttyProfessor: Things have been crazy at work. The semester is winding down and final papers and things are due. These kids ain't gonna drive me crazy, though…LOL

DarkBroNDC: I've been missing you.

NuttyProfessor: That's sweet. I've missed our convo, too.

DarkBroNDC: I hope you'll be online more in the future.

NuttyProfessor: Yeah, I should be around this week.

DarkBroNDC: Maybe we can meet up?

NuttyProfessor: Maybe.

DarkBroNDC: Did you get the pics I sent you?

NuttyProfessor: Yeah, thanx. Very nice pictures. You are really attractive.

DarkBroNDC: Check your email. I sent you a couple other pictures.

As Daryl checked his email account, he looked at the clock on his computer. It was almost three a.m. and he was up working. He couldn't sleep so he decided to take advantage of the

situation and get some things done but, when he logged on, he received an instant message from his Internet buddy.

He stared at the naked pictures in his e-mail. His dick moved as he scrolled through the pictures. It was the perfect body to match DarkBroNDC's face. Daryl knew he shouldn't be conversing with this online stranger. His purpose in chatting had been purely innocent, but it had taken an unexpected twist in the road. He had conversed with DarkBro for weeks before any pictures were exchanged and now that he had a good view of the full package, his mind began to wander to forbidden places.

NuttyProfessor: Damn!

DarkBroNDC: I hope that's a good thing.

NuttyProfessor: That's a very good thing.

DarkBroNDC: What you got on?

NuttyProfessor: Nothing.

DarkBroNDC: You sittin nekkid at the computer talking to me? You so nasty…LOL…but I like it.

NuttyProfessor: Yeah, I'm butterball naked. What you wearing?

DarkBroNDC: Wifebeater and boxer shorts. I want you to do something for me.

NuttyProfessor: What?

DarkBroNDC: I want you to squeeze your nipple. Then, I want you to caress your balls and tell me how it feels 'cause right now I'm doing the same thing as I talk to you.

NuttyProfessor: I can't do that.

DarkBroNDC: Yes, you can. Don't resist. Give in to the moment. You know you want to…I want you to look at my pics and imagine that I'm the one pulling on your nipples. After I do that, I'm gonna lick them and bite them the way you like. I know that'll get your dick rock hard.

NuttyProfessor: Shit, you need to stop talkin' to me like that.

DarkBroNDC: What, you can't handle it? I bet you brick hard now, ain't ya?

NuttyProfessor: I'll never tell…LOL

DarkBroNDC: You don't have to. I know that you are. I want you to stroke that dick. I want you to grab it with both your hands. Imagine it's me doing it to you.

❊❊❊

Daryl paused for a second but then looked at the naked images of DarkBro on the computer screen. He looked into his eyes and felt as if DarkBro was staring back at him. He couldn't resist and did as he was asked. Slowly, he rubbed, tugged, and pinched his nipples, which were hypersensitive. The feeling that raced through his body forced him to take deeper breaths as his dick woke up and stood at attention. The longer he rubbed his nipples, the more his dick throbbed, but he wasn't ready to touch it yet. Instead he rubbed his hands over his smooth balls and pulled on his sack. He loved the way his balls felt in his hands. He continued rubbing and tugging gently at them, while licking his lips.

DarkBroNDC: Yo, you rubbing yo dick, right? You like the way that feels, don't ya? Imagine that it was me with yo dick in my hand. I'd be licking and bitin on yo nipples while I'm jackin you off. You want me to do that?

NuttyProfessor: Shit yea, that shit feels so good.

DarkBroNDC: You want me to suck that dick, don't you? You wanna put it in and fuck my mouth, don't you? Go ahead, put it in.

❊❊❊

Daryl couldn't resist any longer. He stroked his burning dick harder and faster as he imagined he was inside DarkBro. The sexually charged words that appeared in the little box on his screen fueled his fire. The more he read the words and thought of this stranger, the more excited he became. His breathing quickened as the power of his strokes became more forceful and pleasurable. DarkBro certainly had a way with words. Daryl had never been into cyber-sex before, but lost himself in the moment. He stroked himself with speed, alternating his rapid technique with a slower and deeper massage of his muscle. He could no longer contain himself and he closed his eyes and let his head fall backward as he released his frustrations all over his chest. He sat back in his chair, barely able to move, and tried to catch his breath.

During Daryl's moment of self-gratification, he hadn't heard Kevin's approach, but Kevin heard the sounds and the moans that slipped through the partially opened door to Daryl's office. Cloaked by the darkness of the hallway, he peered in and watched the end of his lover's intimate moment. The horror he felt was not born of the simple act of masturbation, but because earlier in the evening Kevin had tried to engage Daryl in sexual relations, but his efforts were rebuked. Daryl said he was tired. Now, Kevin was offended. He thought back to earlier when they were in bed and he climbed on top of Daryl and started kissing him. In the past, that position was a surefire way of getting things heated because it was Daryl's favorite position. Kevin thought back to how he slid his tongue into Daryl's ear and then how he started kissing, licking, and sucking on Daryl's neck, only to be brushed aside. Clearly, Daryl had pent-up sexual energy because he was in his office in the middle of the night jacking off. Kevin felt hurt, rejected, dejected, and angered by Daryl's late-night antics. He backed away from the door and moved closer to the staircase. He took a moment and clung to the banister while he tried to compose himself.

"Daryl, what are you doing?"

Kevin's voice from the hallway startled Daryl and he quickly jumped from his seat. "Uh, uh, oh, I was doing a little work. I couldn't sleep so I decided to check to see if one of my students had emailed me his paper like he was supposed to."

"That can wait, baby. Why don't you come back to bed with me?" he called out from the hallway.

Daryl hit the power button on his computer and the screen went black.

"Alright, baby, I'll be there in five minutes." Daryl held his breath and listened for footsteps headed in his direction. He prayed Kevin wasn't coming into his office because he hadn't had time to clean himself up and he didn't want to have a conversation about it. Part of him was embarrassed about his sexual episode.

Kevin paused before speaking. "Okay. I'll see you upstairs." Kevin turned and shook his head as he walked up the stairs. When Daryl heard his feet on the stairs, he breathed a sigh of relief.

❀❀❀

When they woke up the next morning, Kevin didn't mention anything to Daryl about what he had witnessed. Instead, he pretended as if nothing had happened and cooked breakfast as he did sometimes. Cooking somehow relaxed him and cleared his head. He sipped on his usual cup of green tea and tried to forget what had happened only hours ago. Daryl moved about the house in his usual state of disorganization and barely spoke. The choking kind of silence that filled their morning further highlighted everything that was wrong with them. They each ignored it, as they had for the last few months.

After he finished teaching his two classes for the day, Daryl retired to his office at work. He had a lot of papers to grade as the semester winded down for the winter break. He shuffled the papers around on his desk, pretending to work. He didn't feel like grading the papers because his mind was a million miles away. He wanted to log onto the computer again in the hopes that DarkBro would be online, but he resisted the temptation. In spite of his guilty pleasure from last night, he knew his uninhibited online behavior was becoming a problem. He was spending far too much time thinking about and conversing with DarkBro.

To get his mind off DarkBro, he picked up the phone to call Kevin but got his voice mail.

He paused for a second as he listened to the announcement instructing him to leave a message. He wasn't sure what he wanted to say so he left a generic message and hoped Kevin was having a good day. As he hung up the phone and returned to his lunch, his cell phone rang. It was an unfamiliar number and his first thought was to ignore it and let the person leave a message. Instead, he answered it.

"Hello?" he asked routinely.

"Wassup, man?" the voice delightedly asked.

"Not much," Daryl replied.

"Do you know who this is?"

"No, I don't, but I assume you're about to tell me."

"You forgot me already?" Daryl remained silent. "This is Temple. We met a few days ago at The Fireplace."

Daryl's heart froze. He assumed he wouldn't hear from him. In fact, part of him didn't want to hear back from him. Back when Daryl was single, if he gave his number out to someone and they didn't use it within two days, then he wouldn't give them the time of day. He told himself if they were really interested in him and not playing silly games, it wouldn't take that long to call.

"Hey, man, how are you?"

Temple could detect the excitement in Daryl's voice. "I'm aight. I tried to call you a few other times, but I was getting some weird message."

"Did it sound like some Asian man?"

"Yeah."

"Somehow my line got crossed. I spent two hours dealing with customer service the other day to get it straight."

"Okay. I thought you had given me the wrong number."

"Never that."

"What are you doing tonight? I wanna see you. You wanna meet for a drink?"

"Tonight's not good for me. I'll probably work late and then hit the gym."

"Ah, you're blowing me off. I can take a hint," Temple said.

"If I was blowing you off, you'd know." Daryl's flirtations had intensified and he shook his head when the words escaped his mouth.

"I like the way that sounds. What gym do you work out in?"

"Bally's over by Pentagon City Mall."

"Really? That's my gym. Why don't I meet you there tonight, and we can work out together?"

67

Daryl thought about it for a few seconds. Daryl heard all of the bells and whistles and saw the flashing red lights that served as a warning, but he couldn't resist. He was going headfirst into danger.

"That sounds cool. I should be there by seven. See ya there."

Even though he was wildly attracted to Temple, just because they got together to work out didn't mean something was going to happen. Part of him simply wanted to see Temple again—hopefully, for the last time, to get the image of his face and body out of his head completely. He started working on his defenses now, telling himself he had a lover and that he wasn't a cheater. He would let those thoughts echo in his spirit for the rest of the day.

❦❦❦

Daryl had just gotten out of his Nissan Pathfinder after searching for twenty minutes for a parking space in the underground garage at Bally's at Pentagon Row. As soon as he spotted a car pulling out of a parking spot, he swooped in, not caring that he had stolen the space from an elderly couple. He simply smiled and waved at them as they blew their horn and drove off in frustration. He was in a hurry—a man on a mission. Just as he unbuckled his seat belt, he caught a glimpse of Temple in his rearview mirror driving in a Honda Accord. He took a deep breath. He was so anxious to see Temple. He hopped out of the truck, grabbed his bag and almost lost his step. He gave the obligatory scowl and looked around to make sure no one, especially Temple, had seen him stumble. As he made his way toward the elevator he pointed his keychain at the truck but didn't wait for the familiar flashing of lights to make sure the alarm was set.

As fate would have it, they ended up meeting at the elevator. Daryl tried very hard not to stare, but he was mesmerized. Temple looked in his direction, obviously not caring about the long stare. He looked Daryl up and down and then smiled.

"How are you, Mr. Man?" Temple asked.

"Doing well, but a bit tired from work. It's been a long day."

"See, don't try to punk on this workout. I plan to put it on you," Temple said, his words laced with seduction.

"Hmm, exactly what are you going to put on me?" Daryl asked, his words equally charged. Instead of answering, Temple smiled. "It's good to see you again."

"It's good to be seen." Daryl had been in Temple's presence for less than two minutes and Temple, too, was feeling the heat. "This elevator is so damned slow."

"Tell me about it. There are only three stops, but it still takes forever sometimes." When the elevator finally arrived, Daryl continued with his cool pose. Being confined in the small metal box with Temple brought up so many feelings. He could smell Temple's masculine scent, which was a familiar cologne mixed with Temple's natural body odor. During that very short ride to the surface, it happened. Daryl coolly eyed Temple and Temple coolly eyed Daryl. No words were necessary. In the silence of the elevator, before any significant syllable was uttered, *it* happened. In that elevator, Temple did it without even trying—he took Daryl's breath away. That was the exact moment Daryl knew he was in trouble.

"Gaultier?" Daryl asked, as he tried to name the fragrance.

"What?"

"Your cologne…is it Jean-Paul Gaultier?"

"Nah." Temple smiled.

"Are you going to tell me what it is?"

"Hmm, no."

The doors to the elevator opened at that moment and Temple stepped out.

It had been such a long time since Daryl had felt butterflies in his stomach over someone. He used to have that feeling in anticipation of Kevin coming home or meeting him for dinner, but those days were over. His stomach was twisting into unsettled knots of excitement as he walked behind Temple.

"You ready for this?" Temple turned and asked.

"Trust me, I can handle it."

"I'm going to remember you said that."

There was something sexy in Temple's swagger and something compelling in his voice that reconfirmed what Daryl knew from their very first meeting: this man was dangerous. Daryl had a serious weakness for pretty boys, and Temple was the fairest of them all.

"Damn, what's going on in here today?" Temple asked with some frustration. The gym was more crowded than either of them expected for a late-evening workout.

"Shit if I know. I should have known from the twenty minutes it took me to find a parking space that it would be crowded." He put down his oversized gym bag on the bench opposite Temple who had already taken off his shoes.

Temple let out a small chuckle. "I saw you steal that spot from those old folks. That was cold, man. Just cold." They both laughed.

"No one was supposed to see that. I should feel bad but, hell, I'd been driving around forever. If I had to drive around in a circle one more time I was going to run somebody over."

"I'm sure they were glad to do their part for humanity by keeping you outta jail."

They chuckled, stood up at the same time, and began removing their shirts. When Temple's shirt was removed, the wings of the butterflies in Daryl's stomach started to beat with force and speed. Daryl quickly looked away. Temple's upper body was chiseled to perfection. Daryl had spent many an evening in the gym and was quite proud of his body, but standing next to Temple he felt like Humpty Dumpty.

"Did that hurt?" Temple asked.

Daryl was in a trance. "Huh?"

"Your nipple ring. Did that hurt?"

"I don't want to sound like no punk, but that shit did hurt," Daryl confessed as he remembered the pain.

"I had thought about getting one, but I changed my mind. We're doing upper body, right?" he said as he changed the subject.

"Yeah. You can show me your routine so I can figure out how to get abs like that." Temple was impressed that Daryl was checking him out, but he knew that once he took his shirt off Daryl would be hard-pressed to keep his eyes off.

"Great."

When Temple told Daryl that he was going to "put it on him," he was sure that he'd be able to handle it but, as the workout went on, Daryl realized that Temple's workout was far more intense than he was ready for. *You don't get a body like that without working hard for it*, Daryl thought to himself. They did incline and decline bench presses, shoulder presses, dips, biceps, and triceps and finished off by doing some intense abdominal work. When Daryl thought they were finished, Temple led him to the treadmills that overlooked the courtyard of the shopping complex, and they ran three miles. By the end of the workout, it was almost ten at night and as tired as Daryl was, he was proud of himself for being able to get through it. He knew that unless he did something about it, he'd be tragically sore in the morning so he decided they should relax in the wet sauna before showering. They went back into the locker room, stripped down, and covered themselves with towels. Daryl caught Temple peeking at him a few times, and he was happy his body was drawing attention for him.

When they walked through the double doors that led to the sauna, Daryl really became concerned about how sore he'd be tomorrow and hoped the sauna would prevent his body from stiffening up. When they walked into the empty sauna, he became more concerned about being almost naked in a dark room with Temple. He wasn't expecting it to be empty, but he realized the gym would be closing soon and people had abandoned the gym to go home to their lives. The only saving grace from being alone in the sauna with Temple was the fact that he knew he was in a public place, and he wasn't one of those nasty men having sex in the gym or in public parks.

As soon as they walked in, the heat from the steam beat them both in their faces and caused them to wince. They took their seats on the wooden benches that lined the walls of the sauna. Once they got settled, the heat became soothing. Temple had taken a seat on the bench in front of the one that Daryl sat on and since there was no one else in the sauna, Temple decided to spread out. In doing so, he knew that he'd tempt Daryl. He stood up, removed his towel, and spread it across the bench. The steam had started to rise from the vents in heavy sprays, partially blocking Daryl's view of Temple's naked and nearly perfect body. He knew he couldn't look at Temple naked, not without risking an erection, so he closed his eyes and let his head fall against the wall. Little did he know, Temple was checking him out also.

"This is very relaxing," Daryl said, trying to keep his mind off Temple. Temple didn't respond, but instead found himself thinking about what he had to do to Daryl. In the past, fucking somebody for money or opportunity wasn't something he'd have to think twice about. Destroying lives and hurting people was second nature to him, but something about Daryl was causing him to feel a bit guilty; even before he had really tried to seduce him. Even though he was between a rock and a hard spot and was being forced into this seduction, he was surprisingly unsettled by the thought. He thought for a second that Daryl was the kind of man he could love. However, in the end, Temple would always love himself more.

❀❀❀

After they showered, Temple and Daryl stopped by Starbucks because Daryl wanted to get some green tea; a habit he had picked up from Kevin. They sat at a table in the back and talked and laughed like they were old friends. Anyone looking at them would have known they were lost in their world, enjoying the best in conversation each had to offer. Daryl was amazed at how easy Temple was to speak with. His wit and charm transformed their simple conversation into something deeper than strangers exchanging words and laughter over a cup of tea. Temple had an almost magical way with words. Sounds and syllables rolled off his tongue like enchanting ocean waves but his deep, sultry glances revealed far more than his charismatic words. Daryl found it difficult to resist his gazes and, at moments, realized he was grinning like a schoolboy with a crush on his fifth-grade teacher. It felt as if an epoch had elapsed since his last effortless or flirtatious conversation with Kevin. The fluttering of his heart told him that he was in danger. His heart told him to tread lightly, but he needed this moment. He needed to feel loved and attracted and he needed to flirt and be the center of attention in some man's eyes. He savored each simple word, held onto the sounds of Temple's laughter, and let Temple's gazes burn an indelible mark into his mind.

By the time Daryl got home, it was close to midnight. Kevin was in the den burning the midnight oil. Kevin had decided to work downstairs in part because he wanted Daryl to see his face as soon as he walked through the door. Kevin tried not to be concerned about Daryl's whereabouts; even though he had been. He hadn't heard from Daryl since the voice mail he left earlier in the day in spite of his three attempts to reach him via cell phone. Kevin knew Daryl was ignoring him and avoiding him, but what he didn't know was why.

Kevin's canine-like hearing picked up the sound of the key striking the lock downstairs and when the door began to creak open, Kevin didn't look up until Daryl walked up the stairs and saw him sitting on the couch. He put his gym bag down and planted a kiss on his forehead.

"I see you're up working late. How are things going, baby?" Daryl asked.

"Fine, for the most part. I can't wait for this damned fund-raiser to be over. I can't believe it takes so much planning to pull off one event. The good thing is that I think we'll surpass projections. We've started getting some radio airplay about Danea's concert, and that's boosting ticket sales in a big way. We received a grant from the Department of Health and Human Services. So, things are going well. Do you realize in about three weeks it'll be a new year? I haven't done any Christmas shopping. This whole year has zoomed right by me." Kevin was speaking a mile a minute and had to slow to catch his breath. Daryl knew that Kevin's mind usually raced when he was trying to suppress his anger or to keep from saying the wrong thing. Daryl didn't feel like fighting and he appreciated Kevin's efforts to avoid confrontation.

"Yeah, I know. Time sure flies when you're having fun," Daryl said jokingly. "Things are pretty crazy for me at school, too. I have a shitload of papers to grade." Daryl leaned down and kissed Kevin again, this time on the lips and with more passion. He had to kiss him to get Temple out of his head. He had to kiss him to see if the fire still burned.

"Wow. What was that for?" Kevin asked. "You haven't kissed me like that in a very long time."

"I know. And I've missed your lips." Daryl realized that his love for Kevin was real, but something about Temple's gazes stayed with him. Something wondrous danced in Temple's eyes and connected with Daryl's spirit.

"It's kinda late. Where you been? Did you get my messages? I was checking to see if you wanted to have dinner. I made reservations at that French restaurant in Alexandria that you love so much, but you never called me back."

"I'm sorry. It was a very long day at the school so I decided to work off some steam at the gym. I had a very good workout. In fact, I may be sore tomorrow."

"Ahh, do you need a massage?" Kevin asked, testing the water.

Daryl kissed him on the forehead. "I'm really tired, baby. Can I take a rain check?"

Kevin had grown accustomed to getting the cold treatment from Daryl. "Sure you can but, before you go, let me ask you a question. Are you still attracted to me?"

"Kevin, you know I love you."

"That wasn't my question."

"Baby, please don't start. I'm really tired."

"Don't start what? Am I the only one here who thinks we have a problem?" Kevin looked around the room as if he was expecting agreement from some unseen forces.

"I know things haven't been good lately. We're going through a rough patch."

"Rough patch? More like a rough field."

"Can we talk about this later? I really want to go to bed."

"Daryl, how much later do you think we have?" The stare between them told the story of a love affair gone wrong. "We need to get some help."

"What—you mean like a counselor?"

"Yeah, like a counselor."

"Shit," Daryl said as he audibly sighed in disgust. His parents had taught him that he could handle his own problems. "I'm going to bed."

Kevin shook his head as Daryl walked away. Daryl didn't like therapists, counselors or psychiatrists and thought they were all quacks. His parents had always told him that he couldn't look for anyone else to solve his problems and usually, when there were problems, he already knew the answer and that was true in this case.

Kevin didn't know what else to suggest. He watched Daryl walk up the stairs and disappear. He didn't know what else to do. He sat back on the couch, arms folded, eyes wide, heart heavy, and stared at the walls. As he directed his attention back to his work, Daryl's cell phone—which he had left on the table—began to vibrate. Kevin picked it up and read the text message: "I hope you made it home safely—Temple."

Who the hell is Temple? Kevin thought.

Once upstairs, Daryl thought about Kevin's suggestion. He knew they had serious problems.

His interest in the relationship was waning, yet his love for Kevin held strong. It seemed like such a contradiction. He couldn't figure out why he wasn't running toward Kevin with a solution to all their woes. He didn't want to end his relationship. They had built a life together and it was a life that he used to love. He simply could not figure out why he wasn't more concerned about saving their relationship and right now he didn't have the desire to dissect the dichotomy. Instead of trying to solve their problems, he went into their bathroom, locked the door, and masturbated to thoughts of Temple.

CHAPTER 9

Later, in a different part of the city, Cerina took her fourth shot of Hennessy and looked at herself in the mirror. When she caught a glimpse of her reflection in the full-length mirror on the wall, her face lit up with a smile. She looked sexy wearing her black leather Catwoman outfit with the nipples cut out. Her acorn-sized nipples protruded outward and she ensured that they were at attention by pinching them and rubbing them with ice cubes. She knew that when the men saw her on stage in her tight leather outfit, with nipples screaming *reach out and touch me*, they'd go crazy. She completed her Catwoman wardrobe with a black cat-like mask that covered her eyes and a whip she had learned to snap. She was ready to whip those men into shape so she could make some money. They were behind in rent, her car payment, and Temple's child support. She didn't have the money, but she knew if she really worked it tonight she could get it. *Anything for Temple.*

As she stared at herself in the mirror, her smile hid a secret desire: she longed for a better life. It wasn't that she minded stripping; in fact, quite the contrary. She loved using her body to work the men in the audience into a frenzied state. Being on stage was the only time in her life when she felt powerful and in complete control. When she was on stage, there wasn't much she couldn't get a man to do for her, but she knew she couldn't do this forever. At times, when she thought about her life, she felt sad because this was the only skill she had.

"Cerina, Cerina," a voice called out. "Girl, they are announcing you right now. You better get yo ass out there now before Boss Man comes in here," Nicole said as she looked at Cerina. "You okay?"

Cerina felt short of breath and a bit dizzy. She grabbed hold to the desk to keep from stumbling. She forced a deep breath and sat down in the chair.

"Girl, what's wrong?" Nicole asked with concern. She stepped over to Cerina and tried to put her hand to her forehead, but Cerina slapped it away.

"I'm fine. I have a slight headache."

"You don't look fine. You sure that's all that's going on?"

"I said I'm fine," she said defiantly as she stood up, shook her ponytail, and moved toward the stairs that led to the stage as Nicole looked on. Cerina stopped for a second to collect herself and to push all thoughts of sickness out of her head. She couldn't deal with that right now. It was show time. She could only deal with one hell at a time. Then, all of the lights in the club dimmed and the stage fell into darkness. She listened as the announcer introduced her by her stage name.

"Gentlemen, if you are ready for the show of a lifetime I want you to make some noise!" His heavy voice projected throughout the club and served as a catalyst to charge the crowd. The atmosphere pulsed with ball-tingling energy and electricity that ignited the loins of the hungry crowd. "Welcome to the stage, the one, the only, *Pussy Galore!*" Her stage name revealed so much about her performances. A thunderous round of applause could be heard as she took her position behind the black velvet curtain and waited for them to open. The seductive and easy moving beats that emanated from the speakers filled the room like waves of slow-moving molasses. The energized crowd cheered and hollered for her when her name was announced again. She was the club's celebrity performer and had a large following of fans who flocked to the club for no other reason than to see her on-stage antics.

Cerina prayed that she'd be able to make it through this performance.

The crowd waited with baited breath as the curtain slowly opened. She stood center stage, her legs gapped open, with the whip behind her back giving the illusion of a long black tail. She stood perfectly still. She took a long purposeful glance throughout the crowd. She scanned the room, actually looking for Temple. Earlier in the day, he indicated that he'd come to her show and she hoped he wouldn't disappoint. She needed his presence to get through this show. Unfortunately, she couldn't see very far into the crowd because of the lights. But the show must go on.

Slowly, she started walking around the stage, making the whip crackle and the men howl. She circled the metal pole on stage, sticking her tongue out as if she was going to lick the pole. The crowd screamed. Instead of licking the pole, she threw herself around it and slid down in a spiral pattern with her feet pointed toward the ceiling. Excitement ignited the crowd and money flew onto the stage from all angles.

She moved and gyrated her body in ways unknown to man. She pumped her pelvis and rolled her body as if she didn't have any bones. She squatted in the middle of the stage and flung open her legs several times in rapid succession to reveal Pandora's box—the cat suit she wore was crotch-less. She popped and pumped as her legs opened and closed in a rhythmic spectacle. She then stood up, unzipped the suit and stepped seductively out of it. Now, she was completely naked on stage, except for the black heels and the mask that covered her eyes. She moved toward the edge of the stage, took a seat and with her feet touching the floor, she threw her legs open again. She was close enough to some of the men to read the desire and lust on their faces. She smiled and licked her lips until she noticed Temple in the back of the room near the bar talking to some woman. She grimaced.

On the edge of the stage, she didn't move much, but sat there and let them stare at Pandora's box for a few minutes. She growled at the crowd as if she was Eartha Kitt. She then pushed herself back onto stage and decided that she was going to give them a real treat. She took a quick glance at the money on stage and knew she could get more. She sat in the middle of the stage, and took her left ankle and put it behind her head and did the same with the right until both ankles were around her head, with her pussy on full display. Then, she started smacking it and making it pop. Her antics ushered in a thunderous round of applause, whistles, and boisterous catcalls. And money. Lots of money. Some bills were neatly placed on the stage, others balled up and thrown at her or on stage. The bills, in all denominations, rained down on her as she performed.

She took the handle of her whip, inserted it into herself, and moved it in and out rapidly before she pulled it out and stuck it into her mouth. When she did that, there wasn't a man seated. They all rushed the stage to get a closer look and showered her with more bills—and they weren't throwing singles only. Her performance was extraordinary. As the song ended, the emcee announced that if the crowd was anxious enough they should shout for her to come back out for an encore performance.

Cerina wasn't interested in doing another number. She wanted to know who Temple was speaking to and why she was holding onto his arm. She stood up, licked both her nipples, waved to the crowd, and took a bow. She exited the stage butt naked and the crowd loved every minute of it.

The stage manager collected the dollars for her and brought them to her in the back. While stuffing the bills into her purse, Cerina saw many twenty-dollar bills and a few fifties. She had made a killing on her second and final performance for the evening. She hurriedly put on her clothing so she could go and find Temple.

"How are you making out with Daryl?" RaChelle asked Temple as he rested against the back bar in the 202 Club. She inhaled smoke from her long, thin cigarette and waited for a response. They had watched Cerina give one hell of a performance, and Temple knew she would emerge from the back in a few moments. She always needed a drink after she performed. If she saw him talking to RaChelle, there could be some drama and a scene he wanted to avoid. He wanted to keep this conversation with RaChelle quick and to the point.

"Things are going fine. It's only been a few days." He couldn't believe she had tracked him down at the club. "Why are you here?" he asked, annoyed. He wanted to ask her how she knew he'd be there, but at this point he didn't really care. When he walked in the bar earlier and ordered his Hennessy and Coke, he had turned around and there she was, as if she had appeared in a black puff of smoke.

"Just *fine?*" she asked, ignoring his latter question.

"Look, don't worry. I've already set the trap. It's only a matter of time."

"I don't have a lot of time—you don't have a lot of time. I want this done soon."

"If you want this done right, then you need to stop sweatin' me. I know what I'm doing, or did you forget? Relax."

She glared at him. "I certainly hope you're not losing your touch. You aren't as young or as appealing as you used to be."

"Listen here, Scarface, don't come in here talking shit. I said I'd get it done."

She was momentarily stunned by his brazen words, but then smiled when she realized he hadn't lost his edge. He had never been one to suppress his words or thoughts in the past, and she was happy to see signs of the old Temple. A dry smile formed on her face in awe of his boldness.

She inhaled again and directed her attention toward the anonymous faces spread throughout the room. She wondered how the wives and the girlfriends of these men would feel if they knew their men were in some sleazy club throwing money at a bunch of no-class titty dancers. She thought about all the men throughout time who had thrown away perfectly good lives and wives over some cheap tramp for a blowjob in the backseat of a Buick.

"Some of these men won't even be able to pay their rent 'cause they're giving all their money to these nasty bitches. And speaking of which, your girl is quite talented," RaChelle said, her voice laced with condemnation.

"Leave Cerina out of this," he said. "Look, I gotta pee. I'll be back."

Temple turned on his heels and headed toward the restroom on the other side of the bar. As sleazy as this bar was and as dirty as it made her feel, RaChelle was somehow intrigued by it. There was something forbidden and taboo about stepping into a place like this. A woman with her class shouldn't be caught dead here, yet when she tracked Temple down to the 202, she didn't even hesitate as she paid her cover charge and stepped boldly into the establishment.

She turned to the bartender and ordered a drink as she gazed at the twisted, naked body on the stage. The longer she looked the more fascinated she became. In fact, she was actually enjoying her experience—the sleaze felt good. It brought out her inner freak.

"Excuse me," a voice called out to her from behind. RaChelle cocked her head to the side, saw Cerina standing there, and turned back to pay for her drink. "I said, excuse me," Cerina said, this time with a little pepper in her voice.

"Honey, give me a minute and I'll be out of the way," RaChelle shot back. She picked up her drink and attempted to clear the area for Cerina. When she tried to move out of her way, Cerina blocked her path. RaChelle looked her up and down, not sure exactly what was going on. "Is there something I can help you with?"

"I'm not sure. I saw you all hugged up with my man, and I want to know who the fuck you are."

RaChelle chuckled.

"Did I say something funny, bitch?"

"Bitch? Girl, please. I do not want your man."

"Then, what's yo business with him?" Cerina's frenzied voice conveyed her anxiety. She was used to women coming on to Temple, but this was one night she wasn't having it. She was sick and irritable and was ready to fight.

"I don't have to explain anything to you. Instead of being all up in my face, you might want to ask Temple." Cerina looked at RaChelle as if she couldn't believe that this woman was speaking to her like that. "You don't know me, and I don't want to know you. You ain't exactly in my league," RaChelle said as her eyes cut all across Cerina's body.

"Why you lookin' at me like that? You some kinda dyke?"

"I don't have time for this and I'm sick of talking to you. I'm sure there's a pole somewhere that you should be swinging around."

Cerina raised her hand in an attempt to slap RaChelle but, when she drew back, Temple grabbed her hand from behind. "What the fuck are you doing?" he asked.

"I'm 'bout to knock the shit out of this bitch," she said in a ghetto matter-of-fact way.

"Temple, you need to get this *thing* outta my face. Clearly, she has no idea who I am."

"I know this ho didn't just call me a 'thing,'" Cerina said, more to herself than to Temple.

"Cerina, you need to calm down—shit. Why you always gotta trip?" Temple said as RaChelle eased her way around Cerina. She winked coyly at him when she passed by, making sure Cerina saw it.

"Temple, I'm going to go finish my drink away from this drama. I'll talk to you tomorrow," she said as she turned. "And, Temple, do your fucking job."

"Job? What is she talking about, Temple? If I ever catch you talking to him again, I will kick yo fuckin' ass!" Cerina yelled at the top of her lungs.

RaChelle waved her hand as if she was swatting away Cerina's threat like it was an annoying fly buzzing in her ear.

"Damn, baby, you sure are fine," some man called out as RaChelle walked by. "What time you performing? I got paid and I'm ready to spend all my money on you!"

RaChelle paused momentarily. She looked down at his Payless shoes and then at his cheap leisure suit. "Baby, you could never afford me," she said as she passed, leaving the man speechless and sulking.

※※※

When RaChelle entered her luxurious hotel suite, the first thing she did was kick off her four hundred-dollar pumps. They were fabulous, but they weren't the most comfortable pair in her extensive collection of footwear. What she wanted more than anything was a nice soothing bath, and she started unbuttoning her blouse as she walked into the bathroom. She leaned over the tub and turned the knob to let the water fill the tub at exactly the right temperature. As a final touch, she poured a heavy dose of bath oil and bath crystals into the water. As the water poured into the marble tub, she walked over to the mirror and stared at her reflection. She looked at the scar on her face, as she often did, and grimaced. Her reaction was not born from pain, but was birthed by anger entombed by her need for vengeance.

Slowly, she removed her blouse and looked—almost in horror—at the marks left on her torso by the church fire that almost took her life. She made a point to look at her marred flesh each day. Her fingers traced the rough patches as if they formed a labyrinth that led to some ancient secret. The only thing that was unveiled by the physical scars was the depth of her emotional pain. If she had her way, her revenge would be felt for years to come; just as she would have to live with the pain left by the death of her unborn child. As she lowered herself into the soothing water, her mind flashed back to that fateful day when insanity clashed with reality. She was taken back to that day—the most painful in her life—when her world was seared by fire.

She remembered how angry she was when she found out she was pregnant. She had been getting sick in the mornings and found herself at work darting for the restroom or the nearest trash can to throw up. She didn't want to be pregnant so she tried to ignore what her body was telling her, hoping it was a stomach virus. When she could no longer stand the suspense or deny the possibility of what could be, she purchased one of those home pregnancy tests from Walgreens. She took it home, sat it on the table, and stared at the box. It stared back at her. She was terrified of what it might tell her when it spoke. When she got tired of staring, she'd get up from the table and try to do something productive at home. She cleaned her place, read magazines, took a long shower—anything to divert attention from the small box. Yet, her mind was focused on it. It whispered things to her that she dared not say openly. It toyed with her and mocked her, all while it sat quietly on her table. She asked herself what she'd do if she was pregnant. Would she keep it? Would she abort it? Would she tell the father? Did she even know who the father was? How would being a single mom affect her career if she decided to keep it?

When she had finished her MBA, she had worked very hard at climbing the ladder of success and she now found herself in her twenties near the top of that ladder. She had been recently named vice president of human resources for a large company, and everything that she had hoped for was now within her reach. She had a high six-figure salary, a wonderful home, prestige, and power. She knew that a pregnancy could ruin her reputation at the conservative company, and she had worked too hard and had sacrificed far too much to let an unwanted child destroy her. She thought about all of the conniving, backstabbing and fucking she had done within the company to move ahead quickly. She had never been one to fuck for free. For her, sex was a business proposition. Usually, when she seduced a man, it was usually part of a plan.

But, she had let her guard down with Kevin. Part of her attraction to him was born from his aloofness toward her. She had always used her devastatingly good looks to get what she wanted. There hadn't been one man in all of her life that she wanted to fuck who had turned her down. That is, until she met Kevin. Kevin, she thought, was a fine specimen of a man and she had remembered him from their days back in college in Austin, Texas, but they never traveled in the same circles. That day she ran into him by coincidence in the mall in Houston changed everything for her. She wanted him and would stop at nothing to get him. She went about the business of trying to seduce him—this time out of desire rather than strategy—but he was steadfast in his disinterest. She even got him a job at her company. She practically served *it* to him on a silver platter, yet he didn't want to come to her table to feast. She couldn't understand it. She became even more determined to have him and she pursued him relentlessly until she finally succeeded. She had never had to work so hard to have sex with a man but, when they did, it was the best fuck of her life. Then, the shit hit the fan. She found out he was gay. At a business conference, a video of Kevin having sex with a man was broadcast throughout the luncheon in living color on the big video screens.

She remembered that day.

She'd never forget.

Even before the video, deep in her soul, she knew about him.

Even after the video, she pretended that it was Kevin's twin on the screen having sex with that man. She didn't want to face the truth.

But, she knew.

She had always known.

She remembered how angry she was at herself for getting pregnant by Kevin. She couldn't believe that she had been in denial about his sexuality, but in looking back, it all made sense. In hindsight, you have perfect vision. She had been blinded by lust and that was not something that ever happened to her. She got caught up in the game and ultimately lost. She could offer no forgiveness for him for what she considered his duplicitous behavior. She convinced herself that he seduced her and that his standoffish behavior was his way of making her want him more. Before she found out he was gay, she thought he had played the perfect game: he raised her level of interest in him by pushing her away, knowing full well that would only make her want him more. But, the real reason he didn't want her didn't have anything to do with games.

She remembered screaming at the top of her lungs when she peed on the little strip and it turned blue—a reaction indicating that she was pregnant. Her scream was a blood-curdling, soul-shaking shriek that could cause the deaf to hear. The scream was pulled from the depth of her soul and never would it be replicated. She threw herself onto the floor in a fit. She couldn't raise the child of a fag. Immediately, she knew she had to abort it.

She remembered making the appointment with her doctor to talk about getting rid of the bastard child growing in her womb. After all of the tests were completed, she remembered feeling numb while listening to the doctor tell her that the abortion she had when she was seventeen wasn't performed correctly. She was amazed that RaChelle had gotten pregnant this time. RaChelle was told that if she had this abortion she most likely would never be able to carry a child. *Never. Never. Never.* That word kept echoing in her head as if she had it on repeat. The finality of that word unsettled her. *Never.*

She remembered how her doctor's words affected her. Although she wasn't ready for children now, she had hoped that one day she'd find the right man and settle down and have children. At least, she liked having the option. Now, she was being told that the future she had planned might not be possible. When the doctor uttered those words, it felt like a knife slicing away at the flesh of her future. Wounded and in despair, she left the office without the procedure. She knew that she couldn't make such an important decision on the spur of the moment.

She remembered the pain.

She remembered the fire in her belly.

She remembered.

She remembered telling Kevin about his unborn child. She had thought about how she had never known her father because her mother had refused to tell him that she was pregnant and decided that Kevin, in spite of his lie of omission, should know about his child. However, she made it clear that the decision on whether to keep or abort the child would be hers and hers alone.

Then, she remembered *that* day. It was the day she had decided to tell Kevin that she wanted to keep the baby. She knew Kevin would be at church because his friend Tony was having a commitment ceremony to wed his lover LaMont. She didn't want to go and be a part of that bullshit, but she knew if she didn't tell him that day, she might never tell him. So, she rushed to the church and that's when the madness began. When she walked in, she saw Daryl, who led her to the back where Kevin was busy helping Tony prepare for his ceremony. As soon as the door opened to the back room, a gun was pressed to Daryl's head. Kevin's ex-lover, James Lancaster, had gone psychotic and was threatening to kill everyone in the church. It was a scene straight out of a movie. James beat and tortured a couple of people in the church before he let bullets rain down. Kevin, LaMont and Daryl had been shot. Luckily, their injuries were not life-threatening. In the ensuing madness, a terrified RaChelle tried to push and shove her way out of the burning church when fiery pieces of wood from the collapsing ceiling fell on her. That was the last thing she remembered until she woke up in the hospital days later with tubes sticking out of her body. She remembered her first waking thought: *This is all Kevin's fault.* Even before the doctors had told her, she knew the baby was dead and she also knew her last chance at having a biological child of her own had died also. Kevin had taken her body, her dignity and now he had robbed her of her future. Revenge was her motivating factor in healing. It was like a drug racing through her veins. It fed her. It sustained her. It comforted her. She needed it. She wanted it. And, she would have her revenge.

When she got out of the tub, she put on her robe and moved into her bedroom. She reached into the drawer of the nightstand and pulled out a blue floral book that served as her diary. She always wore the key around her neck on a gold chain—something she had done since she was a small girl. When she unlocked the book, she took a seat in the chair and re-read her entry from the other day.

Dear Diary,

I finally did it! I finally surprised Temple. The look on his pretty face was priceless! I wish some-one had been there to take a picture. It was a Kodak moment. He looked like he had seen a ghost! I know I must have been the last person he expected to see. For a minute, I thought he was going to faint and if he had, I would have left his gay ass on the sidewalk in the cold. Fuck him. If there was one thing I tried to teach him when we were back in Houston it was always expect the unex-pected. So far things are going according to plan, even though I revealed myself a little sooner than I wanted to. I'm sick of this spy shit. It's time for action. Following him and Daryl trying to figure out their routines got boring and has taken a lot out of me. Temple has been to the same bar three times in the last week and each time he left with a different man. Shit, I hope they checked their wallets. I can't believe he spends so much damned time at that bar. I wonder if Cerina knows she's fucking a fag. I hate fags. Anyway, at least he's doing something. Daryl is boring as fuck. All he does is go to work, the gym, and home. I guess Kevin got his ass on lockdown. I was surprised when Daryl ended up at The Fireplace, though. He doesn't seem like the going-out type anymore, but I guess when there's trouble at home…

Everything ended up working out fine, though. Daryl showing up like he did saved me the trouble of having to find a way to get him and Temple in the same room. Temple, being the predictable bastard that he is, did exactly what I wanted him to do. I knew that all I needed was to get the two of them in the same room and his ass would spot Daryl like he had radar. Anyway, Daryl is fine (as far as sissies go), looks classy, and looks like he has money so I knew Temple would flock to him and work his magic. As much as I hate his ass, the bastard still looks good, though. When I saw him, I will admit my panties did get a little wet so I know Daryl was feeling him. This shit is gonna be off da fuckin' hook and much easier than I thought! When I told Temple what I needed him to do, he tried to act like he's changed—a leopard can't change his spots. Then, I showed his arrest warrants and he started singing a different tune. His punk ass is still scared as hell of jail. That time I bailed him outta jail in Houston he looked like he had spent three years in hell, and it was only overnight on a drunk-driving charge. I spent a lot of money getting his ass out that time, but he made up for it when he fucked over and over and over. I'll give it to him, he can lay some pipe—too bad I found out his ass likes dick more than I do. I can't believe I got mixed up with two different fags. When I think about that shit, it still pisses me off. What, do I have a sign on my forward saying "will fuck homos?" I hate Temple, but I hate Kevin more. I know that pretty boy ain't gonna have no trouble working Daryl. I can't wait to see Kevin's face when his world falls apart. I want his tears. He's had mine.

P.S.: On the way home, I saw the perfect baby store I want to check out for Tatiana. She needs some new clothes and maybe a toy or two.

CHAPTER 10

Kevin ignored the sound of the ringing telephone in his office at Jose's, feeling as if he was buried underneath a mound of paperwork. Lately, the fund-raiser had taken up a lot of his time and he had not been able to devote as much time to the restaurant as he would have liked. He passed a lot of responsibility on to Mr. Martinez, but he still felt he needed to be more involved. There were invoices to be paid, food orders to be placed, payroll for the staff to be processed and a host of other things. He didn't want to be distracted by an unnecessary conversation, so he let it ring. Instead, he picked up a bill to renew the property and fire insurance. He thought for a moment. He remembered telling Mr. Martinez to go ahead and renew the policy. The phone rang again. This time, he looked at the caller ID. It was Daryl, but Kevin hesitated a second before picking up the receiver.

"Hey, baby," Kevin said.

"Hey. How are you?"

"Good. What's going on?"

"Nothing. Checking to see if we're still on for dinner tonight." Daryl listened to the sound of shuffling papers through the phone. He knew what that meant.

"Tonight's actually not going to be good. I'm really backed up with work here—"

"Can't you get Mr. Martinez to finish up? I mean, he is the restaurant manager."

"And I'm the owner. There are some things I have to be responsible for. Besides, I have to meet with my attorney tonight to go over some paperwork for Keevan's Room."

"It's always something," Daryl mumbled. He had grown accustomed to Kevin being occupied by something more important than him.

Kevin took a deep breath and removed the glasses from his face and placed them on his desk. He only wore his glasses when the contacts irritated his eyes or when he wanted to appear more professional. "Baby, I know that right now it seems as if I always have some-thing to do, but I promise you things will be different soon. The agreement with Crown Services will be done, I'll have experience under my belt with the restaurant, Christmas will be over, and the New Year's Eve fund-raiser will be over. Can you cut me a little slack right now? I promise I'll make it up to you."

"I guess."

"Baby, please work with me, okay?"

"It's cool, baby. I'll go to the gym with Temple." Daryl's quick and easy delivery of Temple's name struck a bad note with Kevin. He knew what Daryl was doing. Daryl hoped that by casually dropping his name Kevin would think he had heard it before. Kevin wanted to tell him how predictable he was, but he refrained. Kevin had waited for the moment when Daryl would mention Temple. Kevin was certain that he had become familiar with Temple's name from the text message this mystery man had left on his lover's cell phone.

"Who is Temple?"

"Temple, you know Temple, my workout partner. I know I've mentioned him before."

Kevin didn't respond.

"What time will you be home?" Kevin didn't press the issue. He feared their house of cards could not withstand another issue at this time.

"I don't know. Maybe around nine."

"Okay."

"See ya then."

They hung up the phone and Kevin sat back in his chair and tried to make sense of his feeling toward Temple and the growing suspicion in his heart. *His new workout partner?* That didn't sit well with Kevin. He really thought Daryl was trying to run a game on him. First, he introduces Kevin as a "friend" and now all of a sudden he has some workout partner named Temple who is so concerned about Daryl that he has to send text messages to see if he made it home safely.

"Who does he think he's fooling?" Kevin asked himself out loud. He folded his arm as he reclined in his chair. "He must be out his damned mind." Kevin rubbed his face with his hands, hoping he could wipe away his suspicion. He understood Daryl was in a prime position for cheating. He was no fool. And, he felt as if he owned part of the blame for not doing enough to keep the spice in their relationship. He had ceased being attentive and taking care of Daryl a long time ago. It wasn't done purposely, but it was a product of two professional people whose lives were on divergent paths. They both were busy with work and they had forgotten about each other. As true as that was, Kevin also knew if Daryl cheated, then Daryl and Daryl alone would be the blame. It would be a decision Daryl would make and once he decided to cheat, there was no power on Earth strong enough to stop him. If Daryl decided to venture outside the monogamy—and monotony—of their relationship, there would be no forgiveness—he was sure of that. There would be no way for him to forgive him because Kevin knew that he didn't have it in him. Some people can survive infidelity, but he was not one of those people.

As he sat in his office, the magnitude of what they faced clouded his head. It was like a heavy black rain cloud that hovered over the city. At any given moment, the cloud would burst and all of its fury and power would rain down with no apology and no mercy. His relationship was that cloud and he was waiting for it to burst. After all they had been through, Kevin realized he could no longer be content on wondering if Daryl was cheating. It was driving him crazy. He closed the books, grabbed his keys, and told Mr. Martinez that he was out for the evening.

Kevin got into his car and drove the few blocks to his house. Once inside, he hung his coat on the rack and immediately went into Daryl's office. He stood there momentarily while he tried to digest the ramifications of what he was poised to do. He surveyed the room, not sure exactly what he was doing or what he was looking for. He took a seat behind his computer and moved the mouse to awaken the screen. Neither he nor Daryl was in the habit of turning off their machines. With as much time as Daryl spent glued to his computer screen, Kevin thought something had to be luring him there.

Kevin searched Daryl's Internet history to see which websites he had recently visited. Shadows of guilt crept up like a slow-moving fog. He had never before felt a need to spy on Daryl and it didn't sit well with him, but his mind burned with an unquenchable desire to know the truth. He would no longer sit around wondering and he thought that he might find something—some incriminating email or note—on his computer.

For the first few seconds, Kevin felt a sense of relief because everything he saw in the history looked legitimate. When he came across a website with an unfamiliar name, he simply clicked on it and was happy to know Daryl had looked up a couple of photography sites as well as other colleges in the area. He was happy until he saw the website www.adam4him.com. He gasped. Immediately, he recognized the infamous site as a gay dating and hook-up site. When he hit the button that took him to the site, Daryl's login information was already saved and Kevin logged on. The site was divided by city and the user was able to browse ads placed by men in a particular area who were looking to meet someone. Kevin knew this site was designed expressly for men to meet other men for sexual hook-ups. Some folks claimed to be looking only for "friends" but, as far as he was concerned, you don't find platonic friends on a site where every body part and orifice was on display for everyone to behold. This site was about men having mindless, gratuitous, and random sexual encounters with men who have had mindless, gratuitous and random sex probably with everyone else on the site. It sickened Kevin's stomach to find out that Daryl was a part of the madness and what he viewed as the dehumanization of gay relationships. Everyone was reduced to body parts and stats. He looked at the top of the screen and noticed a button that read, "Edit Profile." When he clicked on the button, he wasn't sure if he was ready for the information that Daryl could have in his profile, but he had to know. He wasn't sure how to react when he read the words. The saving grace was that Daryl's profile didn't offer a picture of himself. He read the ad:

"I am a lover, a dreamer, a teacher, a friend, and a poet. I am a work in progress and a diamond in the rough. I am a man of principle and a man of conviction, but I am a MAN, confident in who I am. If you want to chat, send me a message. Just looking for conversation."

Kevin took a deep breath and let the words saturate his consciousness. Neither he nor Daryl had many friends in the area because it was difficult to make true friends in gay D.C. Most of the people they met wanted to have sex with one of them or both of them, so part of Kevin viewed Daryl's ad as a cry for help—a plea for friendship. He knew exactly what Daryl was feeling because he was feeling it also. He missed the closeness he enjoyed with his friends back in Houston. Here, in this brave new world of D.C., it had not been an easy task to bond with people. Even still, that was no excuse for placing an ad on a sex site. *None.* Kevin tried to temper his anger with understanding and calm his disgust with compassion. Yet, he knew in his heart that what Daryl had done went outside the scope of the relationship they shared. It was just wrong. He wondered if Daryl was having an online affair.

Before returning the computer to its previous state, he checked the email section and read a few of the random responses that had been sent to Daryl's account. He deleted each one after he read it. Most of the emails simply said "wassup" or "what you trying to get into" or something of that nature. Kevin wanted to know what kind of people on this site were sending emails to Daryl so he checked the profiles of someone who sent an email. He gasped at what he saw and read. There was a naked man sitting in a chair with his leg draped across the arm of the chair while he was holding what appeared to be a glass of champagne.

Name *Dr. FeelGood*

Location Washington, D.C.

Gender Male

Stats Perfect…look at my pic

Marital Status Available

Orientation Gay

Sexual Role/Position Top Man!

Personal Quote Don't let the smooth taste fool ya!

Kevin pushed himself away from the machine and tried to process what he had discovered. How would he confront Daryl with this new information? Was this information worth the fight? Did it prove that Daryl was cheating? Surely, he could have an ad and not have met anyone, right? Ultimately, Kevin listened to his gut instinct, which told him that that was not the proof he needed. Daryl had not been absolved of sin, but this wasn't the smoking gun that Kevin sought. He hoped that his feeling was wrong but, in his heart, he still knew something wasn't right.

Kevin's initial suspicion of Daryl's infidelity was born from his cozy relationship with Amir—that's when the seeds of mistrust were first planted. Now, Temple was in the picture and another seedling of suspicion had been buried in their garden, and this ad was far more than a seed of suspicion. He didn't know what to do. Kevin hated himself for feeling the way he did and hated Daryl for doing what he had done, but he couldn't help it. He hated looking at Daryl with suspicious eyes. He hated not being sure if he was being lied to. Most of all, he hated the feeling that his relationship was dying. His jealous thoughts used to be staccato flashes of suspicion that only lasted as long as a lightning flash. Now, his bouts of distrust had become more elongated and he had only Daryl to thank for that. That ad on the site convinced him that something was wrong.

Kevin walked into his office so that he could check his email in an effort to get Daryl out of his head. He had to do something to keep his sanity. When he opened his account, there was an email from Daryl saying that he'd be home later than expected because he was running late and had to push back his workout. It seemed a legitimate enough proposition, yet something wasn't right. What was it about Temple that he didn't like? After all, he hadn't even met this Temple. The question lingered in Kevin's mind to the point of distraction. He sat in front of his computer and stared at the curt email his lover sent. Sure enough, the letters he used to form his words looked correct and the words were spelled properly. Even his short sentences made perfect sense, but something was off. Kevin continued staring at the words on the screen hoping somehow—some way—they would show him the truth. There was a grave warning in his heart that told him that Temple was not to be trusted. *Neither was Daryl.* Kevin was so confused. With all the problems they had been having lately and with his suspicion and jealousy over Amir, he wondered whether this was all a product of those feelings and an overactive imagination.

The last thing Kevin wanted to do was become *that* type of man who sought out wrong-doing at every turn. He couldn't imagine devoting countless hours of each day wondering whether or not Daryl was where he said he'd be or if he was out doing something illicit. There was no way Kevin could be with Daryl 24/7, nor did he have a desire to be with him all day every day. He knew that for a relationship to work, both parties needed their own lives and interests outside of each other. They had never smothered each other. Once they became a couple, they gave each other the space and the freedom to be individuals within the context of a relationship. Now, it seemed as if Daryl's freedom had taken him down the wrong road. The feeling kept nagging at him. *Who is Temple and what is he to Daryl?*

The idea of questioning Daryl turned his stomach. It was so against everything that he believed a relationship to be about. You have to have trust. If he said Temple was his workout partner, then that's who he was; nothing more, nothing less. If he had an ad on the Internet, then surely he hadn't hooked up with anyone. Part of him regretted having gone through his computer and his email, but the other part of him knew it was necessary. Part of him didn't want to know the truth. Part of him had to know the truth. Fear gripped him. It wouldn't let him go. Why had he searched? Why couldn't he let it go? Why couldn't he go on pretending not to know the difference? If you looked long enough, you'd always find something; even if it wasn't really there. Someone, a long time ago, said, "When you look into the abyss, the abyss looks into you."

In spite of his contradictory thoughts, the growing discomfort he felt within his soul had to be addressed. He had developed a good sixth sense over the years. If something didn't *feel* right, then usually it wasn't. The uneasiness that dwelled within his heart was never a harbinger of good fortune. He only got that feeling when something was wrong. He had told himself time and time again that Daryl was faithful. *If he says he's at the gym, then damn it, he's at the gym.* He tried with desperation to convince himself that Daryl wasn't cheating. Yet, somehow, he knew that wasn't the full truth of things.

He left his office and went upstairs into the bedroom. He moved over to the fireplace and started a fire. He stared at the crackling flames and momentarily lost himself in its warm glow. He thought about the strange similarities between love and the flame. One minute, the flame can provide much needed comfort. It can protect you from the cruel winter nights. But, if not watched and cared for properly, the same flame that provides warmth, can also destroy with an unmatched ferocity. Once the power of the flame turns on you, you'll feel the heat. Much like love. Beautiful. All-powerful. All consuming...unpredictable.

As he stood before the flame, he made a decision. He didn't want to get burned. If there was nothing going on and Daryl was being faithful, then there would be nothing to find—nothing would validate those suspicions. One thing he would not settle on is being content with his suspicions. He couldn't live like that. He had to find a way to exorcise the negative feelings and the only way to do that was to prove Daryl was not cheating. He needed something to confirm his man's fidelity; he needed to know that it was okay to love again, and he had to know that it was okay to trust Daryl with his love.

He lay across the king-sized bed and wanted to pull the covers over his head so that he could block out the darkness, but there was no protection from his storm. Then, he had a thought. He remembered something he saw the other day when he was shopping in Georgetown. He noticed a sign for a store that sold surveillance equipment. He had walked by it a thousand times but never gave the establishment a second thought. The store sold everything from small video recorders to phone taps to software that would track someone's online movements as well as provide access to their email. The sign in the front window listed many more gadgets and spy equipment, but he only remembered those. By making a few simple purchases he could find out the truth. He didn't want to be played, yet he didn't want to bring himself to the point where he had to literally spy on his man to find out if he was cheating or not. He told himself that if he was at that point in the relationship, then that said a whole lot about what was going on. He never thought there would come a day where he'd walk into that store, but now he was seriously considering tapping the phone lines and installing surveillance software on Daryl's computer. He felt ashamed and needed to talk to someone. So, he called Danea.

"Hello?"

"Danea, it's Kevin. How are you?"

"I'm fine, but what's wrong with you?"

"I'm fine."

"You ain't gots ta lie, Kevin, You ain't gots ta lie," she said in her ghetto-girl voice, in an attempt to be humorous. "I know you too well. I can hear it in your voice."

"It's the same shit. Me and Daryl. Daryl and me."

"What's going on now?"

"I found out that he has a personal ad on a gay sex site."

"What the fuck?" Her sudden alarm rattled Kevin.

"I know. That's fucked up, right?"

"Ain't that a bitch."

"I don't know what to do. His ad simply said he was looking for conversation and he didn't have a picture of himself or any personal information in his profile. I checked his sent mail file and as far as I can tell he hadn't been sending out pictures of himself, either. Maybe he is only looking for friends."

"On a fucking sex site?"

"That's what I say, but maybe it is possible. Who knows?"

"How did you find out about the ad?"

He paused. "I searched his history files on his computer and came across the site. When I clicked on it, his login information was already stored. So, I logged in under his name."

"Damn, I can't believe Daryl is tripping like this. How the hell does he expect things to get better between you two if he is playing around with some Internet trick?"

"I wish I could answer that question. If he hasn't cheated yet, it may be only a matter of time."

The silence on the phone lingered momentarily. Danea had to get her mind around the fact that the perfect couple was facing their demise. She didn't want to entertain that thought but, by the sound of Kevin's voice, she knew that he was convinced.

"Do you think he's already cheated? I mean really *feel* that he has?"

"I get this feeling in my gut and it's telling me something is going on. I don't know what. I have never felt this strongly about any situation. I don't know what to do. If I ask him, he'll simply deny it because I don't have proof."

"Then you need to get proof," she said sternly. "I'll be honest with you. I don't believe Daryl is capable of cheating on you. He loves you far too much, but if you think he is, then you owe it to yourself to find out what's really going on. You can't keep wondering. If you find out that he's not cheating, then you can put these feelings behind you and work to make your relationship better. You and I both know you can't make it better if you think he's cheating. And, if you find out he is cheating, then you do what you have to do."

"Yeah, I guess you're right."

"There ain't no *guess* about it. These are dangerous times and I told Curtis that if he ever cheated on me that I'd fuck him up. I won't have it. I won't let him or anyone endanger my life. When I choose to have sex with Curtis, I assume the risks. We still use condoms. But, if he's cheating on me with someone, then he's putting me in harm's way and I didn't assume that risk. I love him, but I will kick him in his neck and then cut him if he ever cheats on me."

"Damn, you ain't playin', are you?" Kevin asked with a chuckle. "I can't believe y'all have been together all this time and are still using condoms."

"He's my fiancé; not my husband. And, I've seen too many stories where women who think they are in monogamous relationships end up with HIV or some other STD. Like I said, I ain't gonna be a statistic 'cause he couldn't keep it in his pants."

"Daryl and I stopped using condoms a long time ago but, before we did, we got tested three times over the course of a year and a half. Once we stopped, I felt good about it. We were both clean and I never thought I'd have to worry about this kind of shit again. Now, I don't know."

"It's cool that you got tested and waited before you stopped with the condoms, but in this day and age there may not be a time when any of us can ever stop using condoms. I've talked about this shit with a couple of my girlfriends who have been with their man for years and some of them still use condoms. I know most folks—gay or straight—don't get tested together. Most of the time it's like you just roll over one night and do it without the condom. No conversation. It simply happens."

"Yeah, that's usually how it happens. Been there, done that."

"Well, don't put your life and health in danger. I know you love him, but your health is far more important. All I can say is find out what you need to know as soon as possible."

"Danea, I really appreciate your words. You always know exactly what to say."

They chatted for a few minutes longer and when they hung up the phone, Kevin felt a dark sense of release. He finally knew what he had to do, but he also knew that doing so could spell the end of his relationship with Daryl. The blues, jazzy and freefalling, pumping and pulsating, colored his vision. Everything he saw became a shade of blue. Blue teardrops stained the walls as the furniture burned indigo. Each breath he took was invaded by smoky, blue-gray air that smoldered within his lungs and forced him to cough. He took her words to heart and deep within his soul they found life and breath. The love he had for Daryl burned in azure, but the mistrust he felt was deep, dark and navy. His whole world became a deeper blue.

Kevin searched for almost twenty minutes for street parking in Georgetown before finding a spot on M Street. The well-to-do area of D.C. was famous for its shopping and restaurants, which made parking in the area on any given day an exercise in patience. During the Christmas season, it was a hardship. Pedestrian traffic was thick as shoppers sought to find last-minute bargains. Although Kevin was usually a big holiday shopper, this year things were different. He hadn't felt the Christmas spirit with all that had been going on with Daryl and all the other things going on in his world. In fact, the holiday had barely registered on his radar screen. As he walked down the cobbled sidewalk toward his destination, he did take notice of the holiday decorations and lights that highlighted his path. He smiled, if only for a minute.

Once he reached his destination, he paused and looked up at the sign before entering the surveillance shop. He quietly stepped into the well-lit store, not sure what to expect, and tried to remain unnoticed. There were four other people in the store—all women—and Kevin imagined they were in his same predicament of trying to ascertain the fidelity of the one they loved. They were kindred spirits, but he did not dare speak to anyone out of shame.

He crept through the small store looking at the various tape recorders that you could hook up to telephones as well as small cameras—some the size of a small button—that could be planted in various places around a room. The level of sophistication of some of the devices fascinated Kevin. *Hell, if they are selling this shit to the public, imagine the devices the government had,* he thought. He caught the attention of an older Asian lady who smiled at him out of politeness. Was he ready to go through with this? he kept asking. He looked over to his left and saw a display of various software programs that could be installed onto the personal computers. He wasn't ready for this. As he turned to leave the store, a salesman approached him.

"Good evening, sir. May I help you?" Kevin, slightly startled, looked up at the man and tried to gather his thoughts.

"Uh, yeah. I wanted to find out some information about this software. How does it work?"

"Well, I can tell you it is one of the easiest software surveillance programs out there to use and it is highly effective. A lot of employers are using some kind of surveillance software on the computers of their employees and this one is one of the more popular models. Installation is a breeze because it practically installs itself. Once installed, it cannot be traced using normal computer searches or by virus protection programs or spyware programs. The user will absolutely not know that it is installed. It records every keystroke—from passwords to emails to instant messages—made on the machine. It will provide you with the equivalent of a digital surveillance tape so that you can see the exact order of what's happening on the machine in which the software is installed. It's usually one hundred forty-nine dollars, but it's on sale for one hundred twenty-nine dollars. Would you like to buy it?"

Kevin remained quiet for a few seconds.

"Sir?"

"Yeah, I'll take it."

"May I interest you in a tape recorder that you can hook up to a phone line? It secretly records any conversation made on the line it's set up on." Reluctantly, Kevin acquiesced.

CHAPTER 11

Temple and Daryl had worked out religiously the last few days. Daryl was determined not to let Temple keep the advantage and Temple's rigorous workouts were doing him some good. Each day when they'd meet at the gym, Daryl pushed himself harder than the day before because he wanted to see improvement. Even in the short time they had spent working out, Daryl could see a difference in his strength, speed, and endurance when they ran on the treadmill after their grueling bout in the weight room. And, during that time at the gym, they connected. Daryl learned more about his relationship with Cerina than he had asked. He learned about Temple's childhood, and Temple was amazed at how at ease he felt around Daryl. He shared things with Daryl that he had never told anyone; not even Cerina.

His soul confessions to Daryl opened him up in ways unfamiliar to his hardened heart. He wanted to talk more, to bond more, and to share more with this stranger, this man who piqued his interest and this man who made him *feel*. Over the past few days, each time Temple's cell phone rang, he hoped and prayed it was Daryl. He also found himself calling Daryl's cell phone and leaving messages simply to hear his voice. What he was experiencing was new, but he liked it.

Temple tried to get Daryl to open up about his relationship with Kevin, but Daryl resisted. He wasn't in the habit of discussing the intimate details of his personal life; not even with close friends. And, his mother had taught him if you don't have anything good to say, then don't say anything at all.

When Temple thought about his relationship with Daryl, he sometimes became unnerved by the strong and sudden connection. For the first time in his life, he connected with someone and he really wanted to get to know Daryl as much as he wanted Daryl to learn more about him. His often unwanted and unexpected feelings for Daryl troubled him. His feelings for Daryl weren't built on pretense or superficialities, but they were real and diametrically opposed to what he had to do. Somehow, he had to push those thoughts out of his head each time he was with Daryl. He forced thoughts of forced seduction and RaChelle out of his head.

When they weren't working out, they remained in constant communication; either by phone, email or instant messenger. Usually, they talked on the phone at least twice a day while Daryl was at work and saw each other during their workouts. They enjoyed coffee and talks together. Temple's seduction of Daryl was working in reverse. It was he who was being seduced and enchanted by Daryl.

After they finished their workout at the gym, a light snow had begun to coat the area. The flakes fell effortless to the ground as shoppers continued making their way to the stores in Pentagon Row.

"I have an idea," Temple said. He smiled and pointed to the rink in the center of the courtyard. "Let's go ice skating." Daryl looked at him as if he had lost his mind. "I'm serious. I haven't been skating in a long time and the rink is empty right now. I think they close at ten, so that gives us a half-hour."

"You're serious, aren't you?"

"Hell yeah. Why wouldn't I be? Come on; let's get down there before they close up shop."

Temple flashed his pearly smile and Daryl's defenses tumbled. They rushed down the stairs and stepped into the courtyard of the outdoor shopping area. As they approached the booth that rented the ice skates, Daryl remembered the last time he had been ice skating; with Kevin at the Galleria Mall in Houston. He felt a twinge of guilt, but shook it off.

They stepped up to the booth, paid their money and collected their respective skates in the correct sizes. Daryl clumsily made his way to the rink with adrenaline pumping through his veins. He didn't want to fall in front of Temple, but he had never been good at ice-skating. The last time he skated, Kevin spent more time helping him up from the ice than he did actually skating. Even still, Daryl was determined to face his challenger. This was the most exciting thing he had done in a while. He couldn't help but think of how spontaneous he and Kevin used to be before everything went south.

"This is crazy—two grown-ass men out slipping and sliding on the ice like we're twelve years old," Daryl said once he got to the rink.

"Stop complaining. It'll be fun and I never said I was gonna be slipping and sliding. That might be you 'cause I got skills." Temple skated away from Daryl as if this were the Ice Capades.

Daryl was shocked at how well Temple maneuvered the slick surface. He rounded the corners with ease, turned around and even started skating backward while Daryl struggled to keep his balance along the wall.

"Show-off!" Daryl screamed at him. Temple confidently skated his way back over to Daryl.

"Okay. Let go of the railing and take my hands." Daryl wasn't ready to let go of the comfort the wall afforded him. The thought of falling on his ass in the middle of the rink did not appeal to him. "I'm serious. Let go. I got you." Slowly, Daryl released his grip and gave his hands to Temple who slowly and steadily moved them into the center of the rink. "Now, I want you to work on your balance. I want you to stand up straight and get used to the skates and the surface." Temple released his grip on Daryl who managed to stand erect in the center of the ring. Temple started circling him and looking him up and down like a bird of prey. "How are you feeling? You okay?"

"I'm fine, but I'll be better once you take my hands again."

"Nah, I ain't gonna do that. If you want to get back to the wall you're gonna have to make it over there by yourself."

"You are such an ass," Daryl said playfully. Temple positioned himself at Daryl's side.

"Now, just do what I do." Temple slowly started moving forward but when Daryl moved his right leg, he immediately lost his balance. He waved his arms around in erratic circles like a demented fan and when he reached out and grabbed Temple, they both tumbled onto the ice in a flurry of laughter.

"I told you this was gonna happen," Daryl said, trying to regain his composure. Temple stood up and offered Daryl his hand. He pulled Daryl up and into his broad chest and before either of them realized it, their lips made a natural connection, igniting a fire in their loins. They could feel each other's dick pressing against each other, screaming to be released. The snow that fell around them melted as the steam rose from their bodies. When Temple felt his lips connect to Daryl's, a feeling that was foreign to him manifested itself, and he was suddenly overcome with something stronger than desire. He felt a *connection*. He felt his spirit move. And, it shocked him, and he didn't want to let go. During the few seconds that he held Daryl in his arms, he wanted to protect him from the world. Ironically, the only protection Daryl needed was from Temple.

Daryl jerked away suddenly and stumbled his way over to the bench.

"I can't believe you did that," he said to Temple with agitation. "You know I have a lover and you kissed me right out in the open. Are you out of your fucking mind?" Daryl snatched off his skates and demanded his shoes from the man working the booth.

"I'm sorry. I don't know what came over me. I think I'm falling for you and I got lost in the moment. I couldn't help myself. And besides, I didn't feel you pulling away."

"That's not the point."

"What is the point then, Daryl? Don't act like you didn't feel something for me, too." The cashier handed them their shoes with a scowl on his face as he listened to their argument.

"The point is you shouldn't have done that. Not here."

"So, if I invited you over to my house and kissed you there that would have been better?"

Daryl sighed and walked toward the elevator that led to the underground parking garage. They stood in silence and waited for the elevator to arrive. When they got into the slow-moving silver box, Temple pushed Daryl against the wall and kissed him again. And again. And again. In the few seconds it took to reach the lower level, they felt as if they had been kissing for a thousand years. The sound of the elevator door opening broke their embrace.

"Why don't you come over to my place for a little while?" Temple inquired. He knew Cerina would be at the club and he would have the place to himself.

"I can't do that. Kevin is expecting me at home."

"This ain't about Kevin and it ain't about Cerina, either. This is about you and me," he said as he followed Daryl to his car.

"I can't. I can't. I can't," was all Daryl was able to say as he walked away toward his car with Temple right behind him. He tried to put the key in the lock of his car door but he kept missing the lock. Temptation was right on his heels.

"Don't leave me like this," Temple said. "I really need to be near you."

"Temple, I'll call you later. I gotta go."

Temple couldn't believe that Daryl had resisted him. "So, that's it? You're gonna drive away and leave me feeling like this? You're going to pretend what's going on between us isn't real? You need to stop trippin'."

Anger began to sound in Temple's voice. He hated rejection. He couldn't believe after all that had happened, Daryl was going to go home and pretend like everything with Kevin was fine. He was going to get in his car and drive away as if the distance would somehow erase their feelings.

Daryl looked at him one last time as he backed his truck out of the parking spot and drove away. Temple watched his car until it disappeared around the corner. He wanted Daryl more now than ever and it had nothing to do with RaChelle. He felt something real when they kissed and it was a feeling he wanted to experience again. He knew it was only a matter of time before he would have him. Daryl's lips had lit a fire in him that couldn't be quenched by Cerina. He knew what he had to do tonight.

❧❧❧

When Temple arrived at home, he knew he couldn't spend the evening flipping channels. If Daryl didn't want him, there were a thousand other men who would and he wouldn't even have to try that hard to get some. He was hot and bothered, but Daryl had worked himself into Temple's spirit to the point where all he could think about was kissing Daryl. He couldn't get him out of his mind; regardless of what he did. He kept thinking about their fiery kiss and how good Daryl felt pressed against him. He wanted more. If only he could kiss him again. The more he thought about his lips pressed against Daryl's, the more turned on he became. The more he thought about it, the angrier he became. He could see Daryl's truck rounding the corner of the garage and disappearing. Daryl left him alone.

He decided to step out to the Friday night hotspot to see what kind of trouble he could get into. He knew all the *kids* would be packed into The Edge, a gay club in an industrial area of D.C. He knew he'd find what he was looking for. If he couldn't get Daryl to quench his desire, then he'd have to find someone else. In the crowd, the picking would be easy, but the thrill of the hunt still caused the blood in his veins to race. As he got ready, he hoped Daryl would call, but he wasn't going to waste the night waiting by the phone. The more he thought about Daryl's rejection, the angrier he became. He wasn't accustomed to being turned down by anyone; for anything. Usually, all he had to do was smile and the world was given to him. He found it difficult to accept the fact that Daryl had felt the magic of his lips, but was able to scurry away. He didn't like that. He wanted Daryl out of his mind and the club would be the perfect place to forget.

Temple quickly found the blue tank top T-shirt he loved to wear with his favorite pair of jeans. His ass in those jeans had a life of its own and it got all the attention. He put on a pair of boots and his jacket and was out the door by midnight, consumed by lust. As he drove, he could not believe he had gotten caught up so quickly behind Daryl. His nose was wide open. He was supposed to be making Daryl fall for him; not the other way around. He drove with fury up I-395 heading toward the nightlife offered by the District of Columbia. Once he saw the Washington Monument in the distance he knew it wouldn't be long. He smiled wryly as his eyes fixed up on the tower—D.C.'s own larger-than-life phallic symbol—

as its erection pointed toward the heavens. With any luck, he'd have his own erection tonight.

As he parked his truck at the club, a panhandler asking for money to watch his car approached him. Temple had learned the hard way that it was better to give them a couple of dollars; otherwise, you ran the risk of coming out of the club at the end of the night to a vehicle that had been vandalized. Often, the same panhandler you refused to help would be the one to bust out your window or slash your tires. He reached into his pocket and handed the man a five-dollar bill and kept walking in the direction of the club. He ignored the man's *"thank you"* and waved him off without a second thought.

When he got to the window to pay the ten-dollar cover charge, Temple smiled at the cashier, who smiled back. The cashier motioned for Temple to enter the club without paying. Temple winked at him and strutted away. He still had it.

In the club the music was jumpin', bodies were pumpin', and Temple was ready for some humpin'. He made his way through the crowd, got to the bar, and ordered his first drink. Once he got the drink, he lingered momentarily around the bar, taking notice of the guys as they passed by. He diverted a few attempts from folks who eyed him up and down who didn't appear to have much to offer in terms of looks or money.

Instead of sipping on the drink he ordered, he used it as more of a shot and took most of it to the head. He wanted to get into the groove of things quickly and he wanted to get Daryl out of his head for the night. He slid through the crowd and made his way to the room in the back with the house music blaring through the speakers. He assumed his cool pose by the back bar and took notice of the people on the dance floor throwing their bodies around in a hypnotic trance. Soon, the beats and the drink running through his system lured him onto the dance floor and, before he knew it, he was getting his good groove on. He found some of his old dance moves coming back to him from his days when he used to strip on Tuesday nights at the WET, the club adjacent to The Edge. Tuesday nights there were "Hot Chocolate Tuesdays" and the club was usually filled with folks wanting to get a peek of the boys dancing butt-ass naked. Temple remembered those days when he used to dance on top of the bar and hang with skill from the railings on the ceiling as he pumped his body to the music. He hadn't become a stripper for the money—he did it for the attention, but he got bored soon after he started and only danced a few times at the club. Those days felt like eons ago but, tonight, as he reflected, they made him smile. He moved his body so erotically that a small crowd had formed around him adding their energy to the charged atmosphere. Excited by the attention, he gave them a show and used all his assets. At the end of the song, he wiped the sweat from his brow and went to get another drink. Usually, when he went out, he was far too cool to dance but, tonight, he wanted to let go and be free.

As soon as he ordered and paid for his second drink, he saw a familiar face through the crowd. He took a quick gulp of his drink hoping it would mute the nervousness that grew inside. He wanted to have a good time, but didn't need any drama tonight. In order to get out of this fast-approaching situation, he'd have to turn up the charm. Baron saw Temple leaning against the bar and was headed in his direction without missing a beat. Temple knew he was about to get cursed out, but he still admired Baron's physique as he moved toward him. Temple noticed the smoothness of his yellow skin and how the flashing lights glistened off his silky smooth skin. Baron's eyes were set deeply into his head and his eyelashes stood out. It sometimes looked like he wore eyeliner, but he didn't. It was natural. He was about five feet ten inches and when he smiled, his entire face lit up and the dimples in his cheeks gave him a boyish appeal.

"It looked like you were having fun out there dancing," Baron said flatly; with attitude.

"Wassup, B? How you been, baby boy?"

"I've been fine. The question is how have *you* been? I haven't heard from you in weeks. You get me all excited and I pull out all the stops and get whipped cream and strawberries and you leave me hanging. We had a cool thing going on and then all of sudden you stopped calling and coming by. That ain't cool."

"Man, Cerina has been really trippin' lately. I've had to lay low for awhile. You know what I mean?"

"Oh—I guess being out here tonight is what you call laying low? I know you; you out here looking for some ass." Baron folded his arms and clenched his lips together.

"I ain't looking for nothing. I came to get a few drinks 'cause I didn't want to be at home alone while Cerina is at work. But, speaking of ass, you wanna gimme some?" Temple asked as he smiled and reached down and squeezed Baron on the ass. Baron pushed his hand away and shot him an angry look.

"Don't touch me like that. You lost the right to be feelin' when you stood me up."

"Damn, why it gotta be like that? You know how much fun we had together."

Baron fought back a smile as he reflected. Temple could see that his charm, in the small measure he put out, was having an effect on Baron because of the smile that had formed in the corner of Baron's mouth. "Let me buy you a drink." Temple realized Baron had a low tolerance and became sexually charged with alcohol.

"Don't think you're gonna get me drunk and get some booty."

Temple simply smiled. Baron smiled.

A couple of drinks later, Baron's willpower had faded and he and Temple became lost in the beat on the dance floor—slaves to the rhythm. They found themselves in the hip-hop room dancing with complete abandon in the midst of the packed room. Smoke poured onto the dance floor from the machines and the effect of strobe lights hypnotized them. They felt free, alive, and electric and drifted far from reality to a place where only the music and the beats reigned.

Baron's expression of unabashed yearning for Temple showed on his face. He slid all over Temple's body and aroused Temple's interest. Temple thought he was a good dancer, but when he saw the way Baron rolled his body in perfect unison with the beat, he knew he couldn't compete. Baron moved closer to Temple, grabbed him by the waist and thrust his pelvis into Temple's. Temple put his hand around Baron's waist and pulled him even closer. Their bodies bled into one. They united in rhythm. Then, Baron slowly moved a step away from his partner, turned away, and backed his ass into Temple's body. He gyrated, pumped, rolled, and moved from side-to-side like a pro. Temple couldn't remember the last time he had been fucked on the dance floor. This was far more than bumping and grinding. Suddenly, Baron backed off, turned to face Temple, mumbled something, and walked off the dance floor. Temple stood there and watched Baron vanish into the slithery sea of salty bodies and wondered what kind of game he was playing. He waited in vain for Baron to return. Baron never did.

At the end of the night, Temple looked around the crowded club for a brief moment for Baron, who was not to be seen. It was not Temple's style to sweat any man, so he figured it would be Baron's loss. Twice in one night he had been rejected. Instead of pressing his luck, he decided to throw in the towel for the night. He didn't have the mental strength to pursue anyone else. He picked up his jacket from the coat check and stepped outside into the frigid air. Folks gathered in the cold for last-minute conversations. Some were trying to set up "dates" while others waited on their friends or for the club to empty.

Temple was crossing the street when he heard his name being called out. He looked to his left and saw Baron. He kept walking.

"Temple, wait up, man!" Baron called. Reluctantly, Temple stopped.

"I don't know what the fuck you're doing, but I don't have the patience for your games."

"What are you talking about? I'm not playing games. I went to find my friends and then I lost you."

"And you couldn't have told me that on the dance floor?"

"I did, but I guess you didn't hear what I said because of the music."

"So, you just left me hanging?"

"I told you, I had to check on my boys," Baron said. He gestured toward the three dudes who had gathered behind him. They all looked at Temple with impish grins. "I guess you're heading home?"

"Why don't you walk me to my car?"

"Is that all you want me to do?" Baron asked as he licked his lips.

"For starters," Temple retorted with a smile. "We'll talk about the rest on the way." Baron's friends let out some "ohhhh's and ahhhh's" as Baron grabbed Temple's hand. Much to his surprise, Temple didn't jerk his hand away from Baron. He was not one for hand-holding; especially in public.

At the car, Temple leaned back on the outside of the passenger side so he stood face-to-face with Baron. They looked at each other, sizing each other up and smiling. Baron stepped closer to Temple and planted a firm kiss on his lips. Temple wasn't used to the aggressive approach, but something about a man going for what he wanted turned him on. He only wished Daryl would do the same and step up to the plate. When their lips touched, the fire Daryl had started reignited.

"Damn, that was one hell of a kiss," Baron said. "I'm so glad those lips you have aren't wasted."

"You wanna take a ride with me?"

Baron smiled and asked with a wink, "What you want me to ride?" Temple smiled back. "Where are we going?"

"Away from here."

"You're not tryna take me home, are you? 'Cause I'll have you know that—"

"That what? That you wouldn't want to go?" Temple interrupted.

Baron paused for a moment. "I have to tell my friends to go home. I'll be right back."

Temple got into the truck and tried to find a good CD. He wanted something slow and sexual. Moments later, Baron opened the passenger's side of the door and before the door closed, he had his tongue in Temple's mouth.

"Damn, boy, calm down a minute," Temple said. "Let's get outta here." Temple started the car and, as he drove, Baron started rubbing the growth between his legs. When they stopped at a stop sign on L Street, Baron reached over and unzipped Temple's pants. He stuck his hand in and pulled it out. He wanted a preview and a little taste. Temple couldn't wait anymore and found a darkened alley off a side street and parked the car. When Baron went down on him, Temple suddenly remembered how good he was at sucking dick. When Temple finally couldn't take it anymore, he leaned the seat all the way back and put his hands above his head as Baron went about his business. Baron had managed to come out of his pants and underwear before Temple knew it. He then reached into his pocket and pulled out one of the condom packets he had picked up at the club. He ripped open the packet and put the condom in his mouth. He put the rubber on Temple's dick with his mouth. Baron then climbed on top of him and rode him all the way home like a champion jockey.

CHAPTER 12

When Cerina stepped out of her doctor's office and into the hallway, her head started spinning and, for a second, she thought she'd lose her balance and tumble onto the blue-gray industrial carpet that lined the hallway. She fell against the wall and coughed violently as if she was choking. Tiny beads of sweat formed on her forehead while she struggled to regain her composure and her balance. She slid down the wall and anxiously waited for the coughing to subside. Tears formed in her eyes when she thought about everything she had learned and how her life would inevitably change. She didn't know how she would get through this, but she had decided a few weeks back that she wanted to live. She needed to confide in someone who could provide emotional support, but when she thought about the people in her life, there was not one person she could count on. She could never tell Temple. Never. She thought about talking to Nicole, but if she even hinted about it to her, everyone in the club would know. Nicole couldn't keep a secret to save her life. She had no family to speak of and when the realization dawned on her that she was alone, the tears that had formed in her eyes rolled quickly down her cheeks. She was afraid. And alone. She would have to bear this extraordinary burden alone.

When the coughing finally ceased, she shuffled through items in her purse looking for a tissue to dry up the moisture on her face. She feared the makeup would run down her face, leaving her looking like a drug-addicted circus clown. She thanked God the hallway was empty because she couldn't bear the thought of having anyone, not even strangers, see her in such a disheveled state. She ran her fingers through her hair in an attempt to bring some order to her frazzled mane. She gritted her teeth, stood up proudly, and shook her head in defiance of her latest attack and the news she had just heard. She was afraid, but not defeated.

Years before she met Temple, she learned that her health was failing. When they started dating, she initially thought she should tell him of her condition, but her fear of rejection prevented her conscience from giving voice to the words she needed to speak. She needed someone in her life, someone to hold her, someone to make her feel special, someone to make her forget about being sick, and someone to make love to her. She couldn't be rejected. Not again. She could not have another man walk out of her life and leave her alone. That word—alone—occupied a place in her soul and kept her up on those lonely nights when Temple came home late. In those empty moments, when all was quiet in the house and the piercing sounds of sirens filled the night, she feared one of his late nights out with his boys would turn into two, and two nights would become three, and three would somehow stretch endlessly onward until the warmth of Temple's touch was reduced to nothing more than an echo from her past.

She could not be alone.

In the years following her diagnosis, she refused to admit what was going on inside her body and she certainly didn't want sympathy from anyone. So, she kept her secret. She held it in and walked through life as she had never heard the diagnosis. The life-draining words issued by her doctor failed to convey any meaning. She would not yield to it. She would not entertain the thought that she was sick. Yet, in the midst of denial, she knew. Subtle changes in her body and the way she felt told her that much. Still, she refused to face reality. Over the last years she had operated in complete denial, refusing to think about it or acknowledge the truth while she ignored any symptoms of illness. She blamed her lethargy on a bad diet and lack of proper rest. When an occasional blemish threatened to mar her lovely skin, she quickly covered it up with makeup and dismissed it as a factor of aging. But, she knew. Now, she could not ignore the sickness and fatigue that had begun to visit her more often like a pesky relative whose short visit became a permanent stay. Random vomiting spells jolted her back into reality and forced her to deal with her situation. The sudden violence and force that characterized the episodes demanded her attention. And, she decided that she wanted to live.

As she leaned on the wall she shook her head. She could not believe this was happening to her. Not now. She remembered having to run off stage the other night because of her nausea. She darted off the stage, butt naked with her titties bouncing and bobbing up and down. She was lucky not to have given herself a black eye. She barely made it to the restroom before the fluid poured out of her like a faucet. Nicole, who happened to be leaving the stall, held her hair back as Cerina fell to her knees and prayed to the ceramic god. When she had finished, she hurriedly flushed the toilet so no one would see blood mixed with vomit in the toilet. The other girls in the dressing room teased her about being pregnant and she allowed them to have their fun. It was better that they create their own explanation than for them to know the truth.

What was happening now, she could no longer deny. As much as she wanted to continue pretending as if everything was okay, she couldn't. Her body wouldn't let her. She'd have to take care of herself; otherwise she'd risk Temple finding out her terrible secret. If he found out, she was sure he'd leave her.

She could not be alone.

The longer she leaned on that wall, the more determined she became. She clenched her lips and breathed rapidly through her nose while her nostrils flared. She pushed herself off the wall and stood proudly in the middle of the hallway as if she had reached the zenith of Mt. Kilimanjaro. She regained her balance, pulled herself together, then strutted toward the elevator with her back arched and her head held regally high.

❦❦❦

RaChelle strolled through the mall with a smile on her face. She loved Christmas, malls and shopping but, more than that, she loved treating herself to sexy shoes and revealing lingerie, which weren't exactly the typical holiday gifts. As she walked from store to store, she took time to notice the festive holiday decorations and even took a few moments to stare at the huge Christmas tree that rose majestically from the floor in the center of the mall and stretched nobly toward skylights in the ceiling of the four-story mall. At the base of the tree, a long line of children waited anxiously to sit on Santa's lap.

RaChelle grabbed the handles of the bags that she had set on the floor and struggled her way toward the lingerie store. She had paid tribute to Santa, the tree, and the children long enough. Now, it was time for her to treat herself. Even though she didn't have a man to model for, she liked to look good for herself. Walking around her hotel in sexy lingerie, while sipping on a dry martini as the smooth sounds of jazz filled the room, helped her relax and feel sexy. Sometimes, she'd look at herself in the mirror and, in spite of her scars, she'd turn herself on.

The mall was jam-packed. People, wrapped in the details of their own shopping expeditions, zoomed by, darting and dashing in between other shoppers, hoping to find that perfect gift at the last minute. RaChelle had been pushed aside, stepped on, and shoved by hurried shoppers who clearly had forgotten the meaning of the holiday. She remained unfazed by the crazed momentum and the looks of exhaustion on their wearied faces. She was determined not to let anyone steal her holiday joy. In fact, the only person who could turn her into the Grinch was Temple by not delivering on his tasks. She decided now was a good time to light a fire underneath him. She took a seat on the nearest bench and pulled her cell phone out of her purse. She dialed his number and the phone rang several times before he picked it up.

"What?" he said with attitude.

"Good afternoon to you, too," she said. "That's no way to answer your phone."

"It is when you call me this early."

"Temple, it's one-thirty in the afternoon. It ain't early."

"It's early for me. Now, what do you want?"

"First, I want you to stop talking to me like you've lost your damned mind. Secondly, I was checking on your progress."

"Didn't I tell you I would get it done?"

"That's what you said, but I haven't seen anything happen yet. I'm getting sick of waiting."

"Look, if you want this done right, then you have to let me do my thang."

"You've been fucking around for damned near two weeks and you should know I don't play. You have one week from today. After that, I'm calling the judge. And some bounty hunters." She hung up the phone and placed it back in her purse. She stood up and moved over to the escalator that led to the floor below.

When she reached the second level of the mall, she walked by a store that sold baby clothing and toys and could not resist the temptation of entering the store. It had become so natural for her to buy clothing for the child she never had. In Houston, she decorated one of the bedrooms in her townhouse for the baby and had stacked it full of clothing and toys. She'd often go into the room and sit for hours laughing and smiling and enjoying a life and a child who did not exist to anyone else. But her child, Tatiana Amber, existed in her world. In her mind, Tatiana's flesh was as real as hers. And if anyone asked, she could describe in vivid detail everything about the child; from how much she weighed at birth to the small black mole on her left cheek.

"Good afternoon," the saleslady said to RaChelle as she entered the store. "May I help you with something?"

"I'm looking for something for my little girl, but I think I'll browse for a second."

"Well, if you need any help, let me know."

RaChelle continued browsing the racks and looking for the perfect dress for Tatiana. She wanted something that would make the child look absolutely beautiful for the Christmas

Eve church service. After about twenty minutes in the store, she had found three dresses and decided to purchase them all. Nothing was too good for her child.

"Well, look what we have here," a voice said. "If it ain't Ms. Boughie herself." RaChelle turned around quickly and was surprised to see Cerina, who stood there with one hand on her hip, sucking her teeth. Cerina had on a pair of tight, black leather pants that revealed every curve of her shapely frame. Her black turtleneck sweater looked as if it was a size too small and made her big breasts look even larger than they were, and her long black coat came down to her ankles.

"Shit, I should have gone to a mall that wasn't on a bus route," RaChelle said, more to herself than Cerina.

"What did you say?"

"Nothing. Hello, Cerina. You're looking…festive. What, is there a *Matrix* convention around here?"

"Ha, ha, very funny." Cerina walked around RaChelle as if she was sizing her up; trying to decide if she wanted to prance. "What are you doing in this store? You got kids?"

"What I'm doing in this store is none of your business. But, if you must know, yes, I have a little girl."

"Where is she? I don't ever see you with her."

"This is your second time seeing me. Did you expect me to bring my child to your club?" RaChelle moved around her and picked up another dress from the rack. "What are you doing here? I know *you* don't have kids."

"I'm shopping for my friend Nicole's daughter. Today is her birthday and I need a gift for the party."

"How sweet." RaChelle tried to move around Cerina, but Cerina didn't budge. "Is there something you need from me?"

"I'm glad I ran into you 'cause we need to come to an understanding."

"About what?"

"Don't act like you don't know."

"Look, I don't have time for this, so I will let you get to your shopping—or whatever it is someone like you does in a mall like this. I hear they have no tolerance for shoplifting."

"Bitch, I got money. I don't need to steal nothing."

"Guess you had a good time last night on the pole, huh?"

"You want me to slap the shit out of you, don't you? I don't know why you think you better than anybody. You ain't no better than nobody, but I will tell you this. If I see your name on my man's cell phone one more time or on my caller ID, you and me gonna have some problems, okay?" Cerina stepped within a few inches of RaChelle's face. They were almost nose-to-nose. "Do you understand the words coming out of my mouth?"

"I've told you before that I don't want your man, but we do have some business. When he takes care of that, I'll be gone, but not a moment before that, okay? Now, do you understand the words coming out of my mouth?"

They stared at each other until RaChelle stepped back. From the corner the saleslady nervously watched, hoping their exchange of words wouldn't get any louder.

"Bitch, I will break my foot off all up in yo' ass!"

The saleslady stepped over to them, hoping her presence would diffuse the heated situation. "Ladies, is everything okay?"

"Everything is fine," RaChelle said. "I'd like to purchase these dresses."

The saleslady took the dresses from RaChelle and she turned to follow her to the counter. Cerina stuck her leg out in front of RaChelle and gave her a shove to make her fall. RaChelle, with her catlike reflexes, managed to grab Cerina by the arm and they both tumbled onto the floor with curse words flying unchecked from their mouths. They rolled on the floor and into a metal rack of clothing, which promptly came tumbling down on them.

"You clumsy bitch!" she screamed at Cerina as she leapt up from the floor.

"Me? That was you, you fucking idiot!" Cerina shot back.

The saleslady, half in shock, rushed over to prevent another episode. "Are you okay?" she asked of them both.

"I was fine until this hood rat attacked me!"

"Ain't nobody attack you, bitch. You tripped over my foot."

"That's a damned lie and you know it!"

The contents of both their purses had spilled onto the floor. RaChelle reached down and started shoving her items back into her purse. Cerina did likewise.

"I'm going to have to ask you both to leave the store," the lady said.

"Bitch, you ain't gots to ask me to do nothing. I've been thrown outta better stores by better people," Cerina said loudly while she snapped her purse closed and straightened out her jacket. By this time, a small crowd had gathered and a mall security officer was approaching.

"Is everything okay here?" he asked of the saleslady.

"Everything is fine," RaChelle interjected before she could respond. "But, you might want to carefully watch this one," she said, pointing to Cerina. "She steals." RaChelle flipped her hair and marched out of the store, leaving Cerina fuming. Behind her, RaChelle heard

Cerina going off on the guard and telling him to take his hands off of her. She didn't even turn around to witness the spectacle.

Dear Diary,

There were so many people at the mall that it took me almost thirty minutes to find a place to park. I know it's the holidays, but damn! A susta just wanted a parking space…it ain't like I was asking for gold. When I finally got inside, I had a run-in with Temple's ghetto-ass girlfriend in the mall. I still can't believe he'd get with someone so sleazy. That bitch don't have one ounce of class. I'm so disappointed in him. She confronted me when I was in the store shopping for Tatiana and you know how I hate to be disturbed when I'm buying stuff for my baby. It's funny that right before I saw her raggedy ass I had just gotten off the phone with Temple. He has one week to make this shit happen or he's going to be really sorry. I'm putting the final touches on my plan and in one week, right before Christmas, I want to deliver Kevin's special surprise. You know how I like bringing holiday cheer to the ones I love! I have to stay on Temple's ass because timing is essential and he is playing a big part in everything. I want him to fuck the hell out of Daryl and make Daryl forget all about Kevin. Kevin will be sorry he ever met me. Everything he has and loves will be gone by Christmas. Everything! I love the fucking holidays! And, he will know that it was because of me. Revenge is no fun unless you can take credit for it. I can see his pathetic face now. Crying like the little bitch he is.

CHAPTER 13

T raffic was thick in the city for a Saturday afternoon. Kevin darted in and out of traffic, while maintaining a safe distance from Daryl, who was a few cars ahead of him. Kevin rented a car and had decided to follow Daryl so he could find out the truth. This was his second time in as many days tailing Daryl. So far Daryl hadn't done anything out of the ordinary, but things still weren't adding up. Prior to Kevin following him, Daryl would disappear for hours on end without so much as a word. Nothing incriminating had turned up on the computer or the phone as of yet, but Kevin still had that feeling. More than anything, he wanted to prove Daryl's fidelity. He wanted to remove the feelings of doubt and mistrust he felt.

He couldn't believe his relationship had come to this—tape recorders and rental cars. It was definitely a low point in his life, but if his hopes came true, then it would be a new beginning. He would be able to bury his feelings and really start working on making them a better couple. He couldn't fix their problems by himself but, if he could get past the trust factor, then he could invest more of himself in the relationship. That was at least a start.

Daryl had left their house and indicated that he had some things to take care of and then he was going to work out. Kevin told him to be safe and watched Daryl drive off through the window in the den. He then raced out of the house and hopped into the rental car when Daryl pulled off and turned to the corner. He almost lost him a couple of times because of D.C.'s awkward traffic patterns. Luckily, Daryl had gotten stuck at a traffic light a few blocks away. That gave Kevin the opportunity to catch up to him and maintain a safe distance.

As he followed Daryl, his heart raced. This was the kind of madness he saw on TV. He used to laugh at folks when he heard stories about lovers who hid in bushes and put on disguises; all in an effort to catch their mate in a compromising situation. He felt like he was in a bad episode of that show *Cheaters* but, instead of watching it in the comfort of his home, he was living it. Daryl was driving straight down Pennsylvania Avenue toward the bridge that would take him into Maryland, which was in the complete opposite direction of where his gym was located. Kevin remained calm as he tailed Daryl and wondered exactly what business he had to take care of.

As expected, Daryl crossed the bridge and entered deep into Southeast D.C. He continued straight and then took a sudden right on Branch Avenue and proceeded on a direct path into Temple Hills, Maryland. Daryl, oblivious to the clandestine operation in which he was the center of, took a left and then another right and ended up in some ordinary apartment complex. Kevin had gotten stuck right before the complex, but still had a good view of Daryl's vehicle. Kevin didn't want to lose him—there was too much at stake and he wanted to put a final end to his "James Bond" mission. He waited impatiently for the light to turn green but, by the time he reached the complex, the gate had closed and another car was at the box trying to locate the name of the person they were there to visit. Finally, Kevin heard the beep that indicated the gate was opening and he followed the car in front of him closely to ensure he cleared the gate before it closed.

Once clear of the gate and with accelerated breathing, he sped up and drove around the slow-moving car in front of him, paying little attention to the speed bumps in the parking lot until he actually hit one and felt the strong jolt to the car. He tried to brace himself for impact after the first one, but his efforts were negligible. Still, he sped through, looking for Daryl. He had to find Daryl. He had to know why they were there. *Who lived here?*

He slowed his approach through the parking lot, finally noticing signs indicating the presence of children. Running over a child during a mad dash to find his potentially cheating mate and ending up on the nightly news was not something he had in mind. He drove through the complex, looking down every street and every passageway until he saw Daryl as he casually strolled from his car and walked to the building. Kevin turned into a parking space, facing the opposite direction of the building, and watched Daryl in his rearview mirror. He couldn't see much, but he could see Daryl knock on the door and pause for a few seconds. Then, the door slowly opened and Daryl walked into the apartment and the door closed.

Could this be Temple's house? Kevin wondered. After a few moments had passed, he stepped out of the vehicle and slowly approached the apartment. He only wanted to get close enough to view the apartment number.

"Apartment 2D," he said out loud. He was tempted to run up and bang on the door, but decided against that. After all, he had no idea whose apartment it was or who was inside.

Instead, he decided to go back to his car and wait. As he moved toward the vehicle, he saw a young man walking his dog. Casually, Kevin approached him and asked him for the exact address of the complex.

When he got back to the car, his mind raced. Unpleasant thoughts invaded his head and as hard as he tried to shake them, he couldn't. Endless scenarios of Daryl making love to some other man or engaging in some illicit behavior swarmed around him and Kevin felt as if his head was on the verge of exploding. He picked up his cell phone and called Danea. It rang several times before her voice mail picked up.

"Shit," he said to himself as he listened to her voice. "Danea, this is Kevin. I need a major favor. Please call me back as soon as possible." He pounded his head on the steering wheel; accidentally blowing the car horn in the process. He ducked down in the vehicle; in case he had alerted Daryl. When the tension caused by the noise dissipated, he jumped at the sound of his ringing phone. It was Danea.

"You scared the shit out of me," he said with rushed breathing.

"Calm down. What's wrong?"

"Where are you?"

"I'm at home. Why?"

"I need you to do me a favor."

"You sound frantic. What's going on?"

"I'll explain it to you later, but right now I need you to go to your computer and do a reverse address search. I'll give you the address."

"Kevin, you're scaring me. What's going on?"

"I need to know who lives at this address. Now, please take down this information and when you get it, call me back, okay?" He provided her with the information and hung up the phone. He kept his eyes on the apartment from his mirror, but there were no signs. He wondered what was going on behind closed doors. Exactly four minutes later, his phone rang.

"Did you get the information?"

"Yeah, I got it."

"So, tell me."

"First, I want you to tell me what's going on."

"Danea, I don't have time right now. I'll catch you up later. Just tell me whose apartment this is."

"Alright. Amir. Amir Charles."

Danea's words resonated as if she spoke in slow motion, dragging each letter and each syllable of his name into elastic moments that prolonged the initial blow Kevin felt. He ended the call with Danea and sank into the leather seats of the car. He didn't know what to think. Regardless of what numbers he used in the equation, the answer seemed to point to Daryl's infidelity. Late-night phone calls. Temple. Amir. Now, this crazy visit to Amir's house on an ordinary day.

❀❀❀

Daryl reluctantly took a seat on the couch as he waited for Amir to get dressed. Amir surprised him by answering the door wearing nothing but a towel that hung low on his high ass. From the moment he stepped into the darkened apartment he felt uncomfortable. The entire vibe that surrounded Amir spoke of danger and temptation. Daryl realized Kevin was right a long time ago about Amir and he suddenly wished he had not agreed to meet him at his apartment. He suddenly wished he hadn't done a lot of things.

"I'm sorry for keeping you waiting," Amir said as he emerged from the bowels of his unlit apartment wearing a tank top and a pair of small shorts, which revealed his thick thighs. Even though it was in the middle of the day, the apartment suffered from a lack of light. The angle of the windows in the apartment prevented sunlight from shining directly into the room, and the curtains were drawn tightly together, which choked the minute amount of sunlight that dared peek through the curtains.

"It's okay. We just need to get started. I have a lot of stuff to do today."

"You and Kevin have big plans?"

Daryl paused. "Something like that."

Amir moved over to the kitchen and opened the cabinet. He reached up and pulled out a glass. "Would you like something to drink?"

"Nah, I'm okay." Daryl tried to keep his eyes off Amir's ass as he poured a glass of orange juice. He thought about getting a glass so he could set it on Amir's butt. He smiled at that thought.

"I really am sorry about the mix-up with the grades. I don't know what happened and I can't figure out what went wrong. I entered everyone's grade in the spreadsheet like I normally do, but something must've happened," Amir said, recounting the details of his process of entering the grades. Amir placed his glass of juice on the coffee table and then retrieved his laptop and a stack of papers from his bedroom. He sat down right next to Daryl when he returned.

"You might want to get comfortable," Amir said with a slight smile. "This may take a while."

❀❀❀

Two hours later, Kevin was mentally exhausted. During the time he waited in the car, his mind conjured up a thousand different scenarios (and a thousand different positions) about the events taking place on the other side of the door of apartment 2D. Kevin could not believe he had spent so much time waiting on Daryl to leave Amir's apartment. He fought a nagging urge to pound on the door or to throw something at the window—anything to interrupt the pair. His uneasiness caused his mind to think the unthinkable. Finally, when he could no longer bear the disturbing thoughts in his head and when jealousy became his sovereign emotion, he leapt out of the car and slammed the door behind him. He started walking across the parking lot toward the apartment, his head pounding from the torture he had subjected himself to. He felt out of control of his thoughts and his actions. He could not know what his reaction would be when he kicked down the door like they do in the movies. He only prayed they would not be in some compromising position. As he approached the apartment, he noticed the door slowly opening. That shocked him back into reality.

"Shit," he whispered to himself as he darted toward a row of bushes. He tumbled into the wet grass and wedged himself between the building and the shrubbery, cutting his hand on a sharp piece of glass in the process. He pressed his lips tightly together to strangle the yawp he so desperately wanted to let loose. He listened through his pain to their voices and thought he heard the sound of lips touching each other. *Smooch*. It took all of his strength not to jump from the bushes and yell, "Caught ya!" But, he realized he'd look like a madman springing from the bushes; bloodied and scraped up. Instead he waited a minute. He heard recognizable footsteps. He held his breath and peeked through the shrubs and watched Daryl walk briskly to his car. He put the key in the lock, opened the door, and got in while Kevin fumed. Seconds later, Kevin heard the hum of the engine and watched Daryl back out of the parking spot, turn around, and head toward the gate.

Kevin rose from the bushes like the phoenix. The chill in the air turned to steam off his brow and the rest of his body. He examined his hand. The cut was really a minor scrape and his blind jealousy blunted whatever pain he felt. He walked to Amir's door—dirty, wild-eyed, and bloodied—and before he realized it, he was knocking—more like pounding—on the brown door. His heavy fists landed in big thuds on the wooden door. He pounded again. The door shook as the force of his fists reflected his frustration with Amir's delay in coming to the door. Suddenly, terror struck him and he asked himself what the hell he was doing. He wanted to run, to hide in the bushes again, to dart away back to the car, but it was too late. The door swung swiftly open and Kevin stood there like a deer caught in headlights. Amir's twisted face greeted him.

"Uhhhh, Kevin?" Amir stated with concern as his expression morphed from anger to confusion back to anger. "What are you doing here?"

Kevin stared at him.

"If you're looking for Daryl, he's not here. He just left," Amir said with some spice.

"Actually, Amir, I'm looking for you."

"For me?"

Kevin didn't answer his question. Instead, he stepped boldly into Amir's pit and turned to face him.

"Well, come on in, why don't ya?" Amir closed the door, not sure exactly what to expect from this most unusual visit from his boss's lover. "Is there something I can do for you?"

"Yes, there is, and I'm going to get right to the point. I'm not sure exactly what your intentions are toward Daryl, but let me tell you here and now that you need to back off."

"Excuse me?"

"You heard what I said."

"Kevin, I think you have the wrong idea about me. I am simply—"

"His teaching assistant. Trust me; I've heard that song before."

"I really don't know why you're here. There really is nothing going on between Daryl and me." Amir didn't mask the disappointment in his voice. It rang in Kevin's ears like a piercing scream.

"Oh, I get it now," Kevin said as he stepped closer to Amir. "I get it. You have a thing for him, don't you?"

Amir looked deep into Kevin's eyes. "And, what if I do?"

"You better get this straight, little boy. Don't mess with my man."

Amir turned his back to Kevin and walked toward the kitchen. "What if your man messes with me?" he said, with his head cocked to the side.

"Are you saying something has happened between you and Daryl?"

"I haven't said anything like that."

"Then what the fuck are saying?"

"I'm simply saying I can't control who's attracted to me."

"Boy, I will hurt you. You are seriously playing with fire."

The seconds that passed as they stared at each other were filled with so many emotions: pain, rage, jealousy, insecurity, unfilled lust, rejection, anger and danger.

"Would you like something to drink?" he asked to be catty.

"What I want is for you to leave Daryl alone. If I ever find out that you've had your hands on him, trust me, you'll regret it."

Kevin's glare conveyed the seriousness of his words. He looked at Amir one last time before he stormed out of the apartment. When the door closed behind him, he wanted to fall to his knees. He couldn't believe what had just happened. And, he was embarrassed for it. Embarrassed, but still enraged.

CHAPTER 14

When Daryl got home, he found Kevin curled up in bed re-reading his favorite novel. The book, *The Long Blue Moan,* by the very talented writer L.M. Ross, covered his face. Daryl knew when Kevin read that book it took him to a place far from this world. He had read the book so many times that now he only read it when he wanted to escape his reality. When Kevin was engrossed in the words of that passionate and pounding novel, it was hard to disturb him. However, when Daryl walked into the room, Kevin immediately put the book down and stared at him.

Daryl stared back. No words; only emptiness. Neither knew who should speak first.

Kevin sighed.

Daryl huffed.

They stared.

Kevin sighed again.

Daryl huffed, again.

"What?" Daryl finally asked.

"Nothing. I was just looking at you; staring at this stranger in the house."

"You've been listening to Tamia again, huh?" Kevin remained expressionless. He had had a few hours to digest everything and to find that place within him where he could speak without yelling. But, when he got home, he checked Daryl's computer again and could no longer contain his rage.

"No, but I have been doing some soul-searching."

"I think you've been searching more than your soul." Daryl faced him.

"What?"

"Never mind. During your reflection, what did you discover?" Daryl feigned interest.

"Do you really want to know?" Daryl could hear the rising anger in Kevin's voice.

"If I said no, I'm sure you'd tell me anyway, right? So, let's have it. What have I done this time? What didn't I say or do? Did I forget an anniversary or forget to cook dinner or say *I love you*. Please, tell me exactly what I did wrong this time because we both know that I can never do anything right anymore."

Daryl stood at the foot of the bed and watched as Kevin pulled himself from under the covers. He walked over to the dresser and picked up several pieces of paper he had printed from the Internet. "Where were you this afternoon?"

"I told you I was going to the gym."

"Is that all you did?"

"What is this about?"

"I'll tell you what this is about. The reason we're falling apart is because you're so busy spending Saturday afternoons with other men and meeting fuck buddies online." Kevin shoved the papers he grabbed from the dresser in Daryl's hands.

Daryl looked at the papers Kevin handed him. Kevin had printed Daryl's profile from www.adam4him.com and the email exchanges between Daryl and some of his online friends. Suddenly, Daryl felt embarrassment, shame, and indignation. As much as Kevin wanted to wait for something more severe, he couldn't keep the information a secret so he decided to confront Daryl with the evidence. Not after what happened this afternoon. He had installed the software on Daryl's computer a few days ago and all he had to do was wait to get his evidence.

"Where did you get this?"

"Where did I get this? Is that all you can say?"

"This is nothing," Daryl replied as he dropped the papers to the floor. "It's only a stupid ad I placed for conversation. I was merely trying to kill some time at work."

"Oh really? So, you think it's okay to place an ad on a sex site to meet folks?"

"I haven't met anyone."

"You haven't met anyone? Don't lie to me. There is an email exchange between you and somebody named DarkBroNDC. I believe you met him at a bar. Who the fuck knows what you did afterwards!"

"That was nothing." Daryl wanted to press the issue and find out how Kevin had accessed his information. He always left his computer on, so if Kevin wanted to check his AOL email account it wouldn't be hard. However, when he and DarkBroNDC set up their meeting, it was via instant messenger.

"This is the same man who has been sending you naked pictures of himself. What the fuck do you expect me to think? I wouldn't think the worst if you wouldn't give me the worst! You don't think I should have a problem with you flirting with some dude who sends you naked pictures of himself and then you go out to meet him? You must be outta your fuckin' mind!"

"Calm down. All that shit was very innocent. And, with all your righteous indignation you act as if you're the victim here."

"What does that mean?"

"We'll get to that later."

"Is that how you met Temple?" Kevin shot.

"What? No. This has nothing to do with Temple."

"How many people have you met on this site? How many people are you fucking, Daryl? Do I need to go and get myself tested?"

"Don't be ridiculous. I haven't had any kind of sex with anyone since I've been with you."

"I find that hard to believe."

"Are you calling me a liar?"

"I'm saying I don't trust you anymore. I don't know what the hell is going on with you, but I'll tell you one thing. I'm really about sick of all this bullshit. I'm sick of arguing with you. I'm sick of being unhappy with you. I'm sick to death of needing you when you ain't nowhere to be seen. Now I know the reason why we can't fix what's wrong with us. You are too busy on the prowl to focus on us! What the fuck is wrong with you?"

"What is wrong with me? What the fuck is wrong with you? Why the fuck do I have to defend the behavior of my crazed lover who evidently followed me to my teaching assistant's house and threatened him? I'm sitting on the phone listening to him tell me about how you busted up into his home and accused us of fucking, and then you threatened him."

Kevin couldn't hide his shame. "I can explain that."

"No, the fuck you can't. I have never been more embarrassed by you or disappointed in you than I am at this moment. You are out of control."

"If I'm out of control it's because you've made me this way."

"I'll take the blame for a lot of things, but not this. This was all you."

"I'm so sick of all of this."

"If you're so sick of me, why don't I make this really easy for you?" Daryl turned and marched out of the room, with Kevin hot on his heels.

"Is that your answer? You're just gonna leave? You are so pathetic."

"Me, pathetic? Ain't that the pot calling the kettle black?"

"What the fuck is that supposed to mean?" By this time, Kevin was incensed and the depth of his rage sounded in the waves in his voice. Daryl stopped for a moment and glared at Kevin but then continued to walk down the stairs and into the den. "If you have something to say to me, be man enough to say it."

"You wanna know what I think? You really wanna know?"

"I really want to know."

"I think that is some punk-ass shit to go snooping through my shit. If you wanted to know something, you should've stepped to me and asked. Even though we're lovers, I still have a right to some damned privacy. You don't see me going through your shit."

"I don't have a problem with you checking my email or looking at my phone or being on my computer because I don't have shit to hide. You're the one who's suddenly started turning off your cell phone when you get home and taking calls in the other room. You're the one meeting tricks online. I wouldn't be snooping if you hadn't given me reason to. And you're right, I shouldn't be in the business of checking your emails or phone, but I shouldn't feel like I can't answer your phone if it rings."

Daryl turned his back to Kevin and walked deeper into the interior of the room.

"Beyond snooping through my shit, I still can't believe you went to Amir's house. I don't even know what to say. You had no reason and you certainly didn't have any right. That is some crazy-ass shit and I don't know how I can ever forgive you for that. Not only have you threatened a colleague of mine, but you've also put all of our business out in the street. I can't even look at you right now."

For a second, the room quieted and the only sound that could be heard was the emptiness of their lives, which sounded like thunder.

"If you're cheating, I have to know, because you will not put my life at risk."

"Since we're not having sex anymore, that's not something you have to worry about. I'll tell you for the last time that I have not had sex with anyone else since we've been together and I'm tired of trying to convince you of that. I can't prove I didn't do something. I think you want me to fuck someone else because that would give you an easy way out. You'd get to leave the relationship and play the victim like you always do." Daryl moved over to the table and grabbed his keys.

"That's bullshit."

"Is it?"

"Why are you doing this to us?"

"I haven't done anything. All of this is your creation. I only hope you can live with it." Daryl walked by Kevin, shook his head, continued down the stairs to the first level, and slammed the door on his way out.

CHAPTER 15

"Hey, Daryl. What's going on?" Temple smiled as soon as he saw Daryl's number displayed on the face of his phone.

"I know it's kinda late, but are you busy?"

"It's never too late for you. Wassup?"

"I need you. I checked into a room at the Marriott Metro Center. Can you stop by?"

Temple had longed to hear those words from Daryl. *I need you.* It sounded poetic to his anxious ears.

"Why are you at a hotel?"

"I'll tell you when you get here."

"I'm on my way."

Daryl's blood still boiled each time he thought about what Kevin had done. *Snooping. Spying. Playing private detective.* But nothing made him angrier than Kevin confronting Amir. Daryl didn't know how he'd ever face him again. When Amir called him on the phone to report Kevin's behavior, Daryl's heart fell with a thud. He very much wanted to believe Amir was playing a practical joke, but he found out there was nothing funny.

As he lay in the bed, with his hands folded behind his head while staring at the ceiling, he wondered what he would have done if the shoe was on the other foot. Even now, the thought of Kevin being with some other man infuriated him and he would have moved heaven and earth in order to find the truth. Even still, Kevin's antics today bordered on unforgivable and Daryl struggled to find a place in his heart that would allow him to absolve Kevin. In part, he realized he was to blame. He had behaved badly, but nothing he had done warranted this kind of reaction from Kevin.

He got up from the bed and walked over to the window. He pulled the string that opened the curtains and then took a seat in the chair and stared into the dreary night sky. Wild thoughts continued to attack him from all sides. The beauty of the little droplets of light that highlighted the night sky failed to clear the ugliness permeating his every thought. He felt hurt and angered and, more than ever, he felt alone.

When he realized the sky had no answers, he got up and walked into the bathroom. He splashed some cold water on his face in an attempt to shock his system into a sharper state of consciousness. He was exhausted and drained and had tried taking a nap earlier, but each time he lay down, instead of sleep, restlessness became his companion. He tossed and turned until finally he couldn't take it anymore. Hours after their argument and Daryl's abrupt departure, he found himself alone in a hotel room agonizing over his relationship. He had room service bring him a drink, but still he couldn't shake the thoughts of what Kevin had done from his mind. This was the first time he and Kevin had been separated by anger—the first time they had been apart because of an argument. This time, he didn't want to go home. He wasn't ready. He wasn't ready to argue anymore—he didn't have the strength. Nor was he ready to listen to Kevin's feeble explanation for his actions or his apologies. In fact, he wasn't convinced Kevin would apologize at all and that would only make things worse.

About a half-hour later, he heard a knock at the door. He sprang from the bed and rushed over to it, but suddenly realized he was only wearing a wifebeater and his underwear. He put on the sweatpants he had on earlier and opened the door. Temple greeted him with a devilish smile and a lingering hug.

"Damn, you look like you've really been going through it."

"It's good to see you, too," Daryl said sarcastically. Temple walked in and the door closed behind him. He placed his large gym bag over in the corner by the television. "What's the bag for?"

"I wanted to freshen up. I went into the club with Cerina and watched her first performance and now I feel gritty. I don't want to be around you smelling like smoke." Temple reached into his bag and pulled out a bottle of vodka in a shiny blue box.

"What's that?"

"A little nightcap." He put the vodka on the table and pulled out a bottle of cranberry juice.

"See, you know exactly what I need," Daryl said jokingly.

"If you let me, I can take care of all your needs."

Daryl smiled at his titillating comment.

"I'm going to go down the hall and get some ice. I'll be right back," Daryl said.

"Cool, I'm going to hop in the shower for a quick second. If you would, make me a drink while I'm in there."

When Daryl got back into the room, he heard the sound of running water coming from the bathroom and Temple humming some unfamiliar song. He was glad Temple came over because tonight was not a night he wanted to spend alone. When he was alone with his thoughts, he felt powerless.

He couldn't be alone.

He needed someone to talk to. He needed to open up about everything that was going on and the changes that were happening with his relationship. He needed a friend. He was tired of being alone and being lonely. He longed for friendship and affection and attention and attraction and fire and mystery and magic and all of the elements needed to keep life spicy, which were the very things that had long ago vanished from his life with Kevin. If he had one wish, he would have wished for all of those things from Kevin. While he listened to the sound of the water falling from the shower, he assured himself that nothing was going to happen between him and Temple. That was not the purpose of the visit. He needed friendship.

He simply could not be alone.

Moments later, the sound of running water came to a sudden halt. Daryl was halfway through his drink when Temple opened the bathroom door and stepped into the interior of the room, wearing only a sky-blue cotton towel around his waist. Daryl pretended to not notice this nearly naked man in front him.

"I didn't make your drink because I didn't want the ice to melt. Are you ready for it now?"

"That depends on what *it* is," he said flirtatiously.

"*It* refers to your drink. Nothing else."

Daryl realized he had to be strong, but Temple liked the challenge, the chase—the hunt. More than anything, he loved going in for the kill. He loved that moment when his charm and good looks overran his prey's defenses. And, he wanted Daryl and it wasn't to satisfy RaChelle's need for revenge, nor was it to erase Cerina out of his mind. He wanted Daryl for himself. He wanted to feel his skin and lick him from head to toe. He had imagined all of the things they'd do together and he wanted to do it now.

"Damn, that's cold. Let me put some clothes on, but you can go ahead and pour it."

Daryl walked over to the dresser and put some ice in a glass. When he turned around, Temple stood facing him; the towel that stood between him and complete nakedness now laid at his feet. Temple winked at Daryl, and started to apply lotion to his body.

"Dear Lord," Daryl whispered to himself.

"What was that?"

"I asked how strong do you want this drink?" Daryl struggled to keep his mind off the flesh that called out to him like Sirens from a Greek legend.

"Make it as strong as you like. I can take it like a man," Temple said with a chuckle.

By the time Daryl finished making the drink, he was relieved to see that Temple had slipped into a pair of red silk boxer shorts. *At least he has something on,* Daryl thought. Daryl handed him his drink and moved over to the bed and Temple moved over to the couch. Temple arranged the pillows to support his back so he could look at Daryl. Daryl looked at him, sitting on the couch with a drink in his hand, wearing only a thin pair of underwear. Temptation.

When Temple took a sip, he gasped. "Damn, you weren't playing with this, were you?"

"You said you could take it like a man. You can't run away at the first sign of pain. At first, if you're not ready, it can hurt, but if you simply relax, take a deep breath, and let it go down slowly, you'll learn to love it." Daryl took a slow sip in an effort to demonstrate his technique.

"Are we still talking about the drink?"

Before Daryl could answer, Temple's cell phone rang. He jumped off the couch and raced over to his bag so he could silence the device. He saw it was Cerina calling and he was sure she'd keep calling until he answered, so he decided to turn his phone off. He had left her at the club and her set wasn't over so he couldn't imagine why she was calling. Nevertheless, he didn't have the time or the patience for her madness. Tonight was his night. He was in the zone and, at any minute, Daryl would wave him in. Before he turned off the phone, he saw a text message from RaChelle reading, "Time is running out." He knew exactly what that meant and he hoped tonight would be the night he could fulfill his obligation to her and have his record expunged. He wanted to be done with her. And, he wanted Daryl at his side. If he fucked him well enough, Daryl would be his; he was certain of that.

"Booty call?"

"Trust me, it wasn't that." He moved back to the couch. He wanted to climb into the bed with Daryl, but decided to take things a bit slower. "So, when are you going to tell me why you're in this hotel room?" Daryl gazed blankly around the room as he gathered the words to convey all of the madness that had been going on. "Something tells me your relationship has more issues than you've told me. When you first told me about Kevin, I knew something wasn't right."

"And how did you know that?"

"I could tell. There was no joy or excitement in your voice and when you mentioned his name, the sparkle in your eyes vanished. Obviously there was trouble in paradise."

"It ain't been paradise in a very long time. Funny how shit happens and everything changes."

"So, tell me about it."

Daryl took a deep breath and began to confess. He told Temple about how they hadn't been happy in months and how Kevin never has any time for him and when they do spend time together, they end up arguing about something trivial. He spoke about how he found himself increasingly lonely and attracted to other people; including Amir. He wasn't ready to talk about Kevin's unanticipated visit to Amir. When Daryl told him about some of the sexual fantasies he had about Amir, Temple's heart sank a little bit. He didn't like the thought of Daryl being attracted to someone else. Daryl talked about the countless hours he had spent talking to random people on various Internet sites and how he had begun to divert far too much attention to the personal ads.

"I didn't start doing it because I was looking for sex. I did it because I was lonely and wanted someone to talk with. And plus, sometimes it's merely a way to make the day go by faster. I made the mistake of actually meeting this one dude for happy hour and Kevin found all of the email correspondence we had and assumed the worst."

"What happened when you met the dude?"

Daryl took a long swallow before recanting the story of DarkBroNDC.

❀❀❀

Against his better judgment, Daryl agreed to meet DarkBro for drinks at Republic Gardens. Daryl was only a couple of subway stops away, so he decided to go for it. He didn't see the harm in meeting someone for a drink. He had been conversing with DarkBro—whose real name was Corey—for a few weeks and he felt, to a degree, that he knew him.

Daryl walked into the swank Republic Gardens and looked around the dimly lit establishment. He knew what Corey looked like, but Corey had never seen a picture of Daryl. Daryl had described what he looked like and what he'd be wearing and said he would meet Corey upstairs by the poolroom. After waiting for fifteen minutes, Daryl decided he needed a drink, in part because he felt odd being in a bar and not having something in his hand, but also because he was thirsty. He didn't want any alcohol at that time, so he ordered a three-dollar Coke. Reluctantly, Daryl paid for the drink. He then moved away from the bar and stood on the opposite wall. He wanted to survey the crowd. It was a very hip and well-dressed crowd. He could tell that most people there were professionals who stopped in after work to have a good time and to unwind. The ladies made sure their hair and makeup was done properly and the brothers adjusted their shirts and ties to make sure they looked suave. In the process of surveying the crowd, Daryl checked his watch several times and had started to get irritated. He was getting the feeling he was being stood up. He kept eyeing the poolroom, but didn't see anyone in the room or the vicinity who looked like DarkBro.

"Fuck this," Daryl said to himself as he decided to leave and go home. Right as he was about to leave, he heard his name being called. He turned and looked at the person standing before him. "Do I know you?"

"It's me, Corey."

"Corey? DarkBro?"

"Yeah." Daryl wasn't sure how to react to the man who stood before him. He was obviously not the man in the photos that had been emailed to Daryl. The man who stood before him was about 5'4" and weighed about eighty pounds soaking wet and wearing boots. About the only thing that was truthful was the fact that he was dark-skinned. "You don't look like your picture."

"Oh, that's my cousin. Folks say we look exactly alike."

"Folks lied." Daryl turned and walked away. He heard the hobbit calling out to him, but didn't reply.

❧ ❧ ❧

Temple could not stop himself from laughing.

"I can't believe you went on a date with a creature from *Lord of the Rings.*"

"Very funny; very funny. Go ahead and laugh at me. I deserve it. I can't believe folks are stupid enough to send out pictures of other folks and act like it's them. I mean, when you meet them, what do they expect you to say? Thanks for lying to me?"

"Yeah, that's why I don't meet folks from the net. You never know what you're gonna get." Temple took another swig of his drink. "But, truthfully, I haven't heard you say anything bad—yet. So, you met a hobbit for a drink. It ain't like you fucked him—did you?"

"Hell no!"

"My bad. I was only checking."

"Uh-huh. But, I know I was still wrong."

"You haven't cheated on Kevin with anyone, have you?"

"Of course I haven't, but I can't know how long I can be strong. I have really been trippin'. Kevin's right. I got too much going on. Amir. DarkBro. And then—" Daryl stopped.

"And then, what?"

"And then there's you."

"What about me?" Daryl didn't want to say what was on his mind. "What about me?"

"I find myself thinking about you all the time. When you kissed me that time, I almost didn't let you go. It has been a long time since I have felt some kind of passion. It's been so long that I thought I had lost my ability to feel. I felt alive for the first time in a very long time." Temple started inching his way off of the couch, moving toward Daryl to start his seduction. "No, stay over there," he pleaded, but it was too late. Temple was up and standing in his face. Temple grabbed Daryl by the hands and pulled him out of the bed and into his chest. "I can't do this, Temple. I can't." Daryl turned his head in an unsuccessful attempt to prevent Temple from kissing him. The next thing Daryl felt was Temple's heat. And his lips. And his tongue. In defiance of the power of Temple's kiss and the tsunami-like shock waves that rocked Daryl's body, he pushed away. "I really can't."

"Come on, you know you want to. Let me love you."

"No, I can't right now. I just can't." Daryl removed himself from Temple's embrace. "I'm sorry, I just can't."

Temple moved back over to the couch and took a gulp from his glass. He struggled not to show his anger. *Twice rebuffed.* He wanted to keep his emotions in check. He wondered what it would take to bed this man. "It's cool. I don't want you doing anything you're not ready for." He took a long drink from his glass.

"Excuse me for a second," Daryl said as he stepped into the bathroom and closed the door.

Temple smashed his fist into the palm of his hand. He was pissed and horny. He couldn't fathom he'd ever be rejected by a man once—let alone twice. It was new for him. Kevin's hold over Daryl must be far stronger than he thought. Daryl was going to be one tough nut to crack, but with RaChelle breathing down his neck he didn't have that kind of time.

"You okay in there?" he called out, trying to sound concerned.

"Yeah, I'm fine. I feel bad about dragging you over here in the middle of the night. I'm really not trying to tease you. You know I'm very attracted to you, but I also enjoy our friendship as well. I'm not a cheater."

"And, I don't want you to be. Besides, let's say you and Kevin break up and you and I get together. If you cheated with me now, how do I know you wouldn't do the same thing to me?"

"Right, and how do I know you wouldn't do the same to me, too? After all, there is Cerina," Daryl said as he walked out of the bathroom. Temple didn't like Daryl throwing her name into the mix. He sipped again.

"Right. Don't worry about me. I honestly didn't come over here 'cause I wanted to sex you. I came because you were in need." Temple walked over to Daryl and handed him his drink.

"Getting me drunk ain't gonna work, either," Daryl said playfully.

"Negro, I ain't tryna get you drunk. That ain't my style." Daryl gave Temple a peck on the cheek and smiled. "What was that for?"

"For being more than a friend. Now, don't act like everything is rosy with you and Cerina," he said all of a sudden, trying to change the subject.

Temple took a seat on the bed and this time Daryl took a seat with him. He talked begrudgingly about Cerina and her pedestrian ways and her ghetto mentality. As he spoke, his dislike of her was more than evident. Sure, she gave him money and would do anything for him, but there were many classier women or men out there who would do the same thing. As soon as RaChelle got his charges dropped, he planned on finding one. *Or Two.*

"Will you do me a favor?" Daryl asked.

"What is that?"

"Will you lie next to me until I fall asleep?"

Temple thought about it. He thought about being in the bed next to Daryl, body pressed against body. In that compromising position, he might be able to work his magic and really get next to Daryl. As thoughts of conquest filled his head, he looked at Daryl's face. The pained expression on his face connected with Temple on a level much deeper than he thought. Immediately, his thoughts of Daryl's sweet surrender faded. Daryl needed a friend right now and that's all Temple wanted to be.

"Of course I will." Temple put his arms around him and held him as a friend would. His connection to Daryl went far deeper than RaChelle's threats.

They talked for a few more hours and laughed like old friends, but the sexual tension that filled the room could not be denied. Occasionally, when Daryl looked at Temple, he saw his future. And, it was a future filled with hot sex and passionate love. When he gazed into Temple's big eyes, he could see the world and it was a new world he wanted to explore. He imagined being an explorer and trekking over the landscape of Temple's willing flesh. He wanted to travel the roads and its curves; he wanted to dive into the valleys and climb its highest peaks; he wanted to uncover brown stones, trace rounded mountains which would lead to hidden treasures; he could see himself wading through the dark brush and climbing a thick tree that pointed proudly and perfectly toward joy.

He thought about all those things as he looked into the eyes of his friend.

He wanted to explore this Temple.

CHAPTER 16

On that same night, Cerina folded her arms and stormed back into the 202 Club. She pushed her way through the crowd and made her way back to the dressing room. She picked up her cell phone and dialed Temple's number again. Immediately, his voice mail picked up and she hung up. She slammed the phone down on the table and closed her eyes as if she was meditating. Sometimes, she wanted to kill him for treating her so badly. Tonight was one of those nights. It was cold outside, she was tired and all she wanted to do was go home and take a nice warm bath before falling asleep in his arms. Yet, he denied her everything she needed; even in its smallest measure.

She thumbed through her purse for her pack of cigarettes she bought out of the machine in the club. As she fumbled through the items, she came across her pillbox and realized she had not taken her medicine. *Fuck.* She searched for the prescription she had neglected to get filled. It wasn't there, but right now all she wanted was a cigarette. She looked around the room to make sure no one was looking at her as she reached into her purse and grabbed her pill bottle. She poured two small pills into her hand and took a swig of the watered-down rum and Coke she had left on the table.

Moments later, Nicole, who had just left the stage, walked into the room and plopped down in the seat next to Cerina as if she was exhausted.

"Girl, why you still here?" Nicole asked as she pulled, with great effort, the stilettos off her aching feet and dropped them in front of her like they weighed a hundred pounds. She let out a deep breath as if she had been working all day in a field somewhere. Cerina didn't reply to her question but picked up her cell phone and dialed Temple's phone—again. The response was the same.

"Let me guess, that fool left you stranded again?"

"Don't talk about my man. He ain't answering his phone. He's probably been drinking and fell asleep again."

She came to Temple's defense, but the squawk in her voice revealed the truth. She suspected he was out with some other woman when he should have been outside ready to take her home. She couldn't help but think he was somewhere with RaChelle. She was infuriated, but tried to hide it from Nicole.

"Okay, girl."

Cerina swallowed her pride and asked the question she didn't want to ask. "Anyway, girl, can you give me a ride home?"

She didn't want to have to sit through another lecture with Nicole telling her how trifling Temple was and how she shouldn't put up with this mess. Cerina already recognized that, but she wasn't ready to let him go. She wasn't ready to face the world alone and Temple was all she had. *Loneliness is a bitch*, she often thought.

"I guess, girl. For somebody who owns a car, you ain't never got no ride. I know you betta come off some gas money, though," she said, laughing, but Cerina knew she wasn't playing. "Gimme a few minutes to get my shit together."

Cerina took a moment to organize the bills in her pocketbook. She always liked the bills neat and in ascending order. As she was counting up the money, she thought about RaChelle again. She'd never be able to compete with a woman like her. Truth be told, she was envious of RaChelle and she felt RaChelle was a direct threat to her relationship with Temple. If Temple left her for RaChelle, she didn't know what she'd do. Her anger gathered within her like a storm.

"Damn," she said out loud.

"What's wrong, girl?"

"I thought I made more money than this. I'm short and got bills to pay." In order to keep Temple, she'd have to have more money. Money is what glued him to her and she realized that.

"Well, I don't know if you're interested, but Maggie told me a couple of ballers from the Redskins are up in the VIP room. You can make some serious cash. I'm too tired and my feet hurt like hell."

Cerina thought about it for a minute. If there were some serious players in the VIP section, she could make a lot of money in a short period of time, but the thought made her uncomfortable. It had been a long time since she had ventured back into VIP because that was no longer her thing. The men in the back always expected more than a simple lap dance;

especially since they usually put out some serious bills. Cerina wasn't in the mood for it, but she had to do it in order to keep Temple happy. She thought about it some more and decided she needed money more than her pride. Once again, she'd have to become *Pussy Galore*.

When she entered the VIP room, a few sparse candles and red lights in each corner of the room provided the only illumination, making it difficult to see exactly what was going on, but the moaning sounds that filled her ears revealed all. The sound of the door closing behind her sealed her fate. She stood motionless for a few minutes, trying to pull herself together, before she decided to step into the room. In order to get through this she'd have to put on an act—she'd have to become that freak men like to see on the stage. As she scanned the room, she squinted her eyes to see the shapes of women and men in compromising positions. The smell of hot flesh on flesh and sweaty men permeated the thick, smoke-filled air. Cerina wasn't ready for what was in store, but, for the love of Temple, she pressed on.

As she moved seductively throughout the room, she added an extra wiggle in her walk. Her hips shifted from side to side in a fluid, almost poetic style. She held her head high and twisted her hips in tune with the background music. All eyes were on her. As she strutted through, she ignored the initial calls—she couldn't step to the first man who hollered at her. Then, she spotted her man. She took a few slow and deliberate steps in his direction as he motioned for her to come closer. She stopped immediately in front of him, cocked her head to the side, and licked her lips. The man, dressed in a colorful silk shirt, smiled as if he had discovered the secret of joy. Cerina stepped to him and straddled him as he sat in the chair.

"Damn, baby," he said as his hands cupped her ass. "You got it going on."

"Thank you, sexy. How about a lap dance?"

"Is that all I can get?"

"That depends on how much money you got." She leaned in slowly and took his earlobe into her mouth.

"Oh, it's like that?" he asked playfully.

"It's always like that," she said. "Now, what's your pleasure, big boy?" she said as she slid her hand between his legs.

"You got them nice, thick lips. You know how to use them?"

"I can show you better than I can tell you, but you got to show me that you're serious about it." The man reached into his pocket and pulled out a wad of money. "That's what I'm talking about."

"You wanna make some money?"

"That depends on what I gotta do for it," she said, as her tongue grazed his lips.

"You gotta show me the time of my life. I have a plane to catch tomorrow and I wanna see what D.C. has to offer."

Cerina realized what the man was asking for and it had been a long time since she had done that for money and she swore she'd never do it again. In spite of her desire to remain faithful to her lord, she knew Temple had had other worshippers. When she thought about the way he treated her, the anger in her rose to the surface and she felt the need to get back at him not only for leaving her at the club—again—but also for all of the other injustices he had thrust upon her shoulders. She suddenly wanted to get him back for treating her as if she didn't matter, for disrespecting her and for not loving her the way she needed him to. She also needed the money. She glanced down at this stranger, whose eyes were filled with lust for her.

"How much you talkin'?"

"With this phat ass you got and those sexy-ass lips, two hundred dollars."

"Don't insult me, baby boy. Two hundred is pocket change for a big baller like you. Make it five hundred and I'll fuck your brains out. When I leave you, you'll know you've had the fuck of a lifetime."

The man looked at her. Her confidence made his dick throb even harder. "You think you worth all that? For that much, I ain't looking for no ordinary fuck. You betta pull out all yo' damned tricks."

"That—and more."

He smiled and she realized the deal was done.

"We can't do it here though. I got a hotel room downtown. You gotta come with me."

"Give me fifteen minutes to get my stuff and I'll meet you up front."

By the time Cerina reached the hotel with the man, she was fuming because Temple hadn't even bothered to call her back. She had finally had enough of dealing with him treating her as if she didn't matter. She still loved him, no doubt about it, but she decided it was time he respected her and started treating her like she mattered.

"Baby girl, you look distracted," he said as they stepped into the room.

"Nah, I'm okay; thinking about how I'm going to put it on you," she said in a less than convincing tone. "I'm going to freshen up, okay?" She walked over and kissed him on the forehead. As she walked away, he slapped her hard on the ass. It made her clit vibrate.

"Don't be gone too long."

"It'll be worth the wait."

When she entered the bathroom, she took a long, hard look in the mirror and asked herself why she was there. Suddenly, guilt swarmed like a group of angry bees around her head.

"Cerina, girl," she said to herself, "get it together. This ain't yo' first time. You used to be good at this." She took a deep breath and tried to calm herself, but her guilt would not relent. "Fuck!" she said out loud.

"You okay in there?" the voice from the other side of the door called out.

"I'll be right out." She reached into her purse and looked at the five crisp hundred-dollar bills he had passed to her before they left the club. As much as she needed the money, she wouldn't be able to go through with it and that pissed her off. She stuffed the money back into her purse and took another breath. She realized she was acting out of anger and hurt. She couldn't go through with this deed.

When she left the bathroom, he was lying across the bed, fully naked, with his hand massaging the protruding part of his anatomy. Cerina looked at his broad chest and powerful arms, and suddenly felt a surge of fear.

"Listen, boo," she began.

"Get yo' pretty ass over here and take care of this," he said as he eyed his thick flesh. Cerina didn't move, but smiled nervously instead. "I see you want me to come and get you." He stood up, revealing every inch of his powerful frame and tattooed chest.

"I'm sorry, boo, but I gotta go. Something has come up."

"Yeah, me." He moved over to her with outstretched arms and a smile as wide as the ocean. As he approached her, she realized she was trapped. He had her pinned near the bathroom and there was no way she could move fast enough to move around him and out of the door. He moved in closer and embraced her while kissing her neck.

"I'm serious. I gotta go, but I'll take a raincheck."

"No, you won't," he said sternly. "I need this sweet ass now."

She felt his gigantic hands grab her ass. "Let me give you your money back."

He stepped back and the smile that once decorated his face was now replaced with a look of bewilderment. Cerina reached into her purse and pulled out her keys and a tube of lipstick to get to where she placed the money. She pulled out all five bills and showed him that it was all there.

"I don't want that fucking money," he said as he grabbed the money and keys and threw them across the room onto the bed. "I want you. I paid for you, now you gotta perform."

"Hey! Back off!" she yelled as she tried to push him away.

"Oh, I get it now. You one of them bitches that like it rough. I can give it to you rough."

Before Cerina could protest again, he grabbed her and forced his tongue in her mouth.

She pushed him away. Then, she felt his hand strike across the side of her face. She fell hard against the wall and he grabbed her and threw her across the room onto the bed.

"Wait!" she screamed. "Please don't do this. I'll scream."

"You can't scream if you can't breathe," he said. Before she could blink twice, he was on top of her, his hands around her neck. Her legs and arms flapped and flailed as she gasped for air. She tried to fight him off, but was unable to do so. "Yeah, that's right, bitch. Keep fighting. That shit turns me on!"

Cerina found herself unable to move the giant pressed against her. She felt him reach down and rip off her panties and shove a couple of his thick fingers into her. She wanted to scream, but her voice was lost in the choke. Then, the hand around her neck relented—he didn't want to kill her. She coughed and gasped for air. She felt as if she was going to throw up. He then turned her over and forced her onto her stomach.

"I'mma stick this dick so far up yo' ass you gonna feel it in yo' throat! I can't stand you fuckin' hoes. It didn't have to be like this, but you wanted to play games! You come over here and get me all excited, then talk about you gotta go. Fuck that!"

Tears had begun to form in her eyes. She had to make a move. She had been raped once before and it was not an experience she wanted to relive. Out her of peripheral vision, she noticed her key ring was within her reach. She wiggled her fingers and was able to grab them as he was about to enter her. She took the keys and with all the strength she could muster, she reached behind her, aiming for his face. He let out a loud scream.

"You fuckin' bitch! You hit me in my fuckin' eye."

She rolled off the bed quickly and saw blood pouring from his face. He glared at her and she realized he was about to strike but, before he did, she was able to use the pepper spray that was attached to her keychain and she sprayed him directly in the eyes. He screamed and ran around the room like a wild boar. She followed him and kept spraying; making sure she avoided the spray. He screamed as his eyes started to burn. He tried to make it to the bathroom, but Cerina got in front of him and pushed his suitcase in his way. He tripped over it and tumbled onto the floor, cursing and screaming like a wild man. Cerina opened the door to the bathroom, locked it from the inside, and closed it so he couldn't get to the sink to wash his face.

"How the fuck you like that, you muthafucka!" she screamed. She picked up a lamp from the nightstand and threw it forcefully at his head. It shattered and he continued to scream as blood gushed from the side of his face. She then proceeded to kick him in the face and groin while he begged for mercy.

"I'll kill you, you fucking bitch. I'll kill you," he mumbled.

"You gotta get up first!" She sprayed him again. And again, before picking up the money and his wallet and running out of the hotel.

The hot water almost scalded Temple's skin as he tried to wash Daryl off him. He could smell his scent all over his body. He laid with him for a couple of hours, far longer than he needed to and long after Daryl drifted off into sleep. What he felt while holding Daryl was almost unimaginable. It was official—Daryl was under his skin, on his clothing, in his hair, and in his mind. His heart raced. Regardless of how long he stood underneath the falling water, he could not wash him away. It was an intoxicating, bewitching, enchanting, stimulating and strangely hypnotic smell Temple simply could not wash away with soap. It was on his hands and on his lips and he feared he would never be able to rid himself of it. He could still taste him.

When he was in the hotel with Daryl, lying side by side in bed, time stood still. The intimacy they shared could not be duplicated, but Temple craved more. He longed for Daryl's touch. He had never experienced anything like it. In fact, he didn't know that it existed. It went beyond touching, beyond lovemaking, it made his head spin; he was dizzy and dazed and weak in the knees. He scrubbed harder and allowed the water to get hotter, but to no avail. He didn't want to be in love with Daryl. He kept telling himself he wasn't capable of love; yet the pace of his heartbeat would not slow.

Love was a handicap.

He had a job to do—a job he could not refuse and this ill-advised emotional attachment would impede his mission.

He scrubbed and lathered up again. Still, when the soap was gone and the water stopped, Daryl was still there.

As he stepped out of the shower, he grabbed a towel and walked into the bedroom. He found himself at the crossroads of his life. For once, he was concerned about someone other than himself, but he did not want to be the sacrificial lamb spread out upon the altar. RaChelle would either have Kevin and Daryl, or it would be him. Life is full of choices. Everything we do and everything we are is based on a choice we made or did not make at some point in our lives. Temple wasn't sure what decision to make now. He had lived in secret fear for years and now RaChelle offered him the chance to dance in the light. In order to do so, he would have to play his part in destroying the one person he thought he loved. The fork in the road would yield very different results for him and Daryl. Temple was not prepared, at this time, to make the final decision on what to do.

As he slipped on a pair of silk boxers and a wifebeater, he turned to face a frazzled Cerina, who had quietly stepped into the room, looking exhausted and battle-weary. They stood, staring at each other, with the silence masking what could not and should not be said, each with their souls exposed and naked. Cerina could not find words to express what she had been through and Temple dared not express his heart's desire for Daryl because he would find no understanding from her. Face-to-face, with no shields or guards between them, they continued staring at each other, not sure how to offer solace. Even if they had known how to ease each other's suffering, they recognized, in their heart of hearts, the pain they each endured had been self-inflicted.

By the time Cerina made it over to where Temple stood, tears flowed down her face and she couldn't stop crying. She collapsed into his arms and this time, he felt her pain. His soul ached, too. He was, after all, human. And in love.

❧❧❧

When Daryl awoke the next morning, he had found a certain peace. A certain pain. Temple, with all his gifts and talents, had brought clarity last night in the middle of his storm. Temple helped to calm the tides of negative emotion that swept through Daryl. More than anything, he needed peace of mind. He loved Kevin. That was the clarity Temple brought.

When he got home, there was no sign of Kevin, and Daryl breathed a sigh of relief. He didn't feel like talking at that moment. In the meantime, he needed a warm bath. He wanted to soak and forget about all the troubles of the world. He wanted to forget yesterday.

As he was about to lower himself into the tub, his cell phone rang. He jumped out of the tub and raced into the bedroom. When he reached the phone, he yanked it off its charger.

"Hey."

"Hey," Kevin replied. "You didn't come home last night."

"I know. I left you a message."

"I got it."

Silence.

"I don't know what to say."

"Where are you now?"

"I'm at home."

"Are you staying?"

"Do you want me to?"

"I want you to do whatever makes you happy."

"That doesn't answer my question. Do you want me to stay?"

"Did you ask DarkBro or Amir if that was okay with them?"

"Why don't you kick down the door to Amir's house and ask him yourself?"

"That's a good one." Kevin wanted to say so much more, but foolish pride stood in the way.

"Baby, I'm sorry. I don't want to argue with you anymore. I'm tired. I don't know how to convince you that I haven't cheated on you. If we ever had anything between us, I need you to call upon that now. I know things look bad and you have every reason to believe I have cheated, but I promise you now, with God as my witness, that I have not had sex with anyone else."

He hoped that God wasn't listening.

More silence.

"Kevin, we can't keep doing this. I can't keep going on like this. What's wrong with us?" Tears formed in Daryl's eyes and he wiped them away before they fell. His heart raced as he thought about losing him. He would never be able to fill the void if Kevin ever left him. "I love you so much and I'm so sorry for everything that we've become."

"Please don't do this now. I'm at work and I can't be getting emotional. What will my employees think?" Kevin asked, trying to cover his sadness with laughter.

"Tell me you love me, please. I need to hear you say it."

Kevin paused. He wanted to say it more than anything, but the words got stuck in his throat. "I have a restaurant full of people and I have to go. Mr. Martinez will be here in about an hour. When he gets here, I'm coming home, so don't go anywhere."

"I'll be here."

Kevin hung up the phone and took a moment to collect himself. Maybe this was the break they needed to get back to being the couple they wanted to be. They were so close to the end of everything and, unfortunately, it often took the demise of a love for the people involved to realize what they had lost. He didn't want to look back with regret and say they could have or should have done more. He wanted to work on it because deep in his heart, he still believed love could triumph. He actually believed Daryl when he said he hadn't cheated. Trust takes years to build and it can be broken so easily. Once trust is broken, repairing it can take an act of God.

CHAPTER 17

RaChelle delighted in delicious wickedness when she discovered Cerina's secret. It was kismet. She squealed like a giddy schoolgirl, rolled across the king-sized bed onto her back, and kicked her feet into the air wildly. She was on cloud nine. She clutched the small piece of paper and held it to her bosom like it was for dear life. This was a most unexpected discovery and she wasn't quite sure how she'd use this information, but there was no doubt in her mind that she would, in fact, use it. She needed to put Cerina in her place and let her know that simply because she could sling her ass around a pole didn't mean she could threaten and disrespect her. For all of Cerina's low-budget tirades and tantrums, RaChelle would not be out-bitched. *By anyone.*

Earlier in the morning, RaChelle searched her purse for her lipstick when she came across a small white piece of paper that wasn't hers. She didn't keep small pieces of paper in her purse. She looked oddly at the prescription and when she saw Cerina's name, she realized she must have inadvertently shoved it in her purse when they collided in that store in the mall. Her immediate reaction was to tear up the paper and curse Cerina. Then, curiosity set in. She wanted to know what medicine Cerina was taking and for what condition. She tried to decipher the handwriting, but that was an impossible task. If she could have figured out the spelling of the medicine, she would have looked it up on the Internet to see what it was used for. After staring at the paper from every angle for about five minutes, she decided to get it filled. She left her hotel and walked around to the CVS pharmacy on the corner. In about an hour, it was ready. She didn't want to talk to the pharmacist about the drug because she didn't want to seem as if the medication wasn't for her. Instead, she took the small bottle back to her hotel, pulled up a medical website and entered the name of the medication. She gasped when the results were revealed.

Now, malevolent thoughts filled her head. She struggled to keep from picking up the phone and calling Temple, but she decided she wanted to see his face when she told him the news. She wanted to see Cerina's face, too. She wanted it to crack into a million insignificant pieces and blow away in the wind. Then, the thought dawned on her. What if Temple already knew? Nah, he couldn't know. There is no way someone as shallow as Temple would stay with someone like Cerina if he knew what was really going on. There was no way he was going to be caught up in that kind of drama. He valued his life and his health far too much.

She'd have to play this card carefully to get the most bang for her buck. She wanted to devise the perfect scheme to shut her up for once and for all. If she played to win, Cerina would crawl back under the rock from whence she came. When she arrived in D.C, her plan certainly didn't involve Cerina; in fact, she hadn't given a second thought about her, but Cerina had gotten into her face one time too many and she needed to be taught. She needed to lose. *Everything*. And, she would. RaChelle would make sure of that. RaChelle always won.

❄❄❄

Kevin sat in his office at the restaurant taking care of business until he heard a knock on the door. When the door opened, Mr. Martinez crept inside and stood in front of his desk.

"Hey, boss," he said with his slight Spanish accent. "I'm here. What's going on?"

"I told you not to call me that," Kevin said playfully. "It's Kevin." Even though Kevin insisted on being called by his first name, he was never comfortable with calling Mr. Martinez by his first name—Jorge—because of the significant differences in their ages. Mr. Martinez was old enough to be Kevin's dad.

"Okay, Kevin. What's going on? The brunch crowd looks like it's beginning to wind down. So, I guess I'll work on getting things set up for dinner. The upstairs is reserved tonight for that private party, remember?"

"Oh yeah, I remember," Kevin lied. He had so many things going on in his life that certain things didn't even register on his radar screen. He had come to trust Mr. Martinez and felt as if he could leave some of the details about the day-to-day running of the restaurant to him. "I hope you don't mind, but I'm going to have to go home in a bit. Do you think you can handle things by yourself?"

"Of course I can. Remember, I was running this restaurant long before you got to the city," he said with a wink. Kevin smiled and took the comment with a grain of salt. Mr. Martinez still harbored slight feelings of resentment toward him for buying the restaurant, but he couldn't concern himself with that.

"One more thing. I haven't seen the new property insurance policy. Has it arrived yet?"

"I sent the paperwork in a couple of weeks ago. I'll follow-up today and let you know. What time are you leaving?"

"In a few minutes. If you need me, call me at home or on my cell."

"I'm sure I'll be fine," he said as he turned and exited the office. Kevin followed him out of his office and moved over to the bar in the back of the colorful restaurant. He decided to have a glass of Chardonnay to relax before he met Daryl at home.

As he browsed the wine section, with his back to the crowd, he felt a chill. The hairs on the back of his neck stood on end like a cat sensing danger. He turned around—as if in slow motion—and he almost dropped the glass of wine he had poured. Standing in the middle of the room, like an unwanted apparition, was a face he thought he'd never see again. It was a face that had haunted many dreams and crushed a thousand smiles. She looked directly at him, with a full smile. The belt of her overcoat was drawn tightly, but even through the thick garment, he could see her hourglass frame. From a distance, she looked the same—a woman whose beauty was unmatched. She flipped her long hair and waved wildly.

"Kevin!" she screamed as her face exploded into a wild smile. "It has been a long time."

He walked around the bar to greet her. "Oh my God, RaChelle Roland. What are you doing here?" he said as she pulled him into her for an embrace. She wrapped her arms around him and held him there longer than he was comfortable "I can't believe you're here. Let me look at you." He took a step away from her and she removed her coat and did a silly twirl in the middle of the room as if she was a child showing off her new Easter dress. "Wow! You haven't changed at all," he said, ignoring the scar on her face.

"Neither have you," she said. "Neither have you." She took him by the hand and led him over to the bar. "What does a lady have to do around here to get a drink?" Kevin didn't even ask her want she wanted to drink. Instead, he poured her a glass of wine and they took a seat in the big booth over by the window.

Kevin found himself staring at her, wondering what brought this blast from the past into his present. He felt guarded because he sensed she wasn't here on a social visit; in spite of her attempts to veil her true intentions with smiles and flattery. Kevin could also see pain in the back of her eyes; the kind of pain that accompanied a great loss. It was the kind of pain that shone in every smile and was present in every touch, in spite of her feeble attempts to mask it.

Pain is the great equalizer and it is the one thing we all have in common. He had his pain, too.

"I think I'm in shock," he said to her after a few seconds. "What are you doing in D.C.? How did you find me?"

"I'm here on business. My company moved its headquarters here so I had to come in and help set up the office. I heard through the grapevine that you and Daryl had moved here so I tracked you down."

"Well, I'm glad you did. There is so much that I want to say to you, so many things I never got a chance to discuss with you." He took a moment to collect his thoughts. She brought her glass to her red lips and took a sip, never breaking eye contact with him. She already knew everything he was going to say. "I never had a chance to tell you how truly sorry I am for all of the madness you got pulled into because of me. My life was such a mess back then and I did so many things that I'm not proud of. I'm truly sorry you got hurt because of me. I wanted to tell you so many times that I'm so sorry and if I could have lost my life to spare you the pain and to save the life of our child, I would have. When you were in the hospital after the fire and lost the baby, they wouldn't even let me in to see you."

"I know. I told them to keep you out," she said flatly. "Imagine what I was going through. I found out you were gay *after* we slept together—unprotected sex, mind you—and then I get caught up in all the shit with your crazy-ass lover who tried to kill everyone and burn down the entire church. I lost my baby and almost *died* in the process," she said with emphasis. "There was no way you could ever have apologized enough or done anything to make that up. I could never have explained to you exactly how angry and hurt I was. I didn't know how to process all of that, so I shut everyone out. There was so much shit going on in Houston that I had to deal with and I wasn't prepared for any of it. I was forced to readjust my feelings for you. I had started to really get caught up into you and my feelings for you were growing. You may not have realized it, but I really cared for you and when I found out you were gay, it crushed me. And, then, to find out the way I did." She paused. "I remember looking up at the screen during that conference and there you were, having sex with another man for the whole world to see and that was too much for me to handle. Suddenly, nothing made sense and I had to take some time for myself. I had to heal. I had to forgive. I had to forgive you. I felt like I was about to lose it all and you know I could never let that happen. I have worked too hard to get to where I am to have a mental breakdown." The pain she tried desperately to conceal resonated within her voice. He felt her pain, but the pain he thought he had buried was suddenly at the surface. She was a living reminder of the horror his life was when he was with James. James had set out on a path to destroy Kevin and he remembered, with striking detail, that day when the video was broadcast in front of a room of his colleagues—the most embarrassing day of his entire life—and he would never forget the feeling of shame that consumed him.

There were many instances of abuse when he was James's lover, but he had never been more ashamed of himself than when he allowed James to force him into a threesome with a man he didn't want to look at, let alone touch. James was always in control and decided while Kevin was sexing the man, to record the misery and that was the video played at the most important business conference in Kevin's young professional life. Kevin thanked God that those days were behind him and James was dead. But, here in front of him, sat a reminder of what once was but was no more. He wanted to know what she really wanted. She was trying to win him over, but to what end? He wanted to believe her, but he had learned from experience to always keep his guard up. This situation felt *wrong*.

"I'm glad you came by," he said after they finished reliving the past. "I tried so many times before I left Houston to contact you, but I couldn't track you down. I figured after everything that happened, you never wanted to see me again, and here you are, in D.C., in my restaurant of all places. I'm trippin'."

"After time and a couple of years of therapy, I'm better than ever. I let go of all the bad feelings. I ain't bitter. If I was bitter, you'd be dead," she said with a hearty laugh.

Kevin raised one eyebrow. He wasn't amused at her humor.

"I'm only joking," she said as she hit him playfully in the arm.

"Okay."

"Listen, I didn't come here to rehash all that stuff from ages ago."

"Well, why are you *really* here?"

"*Really*, I happened to be in town and I felt it was time to clear the air. The only way I could truly let go of all the pain was to see you and let you know I've forgiven you. Plus, I need an escort around town. I don't know anything about this city and I thought you could show me around."

Kevin smiled.

For the next half-hour, they chatted. He told her about Daryl and Keevan's Room. She filled him in on the details of her life—some true, some imaginary—but as she listened to the lies she told, she almost convinced herself about how wonderful her life was. The only part that was true was her professional success. When Kevin had last seen her, she was the vice president of human resources for a financial firm. Since then, she'd left that company and started an HR firm, which she sold and took a position with her present employer.

"Wow, I can't believe how much time has gone by and all that has happened. Finally, you're living your dream," she said as she looked around the room. "Got your own restaurant, starting a non-profit in your brother's name, and you have your man. I think that's wonderful. I am so happy for you." She reached across the table and put her hands on Kevin's. Her cold touch alarmed him, but he thought it was from the cold wine glass. "It's such a wonderful restaurant. You have pictures of it?" she said.

What a strange question, Kevin thought.

"Uh, yeah. We have lots of pictures. How long are you going to be in town?"

"Hopefully not longer than two weeks. I want to get back to my man. I know he misses me." That lie sounded like sweet music to her ears.

"I'd love to show you around town sometime, but not right now. Give me your number and we'll set something up. Daryl would love to see you, too," he lied.

"Yes, the three of us will have to get together really soon. Call me at the hotel." She kissed him on the cheek and he helped her with her coat. As she walked toward the door, she threw her hand up in a wave and stepped out of the restaurant.

Dear Diary,

It was so hard seeing Kevin face-to-face for the first time in years. I wanted to strangle him. Sitting across the table with him smiling in my face, I wanted to spit on him, but I didn't 'cause I'm a lady. Luckily, I know how to put on an act when I need to. I could've won an Oscar for the performance I gave, acting like I was happy to see him and that I had forgiven him for the shit he put me through and the life he took from me. He had the nerve to put on this act like he was really sorry for what he did to me. Can you believe that shit? Fuck him. Now, he wants my forgiveness. Fuck him twice—with no lubrication. He wouldn't need my forgiveness or my understanding if the fag hadn't lied to me and then fucked me. He knew exactly who he was and what he was doing when he decided to put his dick in me. I hate that nasty bitch. I want him to suffer. I want him to die. He took my life and my future and I'll take his. He has no idea what's in store for him. He's moved on here in D.C. with his man, got a nice restaurant and a nice life. He thinks he's doing some shit. We sat down and talked as we drank wine as he told me about his fabulous life. I had to make up some shit so he would think my life was fabulous, too. I couldn't have him thinking I've been sitting in a dark room for the better part of three years waiting for the day when I would have my revenge. He's moved on with his life like everything is okay. Like he's not the cause of all my pain. Like he's not the reason why I have this scar on my face. Like he's not the reason I almost died in that fire. Like he doesn't know he's the reason my baby is dead. Like he ain't responsible for me never being able to have children. He may not know that yet, but he will. He will soon feel what I feel. He will taste and choke on complete loss and pain, just as I have. I'll make him understand what he's done to me. There is no price too high for me to pay, nor is there a burden too heavy for me to carry to have his tears. I will spend my last dollar, give my last drop of blood, and take my last breath to make him pay. Let the games begin…

The sound of Kevin coming through the door shifted Daryl's attention. As he heard Kevin's recognizable steps on the stairs, his heart skipped a beat. He wasn't sure what to expect. When Kevin entered their bedroom, without words or comments, Daryl grabbed him and kissed him in a way that had become foreign to them. It was a kiss that originated deep within his soul and when Kevin kissed him back, they created an inferno. If either of them had any doubts about the love they felt for each other, it was removed by that kiss.

Daryl took Kevin by the hand and led him over to the chaise lounge by the window. That lounger was of one Kevin's favorite spots in the house and he sat him down on it. When Kevin tried to speak, Daryl put his fingers to his lips to silence him. Daryl needed no words. He removed Kevin's shoes and socks and stepped into the bathroom and returned with a bowl of water. Kevin could smell the lavender bath oil seeping from the water. He smiled as Daryl got down on his knees and, with care and consideration, started to wash and massage his feet. He took his time and was careful to touch Kevin in the erotic and sensual way he liked. As he cleaned his lover's feet and listened to his low moans, he understood and appreciated the benefit of knowing someone's body. Now wasn't a time for him to discover the places on Kevin's feet that would make him moan. Now was a time for him to use the knowledge he had acquired over the course of their relationship. This, for him, was better than a thousand one-night stands where you struggled to discover the sexual secrets of your new partner. With Temple, it was discovery. With Kevin, it was experience, and experience is a good teacher.

After he finished washing, he took the massaging up to the next level all while Kevin's moans deepened. The sensual sounds sparked a smile in Daryl who watched Kevin lean back and enjoy the moment. Kevin liked to be pampered and Daryl liked pampering him.

When Daryl finished massaging his feet, he excused himself for a few moments and went into the bathroom. When he returned, he stood Kevin up and slowly undressed him as they kissed. Daryl took him by the hand and led him into the bathroom, where the Jacuzzi tub was filled with water and bubbles. Again, Kevin tried to speak but Daryl silenced him with a kiss. He motioned for Kevin to get into the tub, which he did. Daryl picked up the remote control and pointed it at the stereo. Instantly, music filled the air as Daryl began washing Kevin's back in smooth circles. Kevin smiled as he listened to Queen Latifah and Al Green sing "Simply Beautiful" from her *Dana Owens* album. The song was a slow-moving and perfectly timed tribute to loving someone and being loved in return.

When Daryl finished washing Kevin's entire body, Kevin pulled him into the tub with him; clothes and all. When Kevin was finally able to get him naked, they made love right there in the Jacuzzi and, for the first time in months, their souls connected. And it was simply beautiful.

Later that night, as they lay in bed, wrapped up in each other, Kevin confessed.

"Baby, I can't tell you how sorry and embarrassed I am for the Amir incident. Everything that has been happening lately has been driving me out of my mind. I got so lost in jealousy and insecurity. I trust you, baby, and I know you would never cheat on me."

Daryl didn't speak. He wanted to forget.

"I don't want to ever fight with you again," Kevin continued. "These past few months have been torture. This is the way I want to be. In your arms. And you in mine."

"And that's where we'll be. You know, even during the times of our most heated fights, I never stopped loving you. *Not for one second*. Maybe it took us going through all the shit to find our way back to each other. I realize now that I can't live my life without you. I can't begin to imagine what that would be like."

"Neither can I."

"I think I love you now, in this moment, more than I ever have." The knots of excitement in Kevin's stomach tightened with Daryl's words. Not only did he hear them, he *felt* them. The words were alive and had breadth and form and were as real as anything he had ever experienced.

"Baby, I have to tell you something," Kevin said. "You're not going to believe who came into the restaurant today." When Kevin mentioned the name RaChelle, Daryl sat up in the bed, shocked at what he had just heard.

"What did she want?" Kevin recognized the concern in his voice because it was the same concern that echoed in his soul.

"I wish I knew. She said she was in town on business and looked me up to let me know she had forgiven me. Somehow, I sense that's not the entire truth."

"I don't know what's going on with her, but we need to be careful. I never trusted that woman. You know she's a little touched in the head, right?" he said with a chuckle.

"A little? She needs treatment. Crack is a *helluva* drug. I really hope she's not up to something, but I'll keep my eyes and ears open." Kevin wrapped his arms around Daryl and pulled him into his body. "Oh shit, I almost forgot. Don't forget about Percy and Keith's holiday party this weekend. There will be some heavy hitters there and I really need us to network to raise some money for Keevan's Room." Daryl smiled in agreement. He was more than happy to do whatever it took to make Kevin happy. He had things to repent for, so whatever Kevin needed, he was only too happy to supply.

CHAPTER 18

C erina pulled out a cigarette from her purse while she sat on the couch. She picked up one of the scented candles from the table and brought the flame to the stick in her mouth. She inhaled and the stick glowed a glorious sunset orange. She didn't care if Temple smelled smoke in the house when he got out of the shower. She had given a lot of thought recently to her life, her health, and her relationship with Temple. He didn't give a damn about her. There would come a day when all her cards would be laid out on the table. No more secrets. No more lies. Her future wasn't the most promising. All she could see were hospital beds, nurses and needles. She could smell that purified hospital scent and see dull white lights. She could hear the beeps of unfamiliar machines, all while she watched a slow drip hooked up to a vein in her arm. Lately, she had been thinking of her own survival. She had to start taking her medicine on schedule. She could no longer go on pretending. She had to face the blinding truth that, when things got bad, Temple wouldn't be there for her. He was destined to leave her. It was only a matter of time. In fact, he was already gone. That was her fault. And his.

That truth stung.

But it was her reality. And, she would face it, when the time came. But now, all she wanted was one day of his love. If she had one wish, she would have put a spell on him so he would love her with the same unrestrained love she felt for him.

She gazed out the window into the drab afternoon. She exhaled. She wanted Temple to take her to the movies. She wanted to see something happy—some movie where in the end the girl got the guy and they lived happily ever after. She loved those movies because she realized she would never experience that. She often wondered what it was about her that made her so unlovable to people. She had been used, abused and tossed aside by so many people—starting with her own family—that she had convinced herself there was something innately wrong with her. Maybe she was hideous, she sometimes thought, but she subsequently dismissed those charges. She was far from ugly. Maybe she wasn't smart enough; even though she had finished high school and had some college credit. She remembered how difficult it had been to graduate from high school with everything going on in her life and within her inner-city Baltimore high school back then. In spite of the crabs in the barrel who sought to pull her down, she prevailed and received her diploma. She didn't feel so dumb.

She thought hard about what she could do to make Temple love her before it was too late. She had already given him everything she had and more and loved him the only way she knew how. What would it take for him to love her? She wasn't classy or sophisticated like RaChelle and she surmised that that was the kind of woman Temple usually dated. If he liked women like RaChelle, then why would he get with her and stay with her so long? She thought the many months of spending time together and their powerful lovemaking sessions would have made him fall in love with her by now. If there was one thing she was confident about, it was her sexual prowess.

Temple walked into the room from the bedroom.

"Are we going to the movies?" she asked.

He ignored her.

She sucked on her cancer stick. "I said—"

"I heard you. Shit, what have I told you about smoking?"

She ignored him.

He walked around the room as if he was searching for something. He smelled shower-fresh and looked good in his baggy jeans and boots.

"Where are you going? I thought we were going to the movies."

"Something has come up," he said, trying to sweet-talk her. "Can we go later this evening? Besides, you ain't even ready. You haven't showered yet."

She exhaled again.

"Are you trying to kill me with that smoke?" As usual, his concern was about his well-being. "I need some money. How much you got in your purse?" he asked as he picked it up and started going through it. She snatched it out of his hands.

"Damn, Temple, you know you ain't supposed to go in a lady's purse." *You ain't a lady,* he wanted to say, but didn't. "I got about fifty bucks."

"Cerina, stop playing. I know you got more than that."

She huffed. "What you gonna give me for this money?"

He thrust his crotch in her face. "What do you want?"

"You know what I want."

"I can't give it to you now 'cause I gotta be somewhere."

"When you coming back?"

"I don't know."

She puffed. "You coming back to take me to the movies, right?"

"Yeah, and I'll break you off a little sumptin' sumptin', too."

She reached down in her purse and pulled out one hundred and forty dollars. Quickly, he took it. He kissed her on the cheek and was out the door before she could say anything else. *Son-of-a-bitch.*

She lit another cigarette. She had smoked two Kool Filter Kings back-to-back. She assumed he wasn't coming back anytime soon, but she wondered who he was going to see. As she sat on the couch, with her mind trying to find a solution to her dilemma, she remembered something. The other night while Temple slept, she had gone through the phone book in his cell phone and copied down a few entries. She wanted to know who he was seeing. They were the reason he wasn't in love with her. She was so sick of bitches throwing themselves at Temple. As much as she smiled and pretended it no longer bothered her, it shook her self-esteem. She still couldn't figure out why he needed someone else. It was their fault. Those bitches. If they would leave him alone, she could have him all to herself.

She had hidden the numbers in the bag she usually took to work. She had almost forgotten about the digits, but she jumped up from the couch, cigarette dangling from her lips, and ran into the bedroom. She tore open the door to her closet and found her bag. She dumped its entire contents onto the bed and rummaged through the various pieces of paper. She had so many numbers from tricks in the club who would shove little pieces of paper in her hand with their phone numbers as she left the club; like she was really going to call them. She sorted through the papers until she found the one she was looking for. It had three names on it and she was feeling bold enough to call. She reached over and snatched the phone off the hook and dialed the first number.

"Hello?" the female voice on the other end answered after the phone had rung three times.

"Who is this?" Cerina interrogated.

"Who is this?"

"I'm trying to reach Ta'Wanna."

"This is Ta'Wanna."

"Ta'Wanna, let me ask you a question. How do you know Temple?"

"Who wants to know?"

"This is his girlfriend and I wanna know why your number is in his cell phone."

"You're his girlfriend? Bitch, please. You can have that trifling bastard. You tell him if he don't pay me back the five hundred dollars he owes me, I'mma get my brother to kick his triflin' ass!"

Click.

Cerina's conversation ended abruptly. She thought about calling her back, but decided to keep it moving. Not to be deterred, she dialed the second number, which was simply listed under the letter B.

"Hey, Temple," the male voice said with excitement.

"This ain't Temple. This is Cerina."

Silence.

When Baron answered the familiar number that showed up on his caller ID, he truly hoped it was Temple.

"Why are you calling me?"

"I want to know who you are."

"Baby, if you're calling me like this, you already know who I am."

"What do I know?"

"Girl, please. You can't possibly be this naïve."

"Who the fuck is you?" Her voice sounded frantic.

"I'm Baron."

"Well, Baron, how do you know Temple?"

"What do you want me to say? You want me to tell you that when he's doing you, he's thinking about me? Or, would you rather I told you that when you kiss him or suck his dick, that it's me you're tasting? What exactly do you want to know, Ms. Cerina?"

"I will fuck you up, you fucking fag! Leave my man alone!"

"You might want to tell your man to leave me alone. He said I'm finger-lickin' good."

"Go to hell! I'll fuck you up!"

"Take care, honey, and don't be calling me anymore with some bullshit like this."

Click.

Another phone call; another abrupt ending. Cerina yanked the phone out of the wall and threw it across the room. She couldn't believe the boldness of Baron; talking to her like that. He evidently didn't know who he was fucking with. She was more upset at the way in which he spoke to her than she was at the words that left his mouth.

She knew about Temple. She had always known. It wasn't the best-kept secret in the world, nor was he the most discreet person with his escapades. She knew. She wasn't happy about it, but she knew. Still, it was better than being alone.

She had decided a long time ago that in order to be with Temple she'd have to tolerate certain things, and one of those things was his proclivity toward pretty young men. She didn't like it, but she'd tolerate it. On the other hand, she couldn't tolerate him running around town with other women. She had good pussy. Gave him good money. Cooked him good food. She could compete with another woman. She didn't have a dick. She accepted the fact that Temple sometimes needed something she was completely incapable of providing. That she could tolerate. She couldn't tolerate another woman running up on her man. She would not lose Temple to another pussy; especially not RaChelle.

❀❀❀

Later on that same afternoon, Temple stopped back by the apartment for a few minutes. He told Cerina they wouldn't be going to the movies because he had to return his cousin's car. She had no real expectations that they'd go anyway. She watched him walk into the bedroom and return with his gym bag. She wanted to say something, to call out to him to let him know about her bleeding heart but, instead, she remained silent. The thought of baring her soul at that moment and watching him walk out the door unsettled her. Her tears would not move him nor stop him from leaving. Instead, she reached into her purse and pulled out a tube of lipstick. She stood in front of the mirror on the wall in the dining room and colored her lips in smooth, calculated strokes. Temple took the bait.

"Where are you going?"

She continued applying her gloss as if his words hadn't reached her delicate ears.

"Cerina, you hear me talking to you. Where are you going?"

She put the cap back on her stick of color and placed it in her purse. "Excuse me?"

"Oh, you wanna act new?"

"Whatever," she said with much 'tude.

"You wanna play games, I see. I got games, too."

"I know you do. Evidently, you're a jack-of-all-trades."

"What the fuck does that mean?

"Nothing."

"You haven't answered my question."

"Well, since you're too busy to take me to the movies, I'm going with Nicole."

"You going to the movies dressed like that?"

She posed for him. "Is there a problem with the way I'm dressed?"

"You look like a two-dollar ho."

"Well, I'm sure I'll find a *real* man with two dollars."

"What? See, you tryna start some shit and I ain't in the mood for your drama. I'm outta here."

Temple had to meet with RaChelle. He had purposely avoided her calls for a couple of days, but he couldn't avoid her forever. He was perplexed by his dilemma, but when her calls started becoming threatening and frantic, he had to meet her. When you sign a pact with the devil, you have to take her calls.

It was a bitterly cold Saturday afternoon and the sun struggled to show through the thick winter snow-laden clouds. The cutting winds, sharp and bold, made no apologies as they whipped through the city with force. Temple sighed as he walked toward their meeting spot. He was perplexed not only because he didn't want to help RaChelle, but also because of his feelings for Daryl and what he was doing—those things weighed on his paper-thin conscience like a ton of bricks. He couldn't pinpoint exactly where the change had occurred within him because in the past, he would not have thought twice about doing what he needed to do to whomever to get what he wanted. But, there was something about Daryl, something in him, that touched Temple's soul and now he struggled with what would be his boldest betrayal.

When he walked into the jazz bar in Georgetown, RaChelle was already seated, having what looked to him to be at least her second Cosmopolitan and her customary cigarette. She seemed mesmerized by the female jazz singer on stage, whose textured voice added grit and sex appeal to the words she sang. Temple didn't know the bar had live singers during the day on the weekends, but apparently it was the best-kept secret in D.C.

When Temple approached her table, she stood up slowly, elegantly, seductively and kissed him on the cheek. He sat down after her, with a heavy heart and made small talk for a few minutes. The plastic moments of empty words and nothingness felt like endless hot sand across the desert of their relationship. She seemed lost in the vocal wonders emanating from the lady on stage and paid little attention to Temple, who quietly watched RaChelle as the music transformed her into something almost human; something with skin and bones and feelings. As he looked at her, she seemed innocent, but he realized this viper was far from angelic.

"Do you have what I need from you?" she asked at the end of the song, still refusing to take her eyes off the stage. Temple looked at the performer on stage and looked at the longing in RaChelle's eyes.

"You wanna fuck her?" he asked.

"You know I don't get down like that."

"Then why are you staring at her like that?"

"Don't worry about what I'm doing. I asked you a question. Do you have what I need? Evidently, you think I'm playing with your ass."

"RaChelle, I know you're not playing, but we need to talk about some things."

"The only thing you can tell me is that you've fucked the hell out of Daryl and now he's ready to leave Kevin for you. That's all I want to hear." Temple didn't speak. He held his head down for a few seconds and focused on a spot on the wooden table. "Is that what you're going to tell me?"

He wanted to protect Daryl. "No, not exactly."

She snapped her head quickly in his direction like she was a snake about to inject venom into its prey. She then took a slow puff of her cigarette. She inhaled deeply and exhaled seductively as if the mere act of smoking itself was an event to behold. She stared into his eyes and he waited for her response.

"RaChelle, surely there's something else I can do for you besides this." He flashed his perfect teeth at her and reached out and touched her hand. He remembered how sensitive it was to touch her body and he could tell that she really *felt* his touch. She looked at him and smiled back. "You and I were really good together back then. At least, we had some really good times. I wouldn't mind a trip down memory lane." His hand glided its way up her arm and her body tightened until she jerked her arm away.

"You must really think I'm a fool. I don't fuck fags."

"I ain't no fuckin' fag, so you better watch your mouth," Temple snapped.

"I can't believe you; trying to seduce me. Your dick ain't gold-tipped so it ain't gonna work. What you need to be doing is fucking Daryl righteously. You need to make him leave his man and be ready to change his god. You used to have it like that. You're Temple, remember? People used to bow to you. I think you're slipping."

"What the hell did they do to you that has you so hell-bent on fucking up their lives?"

"They took my life." Her simple words required no explanation. She did not even blink.

"Okay, but why do I have to be involved in all of this?"

"Temple, what is this?" she asked, as she put out her cigarette in the marble tray on the table. "I'm sick of having this conversation with you. I know you're not growing a conscience all of a sudden." She leaned in close and planted her lips on his. It wasn't a passionate kiss, but one filled with poison. "Remember who you're talking to. I know you for your works."

"Yeah, but that was then. This is now. I've changed."

"Clearly. I can tell by that chickenhead you're living with. Oh, but I forgot, you gotta keep a low profile. See, that's why I'm here—to help you. Scratch my back and I'll scratch yours. As soon as I get what I need from you, I'll give you what you need. Can you imagine a life where you don't have to look over your shoulders all the time? Where you can be in the spotlight you love so much and not have to worry about who might be coming after you? Work with me, not against, and I'll give you your life back." Temple leaned back in his chair and considered his options. He didn't really have any. She had a way of mixing sugar and spice to make it seem worthwhile. After all, he didn't *really* know Daryl, and Daryl would *really* never be his as long as Kevin was in the picture. "Just give me what I came here for."

"There's got to be another way."

"This is the only way." She placed her hand on his cheek. "Baby, don't think about it. Just do it. What's your alternative—a jail cell?"

"Temple!" a voice called out over the crowd. He sighed as he saw Cerina storming in their direction.

RaChelle shook her head in disgust. "Look, it's Cerina. Guess I'll be leaving now," RaChelle said as she pulled out three twenty-dollar bills and placed them on the table to pay her bill. Cerina was the last person Temple wanted to see and he certainly didn't want a scene, so he stood up and tried to cut her off at the path.

"I should've known you'd be here with this bitch," Cerina said with contempt. "I guess that's why you couldn't take me to the movies." She looked directly at RaChelle. "I thought I told you to leave him alone? Now I'm going to slap the shit out of you!"

RaChelle shook her head as she put the straps of her bag across her shoulder. "Honey, how many times do I have to tell you that I don't want your man?"

"Then why every time I look up, you all up in his grill?"

"Cerina, what the fuck are you doing here?" Temple chimed in as he stared at her.

"The question is what the fuck are you doing here with this trick?" Her voice had begun to rise and the small crowd was staring. Luckily, the singer on stage had taken a break right as Cerina had stormed in.

"I have business with RaChelle. How the fuck did you find me? You following me?"

"Yeah, I'm following you and I see I have to. If you have business with her, then *we* have business with her and she betta tell me what it is before I put my fist through her pretty stuck-up face!" She pointed a finger directly in RaChelle's face.

"Bitch, don't let my class fool you. I will wear you out. I am not scared of yo' ghetto ass. You don't know me."

"And I don't have to know you, but I need to know what you doing with my man." As her voice began to rise, she felt a pain in her chest she tried to ignore.

"Your man? Girl, he ain't nobody's man, so stop fooling yourself. He'll never be yours."

"Bitch!" Cerina lunged at RaChelle, but Temple grabbed her by the waist. By this time, the crowd was getting edgy and irritated. Cerina suddenly exploded into a violent coughing fit as Temple held his grip. He wasn't sure if she was faking so he would let her go, and he didn't want to take the chance.

"Damn, girl. You need some Robitussin?" RaChelle knew she needed far more than that.

"Fuck you," Cerina said between coughs. Finally, the coughs subsided and she regained her composure.

"I can't believe you're in here causing a scene." Temple was infuriated and his grip on her was tight. A big dude in a black suit walked over to the dysfunctional group.

"Is there a problem here?" he asked in a husky voice.

"No, I was just leaving," RaChelle said. "Temple, I'll call you later because you're running out of time." She put her hand on his cheek. "And, be careful with Cerina. Sounds like she's got Ebola."

CHAPTER 19

S aturday arrived much faster than Kevin and Daryl had expected. Before they realized it, the big day was here, bringing with it an opportunity to raise funds for Keevan's Room and for Kevin and Daryl to enjoy the holiday festivities. Keith and Percy's holiday party was always the toast of the season and their spectacular home would be packed to the nines. Some of the people at their event would also attend Kevin's New Year's Eve fund-raiser a few days later. They had to turn on the charm and work the room in order to solicit the kind of donations that would make a difference and have an impact. The party was a black-tie holiday affair and after they got dressed in their newly purchased tuxedos, they looked at each other in the mirror and realized what a striking couple they were. Working the room would not be an issue for either of them since they were naturally outgoing.

More important than the party, the dynamic duo really felt their relationship was on the fast-track to being wonderful again. They spoke in great detail of their issues, which included their mutual loneliness and the lack of attention to, for, and from each other. Kevin found his place of peace with Amir and Temple, and he decided to give his lover the benefit of the doubt. He believed nothing sexual had taken place with either of them.

Daryl admitted that he seriously erred in placing his ad on www.adam4him.com and entertaining flirtatious conversation; even if it was all in fun. *It's all fun and games until someone gets hurt.* He didn't want to hurt Kevin anymore. He deleted the ad from the website and changed his email account to prevent folks who already had his information from contacting him. They felt they had a fresh start on being happy. And, for the last few days, their sex had been explosive.

The restoration of their love also restored their festive holiday spirit. Even though Christmas was a couple of days away, they went out and purchased a huge tree and together they decorated it like they had done in years past. Each of them secretly rushed out in a flurry and bought the other presents that were wrapped and placed under their tree. However, the only gift that really mattered to each of them had already been given—each other.

Kevin looked at the watch on his arm and called out to Daryl, who had suddenly gone missing. He called out to him again, assuming he was down in the kitchen getting something to drink. This was one of those times when he regretted not having an intercom system. Kevin was quite surprised when Daryl walked into their bedroom carrying a big bouquet of lavender roses, Kevin's favorite. As soon as he saw them, he rushed over to Daryl and they embraced. Daryl didn't speak, but instead went over to the stereo and turned on some music. He played their song: "I Feel Good All Over." He turned away from the stereo and looked at Kevin from across the room.

"May I have this dance?"

"What are you up to?" Kevin asked with a sexy smile. They moved toward each other and seamlessly fell into position as they slowly danced together in what seemed to be a choreographed number. Daryl had placed the song on repeat so their dance would last longer than merely one song.

"I've missed you so much," Kevin whispered in his ear.

"I don't ever want to fight with you again."

"Me either, but let's not talk about that now. I simply want to enjoy you and this moment before we leave." They took comfort in each other's invigorated heartbeat as they swayed back and forth in perfect rhythm and harmony.

After the song had played three times, Daryl's cell phone vibrated against his leg. He backed away from Kevin and pulled the phone out of his pants pocket. When he looked at the caller ID, he smiled. Kevin stared at him, wondering who was calling.

"Baby, it's time to go. I don't want you to be late for the party. Grab your coat. Your chariot waits." They walked downstairs and when Daryl opened the front door, Kevin saw a shiny black limousine parked directly in front of their house. Then, the driver stepped out and walked to the passenger side of the car and opened the door as he motioned for them to step inside.

"Daryl Harris, what are you up to?" Again, Kevin smiled.

"If we're gonna go to this affair, I wanted you to go in style." They stepped into the back of the stretch limo and it was filled with more roses, chocolate and champagne. Daryl popped the cork on one of the bottles and poured two glasses. "I think it's time we got back to being lovers."

As the limo drove down the dark highway into Prince George's County, Maryland, they laughed and enjoyed each other in ways that were reminiscent of their happier times. They reveled in being in love again and they both realized if they worked hard enough, they could save their life together. Every relationship is filled with peaks and valleys, and it is that enduring love shared between individuals that eventually carries them through and lifts them out of the valley.

By the time they got to the party at Keith and Percy's Fort Washington, Maryland estate, the place was packed. Keith and Percy went out of their way to ensure every convenience for their guests, including hiring a crew of valets so partygoers would not have to struggle to find a place to park their cars. The limo driver let them out at the front of the house and when they walked through the double doors leading into the foyer, Keith appeared out of nowhere with a glass of white wine and a wondrous smile draped across his electric face.

"I was wondering when you two were going to arrive," he said in his usual high-pitched excited voice. He kissed them both on their cheeks. His mannerisms showed that this wasn't his first glass of wine and it probably wouldn't be his last. He ushered Kevin and Daryl farther into the room, where he instructed his housekeeper to take their jackets. He was speaking a mile a minute and they found it difficult to keep up with his rapid thoughts and conversation. He was always full of bold energy and enthusiasm. Kevin and Daryl smiled at each other as they secretly read each other's thoughts. They had always joked that Keith must be on some sort of stimulant because it seemed impossible for one person to have so much energy. Keith kept talking as he led them down the hallway to the rooms in the back where most of the guests had gathered. They walked through the French double doors that led to the deck overlooking the lake in the back of their house. The hosts had installed a heated tent that covered the entire span of the deck, providing a buffer against the outside cold.

When they stepped onto the deck, Keith looked around for Percy but was unable to find him. Instead, a waiter passed by carrying a tray of drinks. Keith motioned for him to stop so Daryl and Kevin could get a drink.

"I tell you, it is so good to see you guys. Percy and I were just talking about you two the other day. We don't see nearly enough of you. It's like we've barely seen you in months."

"I know. We definitely have to hang out more in the New Year. Things have been really crazy lately with getting things together for Keevan's Room, including the fund-raiser in a few days," Kevin said.

"I'm so glad to hear that. And speaking of your party, there are a couple of people I want you to meet. If you work them, I'm sure they'll be more than happy to donate some money to Keevan's Room. I've already told them all about it and they're waiting to meet you. I'm not supposed to tell you, but I know one of them was abused by one of his lovers in the past." Keith put his fingers to his lips and smiled deliciously at the secret. Gossiping was his forte. "Daryl, you'll excuse us, won't you?" Before Daryl could answer, Keith put his arm around Kevin and led him away as Daryl stood back and watched.

Daryl watched them disappear into the sea of people and he stood back and scanned the crowd for a familiar face. He wasn't a fan of these snooty affairs but he understood tonight was important for Kevin and he wanted to support him. He glided through the crowd and didn't see anyone he knew or anyone he wanted to get to know, so he decided now was a good time for a bathroom break. He fought his way back through the crowded deck into the interior of the house. There was a restroom downstairs, and part of him wanted to get away from the crowd. As he was making his way down the stairs, he heard a voice call out his name. He turned to look and lost his breath as his eyes fixated on Temple.

"It's a small, small world," Temple said as a smile spread across his face like the dawning sun.

"You know what they say—six degrees of separation." Daryl was cautious in his greeting of Temple; even while his heart raced. He thought he had dismantled his attraction with the resurrection of his relationship with Kevin, but that's not how the heart works.

"More like two degrees. I'm glad I ran into you," Temple said. "Where have you been? I've been trying to reach you for a few days. You've canceled our last two workouts."

"I know. There were some things I needed to take care of. Listen, I was on my way downstairs to the restroom. Why don't you walk with me? We need to talk."

"Cool. I need to pee, too."

"TMI."

"TMI?"

"Too much information. I don't need to know about your bodily functions."

"That's not what you said the other night." Daryl looked around to make sure Temple hadn't been overheard. Then, they followed the winding staircase to the bottom of the house and made their way down the long, empty hallway to the restroom.

"You can go first," Daryl said.

"Can't we go together?"

"Stop being nasty."

"I'm simply being me." Temple motioned for Daryl to go first and when Daryl walked into the restroom, he locked the door. He didn't want to risk Temple making a bold move and stepping into the room with him. And, if he found himself locked in a small cramped room with Temple, he wasn't sure what would happen. He took a deep breath and tried to pull his scattered emotions together. He couldn't have his feelings for Temple on display. He didn't need to see Temple. Not now. Not when things with Kevin were going so well. He couldn't risk losing Kevin again. He had been avoiding Temple, but they needed to have a serious conversation that would ultimately lead to the dissolution of their friendship. *Remove temptation*. Remove Temple from his life.

As he walked out of the restroom, Temple stepped in and playfully tried to pull him into the space with him. Daryl pushed him away and forced the door closed. When he turned around, he noticed the pictures on the wall. The room was a shrine of Keith and Percy's relationship. There were pictures of them from various exotic vacation spots from all over the world. They were a high-profile, very much out-of-the-closet kind of couple, and a part of Daryl envied them. They were such a good fit and they took pride in their fifteen-year relationship. They had met while in college and were still together. Daryl hoped he and Kevin had that kind of staying power.

"I'm back," Temple said as he slightly startled Daryl.

"Good. I actually need to talk to you, so I'm glad you're here."

"What's on your mind?" Temple already knew where this conversation was going. He didn't imagine running into Daryl here and he wasn't necessarily ready to have the inevitable conversation.

"We need to talk about what happened."

"What is there to say?"

"I need to be clear so there aren't any misunderstandings between us."

"What kind of misunderstandings are you referring to, Dr. Harris?" Temple showed his pearly whites and moved close enough to Daryl to smell him. He was electrified by Daryl's scent.

"This is what I'm talking about," Daryl said as he stepped back. "We need to set some boundaries."

Temple gazed at him in confusion. "How do you set boundaries after we've made love?"

"We are both in relationships and we can't go on like this anymore."

"Daryl, I love you..." Those words shocked them both. Temple had never said those words and meant them to anyone before. When they left his mouth, he felt a sense of relief and a sense of vulnerability. He hadn't meant to say them, but he was glad he did. He did love Daryl. He was sure of that. He wasn't sure when or how or why it happened, but it was true. Love. Love. Love.

"Temple, you can't love me. You don't even know me that well." Temple stepped back from Daryl and turned his back to him for a second. His hands were shaking and he had to calm himself. All of this was new to him. He felt like a fish out of water.

"All I do is think about you. I want to know what you're doing, what you're eating, how your day is going, did you sleep well, are you tired, do you need anything. I can't stop thinking about you. When we made love in the hotel—"

"Temple, you can't mention that. That was a one-time thing. I made a mistake."

"Oh, so now I'm a fuckin' mistake? Was it a mistake when you called me over to the hotel? Was it a mistake when you asked me to lay with you? Was it a mistake when you put your dick in me?"

"Temple, that's not what I meant. I simply meant that, given *both* our circumstances, we shouldn't have done it. I mean, it was great, but we are both committed to other people."

"I have never felt this way for anyone before. I don't give a fuck about Kevin or Cerina. They ain't important. You can stand there and act like you're in love with Kevin, but we both know. We both can feel it. You wanted me from day one. Now, you have me."

"Temple, one night in a hotel does not constitute love." Daryl had to fight Temple's words. Temple *couldn't* be right. He loved Kevin.

"One night in a hotel? We both know it was way more than that." Daryl couldn't argue with him. His feelings were genuine. Was it possible to be in love with two people at the same time?

"Look. Kevin is right upstairs and I can't be down here with you. I gotta go."

"What, you can't take the heat?" Temple stepped close to him and Daryl felt his heat.

"Kevin and I are working on our relationship and for the last few days it has been better than it has ever been."

"Really? What does that have to do with us?"

"It means there is no us. What happened between us should never have happened and Kevin can never find out about it." Temple took another step toward Daryl until Daryl's back was against the wall. He then pressed his body against Daryl and Daryl tried, with a minimal effort, to push him away. "Temple, please don't do this." Temple kissed Daryl on the neck, which sent shivers up and down Daryl's body.

❀❀❀

Temple's powerful kiss forced Daryl to relive that night in the hotel when he made the greatest mistake of his life. It was exactly two-thirteen in the morning and Daryl woke up when he felt Temple release him from his grip. Daryl groaned as Temple rolled out of bed and adjusted his boxer shorts. The lazy light from the candles they had lit earlier provided a sleepy glow to the tranquil room. Daryl's eyes locked on Temple's ass as he watched Temple's shirtless body travel across the room and walk into the bathroom. The door closed.

Earlier, when he asked Temple to stay with him until he fell asleep, he was a bit nervous because the only man he had shared a bed with in the last few years was Kevin. However, when they climbed into bed together, Daryl was shocked at how natural it felt lying next to Temple. He was surprised how easily they fit together; like the pieces of a homoerotic jigsaw puzzle. Daryl lay on his side with Temple's arm draped across his waist and Temple's hips pressed firmly into his backside. Temple had an intoxicatingly masculine scent that lodged in Daryl's nostrils and gave him a tingling feeling in his stomach. *The power of smell is so underrated,* Daryl thought.

When Temple opened the bathroom door, he was startled by Daryl, who stood in front of him. The look on Daryl's face made Temple uncomfortable—just for a moment—and then Daryl took a single step forward and got into Temple's face.

"Wassup?" Temple asked curiously. Then, Daryl grabbed Temple by the waist and pulled his body close—so close there was little room for even air between them. When Temple tried to speak again, Daryl gently—but forcibly—bit Temple's bottom lip to silence him. Then, they started kissing. Wildly. Passionately. Uncontrollably. The heat generated from their kiss burned hotter than the flames in the candles by the bed. Daryl could taste the vodka on Temple's lips when he inserted his tongue into his mouth. With his tongue, Temple fought Daryl's attempts at dominance, but Daryl kissed his lips with fury and fire and sucked his tongue with all the desire that had built up between them over the weeks. Their moans disturbed the silence of the room, but neither of them was concerned about that. Temple rubbed his hands all over Daryl's body and squeezed his ass firmly as he pushed his tongue deeper into Daryl's anxious mouth. Daryl felt as if his heart was going to pound through his chest. Their inflamed kiss stirred up lust stronger than reason and a longing that overpowered rational thought. The kiss broke barriers and fused them together in ways neither had ever imagined.

Temple's dick poked through the hole in his boxer shorts and Daryl grabbed his protruding penis and pulled him to the bed.

He pushed him down and straddled him like he was riding a horse.

He kissed every part of his face.

Temple felt the power of every kiss. Then, he flipped Daryl on his back and yanked off the shorts he was wearing. There it was. Daryl's naked flesh pointed upwardly like a powerful black missile. Temple looked at it. He longed for it. It was beautiful and thick and veiny and Daryl's balls hung low; just like Temple liked. Temple thought he would explode if he kept looking. Daryl reached up and grabbed Temple by his head and pulled his face into his again. He then wrapped his legs around Temple's waist as Temple wildly kissed his neck.

That was Daryl's spot.

He moaned. And Temple kissed and sucked his neck harder.

Daryl pushed him away. If he kept doing that, he'd leave passion marks. Daryl couldn't have that.

Temple's tongue explored Daryl's body with a rapid-fire motion that deepened Daryl's moans. He licked and nibbled on his ears and then slid down his body, stopping at his nipples.

Daryl shivered when he felt Temple's lips. His entire body jerked as Temple sucked on his right nipple and squeezed the left one with his thumb and index finger.

"Oh shit," Daryl whimpered between shudders. His body continued to jerk as if he was having convulsions. The pleasure of Temple's touch was unmatched. Even by Kevin.

Temple nibbled. And bit. And pulled. And sucked on Daryl's hardened raisins until Daryl couldn't stand it anymore. He pushed Temple's head in a southern direction.

Temple licked and nibbled his way down Daryl's body. He pushed Daryl's legs apart and stopped at his left inner thigh. He devoured Daryl's thigh like he was at a buffet.

He looked at Daryl's hard dick again. Moisture had gathered at its tip. Then, without warning, he devoured it. Hungrily, he took it all into his mouth while pulling at Daryl's balls. Daryl let out a loud groan. He looked down at Temple who was sucking him as if his life depended on it.

Temple looked up into Daryl's eyes. He knew he was good at sucking dick. It shone on Daryl's face and in his eyes. Temple smiled from the corner of his mouth as he watched Daryl watching him.

Daryl couldn't take too much more of Temple's power and he wasn't ready to explode. He wanted more. He wanted to take it to a deeper level. A much deeper level. He grabbed Temple by both his ears and pulled him again into his face. Their lips met with heat. Temple pushed away and moved hurriedly to his gym bag. He dumped the contents onto the floor and rummaged through the items until he found a three-pack of condoms and a bottle of lubrication. Daryl stroked himself as Temple bent over, looking through the items. Daryl hopped out of the bed and grabbed two bandanas Temple had dumped onto the floor. He forced Temple back onto the bed on his stomach.

"What are you doing?" Temple asked. Daryl didn't respond. Instead, he took one of the scarves and tied Temple's hand to the bedpost. Then, he tied the other one.

Temple's breathing accelerated. He was completely in Daryl's control. Helpless.

"Daryl," he began.

"Shhhhh."

Daryl went into the bathroom and returned with a towel that he fixed around Temple's eyes.

"Wait, Daryl," Temple said between nervous breaths. He was now blindfolded and panting like a dog.

"Trust me. It won't hurt."

Daryl ran his tongue up and down Temple's back. Temple wanted to scream with pleasure and anticipation, but all he could muster was a moan. Daryl licked and nibbled until he got to the crack of Temple's ass. He squeezed Temple's ass cheeks and slapped them with a bit of force. Temple liked the sting.

Daryl took the lube and applied it to Temple. He used two fingers to probe his willing partner. Temple's breathing quickened.

He wanted it. He wanted to feel the burn.

"I want you to fuck me," Temple groaned.

Daryl slipped on the black condom.

He eased his way into Temple.

Temple grimaced, but did not shy away from it. When Daryl entered him, Temple raised his ass a little higher and used the pillow to muffle his grunts.

What they felt was beyond pleasure and far past joy. Daryl felt as if he was inside happiness. Their moans grew louder and more intense with each thrust. They had connected.

Daryl didn't want to merely pound away. He wanted to enjoy the moment. He wanted the pleasure to outlast time itself. Daryl squeezed his ass cheeks together and continued his thrusts in rolling motions.

"Oh, shit. What the fuck are you doing to me?" Temple asked. He felt like he was going to bite a hole into the pillow. His question needed no answer.

Daryl's freaky nature came to the surface. He reached over and grabbed a candle from the nightstand.

"Baby," he said, "are you ready?"

"I'm ready for anything you've got. Just don't stop fucking me."

Slowly, Daryl let a few drops of hot candle wax hit Temple's back.

"Fuck!" Temple screamed. When the wax hit, he felt Daryl's thrust in the small of his back. Temple screamed again.

More drops of candle wax fell on Temple's yellow skin.

The maddening mix of pleasure and pain sent Temple into a tailspin. He was excited by the experience. He pushed his ass back at Daryl, who had placed the candle down and was concentrating on his in-and-out motion. The thought of being inside Temple excited Daryl more than the actual act. He couldn't believe Temple's sweet surrender. He looked at his dick moving in and out, in and out, and couldn't take it anymore.

"Shit, I'm gonna cum!" Daryl shouted as he pulled out and yanked off the rubber. Temple felt Daryl's hot release on his back. Daryl yelled and his body jerked as he stroked himself.

The restraints had loosened and Temple was able to free himself. He rolled over onto his back and grabbed Daryl by the back of the head. He forced his tongue into Daryl's mouth and, with three strokes, he shot his load into the air. He kissed Daryl harder and bit down on his tongue as he continued to cum in big bursts. He didn't think he'd stop. His body shook uncontrollably. He had never shot like that before.

❧❧❧

The sound of Temple's voice brought Daryl back to reality. "What were you saying about us?" Temple asked between deep breaths. He pushed Temple away, this time with so much force it startled Temple.

"Stop it. We can't do this anymore. I love Kevin. You were a mistake." Daryl's words stung Temple.

"A mistake? A fuckin' mistake? Your dick is so hard right now that it's about to bust through your pants. Is that a mistake, too?"

Daryl didn't respond. Temple's voice grew louder and Daryl feared they would be discovered in the abandoned basement. Ever since they had made love in the hotel, Daryl had fought desperately to forget that night. He struggled with forgetting about Temple's embrace and the feel of his lips on his body. More than anything, he needed to forget Temple's touch and how every part of his body came to life with even the simplest touch. In order for his relationship with Kevin to work, he'd have to forget, but when Temple pressed his lips against his, everything came back to him.

Temple was offended by Daryl's rejection. He had fallen hard for this man, who was involved with someone else. He had struggled to keep RaChelle at bay and had not yet told her about their affair. His emotions were unstable and erratic. All he wanted was to be near Daryl. The night they spent together in the hotel he experienced something far deeper than sex. It was truly the first time in his life that he felt connected with someone. Finally, he understood that there could be a difference between having sex and making love.

"Temple, we can't." Daryl put his hand on Temple's face. "I need to get back upstairs before Kevin comes down here and finds me with you." He turned away from Temple and made his way back up the long and winding staircase. Temple watched him walk away.

When he got upstairs, the sounds of boisterous laughter filled the area, but he was in no laughing mood. He saw Kevin over in the corner, smiling and laughing, without a care in the world. *If only he knew*. He stood back and studied Kevin. In that moment, his love for Kevin had never been clearer. It was so bright it almost blinded him. It severely dulled the background noises and the sounds of glasses clinking and of people laughing and of waiters shuffling by. It was the most powerful thing. *Even more powerful than his lust for Temple*. He loved watching Kevin when Kevin didn't know he was being watched. Daryl liked to watch his facial expressions and the way his body reacted to laughter and emotions. Kevin was very expressive and it was difficult for him to hide his feelings because they usually were revealed in his face, his eyes, and his bodily movements.

When the waiter walked by, Daryl quickly took another glass of champagne. He decided he needed to mingle and took his place at his man's side.

"Hey, baby," Kevin said as he pulled Daryl into him. "Are you having a good time? You look a bit flushed."

"I'm fine. How's it going over here?"

"Your husband has been charming the money right out of everyone," Keith chimed in with his usual zeal. "And speaking of husbands, where is mine?" He looked around the room to find his mate, but couldn't locate him.

"I saw Percy greeting some folks in the foyer a few minutes ago," Daryl offered.

"Oh, he's the greatest host. I'll find him in a minute but, before I do, I want you two to meet someone. Don't go anywhere. I'll be right back." Keith went through the crowd and disappeared momentarily.

"Thank you for coming with me, baby," Kevin said.

"There's no other place I'd rather be than at your side." Right as those words exited his mouth, he heard Keith's voice. When he returned, Temple was on his side, standing with an impish grin.

"Temple, I want you to meet a couple of friends of mine," Keith said. "This is Kevin and—"

"Nice to see you again, Daryl," Temple said, with a sexy enigmatic grin. He extended his hand to Daryl. Kevin felt as if he had just had the wind knocked out of him. *So, this is Temple*. He looked at Temple and then noticed the nervous look in Daryl's eyes.

"Oh, so you're Temple?" Kevin said. "I've heard so much about you."

"I should've known you would have met them already. D.C. is such a small place," Keith inserted.

"Yeah, Temple is my workout partner," Daryl said to Keith as Temple's gaze fixated upon Daryl's face.

"Yeah, we met at the gym some time ago. Daryl saved me from a horrible accident on the bench press," Temple lied.

"That's *my* Daryl," Kevin said as he put his arms around his partner. "Always willing to help out a stranger." Kevin's tone was peppered with disapproval. Keith looked at Kevin and saw the expression on his face and decided to take action.

"Temple, come with me please. There's someone *else* I think you should talk to," Keith said with all due seriousness.

"It was nice meeting you, Kevin. And, Daryl, let's talk soon." With those last words, Keith took Temple by the arm and led him away.

"Hmm," Kevin said out loud. Daryl took another sip of his champagne and hoped he could dodge this bullet.

"What does that mean?"

"What does what mean?"

"That sound you just made."

"Nothing. Nothing at all." Kevin watched Temple slither through the crowd. He had heard about Temple, but this—their first meeting—left a lot to be desired.

CHAPTER 20

B y the time the party was over, Kevin was exhausted. He felt like he had put in a full
day's work strolling through the room; smiling, laughing, and casually flirting with
folks all in the name of service to the community. He hadn't worked so hard for
dollars in a very long time, but he was happy with his return on investment.

When he and Daryl got into the limo to go home, there was a palpable change in Daryl's
demeanor and it had started to get underneath Kevin's skin. Each time he asked him what
was wrong, Daryl responded that he had a headache. Somehow, Kevin knew that wasn't the
full truth. He wasn't sure what happened at the party, but it had something to do with
Temple. The strained looked on Daryl's face, the uneasiness in his voice, and his slumped
posture revealed so much. Kevin shifted uneasily back and forth as the limo navigated the
darkened streets. He looked out of the window into the wounded night sky. Large clouds
had formed, partially obscuring the moonlight. In the darkness, the truth is all that remains.

During that ride home, Daryl's amplified guilt returned with a vengeance. He realized he
had fucked up. Big time. He had tried desperately to forget about the affair and had told
himself that if Kevin didn't find out about it, then it never happened. Kevin never had to
know. After all, the affair happened in the midst of their hardship, when everything seemed
lost and when he was emotionally weakened by Kevin's accusations and words. In part, he
blamed Kevin for pushing him into Temple's arms, but realized he probably would have
ended up there anyway.

In the aftermath of his infidelity, he thought about how he had compartmentalized his
mistake. He kept his affair with Temple in a box and tried to bury it deep in his backyard, but
when he saw Temple tonight, the hole he dug seemed shallow. Tonight, the box had been completely exposed. He couldn't hide or even contain his lust or his guilt. It was all over his face.

He should avoid Temple at all costs. No phone calls. No contact. But, in spite of his promise to remove temptation, he wasn't entirely ready to give him up. *How strange,* he thought. He was being pulled in different directions and he felt as if he was about to lose control.

When they got home, Daryl tipped the limo driver and sent him away. Kevin grabbed his hand and they walked hand-in-hand from the car to their house in a hollow display of emotion. Daryl opened the door, entered the four-digit code to turn off the alarm, and practically raced up the stairs to their bedroom. Shooting pains of guilt and horror pierced his thoughts and he seemed powerless to protect himself from them. Moreover, he was powerless to protect Kevin. His actions and lack of self-control would eventually destroy them. He recognized this. He could smell it in the air. *It's only a matter of time,* he thought. *Secrets don't stay buried forever and what's done in the dark always comes to the light.* But, he would fight tooth and nail to keep the secret. How could he have let this happen? He entered the master bathroom and sat on the side of the tub as his heart threatened to pound through his chest.

Kevin knocked on the door.

"I have some aspirin for you."

"I'll be out in a second."

Choices. Decisions. Life is simply a collection of choices and decisions, and everyone's life is a reflection of their decisions and choices. Daryl had made the wrong choice by inviting Temple over to the hotel. If he could relive everything, he would choose differently. Never invite temptation into the room with you. Never invite temptation into your bed. He wished everyone in life was blessed with one "do-over" so that when they made a horrible mistake, at least they'd have one opportunity to correct it. Now, he was faced with uncertainty. Should he tell Kevin straight up and beg for forgiveness, or should he remain silent and hope it would pass? Could he rely on Temple to remain silent? Temple hadn't given him any indication he would reveal the secret but, at this point, Temple had a lot of power over him he could wield at his will. Would he be able to keep Temple at bay? Love is irrational. If Temple loved him as he claimed, unrequited love can be dangerous. Was Temple volatile enough to tell Kevin? He thought about how Kevin, one of the most stable people he knew, confronted Amir on the thinnest suspicion. If Kevin could react so emotionally, there's no telling what Temple would do. He had only known the man for a relatively short time and Daryl wasn't sure how he'd react when his back was against the wall. Daryl's head spun in circles.

"Baby, unlock the door. You're worrying me."

"I'm sorry, baby. I'm having one of those crazy headaches I used to get. I'll be fine. I just need to go to bed," Daryl said as he opened the door.

"Are you sure you're okay?"

"I'll be fine, baby." Daryl started to undress and forced himself to think of other thoughts than his infidelity. "So, how did you do tonight?" he said, trying to change the subject.

Kevin's face lit up. "I did well. I had a long conversation with Max Tomlin, the Director of Corporate Giving for District Health Plans. He's very interested in Keevan's Room and he practically guaranteed a fifty thousand-dollar grant from his organization! I have to fill out a grant application and get it to him by the end of January." Kevin did a happy dance and then smiled wildly.

It brought joy to Daryl's glum spirit. "Damn! My baby got skills!"

Daryl stood up and joined in the dance. Anything to forget Temple's kisses. His dance momentarily pushed his infidelity out of his head and he basked in Kevin's happiness. That joy, he knew, would soon be replaced with heartache.

After the celebration faded, Daryl took a shower and decided to get some rest. He hoped the morning would bring clarity to his dilemma. He didn't want to live the rest of his life with some dark secret that could surface at any moment and tear their lives apart. Why had he been unable to resist? Temple wasn't the first attractive man to try to seduce him since he'd been with Kevin and with all those other guys, he was resolute in his fidelity. Maybe it was the fact his relationship had been weakened and he was an emotional wreck. Constantly arguing with Kevin and being accused of infidelity, in one way or another, took a lot out of him. Add alcohol and a seductive man who has been clear in his desire and that is the perfect recipe for disaster.

Even though Kevin was tired, his excitement prevented him from sleeping. He decided to do some work on the upcoming party. He took some papers into the den and rested on the couch, with soft jazz playing in the background. He had spoken with the party planner, Desiree, a couple of days ago and she had assured him everything was on schedule. He still had butterflies in his stomach. It was not unusual for him to be nervous because he was such a perfectionist. The party that had once seemed so very far off in the future was rapidly approaching, with less than a week to go.

As he sat down and plotted out the remaining details of what needed to be done, he heard a phone ring. It wasn't coming from the house phone, but a cell phone on the table. Instantly, he recognized the ring as being Daryl's phone. He didn't want to run the risk of Daryl being awakened by the loud melody that emanated from the phone with each ring. Kevin raced over to the table by the door where Daryl had dropped his keys and his phone. He picked it up. He looked at the caller ID and didn't like what he saw.

"Hello," he whispered into the phone.

"Hey. I wanted to check on you to see how you were doing. I think I freaked you out at the party."

"Temple, this is Kevin."

Silence.

"Oh, wassup, man? I was trying to reach Daryl."

"I know you were, but it's three-thirty in the morning and I can assure you that Daryl is sleeping. I can't imagine why you would be calling so late. Is there an emergency?"

"No. He seemed kinda *off* when you left the party, so I wanted to check on him."

"*We* appreciate your concern, but don't trouble yourself. Daryl has me and I take very good care of my man."

"You don't say? Look, I didn't mean to cause any shit. I was concerned. That's all."

"Something tells me that's not entirely true."

"What does that mean?"

"It means I think you're up to something, but whatever you have in mind, won't work. Daryl loves me and I love him and you can never come between that. Do you understand what I mean?"

"You don't know anything about me." Temple couldn't stand being chastised or challenged in this manner. *He has no idea of my powers,* he thought. He would not let Kevin arrogantly question his ability to have any man he chose at any moment. He would not allow Kevin to have this victory. Temple had called out of concern and guilt and hadn't expected to be talking to Kevin.

"I understand exactly what you mean, but I wouldn't be so cocky about your relationship, if I were you."

"What the fuck does that mean?"

"Ask yo' man."

"I'm asking you."

Silence.

"Let's just say everything ain't always as it appears to be. If I wanted Daryl, trust me, I'd have him."

"You think you got it like that?"

"I know I got it like that. Since you so big and bad all of a sudden—"

"Look, I don't have time for this bullshit."

"Neither do I. Tell Daryl the next time he's at the Marriott alone and needs some more company to call out my name. I'll be there again like I was before."

The phone went dead.

Kevin felt as if he had been slapped. The heavy-fisted fury of Temple's words struck him hard and sent him in a loop. In his conversation with Daryl about the Marriott, he never mentioned—not one single time—about Temple stopping by for a late-night visit. *Was that something Daryl should have mentioned?* Kevin asked himself. After all, he never asked Daryl if anyone stopped by or if he had spoken to anyone about the fight they had that night. So, many questions; so many things running through his head. That mistrust was back. The feeling that something was wrong was back. Right when he felt things were getting better, doubt moved back into his heart.

He wasn't sure what to do. Temple's words cut like a dagger into the heart of his relationship. Just when things were looking up, the worst possible scenario was thrown into the mix. Over the course of the years, Kevin had learned and had witnessed jealous and vicious folks who would stop at nothing to destroy someone else's relationship. It was that whole "misery loves company" mentality that was the catalyst that destroyed lives. Once the seeds of mistrust were planted, it was hard to prevent them from taking root. Those seeds, if you let it, would spring into wild vines that gripped the neck of the relationship and cut off its air supply. Yet, somehow knowing the evil ways of man, Kevin simply couldn't dismiss Temple's allegations. There was something in the sound of Temple's voice that was more than a cause for alarm. There was some truth and some legitimacy in his callous tone Kevin simply could not deny. He stood in the middle of the room and watched the world he knew become its deepest shade of blue.

CHAPTER 21

K evin didn't bring up Temple's phone call. He certainly wasn't about to mess up their groove now that they had reconciled and Christmas was upon them. Yet, he couldn't get the words out of his head. Did Daryl have an affair with Temple and was he still having it? Thoughts of a cheating heart drove him to distraction, but he managed to stay in the groove with Daryl by focusing on the holiday and Danea's impending arrival. He tried, as best as he could, not to let Temple's toxic words kill what he was trying to accomplish with Daryl. Instead of focusing on Temple, he wanted to get everything ready for Danea's arrival.

It was the morning of Christmas Eve and Kevin and Daryl were awake. Because neither of them had close families, Danea usually spent Christmas with Kevin and Daryl, but she had missed last year because she decided to go home with Curtis. Once again, Curtis had tried to convince her to go to New Orleans with him, but she declined. She wanted to see her boys—her family. She was going to stay with them for a couple of days and when Curtis arrived in time for her concert at Kevin's party, they would move to a hotel so they'd have some privacy.

"I finished up the guest room," Daryl said as he walked into the kitchen with Kevin, who was busy preparing a feast.

"Cool. She should be here any minute and I can't wait to see her. I only wished Tony and LaMont were here, too. Then we'd be all together like it used to be; except Keevan would still be gone. You know I still miss him? Not a day goes by that I don't think about him."

"I'm sure Tony and LaMont are enjoying Houston; like always. You know that old married couple doesn't have time for us. It's been almost a year since they've been for a visit. And, as far as Keevan, I know he's smiling down on us right now," Daryl said, trying to offer some comfort. He walked over to Kevin and put his arms around him.

"Yeah, I know." The sound of a car horn blowing out front made them both smile. It was Danea. They had been eagerly awaiting her arrival for some time now and could barely contain their enthusiasm. They raced from the kitchen to the front door to greet their friend. They first peered out of the window to visually confirm her arrival and when they saw the limo outside, they knew. Kevin flung open the door and laughed as the driver stepped out into the cold to open the door for the superstar. Snowflakes spiraled gently from the heavens and were carried by a light breeze. Danea stepped out of the limo in a white fur coat, big Jackie-O sunglasses and three-inch heels; in spite of the weather.

"Danea!" Kevin screamed as he stepped out of the warmth of his house and hurdled the stairs leading to the sidewalk. Daryl wasn't far behind him. When they reached the limo, the three of them hugged each other with force and held on for dear life. It had been a long time since they had seen each other.

"It is so good to see you both!" she yelled.

"It's good to see you, too," Daryl said, "but it's freezing out here. Let's get in the house." Kevin and Daryl helped the driver with some of her luggage to expedite the process.

As they stepped into the warm interior of the house, Danea took off her hat and fur and looked around the room. "I like what you've done with the place. It looks amazing." The wide smile on her face lit up the room and she acted like it was the first time she had been to their house.

"That was all Daryl," Kevin said, giving credit where credit was due. "He truly has done a remarkable job on the place. Wait until you see the rest of it."

"And, what is with you and this long-ass limo outside? You got fur coats and diamond rings. I ain't mad atcha!" Daryl said playfully.

"Hey, I gotta look the part. It's all image, but I'm still the same old Danea. Now, y'all know this country girl is hungry. I haven't had breakfast yet. What you cooking up 'n through here?" she said with a laugh as she rubbed her stomach.

"Come on into the kitchen and find out." Kevin hung her mink coat in the closet and took her hand as they walked to the kitchen. Kevin commented on her remarkable makeover that she underwent. She had lost thirty pounds and gotten rid of the shoulder-length braids she had worn for a couple of years. Her auburn hair was midway down her back and it blended well with her café au lait skin tone.

Danea feasted on the soul food brunch Kevin had prepared and, for the rest of the afternoon, they chatted and caught up on old times. She filled them in on her Hollywood escapades and dished a little dirt on some of the celebrities she had encountered. She was truly a breath of fresh air. Her playful demeanor made Christmas Eve much more special. Before becoming a professional singer, Danea had been a successful attorney and had a powerful courtroom presence. She was the mother hen of their group of friends; encouraging each person to do the right thing and make the best decisions so they could live their best lives.

By late evening, they had finished off a couple of bottles of wine and watched two movies. It was a nonstop laugh fest. They were in the den listening to music and playing cards when the doorbell rang. Kevin and Daryl looked at each other because they weren't expecting any visitors. Kevin walked downstairs to the front door with a baffled look on his face.

"RaChelle. What are you doing here?" he asked, more out of shock than excitement when he opened the door. When they were back in Houston, she had an annoying habit of showing up unannounced. Clearly, it wasn't a habit she had broken.

"Well, I was in the neighborhood and saw your lights on, so I thought I'd stop by and bring some holiday cheer. And, I wanted to give you your present."

He knew she was lying. His home wasn't anywhere near her hotel. He looked down at the gray envelope she held between her delicate fingers and the small box wrapped in metallic silver paper in her other hand. "A present? I can't take this."

"Sure, you can. It's nothing big. Just something I thought you'd like to have. Here, take both of these. They go together."

Reluctantly, he accepted the gift. As much as he didn't want to invite her in, the Southern gentleman in him prevented him from cursing her out and throwing her back out in the cold.

"Would you like to come in?"

Without hesitation, she walked in, then kissed him on the cheek. She handed him her coat and followed him upstairs into the den. When Kevin walked in with RaChelle behind him, everything stopped. Daryl and Danea collectively held their breath and had to refocus their eyes to make sure they weren't seeing things. Daryl knew she was in town, but certainly wasn't expecting to see her now. Danea was completely taken off guard. Kevin walked over to the tree and placed her gift next to all the other boxes.

"RaChelle," Daryl said as he stood and greeted her. She kissed him on both cheeks and showed a dainty smile. Danea remained on the couch, drink in hand, and shot RaChelle a fake smile. Danea never liked her. RaChelle was not the kind of person any of them needed in their lives. "It's good to see you. Kevin told me you were in town. I was wondering when I'd get to see you."

"Well, here I am. Take a good look," she said as she struck a pose. Danea turned her head in disgust. "Danea, I had no idea you were here. It's been what? Three years since I've seen you?"

"Yeah, it's been a very long time. How have you been?"

"I couldn't be better."

"Would you like something to drink?" Daryl asked her.

"A Christmas martini would be great," she said as she took a seat on the couch next to Danea.

"Oh, Danea, I wanted to tell you that I thought your *little* CD was good; for a first try. I can't wait to hear your sophomore act." Her catty words stung Danea.

"Excuse me? *Little* CD?" Danea asked with much attitude.

"Girl, you know what I mean," she retorted with a smile. "Kevin, how has your holiday been so far?"

Kevin pretended not to hear her and joined Daryl at the bar where he was making RaChelle's drink.

"What is she doing here?" Daryl whispered.

"I don't know. She showed up at the door like some stray cat."

"That's what happens when you feed one. They never go away."

"I know if she keeps up this attitude with Danea, she might get punched."

"I'd pay money to see that."

"Hell, so would I. Okay, let's try to get through this without bloodshed. Maybe this will give me an opportunity to really find out what she wants."

Kevin and Daryl rejoined the ladies in the den, but the rest of the evening passed without any meaningful event. RaChelle put away her claws, relaxed and the four of them had a good time listening to Danea's *little* CD, playing cards and drinking. Christmas Eve, in spite of the interloper, turned out pleasantly.

"Well, guys—and Danea—I have had a really good time, but I've got to go. I've got a couple of deliveries to make tonight. I didn't mean to crash your party. Kevin, thank you for the drink and y'all have a merry Christmas."

❄❄❄

"Girl, them fools out there tonight are rowdy," Nicole said as she sat in the chair next to Cerina. "It's Christmas-fucking-Eve and this place is mo' crowded than it usually is. You'd think these Negroes would want to be home with their families instead of here."

"I'm glad they tired asses are here. I gots bills to pay," another girl chimed in from the back.

"Cerina, you ready to go out there? I think you're up next."

"I'm so sick of this shit, Nicole. There's got to be a better way."

"If you find one, be sure and let my ass know. If one mo' greasy ass man puts his hands where they don't need to be, I swear I'mma kick him in the face."

"I know that's right, girl," Cerina said as they gave each other a high-five. "Did you see Temple out there?"

"Yeah, he's out there talking to Rose."

"Rose? What's she doing talking to my man?"

"Wait, Cerina, you know it ain't like that with Rose, so don't start trippin'. You know how you get."

"My bad. I'm only tired, I guess."

"Did you hit your head?"

"What?"

"You have a bruise on your forehead."

Cerina panicked. She leapt up from the chair and looked at herself in the mirror. Nicole was right. There was a dime-sized purple discoloration on her forehead. "Damn."

"You see it now? What is it?"

"I ate some cherries this morning and you know my ass is allergic."

"Cerina, you know better than that. The last time you had some cherries you broke out in a rash all over your body."

"I know. Don't remind me. I only had one this time. Let me borrow some makeup so that I can cover it up."

❧❧❧

Outside in the main part of the club, Temple leaned against the bar in the back; striking his usual sexy stance. He sipped slowly on the drink Rose charmed out of the bartender and then pulled out his cell phone and dialed Daryl's number again, but he knew he'd only get a voice mail. He left his third message in two days anyway. He didn't like being ignored.

He watched with disinterest the girl on stage popping her ass to the hard-hitting bass of the song that pumped through the speakers like thunder. He looked around the room and had never been more disgusted by the environment. He had been to strip clubs before, but none as sleazy as this. Cerina often talked about how the girls used this club as a means to propel their lives to a better place. Temple knew better. This wasn't the kind of place that launched a thousand professional careers. These girls would never be doctors or lawyers or teachers. This was the kind of place you worked at when you couldn't get a career and didn't have any options. Even the clientele of the club reflected the images of broken dreams and shattered lives. The stench of flesh and cigarette smoked filled his lungs; like hopes and dreams left rotting on the vines of life. He couldn't wait to be done with Cerina and this entire scene. When he first met her, he never imagined he'd stay with her so long—she was something to do for the moment. Quick cash and easy ass became his addiction, all while he played the field searching for something a bit more to his liking.

He had decided to break it off with her; regardless of what happened with Daryl or RaChelle. He was over it and her and could no longer bear such a low-class spot and a low-life existence. It was time for him to dance in the sun again; to play the strings of life and to reap the benefits of being beautiful and available. He wanted to dance with Daryl. He pulled out his cell phone again and dialed the number. This time, Daryl picked up and Temple pushed his way through the crowd into the restroom so he could hear.

"Temple, are you okay?"

"Yeah. I wanted to talk to you. I was wondering when we're going to hang out again."

"Look, Temple. That's not a good idea."

"I mean, can't we still be friends?"

"Temple, come on, man. Let's not go there."

"Daryl, baby, why are you doing this to us? We could be so good together."

"I can't have this conversation with you right now. I'll call you in a few days."

"A few days?"

"Bye, Temple."

Click.

If Temple could have crushed his cell phone with his bare hands he would have. Instead, he punched the paper towel dispenser hanging from the wall and left a big dent. He needed to shout, to yell, to fight, and to fuck away his anger. He pulled out his phone again and dialed Baron's number. It rang until the voice mail picked up. He didn't leave a message. He picked up his drink that he had set on the sink and walked out of the restroom; angered and humiliated.

When he made it back to his spot by the bar, he shook his head at the sight of RaChelle. She was truly the last person he wanted to see on this night. Couldn't he enjoy the rest of his Christmas Eve without having to deal with her ass? He knew why she was there and he hadn't yet delivered the goods she needed.

"Temple! Merry Christmas!" she screamed. She pulled him into her body and grabbed his ass.

"Look, I know why you're here. I told you already that Daryl and I had sex and I even gave you proof, but—"

"I'm not here about that. I'm here to spread some holiday cheer. You know how Christmas warms my soul."

"Right. How could I have forgotten?" he asked sarcastically.

"Has your girl performed yet?"

"She's up next; I think. RaChelle, if I didn't know any better, I'd think you were beginning to like this place. You into coochie now?"

"Temple, you know that ain't my style. Beside, I like dick far too much." She put her hand on his crotch and squeezed.

"Hey, take it easy. What's gotten into you tonight?"

"Must be the Christmas spirit."

A booming voice poured out of the speakers announcing *Pussy Galore*. The lights flickered and flashed as she made her entrance. She was dressed like a Catholic nun; complete with big black block-heeled shoes. As usual, she carried her black whip and made it pop a few times while the crowd worked itself up into a frenzy. From opposite sides of the rooms, three waitresses passed gray envelopes marked, "Merry Christmas From Pussy Galore. Open now," to the club patrons.

While Cerina worked the crowd, she didn't know she was being worked. She ripped open her uniform and stood there in a black leather bra with a g-string and garter belt. She twirled and tumbled across the stage all while patrons' smiles changed from excitement to confusion to repulsion to anger. She sat in a chair with her legs open while she read what appeared to be the Bible.

"Boo!"

Cerina didn't pay the sound any attention.

"Boo!" This time the singular boo had become a growing chorus of discord. Within seconds, that small chorus had become a catastrophe of voices all yelling, "Boo!" She stood up from her chair and looked out into the crowd with her hands on her hips.

"Shut the fuck up!" she yelled back.

RaChelle smiled.

Temple sat back and watched and wondered what was going on.

"Boo, ya' stank nasty biatch!" a voice yelled out above the others. Balled-up pieces of paper and gray envelopes were hurled at her like baseballs. She ducked and dodged and fought back her anger. And her tears. "Get yo' nasty twat off stage, you sick ho!"

Temple wanted to move, but didn't. RaChelle grabbed his arm.

Balled pieces of paper from every corner and every angle assaulted Cerina as security tried to exert some control over the maddening crowd. She didn't know what was going on until she picked up a piece of paper with her face on it. As soon as she saw it, she wanted to die. All of her business was now everyone's business. The secret she held tight for years had escaped. Everyone knew. She looked out into the angry crowd and tried to run off stage, but she tripped over her whip and tumbled to the stage in a sad display. The crowd continued yelling and throwing things at her until she was able to pick herself up and exit the stage.

Temple stood back in horror. He didn't know what to say or do and wondered what had made the crowd react so violently toward their favorite dancer. RaChelle had been holding onto him to keep him from moving forward; not necessarily out of protection for Cerina. She wanted him to witness the entire scene. She let go and handed him a gray envelope she pulled from her purse.

"You might want to see this, too."

He looked at her fearfully and wondered what was in the envelope.

"What have you done?" he asked.

"This is not about me. You might want to read it."

When Temple opened the envelope, his heart stopped. Time stood still and he almost choked on the words. His head spun and he felt anger and fear unlike he had ever felt before. In fact, his hands trembled as he held the piece of paper.

"I'm sorry you had to find out like this."

He glared at her and gritted his teeth to keep from punching her. He then pushed his way through the crowd, ignoring her calls.

Once he got back in the dressing room, the scene wasn't much better. Cerina had retreated into a corner as a horde of half-naked women yelled and tormented her. Tears stained her face. Her mascara left muddy rivers that streaked down her cheeks.

"I gave this bitch CPR once when she fell out back here!"

"Fuck that! I used the toilet after that trick!"

Temple pushed his way through them and pulled Cerina up by one arm. The anger in his eyes could be seen from across the room.

"Back up!" Temple parted the room by the sheer sound of his voice. He shoved Cerina into a corner in the back and held her shoulders firmly against the wall. He took the crumbled piece of paper in his hand and held it up to her face. His eyes burned with maddening fire and his hot breath singed her eyebrows. All of the fear that she had kept inside suddenly released in a torrent of tears that flowed down her face.

"Shut the fuck up!" He grabbed her by the shoulders and shook her repeatedly as her head bobbed back and forth while hitting the wall. "You better tell me this is a lie or so help me God!" He let the paper fall to the floor and waited for her answer. She found it difficult to even look at the man she loved. Her nightmare had come to life in bold and blinding colors. There was no way to escape it. There was nowhere to hide from the truth.

"Temple, I can explain," she said in between hysterical sobs. "Let me explain."

"Tell me this is a lie. Tell me that you haven't fucked up my life."

"Baby—"

"Tell me this is a fucking lie! Tell me this is RaChelle's idea of a sick joke." The power of his voice shook the room. The girls stood back, wide-eyed and with gaped mouths, and watched her ordeal unfold. Their anger at her had almost been replaced by sympathy. *Almost.*

She wanted to lash out at RaChelle—to curse her and damn her to hell—but the vixen was not around. Cerina's heavy, tear-stained eyes revealed the truth, but she couldn't say the words. Temple needed her to say the words. Through her teary eyes, she looked out at her coworkers and the looks that colored their faces. Then, something in her hardened. She retreated back into the space that had kept her alive so long. She became that person who fought her way through her inner-city high school, who fought back the hands of tricks and johns who tried to skip out on paying her; she found that place that allowed her to survive the abuse her father inflicted and the abandonment by her mother. She looked at Temple again, who waited for her to tell him what he needed to know. He needed to know this was a lie. He needed to know she hadn't given him her disease through their sexual relationship. He needed her to be his savior. He needed her to say three little words. *I'm not positive.* But, those words would never come.

"Please, Cerina. Please tell me you haven't fucked up my life, too!" This time, his voice was weighed with fear and sorrow and pain.

She wiped her snotty face. Through streaming tears, uncontrollable sobs, fear, and hurt she spoke; from that blackened place in her lonely soul, her hurtful words sliced away Temple's assaulting stare. In that moment of brevity, her tears dried and her sobs ceased as apocalyptic words shot from her mouth like toxic smoke smoldering from a pile of burning secrets.

"Your life wasn't worth that much anyway."

She braced for impact.

Instead of punching her like she was expecting, he put his fist through the wall. If he wasn't afraid of her blood, he would've hit her in the face.

CHAPTER 22

B efore sunrise on Christmas Day, Daryl was awake. He loved waking up early on Christmas morning to open gifts before the first morning light—a ritual left over from his childhood where it was customary to be up before six in the morning, opening gifts and playing with toys. Even to this day, he woke early and always woke up Kevin, who had grown unhappily accustomed to his ritual.

By six-thirty, Daryl could no longer contain himself and pulled Kevin out of bed before going into the guestroom to awaken Danea. Daryl rushed into the den and started dividing up the presents underneath the tree. He made three neat little stacks in the middle of the floor; one stack for each of them. For someone who started Christmas shopping at the last minute, he was able to find a lot of things for Kevin and Danea and couldn't wait for them to open the presents. Danea had unloaded her suitcase full of gifts and placed them underneath the tree before she had gone to bed the previous night, so she was happy to see the expressions on their faces when they saw presents from her with their names on it.

"You know you're too old to be this excited," Danea said as she slid into the den in a headscarf, pajamas, and fuzzy slippers.

"You're never too old for Christmas," Daryl replied.

"Baby, it is very early," Kevin said, wiping the sleep from his eyes.

"Y'all need to get into the spirit of things. It's Christmas!" Daryl yelled.

"I think we're fighting a losing battle, Danea. Let's just go with it."

For the next half-hour, they unwrapped everything from sweaters to watches to iPods and everything in between. Daryl hollered in delight each time Kevin's face lit up in excitement at one of his presents. In Kevin's pile, he noticed a plain, letter-sized envelope and tossed it aside until Daryl made him open it. Inside was an itinerary for a trip to Boston at the beginning of April. Kevin looked at the ticket in confusion. Boston wasn't at the top of his list of vacation spots so he couldn't figure out why Daryl wanted to go there. That is, until Daryl knelt before him with a small box. He opened the box and revealed a diamond-studded platinum ring.

"Kevin, all of my life I have waited and dreamed about *the one*. I have dated and loved others, but no one has completed me the way you have. These past few months haven't always been the best, but it was during those times I realized you were the best for me. You make me want to be a better man and I can't imagine my life without you. I'm asking you to spend the rest of your life with me. Will you marry me?"

Danea's eyes grew wide in anticipation of Kevin's words. Kevin looked at his lover, on one knee before him, with tears welling in his eyes. Everything they had been and would be was in that moment. This moment was real. This was their moment—their one moment in time. He couldn't imagine *not* flying off to Massachusetts—the only state with legalized gay marriage—and marrying this man.

"Yes, Daryl, I'll marry you!" As soon as the words were uttered, Danea jumped up and squealed in delight. Kevin kneeled down next to Daryl, who placed the ring on Kevin's finger, and they kissed like it was their first time.

"Oh my God! I can't believe it!" Danea yelled. She seemed happier than either of them. "I'm so happy for guys! Give me a hug!" The three of them hugged, hollered, and danced around the room with glee and celebrated the Christmas miracle.

Although they had papers already drawn up granting each other certain rights, like the ability to make medical decisions for the other and their house was jointly owned, marriage would take it to a new level because D.C. had decided to recognize and grant all marriage rights to gay couples who wed in other places but resided in the District. Once they were married, they'd have to take their paperwork to the proper government agency, and their lives would officially and legally become bound.

"This calls for a celebratory Mimosa," Danea said as she scurried out of the room.

"Wow, I can't believe this," Kevin started. "A short time ago, I was preparing for our break-up and here we are, heading off to get married. Ain't that some shit. It's funny how life can turn on a dime." On the table in the corner was a small gray envelope from RaChelle and the small box.

Fantasies of exotic honeymoon spots filled Kevin's head. He had never given too much thought about the issue of gay marriage. He already felt like he was married to Daryl and a piece of paper wouldn't change his attitude. Yet, the thought of being validated and recognized intrigued him. He looked at the ring on his finger and smiled.

"Oh, Kevin," Danea said as she handed him the envelope and the box from RaChelle. "You didn't open your gifts from the Wicked Witch of Houston." Kevin put down his Mimosa and took the gifts from her.

"I forgot about that. I can't believe she would give me a present. We ain't that close."

"Well, y'all have been pretty close considering she was pregnant with your child once upon a time," Daryl said playfully as he got up from where he sat and decided to put on a little holiday music.

"See, why you gotta bring up old shit?" Kevin shot back playfully. "Silver Bells" sounded from the stereo as the smile from Kevin's face suddenly left. The box simply contained a pair of underwear—a pair he recognized as one he bought for Daryl. Danea put down her drink. Kevin slowly opened the envelope, which contained Cerina's test results.

"Who the fuck is Cerina Ford? Why does RaChelle have a pair of your underwear? Daryl, what's going on here?" Kevin asked, almost frantically. Then, he found and read the other note.

Dear Kevin,

I wish I could see the confused look on your face right now. I'm sure you're thinking what the hell is going on. Well, don't stress out about it. I'll explain.

The pair of dirty underwear you're holding belongs to Daryl. I bet you wanna know where I got them? Well, I got them from Temple. You know Temple, right? He's the man fucking your lover. I believe you've met him before, haven't you? Pretty, ain't he? Now, I really wish I could see the look on your face. Yes, your man has been having an affair. He's been fucked every which way by Temple. Up, down, sideways, on his back, on his stomach, legs in the air. You know how you fags do.

Now, this is the interesting part. Cerina Ford is Temple's girlfriend. And yes, Temple fucks her, too. So, guess what that means? If Temple has been fucking her and Daryl has been fucking Temple and you and Daryl are still doing the nasty, guess what? All you hoes get to share in the same fate!! See, I just wanted you and Daryl to break up. I didn't know about Cerina's "condition." I couldn't have planned this any better. You see how the universe works things out for you? Karma is a bitch. You took my life and now you'll lose yours.

Ho, Ho, Ho, Merry Christmas

P.S. You might want to see a doctor really soon.

"Daryl, what have you done?" was the first thing Daryl really heard. Danea's frantic voice was filled with concern. Kevin sat immobile on the couch, looking up at Daryl as he read the note.

"Baby, listen. Let me explain."

"The only thing you need to tell me is this note is a lie. This isn't true."

"Baby—"

"Baby, nothing! Did you or did you not fuck that motherfucker?" Kevin shot up in a flash and was inches from Daryl's face. "Look me in the eyes and tell me the truth. Have you put my fucking health in danger?"

"Kevin, I didn't know. It only happened once. It was that night I stayed in the hotel overnight." Before Kevin even realized it, he had struck Daryl in the face, who tripped over the presents and landed on the floor. Daryl held his jaw as he looked up into the twisted face of his lover.

"Get out! Get out! Get the fuck outta here before I kill you!"

Daryl had never seen the face of rage until now. Kevin's face was warped into a caricature of what it used to be. Somehow, his expanding features pulsated as his red-hot emotions flashed and burned away any merriment the holiday brought. The scowl on his brow dug deep into his face like trenches on a great battlefield. His fists were tightly wound and ready to pound again at the slightest provocation. He towered over his fallen Daryl and glared down at his traitor as disease-infected thoughts blurred his vision. *Lies. Deceit. Betrayal.* Thoughts of lustful duplicity burned his spirit to gray, crumbling ashes that disintegrated into the nothingness of his now-vacant soul and lit a fiery rage within that consumed all rational thought and feeling. At this moment, in the ignited, blue-flamed, twisted and heated night, there was no room for rational thought. In this moment of ultimate betrayal, violence threatened to burn the house down.

Daryl had never seen such pain in Kevin. He knew at that moment Kevin would be capable of the unthinkable and the unspeakable and he did not want to press his luck. He did not want to light that bomb. If he exploded, there would be casualties. Danea stood back, her arms folded and with tears in her eyes.

"Daryl," she simply said in a piercing whisper that carried far more weight than his name. When he heard his name on her lips—the way it sounded wrapped in sadness—he could not prevent tears from falling from his eyes. He rose slowly and held his head low. All was lost. Their love died in that instant. The life they had built together for years was swept away in a torrent of emotions caused by Daryl's fleshy weakness. He wanted to say something to ease Kevin's burden but no apology would ever suffice. There were no words that fit his crime and there would be no forgiveness. Not in this moment.

"Baby, you don't have to worry about your health. We used condoms," he said in a voice that would forever echo in Kevin's heart.

CHAPTER 23

Daryl drove around the city aimlessly while his heart continued to break into jagged pieces of fragmented love. Each time he thought he was feeling the worst, a jarring pain in his chest told him that pain was boundless. He tried to swallow the bitter pill of his bitter reality as he drove blindly through the barren and broken streets, but the pungent reality that he had lost the best love he would *ever* know stuck in his throat. In his young life, he had dealt with many tragedies, including the death of both of his parents, but this death felt like a knife wound that pierced through his entire body. As much as he tried to cover his wounded spirit with his hands, the blood continued to flow in powerful red gushes. This wasn't his idea of a Merry Christmas.

Daryl had been cast out of his heaven like the fallen angel and the empty streets of D.C. became his companion. He drove on the frozen roadways, over the bridges, near the White House, and around the Washington Monument all in an effort to forget, but everything he saw reminded him of his betrayal—he couldn't escape it. It was everywhere. It shone in the ash-gray sky and the hollow eyes of strangers he passed on the streets. The wind carried his treachery on its icy lips like a kiss of death. It was a part of the landscape and it was all he could see on the dull horizon. He wanted to run, but the guilt would overtake him; even if he sprinted. He wanted to hide, but the pain would seek him. He wanted to yell, but he had no voice. So, he drove. Without direction. Void of purpose.

He had called Temple three times in the last fifteen minutes but only got his voice mail. As angry as he was at Temple, the blame was his to bear. He was the one who invited Temple over to the room that night. It was he who initiated the sexual contact. He did it all. And, he was responsible for his ruined life and for hurting the one person who would walk through the fire with him. Why he had lost control over someone who didn't matter, he didn't know.

Things would never be the same. It was only now, at the end of things, that he knew. As he curved through the narrow streets, he thought about all the conversations Kevin had started in an effort to fix their sick relationship. Kevin suggested counseling, suggested choosing one day a week they would dedicate to each other, suggested taking a weekend trip to the mountains, but all those things Daryl rebuffed because he was too busy *working out* with Temple or flirting on the Internet. Sure, his body looked good, but his soul bled. The price he paid for the flirtations with Amir and the cost of Temple's touches proved to be far too high. Going in, he assumed the risks. It didn't *just* happen. Yet, he gambled anyway. And lost. You always have to pay the price of your actions.

❊❊❊

By the evening, the sun had almost finished its slow trek across the sky and darkness was set to be the new order. Danea waited for Kevin to emerge from the confines of his room, where he had locked himself since he threw Daryl out. She placed her ear to the door as she knocked, but didn't hear any sounds. She hoped he was sleeping, but there was no way to be sure. She knocked again; still no answer. She called out his name but her voice seemed to fall on deaf ears. She was beginning to worry.

"Kevin," she called out once again as she banged on the door. Her shaky voice carried her concern through the thick door.

On the other side of the door, her voice finally connected with Kevin, who looked toward the door. He had been sitting in the chair, gazing out of the window for the last few hours. He had barely moved and his mind was blank. Christmas had started off so wonderfully with gifts and proposals of marriage, then it suddenly exploded into a winter nightmare. He sat in silence and listened to D.C.'s symphony play its familiar song. That symphony, as D.C. residents knew, wasn't music at all: it was the constant sound of sirens from emergency vehicles that filled the days and nights like an urban sonata. The sirens that blared on this Christmas evening seemed louder and closer than usual. Kevin got up from the chair and walked quietly over to the door. It was almost as if he was gliding on shattered emotions. Everything seemed so surreal. He placed his hand on the knob and watched his hand turn it to open the door. Even that simple motion felt out of place. Danea rushed into the room and immediately threw her arms around him. She had no words of solace or consolation to offer.

Then, Kevin began to speak. "My life is over."

"No, it's not," she said as released her hold. "You have so much to live for. I know it doesn't seem like it right now, but this, too, shall pass."

"Please, spare me the tired clichés. I can't believe he would do this to me. It seems so unreal."

"Kevin, have you thought about RaChelle? That bitch had a lot to do with this. I mean, she delivered the note and the underwear. I think she set up the entire thing."

"I've thought about that, but she didn't make Daryl have sex with Temple. She may have set the stage, but the decision to play the part was all Daryl's. Fuck RaChelle and fuck Daryl." He moved over to the bed and shook his head. "But, that's not even my main concern. What if, because of Daryl, I'm positive? I don't know what he did with Temple and even though he said they used condoms, how do I know he's telling the truth? He's been lying to me for weeks so why should I think he'd tell the truth about this?"

She had no words. She moved over to him and rubbed his hand, hoping her touch would ease this burden.

"Now, I have to get tested and even if it comes back negative, I've got the next six months or longer to worry. I hate him so much."

"You don't hate him, but you hate what he's done, and so do I. I believe him when he said he used condoms. He couldn't be that dumb. He wouldn't jeopardize his health and life like that, so I don't think you should worry about that."

"That's easy for you to say."

The sudden sound of the ringing telephone startled Danea, but Kevin didn't flinch. He thought it might be Daryl calling to apologize to throw himself on Kevin's mercy. For Kevin, there would be no mercy and no forgiveness. *None.* He wanted to tell her to let it ring, but she quickly snatched the phone from its base.

"Hello? No, I'm sorry Kevin is unavailable. Is there something that I can help you with?" When Danea yelled and dropped the phone, Kevin realized something was wrong. "Danea, what is it? Is it Daryl? Is he alright?"

"Grab your coat. We've got to go."

❀❀❀

Kevin completely zoned out of the conversation as he listened to the fire chief tell Danea that the blaze had been too intense for them to save most of the building. The chief surmised that some flammable liquid or incendiary device had been used which contributed to the intensity and the ferocity of the fire that destroyed Jose's. Kevin stood on the corner of Eighth Street in Eastern Market, alongside a small crowd of people that had come to witness the Christmas carnage, and looked at the rubble that used to be his restaurant. He couldn't conjure up the appropriate feelings or indignation that would be appropriate for the destruction. He wanted to yell, but it simply wasn't in him. He thought he should fall to the ground and scream like he had seen the folks do on television whenever there was a horrific and life-altering event. He even thought about pulling a Florida Evans and screaming, "Damn, Damn, Damn," but that would be far too contrived. Everything that he had was now gone—including Daryl—but the invocation of those kinds of soul-draining emotions was not something he could do; the emotions simply weren't there. He was drained. His relationship and his business were both destroyed by the heat of the flame. The smoldering pile of debris reflected the way he felt, and it spoke in far more dramatic terms than Kevin ever could express.

"I'm sorry for your loss," the fireman said as he walked away.

"Shit happens," Kevin replied under his breath. Danea looked at the glassy look in Kevin's eyes. She wasn't convinced this tragedy had registered with Kevin.

"Kevin? Kevin?" she said. "Kevin!"

"What? Shit, stop yelling. I ain't deaf."

"You're scaring me."

"Don't be scared. I'm okay. Well, this certainly has been the most memorable Christmas I have ever had," he said sardonically. "I can't wait for New Year's." As Danea hugged him, she saw Daryl rushing through the crowd. She released Kevin and pointed to Daryl, who was approaching.

"Damn, did you call him?"

"No, I didn't, but he's here for you. Let him be there for you."

"Fuck him."

"Kevin, are you okay? What's going on?" Daryl said as he looked at what was left of the restaurant. "What happened?" he asked as if the day's earlier events had been forgotten.

"We don't know yet. The fire department is still investigating," Danea offered. "I'll be right back." She wanted to talk to the fire chief again but also wanted to give them time alone.

"I am so sorry, Kevin."

"Yes, you are."

"Is there anything I can do?"

"Haven't you done enough to me already?"

"Kevin—"

"Don't say my name." Kevin stared at him.

"Baby—"

"And certainly don't call me baby. I'm not your baby."

"What am I supposed to call you, then?"

"Don't ever call me. How about that? You'll have to excuse me. I need to call my doctor for an AIDS test."

Kevin walked away in a huff and joined Danea while she was interrogating the fire chief. Daryl stood back and watched and waited and hoped for some sign—some invitation—to be a part of the conversation, but he wasn't going to push it. When Kevin glanced back at Daryl, he shot him a look of pure disgust that made Daryl feel like less than nothing. Even still, Daryl felt compelled to help, to do or say something—as he had always done—to ease Kevin's pain. However, they had been through so much on this day. Kevin needed space and time, but his paternalistic nature wanted to take care of Kevin and make everything all right. No amount of wishing or hoping was going to turn back the hands of time and erase this merry Christmas.

CHAPTER 24

T he day after the fire, the demise of Jose's had very little effect on the life of the city. The sounds of car horns and screeching vehicles careening down the narrow streets awakened Kevin from his restless night. Outside his window, the motorized sound of a snow blower could be heard over the customary sounds of emergency vehicles. Out of habit, he reached over to put his arms around Daryl, but the emptiness of the bed brought back the memories of the past day. He leapt up and hopped into the shower, hoping the water would wash away the blues.

Thoughts of a love lost, a flaming building and disease filled his head. The warm water continued to stream over his body and he continued to be assaulted from a thousand different angles. All at once, he felt suffocated and enraged and frightened by his new reality. With everything that had happened, his most troubling thought was the test he needed to take. He stood underneath the shower and his mind was focused on taking the test. He could not imagine what he would do if it came back positive. A part of him really believed Daryl when he said they had used condoms, but how could he believe any words that left his mouth? He felt like a time bomb had been placed in his bloodstream and was simply waiting for the right moment to detonate. He had never known such fear.

By midday, Kevin had said very little to Danea about anything; in spite of her attempts to share his pain and ease his burden. There were times during the day when tears stained her cheeks, and she walked around with a small towel to wipe her face when the waterworks started. She tried to be strong for him, but she felt as if a part of her had died as well. She was a living witness to the destruction of the best relationship she had ever known and it was taking a toll on her. She had always imagined they'd be together forever. She wished there was something she could say or do to make things better, but she was powerless. She tried to pull herself together so she could be strong when Kevin needed it. The silence that filled the house was weighed with worry. She watched him moved back and forth casually from room to room as if today was an ordinary day.

The more she pressed, the more he shut down. When they did speak, it wasn't about Daryl or the fire, but usually about the upcoming party. His words were brief and his voice was strained. He asked her if she was ready to perform and inquired about the arrival date of her backup singers. In spite of the personal tragedies, he wanted to make sure she was ready to give the performance of a lifetime and that everything at the masquerade ball would come off without a hitch. Kevin spoke with the event planner, Desiree, at length, and everything was on track. Danea's dancers would be arriving the day before the event so they could have a couple of rehearsals, but they had done the show a thousand times before so she wasn't worried about it. She was worried about Kevin.

"Kevin, are we going to talk about this?"

"About what?" he asked as he peered at her from around his computer monitor. "There's nothing really to talk about. All I know is that I've got a big party coming up in a few days and there are a million things to do."

"Daryl called again," she offered softly.

"So."

"You can't pretend like nothing has happened."

"Why not? Why can't I simply go on living my life without a care in the world? Why do I have to deal with this fucked-up reality?" His stare bore a hole through her heart. She knew exactly from where he was speaking, and it was a place born from pain and nurtured in misery. His words rang with thunder and lightning and he felt poised to strike out at anything and everything. "I can't let some cheating-ass man fuck up my party. Or my life."

"Kevin," she said softly as she stepped into his office and moved over to the chair against the wall. "You don't have to do this alone."

"See, that's where you're wrong. I am alone."

She struggled to keep her composure. The last thing she wanted to do was fall apart in his presence, but the weight of his words was almost too much for her to bear. She was the strong one. She was the one who was always together. She had to hold on to that for him. *And for herself.*

"I know it feels like you're alone, but you have me. I'll always be there for you. And you can't bury yourself in work. You've got to deal with everything. I know, I know, it's a shitty deal, but you can't ignore it."

"Danea, I have nothing. Daryl is gone. My business has been burned to the fucking ground. And yes, my health may be gone, too. So, do me a big favor. I want you to sit there and tell me how to deal with that shit." He folded his arms and waited for her response.

"I wish I had all the answers. I wish I could tell you that tomorrow everything will be better, but I can't. There's so much to deal with, but I can tell you that you can—we can—get through all of this. But, we have to take this one step at a time."

"Uh-huh. I don't know what kind of karmic hell I'm paying for this time around. When I was with James, he used to kick my ass on the regular and that was fine. I thought I deserved it because I blamed myself for Keevan's death. But, I don't deserve this bullshit with Daryl and the rest of the crap that has been dumped in my lap. I have been perfectly good to that man and how does he repay me? By fucking every Tom, Dick and Temple."

"Have you contacted the insurance company about the fire?" she asked, changing the subject. She wanted him to get his mind off Daryl; even if for only a moment.

"When it rains, it pours. I called them and those bitches told me my policy had been cancelled for nonpayment and that I need to fax them proof of payment before they can take any action. I know Mr. Martinez sent payment weeks ago, but I can't check the books because they were in the fire. I called the fucking bank and they can't find proof of payment either so I'mma have to go up to the bank at some point today. I've left Mr. Martinez two messages but he ain't called me back yet." Danea was happy to hear that he had taken some steps to deal with the harsh reality. "But, the fucked-up part is that I have this really bad feeling. I mean, what if he didn't pay the policy? The way my luck is going these days, that wouldn't surprise me at all."

"Don't sweat that. If he was that irresponsible, I'm sure you wouldn't have him working for you. I'm sure he's going to call you today."

"Danea, he was scheduled to open the restaurant a few hours ago and I haven't heard from him. None of this makes any sense."

"You don't think—"

"What, that he burned down the restaurant? Hell, I don't know what to think. All I know is the fire has been all over the news, he was supposed to open the restaurant today, and now, all of a sudden, he's ghost. I have a bad feeling."

"None of this makes any sense. All of this shit happened on the same day. I swear to you that RaChelle has a lot to do with this."

"I've been thinking about that, but why would she want to do any of this?"

"You can't rationalize crazy. That bitch is a loon and it wouldn't surprise me if she burned down the restaurant herself."

"I think it's time I paid a visit to Ms. Roland."

"You mean *we*."

❀❀❀

When they walked into the spacious lobby of the hotel, Kevin marched directly to the desk and asked for RaChelle's room number. Instead of providing the requested information, the clerk called her room, but it simply rang. At least she had not checked out and was still lurking around the city somewhere. Kevin took a seat in a chair in the corner and Danea joined him.

"I don't care how long it takes; I'm waiting for her ass. I'm going to get some answers today."

"She's not going to admit anything, I'm sure," Danea said.

"She will. If she is behind this, she'll want me to know. I'm sure she wants to gloat. She's trying to take my life and I won't let her. I have been through too much and worked too hard."

He and Danea sat in the grand lobby of the hotel and watched patrons enter and exit the building. The hotel was bristling with activity. The bellhops were busy with carrying bags, the front counter clerks were overcome by a vanload of passengers checking in, and the concierge was swamped with questions from the hotel guests who wanted to know how to get to restaurants and what the city nightlife had to offer. In the midst of the flurry of activity, Kevin and Danea patiently waited for RaChelle. Time crept by as Kevin's anger and curiosity rose. Why was she doing this to him?

Three hours later, they saw her enter the lobby. She strutted into the room as if she was a celebrity, with her attitude preceding her. Kevin eyed her with contempt as she walked toward the elevator. With cat-like movements, he leapt up from where he sat and accosted her. She was startled by his sudden approach.

"Kevin, darling, how are you?" she asked as she air-kissed him. "Oh, I meant to call you when I heard about the fire at Jose's. That's so tragic. I hope your insurance pays for everything," she said with a coy wink. "Now, what brings you here?" She turned and faced Danea. "Oh, hi, Danea," she said plainly as she rolled her eyes.

"I need to talk to you; right now." He grabbed her by the arm and snatched her into a corner.

"Hey, you're hurting my arm. I don't appreciate you man-handling me like this. The last time you did, I ended up pregnant, remember? What is your problem?"

"My problem is you. I know what you've been up to and it won't work."

She scowled. "What have I been up to? I'd like to hear this."

"You set Daryl up with Temple and you burned down my restaurant, you vicious bitch."

"Stop with the name-calling. It's so junior high. Why would you think I would do something like that to you? That's ridiculous."

"You think you're so smart, don't you? Don't make me slap that smile off your face," Danea said.

"Can you tell your pitbull to sit down? This has nothing to do with her," she said to Kevin.

Danea made a sudden move toward RaChelle and Kevin had to restrain her as a couple of people in their immediate vicinity raised their eyebrows as their voices rose.

"I know you're behind all of this shit," he said. RaChelle didn't respond verbally. Instead, she lifted her head proudly and looked into his eyes. In the glare that she gave him, everything was revealed. "Why are you doing this to me?"

"I will kick yo' ass, bitch," Danea said in an excited tone.

"Danea, sit down and let me handle this."

Danea looked at Kevin and realized he meant business. This was his fight so she took a few steps to the left, but remained close enough to hear the entire conversation.

"You always try to blame your problems on someone else. For once, be a man and take responsibility for your life. I mean, is it really my fault your man is so easy? You can't blame me 'cause he's a ho." She chuckled. "And, if your *little* restaurant burned to the ground, how is that my fault? You should be blaming Mr. Martinez; not me. You should really be more careful about the people you let work for you."

When she spoke of Mr. Martinez, her eyes tightened into a squint. She was ready to lay it all out on the table. Kevin thought about all of the conversations he had had with Mr. Martinez about renewing the policy. He trusted his manager to do it and thought it had been done, but somehow RaChelle had gotten to him. All of the little jabs and comments he would make about Kevin and the restaurant all made sense. Evidently, he was still bitter about Kevin buying the restaurant in the first place. Kevin was enraged.

"What do you want from me? What have I done to you to deserve all of this?" he yelled. Again, folks in the hotel turned their heads in his direction.

"Like you don't fucking know, you lying faggot! You took my child and my life away!" RaChelle yelled back, unable to keep her erratic emotions in balance. "And everything that has happened to you has been well-deserved for what you did to me!"

"I didn't intentionally set out to hurt you. You were the one who kept coming on to me!"

"Oh, you didn't mean to fuck me? Oh, it's not your fault I was in the church the day of the fire and lost my baby and almost my life? Well, since you didn't mean to do anything, all is forgiven," she said with thick sarcasm.

"You won't get away with any of this."

"Darling, I've already gotten away with it. And, if you think what's happened is bad, wait until you see what's coming."

"I want you to look into my eyes and know that you will pay for this. If you ever come near me, Daryl or Danea again, I'll fuckin' kill you! Do you understand me?"

She chuckled. "Look at you; all dressed up in big brother's clothes. Oh, wait, I forgot. Your big brother is dead."

"Fuck you!" It took all of his strength not to slap the smirk off her face.

"No, fuck you!"

"Excuse me. Is there a problem here?" asked the hotel manager who had been alerted to the confrontation by a concerned guest. In the midst of their conversation, neither of them had seen him approach.

"No, everything is fine. We were about to leave," Danea said as she took Kevin by the hand.

"Just know that this is not over," Kevin said to RaChelle before Danea led him out of the building.

CHAPTER 25

The ride home from the hotel was filled with anger and curse words directed at Kevin's nemesis. Danea was speaking, but Kevin wasn't listening. In all of the yelling and threats, Kevin realized he had severely underestimated the extent and the depth of her hurt and rage. She had clearly devoted a lot of time and energy into launching this diabolical plot of revenge. She had waited over three years to strike and that had given her plenty of time to plan out every little detail. He had to take her seriously when she indicated there was more to come. What more could she possibly do? She had destroyed his relationship and his business. What was left for her to destroy? The fact that he and Daryl were having issues long before she burst onto the stage made her job that much simpler.

When they pulled into the parking spot in front of his house, there were two people walking down the steps leading from his house. The man, dressed in a long gray trench coat with a very thin face, appeared to be in his late-forties and Kevin could see the gray in his beard from the curb. The white lady accompanying him stood about 5'4" with reddish-blonde hair.

"May I help you?" Kevin asked as he approached the couple, hoping they were from the insurance company.

"You can if you're Kevin Davis," the man said with a deep bravado.

"I am."

"Good. I'm Detective Shields and this is my partner Detective Mahoney. We're with the Arson Unit of the Metropolitan Police Department. May we have a word?"

In one seemingly coordinated gesture, they both reached into the left pocket of their trench coats, pulled out badges and flashed them at Kevin and Danea.

"We were wondering when you guys were going to show up," Danea said. "We've been waiting."

"Sorry for the delay, ma'am. We've been pretty busy the last couple of days."

"I'm sure," Danea said skeptically.

Once they entered the house, Kevin offered to take the coats from his visitors, but they declined. He then led them upstairs into the den and offered them a seat, which they also declined. Danea took her place in the chaise lounge by the window. She listened and watched the routine of the detectives as they shot off questions about the fire. Their staged routine was almost comedic as they alternated questions and wrote notes on matching blue pads.

"What reason do you have to suspect this RaChelle Roland was involved?" Detective Shields asked as he shot his partner a curious look.

"We just left her hotel and she practically admitted to it," Danea interjected.

"Practically?" Detective Mahoney asked. "What did she say?"

"It was more of what she didn't say," Kevin said. "She's out to get me. She'll do anything to destroy my life."

"She's crazy—certifiably insane," Danea said.

"Let me get this straight," Detective Shields started. "This woman, whom you impregnated three years ago, has now come back to destroy your life? And, you think she bribed your restaurant manager to not pay your insurance so she could then burn down your restaurant and leave you penniless?" Detective Mahoney chuckled.

"Is there something funny, detective?" Danea asked with a measurable amount of attitude.

"It sounds a bit far-fetched," she replied.

"Look, I know how all of this sounds, but it's true."

"Do you have any proof?"

"What, you think I have a video of her burning down my spot? You think she stopped for a Polaroid with a can of lighter fluid and a match outside Jose's? I don't have it yet, but I will," Kevin snapped.

"Leave the detective work to us," Detective Mahoney said. "I do have a question for you. I understand that you're raising money for a project called, let's see, Keevan's Room. How is that going?"

"What does that have to do with anything?" Kevin asked suspiciously.

"How close are you to raising all of the money you need?"

"I still don't see the relevance," Kevin said.

Danea jumped to her feet. "Wait a damned minute. I hope you're not implying what I think you are," she said sternly. "That is completely preposterous."

"We're not implying anything," Detective Mahoney said. "We're merely asking questions."

"This is ridiculous. If you think Kevin destroyed his own restaurant in order to collect insurance money for Keevan's Room, you seriously need to have your heads examined."

"What the fuck?" Kevin exclaimed.

"We didn't say anything like that," Detective Shields replied. "I think we have all the information we need right now. And, thanks for providing information about RaChelle. We'll go and talk to her now."

"Detectives," Danea said, "I really think you need to thoroughly investigate this woman and not spend time spinning your wheels on Kevin. Right now, we can't even verify that his insurance policy is current and if he was going to burn down Jose's for money, of course he'd make sure his policy was paid. Don't waste your time here. Investigate RaChelle and you'll find out everything you need, if you're good."

"We appreciate your input," Mahoney said as she followed her partner down the stairs. "We'll keep you abreast of any significant developments."

Kevin walked with them downstairs and locked the door behind them. There were so many thoughts swirling around his head that he was getting a headache. Too much was going on and RaChelle's lastest threat concerned him. What else did she have planned for him?

"Kevin, we've got a problem," Danea started when Kevin reached the top of the stairs. "I don't have a good feeling about that conversation. And, I don't like the way she was looking at you and asking you questions. We've got to find a way to prove RaChelle is behind all of this before they really think you're responsible for the fire. I don't have a lot of faith in police departments these days."

"Yeah, I didn't get a good feeling about any of it, either. The question then becomes how do we prove it?"

"We've got to find Mr. Martinez."

Just then, the phone rang and Kevin picked it up. Immediately, he recognized the voice

"What do you want, Daryl?"

"I wanted to check on you."

"How sweet. Thanks for calling, but I'm really busy."

Click.

"Kevin," Danea said.

"Don't start," he said as he put his finger up.

"I have an idea. Let's go to church in the morning. This is certainly a time for God."

❀❀❀

Danea walked out of the guestroom wearing a nice black dress complemented by a white blazer and three-inch black heels. On top of her head sat a huge black and white church lady hat with a big round brim and a veil. She looked like she had stepped out of a soap opera. Danea was hoping she could be discreet in church and that her celebrity status wouldn't be a distraction. After everything he had been through, Kevin definitely needed some church in his life. She stood at the bottom of the stairs and called up to Kevin as if she was his mother trying to get her child into the car so they wouldn't be late for Sunday School.

When Danea was out of town, she always made it a point to attend somebody's church and during her frequent visits to D.C. she had found an inviting church in Prince George's County; right across the District line. It wasn't a huge congregation, but they were a spirited bunch and made Danea feel welcomed each time she worshipped there. Upon her first visit, Pastor Stanley announced her presence and actually asked her to sing a song. When she did, the congregation rejoiced in the joy that was her voice. She hoped that today she could slip in, unnoticed, and blend with the congregation.

On the way to the church, they didn't speak much; instead opting to let the gospel music from the radio fill the air. They had so many thoughts about what was going on that even the powerful sounds of the music failed to block images of RaChelle. Kevin hoped he would find some comfort in the Word today because, more than anything, he needed strength, peace of mind, and clarity of thought. He kept thinking about that old saying, "Let go and let God." He wanted to turn it all over to God, but wasn't sure how. It had been some time since he had been to church and he wondered if he prayed, would God listen to his cries.

When they arrived at the church, they parked the car and walked into the hallowed sanctuary. The room, dimly lit by several chandeliers hanging from the ceiling, felt warm and inviting. It made Kevin smile as they walked deeper into the interior. He was already feeling a sense of comfort.

They walked through a densely populated room to cushioned blue seats in the corner toward the front of the room. It was barely 9:00 a.m. and service didn't start until 9:15. Danea liked to be early. They were quite impressed that so many people had showed up early instead of the stereotypical lateness of black people that had come to be known as CPT—colored people's time. Kevin recognized the gentleman who sat in front of the organ from a couple of gay parties he had attended. When the man saw Kevin, he smiled, nodded his head in tacit acknowledgment and Kevin did likewise.

Danea grabbed Kevin's hand and smiled. "This'll be good for you," she said as she clung on to hope. "All you have to do is have faith."

"Yeah, you might be right." Kevin had never been one to regularly attend church, but that didn't diminish his belief in a higher power. He had always thought that church was far too organized, far too politicized and sometimes very polarizing. Instead of coming to church and getting the Word, trivial things such as what folks were wearing often distracted people. He also thought church gossip that spread like a virus throughout the congregation diminished the experience for him. As he looked around the room, he hoped this experience would be different and that people who came were really there to praise God. They took their seats in front of a couple of younger-looking ladies who giggled like they were at a party instead of church.

"Girl, I heard Pastor invited Reverend Dean back to preach this week," one of the ladies said. "Who is that?"

"You know, the one from North Carolina. Real scary-lookin'—the one who can't never keep no wife. Ev'rytime he come here, he got a new woman."

Daryl tried not to laugh at the girl who sounded like that animated ghetto character Cita who used to be on some BET show.

"See, you wrong for that," the other said as they broke out into laughter. "Yeah, I don't really like him. I don't know why Pastor keeps asking him back. If I had known he was preaching, I woulda went to church wit my mama."

"Sharita, gurl, is that Danea in front of us? You know, the singer?" she asked in a voice that wasn't anything near a whisper.

Danea, in her periphery, could see the other girl stretching her neck to get a look at her. She ignored her and continued her conversation with Kevin.

"The pastor is really good. He's pretty young and the first lady of the church is very nice. I think you'll enjoy the service," Danea said. As she finished her sentence, three women and three men dressed in black took center stage. The pianist started playing and the group started singing. They sang an upbeat song and the energy generated by the song was electric. Folks started wildly clapping and shouting as if the Lord was hard of hearing. Kevin looked at Danea, but she pretended not to notice his gaze.

"When folks get full of the spirit, sometimes they gotta let it out," Danea said with a chuckle, as a way of allaying his concerns. A song that should have lasted about five minutes was stretched into twenty minutes. Then a soloist took center stage and belted out a tune that brought tears to the eyes of the congregation. Kevin kept his eyes fixated upon one of the ladies who originally sang because she was really caught up in the spirit. Anytime there was a scream or an "amen" or "hallelujah," it came from her. During much of the song, she was laid out prostrate on the floor; screaming and speaking in tongues and shouting praises. Again, Kevin looked at Danea who shook her head. The lady apparently was having a fit and when she rose up, she started dancing and running around the church. Within seconds, others followed until there was a line of parishioners running throughout the room like the aisles were part of a track.

"What are they doing? Jogging for Jesus?" Kevin whispered to Danea who quickly silenced him as she tried to mask her laughter with song. "What's really going on? I guess in order to attend service here you need to be able to run three miles. I wonder if you get a free membership to Bally Total Fitness when you join."

"Shhhhh, be quiet and enjoy the service," Danea said, trying not to laugh.

"They are a lively bunch, aren't they?" he asked. Suddenly, he felt a blow to his back and, when they turned around, one of the young ladies was spinning in circles and shouting toward the heavens like a woman possessed. Then, she fell out in the chair with her limbs spread out. The ushers rushed over to her aid and started fanning her and shaking her, but the rest of the church didn't miss a beat. Danea tried hard to not snicker because of the priceless expression of shock on Kevin's face.

Finally, the energy in the room subsided as the attractive pastor took his place behind the pulpit. He stood there, smiling out at the sea of stimulated faces. He started his sermon. And, he preached a good word about the value of hard work and how God has attached a blessing to that hard work. He pointed out the difference between working hard and doing hard work, and the crowd clung to each of his powerful and inspiring words. Right when they thought the sermon was over, the pastor introduced a visiting preacher from North Carolina. The older gentleman rose to his feet and stepped with deliberate authority to the pulpit. He stood menacingly in front of the eager room, surveying the landscape, giving the congregation a moment to take in his formidable presence. Kevin didn't get a good feeling. When the preacher began to speak, his voice carried a booming bass as if he were trying to command the heavens themselves to part with his words.

"Ladies and gentlemen, let me tell you about hard work. I grew up working the fields in North Carolina underneath a blazing Southern summer sun, my back bent over, my fingers aching and the sweat running from my brow. I didn't complain one time because, like your pastor said, I realized God had attached a blessing to that hard work. That hard work helped put food on the table so we didn't go hungry. It helped put clothes on our backs so we weren't naked. It was hard, but it was a blessing because we didn't go hungry or naked. Nowadays, folks don't believe in working hard. They like to duck and dodge the hard stuff," he said as he moved his body the way a boxer would in the ring. "Back in the day when men were men and women were women, we used to have pretty women and hard-working men. Nowadays, we got hard-working women and pretty men." The congregation rose to its feet at his words. A feeling of dread, in the house of the Lord, suddenly presented itself to Kevin.

"Oh, Lord, if this is going where I think it's going, we're outta here," Kevin said to Danea.

"Nowadays, folks are working for the wrong thing. Working for that new car. Slaving for that new pair of shoes. Working their fingers to the bone so they can be better than their neighbors. Working two jobs to pay a mortgage on a bigger house. Working hard to uphold the killing of babies before they leave their mama's belly. Sweating while they out marching trying to keep God outta schools. Wasting their energy on trying to pass rights for the homosexuals. What sense does that make? Ain't none of that mess gonna be blessed by God!" When he spoke, he jumped up and down in excitement and the fevered pitched of his fiery words raced through the church at lightning speed. "What kind of rights do the homosexuals need? They want to have a right to work in your school with your children. They want to have a right to live next door to you and want to have a right to come into your house with their filthy ways. I ain't gonna live next door to no faggot because when God strikes down that house, I don't want to be hit in the crossfire! They need to be taken out and horsewhipped like my daddy used to do me when I did something that wasn't pleasing in the eyes of God."

Once again, the church greeted his words with thunderous applause. Kevin nudged Danea. He felt ambushed by the harshness of the minister's attack. He looked at the organist, who sat with his arms folded and his head bowed. Kevin wanted to tell him that he could pretend to not hear the words, but that wouldn't do anyone any good. The preacher paused long enough for the shouts to subside and for the congregation to sit.

"This is some bullshit. We shouldn't have come. It's always the same thing. I'm outta here," Kevin said out loud, much to the chagrin of the lady to his left. As Kevin listened to the preacher's words, he felt something manifesting itself inside of him. This had been a week from hell and he had hoped by coming to church, he could be washed in the blood so he could find the strength to stave off RaChelle's merciless attacks. Instead of finding peace, he felt blindsided by hate. *In God's house.*

When they got up to leave, Danea dropped her purse and a lot of her belongings fell into the aisle; causing a minor scene. The pastor stopped preaching, clearly disturbed by the noise they made. He was not the type of man who liked to be interrupted and, at his home church in North Carolina, the parishioners knew not to walk out or even get up during his ceremony because of the fear of God he instilled.

"Is there a problem here, my young brother and sister? I know you aren't leaving during my sermon," he said, directing unexpected attention toward them.

"Yes, we are leaving," Danea said in defiance as she put the remaining items back into her purse.

"Was it something I said, young lady? Are you running from the truth?"

"No, we simply don't need to sit here and listen to you rant and rave about things you're not compassionate enough to understand!" Kevin shouted as he stepped forward. He had had about enough of the hate.

"It's not merely what you said; it's this entire experience. Every time I come to church I'm forced sit and listen to some *minister* spew hate from the pulpit under the guise of it being the Word of God. I've had a very bad week and I was hoping to feel the love of God here, but you're twisting that love and His Word into something wicked. Is homosexuality the only *so-called* sin in the Bible? Surely there are people still out there fornicating, committing murder, lying, and stealing, too. Yet, I never hear any one of you ministers condemn the liar or the adulterer with the same fire and brimstone. It's like ministers today only have one thing on their minds and, quite frankly, I'm sick of it."

"Young man, homosexuality is an abomination in the eyes of our Lord and the homosexual is destined to the fires of hell," the preacher retorted. "It is something that we cannot tolerate and we will not sit by and watch them pervert our nation and our children with their homosexual agenda."

"So, you think the way to counter this homosexual agenda—whatever that is—is to instill hate within the hearts of people? With all your holier-than-thou words, you think you can erase Jesus's message of tolerance and love? All I hear you yelling about is hating people. Where is the love that is the central tenet of Christianity? Do you have any idea of the kind of violence gay people have to put up with because people like *you* tell folks it's okay to hate people who aren't like them? Do you have any idea how many children are tortured and ultimately commit suicide because people like *you* tell them they're going to hell? Do you know how many men and women have been murdered or beaten and left for dead in the streets of this nation because people like *you* give open approval for people to hate an entire group of people they don't know? You, dear Reverend, don't have the power to send me to Hell or anywhere else." Kevin stepped a bit closer and took a position near the organist. "I'm

amazed that all of you don't find the words of this man and men and women like him contradictory to the Word of God," he said to the room. "You think it's okay to tell everyone
in this room to hate me and people like me and they don't even know me," he said to the
minister, who took a cloth and wiped his face. Danea watched Kevin become transformed.
This week had been over the top and clearly he felt the need to stand up for himself.

"Son, change your wicked ways before it's too late," the preacher commanded as he pointed
at Kevin with his long, curved black finger. "Change your ways. Leviticus says it is an abomination. You can't change the Word of God to fit your evil ways. The Word of God is unchang-
ing. Leviticus, chapter eighteen, verse twenty-two, says, *'Thou shalt not lie with mankind, as
with womankind: it is an abomination.'* You are an abomination!"

"Do you not think encouraging hate is an abomination? Using the Word of God to teach
hate is a trick of the enemy, but I guess you're so caught up in being righteous and holier
than thou that you can't see it!"

"You can't defend your choice of lifestyle."

"You people are so quick to use scripture to justify your hate. The same Bible that you use
to condemn me I use to love you. And, let me tell you something, the devil can quote the
Bible with the best of them. So, don't act as though just because you know what the words
of the Bible are, you're some expert on the will of God. Do you think it's pleasing in the eyes
of God for a room full of people to jump to their feet and applaud the idea of going out and
beating another human? How Christian is that? I can't believe how much hate there is in this
room now." With those words, a noticeable change infected the room. The people still
standing, who once cheered at the reverend's words, slowly began to sit, one by one, like
dominoes, with lowered heads. The reverend looked around in dismay and disgust. "I've
never asked anyone to be overjoyed with my *life*. I'm gay. I've always been gay. I wasn't
molested or raped as a child, nor did I grow up around anyone gay. I'm not asking for your
embrace. I'm not asking for your acceptance, but only your tolerance; in the same way we
have to tolerate things we don't like about you. We're not after your children or your
husbands. I simply want to be able to live and work in peace and harmony. And, if at the
end of all things, it is a sin in the eyes of God, it is my sin to bear; not yours. So, stop wasting
your time hating us when you can be loving your families. Stop wasting your time trying to
deny me the same rights I should have as an American—not as a Christian—but, as an
American, that you have. I pay the same taxes as you and I should receive the same benefits
from our government you receive. You Christians need a good lesson on how to be good
Christians."

"We're not about to sit around and let you destroy the family and marriage. God made Adam and Eve, not Adam and Steve, and we will defend the sanctity of marriage from the likes of the homosexual," the reverend spouted out, trying to regain some control of the room.

"Actually, Reverend, God made Adam, Eve, Steve, Bill, Susan, Bobby and everyone in between. You're so worried about us, but how many times have you been married, Reverend?" Danea shouted, recalling the earlier conversation of the ladies behind her. The reverend mumbled something under his breath. "I didn't quite hear you. How many times? Once, twice—more? Which marriage of yours are you defending? Your first or your second? Is there a third?"

The congregation gasped.

"My marriages have nothing to do with this conversation!"

"They have everything to do with this conversation. If I'm not mistaken, the last time I checked, God didn't condone divorce. But, that's not what this conversation is about. I'm tired of all the hate. I'm just tired."

"I'm tired of it, too!" the organist exclaimed as he suddenly jumped to his feet. "I come to this church every week and I've gotten to know a great many of you. Many of you have talked to me about a lot of things and I can tell you, let he who is without sin cast the first stone. I know no one in this room—not even you, Reverend—is qualified to do that. I thought we were supposed to treat each other with love and kindness—as brothers and sisters, but that's not what happens here. I'm tired of the gossip and backstabbing, too. I'm tired of folks talking about each other and being mean-spirited. We gotta do better. This is the house of God. This is a place of love."

From the back of the room another voice boomed out. "I'm tired of it, too." Everyone turned and looked at the small-framed woman. "I'm a proud lesbian and I can also love and be loved by the Lord." In the front of the room, from the choir stand, there was another rustling of bodies.

"I'm tired of it, too," said one member of the church choir as two others stood alongside him.

"We can sing about love and being good people, but we don't practice that around here. I'm a gay man and I've been at the point in my life where I wanted to kill myself because I couldn't go on with my feelings. I prayed about it and cried about it until I couldn't cry any more, but the Lord told me that if Jesus could love a prostitute, then He could love me also. I will not tolerate this abuse and these attacks upon my soul."

Kevin and Danea stood in amazement as folks stood up, one by one, and proclaimed their lives or their support for others in their lives.

"I ain't gay, but this is my niece," an old lady said as she struggled to stand next to her niece who was first to confess. "I raised this child and I always knew she was gay and I don't love her any less. I don't see how all this gay talk is doing any of us any good."

The reverend struggled to say something that would reestablish his authority over the room, but the spirit of love was infectious. It passed from person to person, from one touch to another, in one word to the next until almost half of the church stood. Most of the standing members stood, not because they were gay or lesbian, but because they were tired of the hate, too. Kevin could not believe what he was witnessing. It was an unprecedented act, but he knew at some point, it had to be done. He didn't know what had come over him to start this conversation but, based on the reactions in the room, it was long past due. At some point, Kevin realized people needed to stop allowing themselves to be attacked and beaten into the ground by people who didn't know what it meant to be Christian. Kevin gave one last glance around the room and the looks that greeted him ranged from outrage to understanding. He walked toward Danea and took her by the hand.

"If you think you and your hate will force us back into the darkness, look around this room because we're standing in the light. If you think your words will force us to the back of the bus—or church—think again. We are center stage. If you think, for one second, that you speak for *my* God, think again. He loves me. Hate is not a Christian value and if you keep preaching it and this congregation keeps embracing hate in the name of God, then a plague will land upon each and every one of your houses," he said, pointing around the room. As the duo left, they heard a cacophony of voices—some in support and some in condemnation—of what had transpired. When they exited the building, they never looked back, but Kevin smiled.

CHAPTER 26

After much anticipation and preparation, New Year's Eve finally arrived. Kevin had managed to put thoughts of Daryl and infidelity and doctor's visits and false churches out of his head enough to really focus on the event. The weather was chilly, but not too cold and no snow was predicted. That had been one of Kevin's worries in the past. Planning large events in D.C. in the wintertime was always a risk. D.C wasn't like Chicago or New York where, even in eight inches of snow, the city carries on. Whenever an inch of snow was predicting to fall, D.C. would shut down. Had that happened, that would have been tragic for Keevan's Room.

Kevin arrived at the club for one last inspection at seven p.m. and when he walked in, he was awestruck by the enormity of the room and the magnitude of the event about to occur within a matter of hours. He had been to the club more times than he could remember, but it looked and felt very different on this day. He stood at the front and noticed the decorations adorning the room. Colorful balloons—purple, yellow, green, blue, and silver—were tied to tables, the railings of each of the staircases, and the railings of the bar, while colorful napkins decorated the tables. As he stood at the front, he glanced across the room at the main dance floor—affectionately called The Pit—that was lowered by five small steps so anyone desiring to dance had to climb down. Kevin looked up at the ceiling and saw the net containing hundreds of balloons and confetti, which was going to be released at the stroke of midnight to rain down on the room in a New Year's flurry.

Kevin looked around the room for Desiree. She wanted to discuss something but he couldn't make out the message she had left on his cell phone earlier. He surveyed the room a little longer and headed upstairs to search for her. He walked up the long metal staircase and entered the lounge area on the second floor. The color purple served as a backdrop for the velvet maroon chairs and sofas. He didn't see her so he took the stairs to the third level and saw her speaking with a technician on the catwalk. He climbed those stairs to reach her, but gave her a few moments to finish her conversation. He loved the catwalk that encased the perimeter of the club. From that height he could see everyone on the floor in The Pit below.

Desiree was dressed in a blood-red dress with matching heels. Her hair was pinned up in a tight bun that elongated her thin neck. She was a petite woman, about five feet four inches—while wearing heels—but she was a formidable event planner and recognized the ins and outs of putting together a first-class event.

"Hey, Kevin," she said with a warm smile as she finished her conversation with the technician. "We were adjusting some of the lights up here. When the show starts, I want things to be perfect."

"Cool. So, everything is okay?"

She took him by the arm and led him down the stairs. "Everything is fine; trust me. The caterers are in the back setting up, the wait staff, bartenders, valet parking attendants, and security personnel are arriving even as we speak. Danea's dressing room is set up, as is the changing area for dancers. The DJ's are excited and ready to get the crowd pumped up. So, all is well. I can't wait. I tell you, this party is going to be spectacular."

"You're absolutely the best. I couldn't have done this without you."

"Of course you could have. I'm only glad you didn't." She giggled. "So, don't worry about anything. I have everything under control."

❀❀❀

A couple of hours later, Kevin changed into his costume in the office he commandeered for the party. He was dressed as Prince Charming, complete with cape and hat, and looked as if he was about to ride off into the sunset with Cinderella. He stared at himself in the mirror and couldn't help feeling a certain emptiness inside. He felt hollow—like a part of him was missing. He wished things were better with Daryl. He wanted to share this magical night with him, but he was alone and wasn't sure if his heart could take another break so he thought he might be alone forever. When he thought about Daryl, a rush of emotions over-came him like floodwaters. He missed him and hated him and loved him in ways that words could never describe. Even still, that didn't change the fact of what he did. No amount of love could erase the betrayal. No amount of missing him would wipe the slate clean. He took a final look in the mirror and wiped a solitary tear from his eye. He needed to pull it together for the sake of the party. He picked up his cell phone and dialed Danea's number. Her voice mail picked up. He was confident she'd be there and on time, but wanted to check in on her anyway. Finally, he picked up a chart and walked out of the office. It was party time.

When he got into the area near the main dance floor, the room was far more crowded than he had expected. Waiters in black and white uniforms walked by carrying champagne on trays, and the music blared as folks continued to stream into the party of the year. A vibrant parade of costumes and color added flare and style to the festive evening. Angels and devils, fairies and trolls, super heroes and heroines, creatures from fairytales, nymphs and seductresses, gladiators and animals and legendary movie characters all marched past each other in a dazzling spectacle of pageantry. Kings and queens, princes and princesses, wizards, witches and warlocks all strutted by with much pomp and ceremony as if the party was a royal court. The costumes were bold and daring and some were even scandalous, revealing taut skin and slick body parts that glistened underneath the electric lights. Kevin smiled and thought about how proud Keevan would be of him if he were alive. It was still early, but it was already one hell of a party.

Kevin and Desiree played a game of trying to recognize people through their elaborate disguises. Percy and Keith were easy to spot: Percy was Superman and Keith was dressed as Wonderwoman. He even had a golden lasso. There were women out there who would kill to fill out that costume the way he did. Lynda Carter would be jealous.

"Hi, Kevin," a familiar voice spoke from behind.

The sound of the voice struck deep in his heart and he struggled a bit to maintain his composition. He turned around to face Daryl.

"Nice costume," Daryl said with heavy eyes and a solemn voice. He was dressed as a pig, complete with a big pink snout. He wasn't sure what Kevin's reaction was going to be, but he had to be there to support him on this night; regardless of their personal issues.

"Your costume. Interesting. And appropriate," Kevin said. "Desiree, could you check on Danea for me and make sure she's okay?" Desiree got the hint.

"Before you say anything," Daryl began, "I know I'm the last person you want to see right now."

"You got that right."

"But…" He hesitated. "I wanted to be here for you. I wanted to support you and all the work you've done putting this event together. Please, Kevin, please let me stay."

Kevin took a deep breath. Looking at Daryl brought back so many feelings. He could see the hurt in his eyes that was entombed by sorrow. He looked pitiful, almost like a child begging for recognition from an indifferent parent. Kevin wished he could turn a knob and turn the love off like an annoying drip from a bathroom faucet, but he couldn't. The love was still there. Part of him wanted to reach out and grab Daryl and pull him into his body, but the other part wanted to reach out and strangle him.

"You can stay."

"Thank you so much." Daryl wanted to weep at Kevin's feet and touch the hem of his garment, but he stood tall with teary eyes. "Do you need me to do anything?"

"Yeah, stay out of my way." With those chilly words, Kevin turned and walked away. Daryl followed him with his eyes until he could no longer distinguish him from the mass of bodies. More than anything, he wanted to know if he would ever win back Kevin's love. He was in for the fight of his life, and his love.

Daryl causally strolled over to The Pit and gazed into the crowd. As he scanned the landscape of revelers, he saw an image that caused him to lose his breath. He focused his eyes on a body slinking through the crowd like a specter. The man, dressed in a *Phantom of the Opera* costume, weaved through the crowded room, but there was something familiar and electric in the way the phantom slid around the dance floor with his head high and his back straight. It wasn't an ordinary walk; the body moved with the gallop of a magnificent prized stallion. Daryl was intimately familiar with that walk. He tried to get a better look. The crowd, the flashing strobe lights, and the costumes prevented him from making a positive identification from his distance, but it had to be Temple. From the haughty way in which the phantom navigated the crowd, it could only be Temple. When Daryl attempted to move through the room, people chitchatting and laughing gaily cut him off at the path. He had to get a better look. He didn't want any surprises. He didn't want to talk to Temple, but his heart fluttered; if only a little bit. He wanted to know what would possess Temple to show up here. Surely he had to know this was not the appropriate time to talk. Suddenly, Daryl wished he would have responded to some of Temple's frantic messages. He suspected Temple was on a search for him. Daryl could not deal with any more of his confessions of love or lust or longing; especially not tonight. He had tried to let him down easily, but Temple remained convinced that what he felt for Daryl was real and he wasn't ready to let it go so effortlessly. Daryl had explained, on more than one occasion, that their one sexual encounter was a mistake, but Temple could not let it go. Daryl wiped a few gathering beads of sweat from his nervous brow. If Kevin spotted Temple or saw him speaking to Temple—for whatever reason—his chances of reconciling would be over. As he moved through The Pit, someone grabbed his arm. It was Percy.

"Daryl, man, this party is great. I haven't had so much fun since, well, since our holiday party," he said with glee. "I spoke to City Councilman Stanley and you should see his costume. He's dressed as some kind of African warrior. I didn't know he had that much ass," he said with a hearty laugh. The councilman was one of two openly gay members on the council and he had served the D.C. population for over ten years. "I'll have to introduce you and Kevin to him. Speaking of Kevin, where is your man?"

Daryl didn't have the heart or the patience to tell him the truth. The last thing he wanted was to hear "I'm so sorry" or "what happened?" or "I thought you guys were the perfect couple." So, he didn't say anything.

"Kevin is around here, probably taking care of some minor crisis. You know how he is. Will you excuse me for one second?"

Daryl didn't wait for his response before taking off through the mass of people. He fought his way through The Pit, trying to slip by bodies electrified by music. He searched around for the phantom, but he was nowhere to be seen. He continued peering through the crowd until he realized his effort was futile. He exited The Pit on the other side and marched toward the back bar and lounge, which was equally packed. He thought if he went to the second level he could look down on the crowd and locate him.

Kevin walked around the club silently checking on partygoers and to see how things were going. Desiree was right: she had this thing on lock and the party was wonderful. As he moved through, his ears were overcome by boisterous laughter and animated conversation. People "ooooo'ed" and "aaaaa'ed" at some of the costumes, and would often stop strangers to compliment them on their creative attire.

Kevin walked to the front of the club to make sure everything was working well with the valet parking and was pulled to the side by Desiree. She wasn't wearing a costume, but remained in her red dress. She carried an official-looking clipboard and had an earpiece in her ear to make sure she stayed in communication with her people.

"Whew, I'm glad I found you. I called you a few times, but you didn't respond."

Kevin reached into his pocket and pulled out his phone. It was set on vibrate but he hadn't felt the familiar jolt. "I don't know what's wrong with this phone. Wassup?"

"There are two reporters here with photographers. I need you to do a quick interview with a reporter from *The Washington Post* Style section and *The Washington Blade*. They're both covering stories on the parties this evening and they have to leave in a few to get to some other places. They've already interviewed Danea. I took them to her dressing room. She gave a quick quote and took a few pictures. I need you to do the same. Make sure, of course, you mention Keevan's Room and the purpose of this party. It makes a good story." Without further comment, she grabbed him by the arm and took him over to the reporters who were busy interviewing folks as they streamed into the club. Desiree cleared her throat to let the *Post* reporter know they were ready for the interview. She mentioned that while he was interviewing with the *Post*, she'd go and find the reporter from the *Blade*, which was D.C.'s weekly paper that covered local and national stories of interest to gay people.

"Hi, I'm Zoe Cohen from the *Post*. I wanted to ask you a few questions about this fabulous party and take a few shots that will run in tomorrow's paper. Will that be okay?"

"Of course," Kevin replied.

"Since you're the organizer of this event, why don't you tell me about the party?"

Kevin started telling her the purpose of the party as she took notes on a little blue pad. As he continued to talk, he looked up toward the door and his eyes froze. Walking through in a long gold and diamond beaded dress was RaChelle. She wore a huge crown on her head and carried a golden scepter as if she was the Queen of England. Kevin gasped.

"Are you okay?" the reporter asked.

"I'm sorry. Where was I?"

As he regained his composure, RaChelle looked over and saw him. She smiled as she headed his direction.

"Kevin, darling, how are you? The cars are lined up outside. It took twenty minutes for my limo to reach the door, so I know it must be packed in here. I'm so excited to be here and to support such a wonderful cause." She kissed him on both cheeks and then linked arms with him. He wanted to punch her in the kidney, but didn't want the reporter to be privy to such hostility.

"Hi, I'm Zoe with *The Washington Post*. Your costume is wonderful. You look so regal."

"Thank you, dear. It wasn't the one I was originally going to wear, but when I saw it the other day, I realized it would be perfect for this wonderful event."

"Would you mind posing with Kevin for a picture?"

"Of course not. We'll be the king and queen of the ball."

Kevin grimaced. Zoe instructed them to get close together and, right before the photographer snapped, Kevin turned on his million-dollar smile. He was not about to let her ruin his photo op.

Once Zoe left, the other reporter approached and essentially the same scene was repeated. RaChelle beamed like the belle of the ball and had the reporter blushing and smiling all at the same time. She gave wonderful quotes and really helped Kevin sell the event to the reporter. By the time they were done, he said he had more than enough for a terrific story and that the paper would even include an address for donations to Keevan's Room. Kevin smiled as the reporter exited the building.

"What the hell do you think you're doing?" he asked her, trying to maintain some decorum.

"I came out to support you. I know your little project still needs money."

"Do you really think I'd want anything from you?"

"What's wrong with you? Why are you acting like this?"

"You must be out of your fuckin' mind."

"I know you still don't think I burned down your restaurant, do you?"

"You practically admitted to it."

"No, I didn't. That was merely your imagination, baby."

"I want you out of here." Kevin grabbed her tightly by the arm.

"Let go of me. My arm is still bruised from when you grabbed it at my hotel. If you don't let me go, I'll scream and cause a major scene." He wanted to avoid a confrontation right now. Every dog had its day and she'd have hers, too.

"If you do anything to mess up this evening, I'll make you wish you were never born." He released her and smiled at Desiree, who had approached from behind. She had a startled look on her face.

"Is everything okay?" she asked Kevin as he breezed by her and nodded his head in the affirmative. RaChelle looked at Desiree, nodded, and walked into the club with her head held high.

Then, the DJ started speaking on the mic and the lights dimmed. "Shit, it's time for Danea to hit the stage. I didn't even get a chance to wish her luck," he said to Desiree.

"You've seen her perform. She doesn't need luck. She lives to perform."

The lights in the club started flashing in a colorful display of choreographed beams. The curtains that covered the stage slowly began to open to reveal psychedelic patterns of colors shown against a glow-in-the-dark background. The sounds of one of her dance hits started pulsating from the speakers. It was a slow, thudding kind of beat you could feel deep down in your bones. Kevin followed the spotlight to the third-floor catwalk. Descending slowly from the top was a body, wrapped in some colorful material, moving its head from side to side in rhythm. The crowd whistled and screamed in awe. Danea eyed the crowd as she made her perfect descent onto the stage directly in front of a microphone on a stand. She landed with perfect timing to start the first verse of her song. Her wild, glittered hair and makeup reflected the lights in the club. She let out a piercing, soul-shaking note that excited the crowd. She was completely wrapped in a cocoon, hands and body unseen as if this was her natural condition. Her thrilling voice filled the club with a throbbing and emotional intensity. The crowd loved it. She stood in place, still wrapped, and sang effortlessly. As the song's tempo accelerated into her dance single, she burst from the cocoon to reveal these bright yellow and black butterfly wings that she flapped around wildly. Again, the crowd hollered and yelled with delight. She excitedly raced around the stage as if she was trying to get airborne, working those wings for what they were worth. The short green and bedazzled dress she had on did not stop her from giving one hell of a performance.

"Your girl is awesome," Desiree said with awe.

"I know. She's out of control, but I love it!"

"I know you do. Listen, I've got something to check on, so I'll catch up with you in a few."

"Cool."

❀❀❀

As the midnight hour neared, Danea was still on the stage, microphone in hand, and was gearing the crowd up for the countdown. Kevin had made his way up to the third level of the club and looked around the room and the couples hugged up waiting for the stroke of midnight. He couldn't help but feel a longing for Daryl. When the clock struck that magic hour, he'd be alone.

"Ten! Nine! Eight! Seven!" Danea yelled into the microphone as the crowd chanted in unison. "Six! Five! Four!" she kept yelling. "Three! Two! One! Happy New Year!"

The fevered crowd jumped up and down as the confetti and balloons rained down on them. The strobe lights flashed and made everyone seem like they were moving in slow motion and as if lightning was illuminating a darkened field. Whistles blew and horns blared in excitement. With all of the noise and the screams, the crowd was oblivious to a blood-curdling call on the catwalk. Kevin heard the cry and thought it sounded peculiar. It didn't sound like a celebratory yelp, but one of excruciating pain. He raced up the set of stairs that led to the catwalk in a frantic dash. He now recognized the blood-curdling yell wasn't part of the festivities—it was truly a cry for help. When he got to the top, he looked toward the other end of the catwalk and tried to adjust his eyes to the rapidly flashing lights. He squinted and focused in on two figures at the end of the runway. He saw a figure pull what looked like a long, bloody butcher knife out of her body. *This can't be real*, he thought. He needed and wanted to move. His feet felt cemented to the metal floor, but he managed to take a few steps. He gasped for breath, not sure if his eyes were playing a sadistic trick on him or if what he saw was, in fact, real. She looked at Kevin. Even from their distance, he could see the look of panic in her eyes. Her shocked stare pierced through the flashing lights and falling confetti. Kevin would never forget her empty eyes as her stare bore through the night.

In spite of the maddening screams from the crowd below, in defiance of the lights that flickered and the balloons that danced, her glare remained steady. Kevin found himself focusing more on her face than the knife-wielding hooded figure who embraced her and stared at him. Her last gaze pulled him into her. The expression on her face was an amalgamation of pain, fear, confusion and ultimately acceptance. Acceptance of her fate. Acceptance of this reality. Acceptance of the inevitable. In spite of it all, her eyes bore no apology and no sorrow.

In this moment, in her last moment, Kevin expected more humanity from her, but her eyes were vacant. She tried to speak, but no words could be heard. The masked figure waved the knife slowly, back and forth, in a threatening manner as her blood ran down the blade. Kevin's eyes focused on the knife. Suddenly, the figure jabbed her body with the knife over and over in a carefully timed motion. The fact that the blade had just been pulled from the body of a living and breathing human being seemed surreal. This couldn't possibly be happening. He took a step backward and almost fell down the stairs.

She looked at him but still she could not scream. It was already too late. She knew it. Kevin knew it. The figure, in one last violent act, bucked and pushed her over the railing before running down the catwalk with the black cape flapping in the air to exit on the other side. Kevin made it to the railing just in time to see the body splatter onto the table near The Pit below. When her body hit, her warm red blood splattered on the faces and clothing of those unfortunate enough to be in the near vicinity.

Immediately, the screams started. The crowd realized this was not a joke. Death was in the building. The music instantly halted, the lights came up in a hurry, security rushed Danea off the stage, and folks scattered. The crowd on the second floor looked up and saw Kevin gazing down in horror and disbelief. He had no doubt RaChelle was dead.

Never had Kevin run so fast. Not even when he ran track in college. He raced down from the catwalk, hurdling tables and pushing people out of the way. He had to find that person who committed this horrific act of violence. People raced around the club in frenzied bursts, knocking other people down and not taking time enough to help them up. They forced their way out of the three exit doors and never looked back. Once he reached the first floor, he stopped to help a lady off the floor who had been partially trampled. Kevin didn't want to believe this maddening and chaotic scene was real, but the destruction he witnessed could not be denied. Tables laid overturned, champagne bottles and glasses littered the floor along with purses, capes, masks, wands, pitchforks, angel wings, and other costume accessories. People abandoned the area with all due speed and purpose, not sure exactly what happened, only knowing that a dead body lay in the middle of the floor. Screams could still be heard as people continued pushing their way forward to the front. Kevin didn't know where Daryl or Danea were, but hoped they had gotten out safely. He scanned the room to try to locate the murderer, but things were too chaotic for him to focus. Then, he saw her body. Lifeless. Bleeding. Ripped apart. Her eyes were still open. Kevin knelt down beside her and looked at her bloodstained face. Her beauty faded.

"Kevin? Kevin?" Daryl screamed out as he raced from the back and saw Kevin kneeling over the body. "Oh my God! What happened? I was in the back and heard all of the screaming."

Kevin remained silent.

He studied her bruised face. Her curious expression prompted him to wonder about her final thoughts. In those last seconds, when she teetered between life and death, when all that she had and all that she was no longer mattered, when her beauty became irrelevant and her money was rendered worthless, what thoughts occupied her mind? Was she regretful? Fearful? Ashamed of life? Proud of her accomplishments? Satisfied? Was she angry at the world? Did she forgive him? As he stared down at her face, a face that would no longer smile with eyes that could no longer shed tears, he wondered about her soul and its place in perpetuity. Then, he felt a warm hand on his shoulder. It comforted him, yet he didn't need comfort. RaChelle's last efforts were used to destroy his life and, as much as he wanted to feel sorry for her, he could not muster up any warm feelings. All he felt was pity. You live by the sword and you die by the sword. She died never having seen the face of her killer.

CHAPTER 27

Temple walked into the apartment he shared with Cerina with trepidation. He hoped and prayed she would not be home. All he wanted to do was get his stuff and leave. He didn't want to see her and he certainly didn't want to talk to her. He couldn't be sure he wouldn't kill her if he saw her. It was still in the very early hours of the New Year and he figured she'd be out drunk somewhere. Parties were taking place all across the city, but Temple had nothing to celebrate. He had spent the last few days bouncing back and forth between Baron's crib and his cousin's house.

When he stepped into the blackened room, his breathing quickened as a rush of rage overtook him. He pulled out a chair from the dining room table and plopped down, burying his hands in his face. No sounds could be overheard in the apartment beyond the sound of his fearfully beating heart. Suddenly, the reality of health rushed in with gale force winds and he couldn't stop crying. He wept. He wept for himself. He wept for hurting Daryl. He wept for all the people he had wronged in his tragic life. He even wept for Cerina. He always thought crying made a man soft, but now he didn't care. He had the darkness to cloak his pain. He let the pain out. He let the fear have its voice. There was no doubt about it; he was scared. He was so scared he resolved not to get tested. He wouldn't be able to cope with what he assumed would be a positive result.

Why had she done that to him, he kept asking himself.

After about ten minutes of tears, he got up from the chair and turned on a light. He'd hate for her to walk in and see him crying. He had to leave. He needed a suitcase to pack his things. He walked toward the hall closet but stopped to pick up a black and white mask that lay on the floor. It seemed ironic to him, for her to be masked when all of the truth had been revealed. He held the plastic phantom mask and studied it carefully for a few seconds before letting it fall to the floor.

Then, he heard a sound coming from the bedroom. It was a muffled, barely audible sobbing sound. He froze. He didn't want to see her. Part of him wanted to leave and come back another time. The other part prodded him to march into the bedroom and strangle the bitch.

When he walked into the dark bedroom, he turned on the lamp near the bed.

Then he saw her, dressed in a bloodied, black and hooded costume. She sat on the floor with her back against the bed facing the window. He slowly walked over to her. Blood stained her face. An empty bottle of whiskey and a bloodied knife were at her side. She looked up at him as he looked down at her.

Neither spoke.

There were no appropriate words.

He gritted his teeth and clenched his lips tightly. He felt his fists balling into tight knots. He wanted to bludgeon her to death.

Tears fell from her face.

He relented. He glared at her, but eventually turned his back on her and walked toward the bedroom door. He didn't want to see her.

A gunshot shattered the silence.

Temple died instantly when the bullet entered the back of his head.

Cerina crawled over to him and put his lifeless arms around her. Then, she raised the gun to her head and pulled the trigger.

CHAPTER 28

K evin sat in the chair in his bedroom sipping on a cup of green tea while reading a wonderful novel entitled *I Wrote This Song* by Dayne Avery. He tried hard to divert his attention away from Daryl. It was five days into the New Year and so many things had happened that it was hard to keep things straight. RaChelle was dead. And so were Temple and Cerina. His restaurant was gone and he would not be paid by the insurance company because his policy had been cancelled due to nonpayment. The officers who previously visited Kevin told him that Mr. Martinez boarded a plane to Argentina at Dulles airport on Christmas morning. Kevin knew he'd never be heard from again. The cops found RaChelle's diary in her hotel in which she had written out the explicit details of her plot. That plot included paying him seventy five-thousand dollars to torch Jose's. Her diary revealed other things she planned that shocked Kevin. He had no idea he had caused her so much pain. He wanted to feel sorry for her, but he could not. He wanted to weep for her, but he had no more tears. He wanted to be angry, but he forgave her. All that remained was pity for both her life and her death.

Daryl and Kevin had taken HIV tests, which yielded a negative result for each of them. They would both have to be retested in a few months to be sure. Kevin closed the book and took a deep breath. He watched Daryl pack his remaining items in a brown box and tape it closed. The sounds of the tape being torn from the dispenser and being applied to the top of the box brought finality to their failed relationship. Daryl bent over and picked up the box, pausing long enough to face his greatest love. All he had now was love and regret.

"When my home phone gets connected, I'll call you and give you the number," Daryl said as he moved toward the door. He had to leave before he broke down again.

"Okay," Kevin said, holding in his emotion.

Daryl moved closer to the door, box in hand, and stopped.

"Do you think, one day, I could take you to dinner?"

Kevin closed his eyes. "I don't know, Daryl; maybe. Everything between us is so different now."

"You know I still love you, right? I never stopped loving you and probably never will."

"Yeah, I know."

Kevin wasn't sure if love was enough.

He took another sip of tea and picked up his book. He had a song to write, too. Something about the blues.

AUTHOR BIO

Lee Hayes is the author of the bestselling novel, *Passion Marks*, and he just completed his Master of Public Administration degree from Baruch College in New York City. He is a native Texan who graduated from the University of North Texas with a degree in sociology. He is single and currently resides in Washington, D.C. Visit the author at www.passionmarks.com or email him at leehayes@hotmail.com.

PASSION MARKS

LEE HAYES

AVAILABLE FROM STREBOR BOOKS

CHAPTER 1

The black cordless phone slammed against the right side of my face with such force that it sent my entire body reeling over the white sofa. I rolled over it and onto the coffee table, shattering the glass top. Instantly, my face went numb. I lay on the floor in a daze, trying to ascertain the extent of the damage: the pain was intense. I rubbed my face with my hands while I tried to ignore the warm feel of blood as it oozed out of my back and soaked my shirt. When I found the strength, I looked above me and saw him looming like a volcano suddenly compelled to erupt. His savagely contorted face burned with the fire of his words and the anger that dripped from his thick breath. When I attempted to sit up, I felt his shoe in my chest, kicking me back to the carpet. His words failed to convey any meaning through the depth of my pain, but the anger on his face spoke volumes. I closed my eyes, praying this nightmare would end; instead of ending, his body suddenly pressed down on my chest, and unrelenting fists pounded my face. I tried to shield my face from his blows with my arms, even while his frame weighed heavily upon me.

By this time, my lungs were on the verge of collapse and I gasped desperately for air. I was far too weak to force him off me, and when I struck him in the eye with my fist, it only made him pound harder. Through his anger, and between the unbroken chains of profanity, he yelled something about blood on the carpet, *as if it was my fault*, and then pulled me up from where I lay like a rag doll. He stood me up so I could look directly in his brown eyes, and then he slapped me so hard across the face that I crashed into the wall, narrowly escaping the flames of the fireplace. Just as he raced toward me, I stood up, and with all the force I could muster, I slammed my fist into his face. He stumbled. I threw my body into him with the force of a linebacker. He tried to withstand the force, but he lost his balance, and we both tumbled onto the floor. His head hit the side of the entertainment center, and blood began to run down his face from the open wound. I pounded his face with my fist, and then slammed his head onto the floor repeatedly like a man possessed. He looked worn out. It was over.

I rolled off him and onto my back, taking a moment to breathe as I looked up at the ceiling. Slowly, I moved away from him. That's when I felt his fist connect with the back of my head. He plowed into me like a truck from behind, and I flew into the fifty-gallon aquarium, shattering the glass and sending the helpless fish to the floor. They flipped and flopped, gasping for air; within moments they'd be dead. He grabbed my left leg and pulled me with ease across the carpet, unmoved by my struggle for freedom. My attempt at liberation from his massive hands proved futile, and he continued dragging me across the white carpet, leaving behind a trail the color red.

When we reached the staircase, he gave my body a tremendous yank to assert his control. With sudden prowess, he moved behind me, pushed my body down, and forced my stomach into the stairs. I could feel his gigantic hands on the back of my neck as he pressed my face into the carpet. I was pinned down, unable to move. He ripped off my bloodstained shirt and tossed it aside. As he whispered something in my ear, his hands grabbed my ass. The heat of his breath scalding my neck was far worse than the words he spoke. He grabbed me by the waist and raised my body up just enough for him to undo my belt. As he pulled down my pants and underwear in one swift motion, I braced myself. His accelerated breathing became louder and louder in anticipation. I tried to prepare myself for the violation. I knew that he would do everything in his power to make it hurt—to make me scream for mercy. He had a special affinity for delivering pain. This time I would deny him the perverse pleasure of hearing me scream.

Behind me, I heard him unzip his pants; that was the catalyst that brought tears to my eyes. I would not let them fall. My tears would only add to his callous joy, so I withheld them. My legs were then forced apart, and I knew there was no turning back. With his arm still pressed against the back of my neck, and my face forcibly held against the floor, I felt his thick flesh force its way into me, connecting in a vile union. The pain of that first thrust when it broke through my barrier almost caused me to let out a loud scream, but I held it in. His bursts rocked my body, and the pain increased the longer he stayed in me. I reached my hands behind my back and tried to push him off me, but my effort proved pointless. He pushed harder and harder, while his inhuman grunts filled the room, like the howl of a wolf in the darkness of night. The force of his thrusts rolled my body back and forth, back and forth, back and forth, for what seemed like an endless moment in time. My face dug deeper into the stair, and the burn from the carpet on my face was becoming painful. His panting was vicious, much like an animal that suddenly realized the extent of its power and its victory. All the while, his voice shouted despicable words, and with each debilitating push from his body into mine, his voice became louder. *This had to end.* All of the hurt my body suffered now went to my head, and I could feel myself losing consciousness. He turned my head toward him, forcing me to look into his hollow eyes. Blood stained his face. His muscles inside of me began to contract, and I knew it would be over soon. He pushed harder, faster, harder, and still faster, until I felt the release of his hot fluids. He pulled out of my body while still enjoying his eruption. His juices spilled on my back, and then rolled down my side. It was over. From behind, he wrapped his hands around my waist and pulled me into his powerful chest. He held me there for a few seconds, gently kissed the back of my neck, and released me. *"Clean up this mess,"* he said as he motioned toward the war-torn room. He climbed over me, and made his way up the staircase. When I looked up, I saw the back of his naked body reach the top of the stairs and disappear into darkness.

There were no words with enough power to capture the way I felt. I remained laying face down in the carpet, naked except for one sock dangling off my foot, unwilling—perhaps unable—to move. I felt stinging sensations pulsating on my back from the glass still buried beneath my skin. I tried to check my back to see if it had stopped bleeding, but I really wasn't concerned about those cuts; my attention was singularly focused on bigger issues. My entire body, wrapped in a throbbing blanket of pain, felt limp. After a few deep breaths, I managed to regain some control of my tattered frame, and forced myself to slide slowly to the bottom of the staircase, where I pulled my knees into my chest, and rested in the corner like a small child hiding from monsters under the bed. The sweet smell of jasmine still clung in the air, much like a damp mist over a lake in the early morning. With my right hand, I caressed my face—the swelling had already begun. I needed to crawl into the kitchen to get some ice, but that distance seemed unconquerable. The dimly lit house, once full of noise, now sat quiet as if the weakened sky had nothing left to give after its storm. The only audible sounds came from the rain lightly pounding against the windows, and the murmur of the rolling thunder. The lightning flashes offered a brief illumination, but I longed for the darkness to bury my shame.

The entire evening replayed in my head like a big-screen horror movie. I paid close attention to the details to see if I could figure out where it went wrong. Alluring candles, sweet incense, and a basket full of fabulous seafood in front of the fireplace. Sexy love ballads from the stereo, expensive wine, and vases full of freshly cut colorful roses all over the house. It all seemed so perfect. James and I had held each other closely while staring seductively in each other's eyes; this was the man that I adored. The evening conversation had been full of love and comforting smiles. His soothing caresses brought me to the ultimate state of relaxation. I thought the dark days were long behind us, forever sealed by the hands of time. For the first time in months, it seemed that we could be the happy couple I envisioned.

This wasn't the first time I had felt his fists and been burned by his quick temper. Throughout the course of our relationship, violence was not uncommon, especially during his times of stress related to his firm, Lancaster Computer Systems. A year ago LCS made an acquisition of a smaller computer firm in Austin; this transaction brought out the worst in James. Some nights when he came home, I feared for my safety, and at times, for my life, not knowing what to expect when he walked through the door. It was like rolling the dice.

Partly, it was my fault. I knew this. Sometimes, maybe out of boredom, I would intentionally antagonize him just to get a reaction. I wanted to see how far I could push him. I wanted to know whether or not I had the power to make him lose control. During stressful times, instead of being supportive and appreciative, I managed to say or do the wrong thing. But this attack was by far one of the most vicious outbursts I'd suffered at his hands.

Over and over again, I replayed the evening. The phone rang and he picked up. While he was on the phone, I decided to go into the kitchen for more wine, and when I returned something in him had changed. He seemed irritable and ended the phone call by slamming the phone on its base. As I approached him, the phone rang again. I answered it without thinking. By the time I heard his commands to let it ring, it was too late. I should have noticed the look on his face. I should have heard his words. I should not have let anything interrupt the mood. He stood up and held his hand out for the phone, and I innocently gave it to him. That's when everything changed. *It was my fault.* If only I hadn't answered that call. If only I had listened to him. I would have to start paying more attention to his needs. The phone call could have waited.

As I dragged myself up from the corner with considerable effort, I wondered how many men and women were in situations similar to mine. The lyrics to that old song "How Could You Hurt the One You Love?" came to mind. I managed to limp slowly to the restroom without losing my balance. I held a firm grip on the black sink for support, and when I flipped the light switch on, I let out a shriek as I looked at the broken and tattered image that stood before me in the mirror. *Surely, this wasn't me.* The mirror played a cruel joke. My eyes were beginning to close from the swelling, and bloodstains covered my face. My swollen lips pulsated with a heavy pain. Numerous purple and black bruises covered my chest, and the gentlest touch of my passion marks caused a horrible sensation. Still holding onto the sink, I turned to examine my back in the mirror, but when I turned, a sudden explosion of pain enveloped my body. The room started to spin, and before I even realized what was happening, I collapsed to the floor in a fit of pain. The plush mauve rug did little to break my fall. I heard the sound and felt the thump as my head hit the porcelain tub, and everything went black.

✖ ✖ ✖

"Sometimes, Kevin, you reap what you sow." I was startled by the familiar voice and when I opened my eyes the apparition stood before me, part flesh and part fantasy, and then vanished into the darkness.

"Keevan? Where are you?" I asked in fright. My heart palpitated with the rapid speed of hummingbird wings, and it felt as if it would beat through my chest.

"I came back." I followed the voice into the den. Keevan stood there, dressed in the same clothing he wore when I found him dead. I walked slowly toward him, with carefully chosen steps. "I'm your brother. I came back." His words haunted me and his expressions taunted me while his eyes mocked, offering no absolution. He vanished in the same mystery that allowed him to come forth.